SLEEPLESS NIGHTS

ALSO BY SARAH BILSTON

Bed Rest

SLEEPLESS NIGHTS

SARAH BILSTON

HARPER

An Imprint of HarperCollinsPublishers

FIRST EDITION

Library of Congress Cataloging-in-Publication Data is available upon request.

ISBN: 978-0-06-088994-4

09 10 11 12 13   OV/RRD   10 9 8 7 6 5 4 3 2 1

For Rosa and Karl

We held hands once and were beautiful. But what followed? Sleepless nights, oh, sleepless nights.

—JAMAICA KINCAID, "AT LAST"

ACKNOWLEDGMENTS

~

A number of friends have given me advice or information on issues confronting lawyers and the practicalities of the lawyer's existence; special thanks to Sharon Volckhauen, John Buretta, and Sarah Stevens-Cox. Thanks to Margaret Mary O'Rourke for providing me with such a vivid and arresting portrait of a small-town lawyer's life, and to Richard Falkenrath for putting us in touch. For advice on family law, warm thanks to my mother-in-law, Inga Markovits. And finally thanks, as always, to my husband, Daniel Markovits, for his always engaging, always thought-provoking observations on the ethical issues of lawyerly life.

SLEEPLESS NIGHTS

1

Q

New York

The party was in a Brooklyn brownstone. I stood on the sidewalk, staring up at the rearing expanse of red-brown brick, on a hot evening in late June. Above the door, gargoyles grinned and glowered at the street and at the gorgons bulging over the casement cornices. A hot, oily breeze stirred fronds of trailing ivy in two giant, swollen urns beside the door. Little piles of itchy grit swirled in the air, down the long flight of steps, and into my eyes. An old man enjoying the evening grinned as he passed, and touched his hat. "Waiting don't make it any easier, you know," he said softly, chuckling.

I rearranged my acre-wide blue dress across my belly, shapeless as a burst balloon, and began to mount the stone stoop. With each step I felt the sharp pull in my scar, a hot, numbed mouth pressed awkwardly closed. At the top I checked my cotton overshirt, re-clipped my snarled red hair, and hit the buzzer.

Inside I could hear voices and the deep pound of a bass. There was a pause, a shout suddenly close by ("Don't worry, I'll get it!"), and the door flew open; a pale, glamorous woman of forty appeared, dressed in a microscopic black shirtdress, long dark hair flowing glossily over one shoulder. "Oh—Quinn, it's you," she said dubiously, looking me up and down. "People call you Q, yes? Congratulations, and all that. Come in." She ushered me into the rich, air-conditioned coolness. "There are a few other associates here—over there some- where, I think." She gestured vaguely.

Caroline was the youngest woman ever to be partnered at my law firm, Schuster and Marks. She'd had a string of lovers in the five years I'd known her but no husband, and she swore she didn't want one "until I've lost my looks. The only reason to get married is so you can fuck when you're too old to get it any other way, y'know?" She spent every penny she earned at Schuster on herself—whenever she was away from work long enough to spend it, which was not of- ten, especially in recession-era New York. She thought she was a role model for me and the rest of Schuster's female associates.

Caroline pushed her way off into the throng, bony arms swing- ing by her side. I could see the points of each sharp elbow, little pink eyes glaring back at me. Knots of people were collected on each of the three dove-gray silk sofas, while others milled restlessly on the polished parquet floor. Three men were having an intense conver- sation around the fireplace while a fourth listened, tapping his fin- gers edgily on the marble surface. There were at least ten people in the kitchen area, spilling off bar stools or talking across the gran- ite countertops while a man with hooded eyes stirred something steaming and blackberry-colored in a copper vat on the stove. A few more were smoking out on the balcony overlooking the slim strip of garden.

"Q—my God, I can't believe it's you." It was Fay, another of the partners from the firm; there were new lines above her mouth, I noticed, as she slipped her arm around the waist of a young blond woman. "How did you manage to get away? Can I get you a drink? Caroline had vodka imported from Russia specially for the party. It's over there—" and she gestured to a white table on which stood twenty unlabeled bottles beside several towers of stacked shot glasses. "Af- ter the first six you don't notice the shit-awful taste anymore. Karen, why don't you get her . . ."

I reached out to stop the girl, whose vacant wide eyes slid over my face. "Thanks, Fay, and Karen, but I can't. Drink, that is. I'm—I'm nursing," I explained.

Fay blinked. "Right," she said cautiously.

"Breast-feeding I mean," I went on, laughing a little, looking down at my body, feeling a start of shock at my own extraordinarily unfamiliar shape. Since Samuel was born, my nipples, new brown moons, have taken to poking through my clothes to see what's up. My shirt, I realized suddenly, had fallen aside.

Sometimes, for what seems no reason at all, the waves of conversation at a party crash into silence, and for a moment there is nothing but an awkward flutter. Women look askance, men grin foolishly. As it happened, I was in the middle of the room at the time, a little gap opened up about me; about thirty pairs of eyes swiveled in the sudden hush to my ludicrous, pornographically swollen chest. Milk: I felt it, warm and dark and spreading. Blushing, I readjusted my shirt over my navy dress--too late; a man six feet away turned his head hastily, and there was an audible snicker from somewhere in the kitchen. Fay made a noise that was half a cough, and backed off. "I see. Of course. I think--" (touching her moist brow with the back of her hand)—"there's water over there, or juice, or whatever it is that—that nursing—or -people drink. I'll catch up with you later . . ."

She pushed her way toward the garden, dragging the bewildered girl behind her. *Oh that this too, too solid flesh would melt . . .* I fixed my gaze on a vast modern art canvas on the opposite wall, a block of shining black slashed with hell reds and oranges, and, as the noise picked up its hum, tried very hard to look as though I was appreciating its aesthetic complexity.

Bland faces with sharp, glittering eyes moved like other-worldly shadows around the room. I didn't recognize most of the people (lawyers from other firms, most likely) although nearest the fireplace sat Michael, a Schuster partner, now deep in conversation with

Marta, an associate hired a few years after me. Sitting beside her was a cohort of mine, named Julie. Very slim, seemingly self-confident; we'd never quite managed to be friends. I watched her face covertly. Julie didn't seem to be actively ignoring me.

Tom, why did I ever let you talk me into this . . . Pushing my way past elbows, navigating wafer-thin cocktail glasses, I lumbered over to the little circle, positioning myself on its periphery.

"I thought you pulled triumph from the jaws of defeat, Michael," Julie was saying. She was still in her suit, but had pulled her shirt an inch or two out from the waistband. "When the chief financial officer took the stand my heart just *sank*. You could see how confident he was. But then you confronted him with those receipts—"

Michael shrugged. "It helped that the prosecutor was an absolute idiot, obviously."

Julie took a swig from her vodka glass. "Your cross-examination was masterly—don't you think, Marta? Once you'd shown the jury the CFO's hands could be dirty, Michael, tapped into their 'Wall Street fatigue,' I knew we were—oh, hi!"

Seeing my shadow fall over her hands, Julie looked up: "Q! I can't believe it's you." Michael stood up and shook my hand formally; Marta nodded briefly, murmuring something I didn't catch.

Julie, however, patted a small space beside her. "It's really nice to see you. You've been away for—what, four months? Seems longer. So much has happened," she added, more quietly now, as Marta and Michael fell back into conversation. "What a crazy time. Alex and Miranda were fired as part of the restructuring, and quite a few new jobs were cut, but in other ways we're doing okay, relatively speaking—well, I'm sure you've kept up with the blogs. Helps to be a big firm in times like these, although as you'd expect, the associates are still very nervous" (with a quick side glance at Michael). "I take it you heard we won the Litchfield case?" she went on, more loudly. "You could hardly have missed it, it's been all over the *Times*, together with smiling photos of that smug CEO. I hear he's just bought a new house in the Hamptons—recession be damned . . ."

I didn't like to tell her that I'd barely had time to switch on the computer since my son was born, although I had heard of the fate of several associates hired after me, not to mention the expiration of three century-old law firms based near our office and the resultant hemorrhaging of lawyers onto the streets. Schuster and Marks still, for the moment at least, had its head above water. But things could turn around quickly.

"Now tell me: what have you been doing with yourself all this time?" asked Julie at last. She clearly expected a list.

"Well. I was on bed rest for three months at the end of the pregnancy. I had a problem, you see, with—"

"Yeah, I heard all about it. Crazy. I broke my leg skiing in Vail once, couldn't get into work, almost went off my head. And it's not clear bed rest even works, right? *I* would have told the doctors to stick it, but that's just me. Not," she went on, seriously, "that *I'll* be getting pregnant any time soon. Christ! Ed was talking the other night about starting a family; I said, 'Unless you can find a surrogate mother, forget it. I'm not turning *this* body into a baby-making machine. With the economy the way it is, this is hardly the time.'"

She began to laugh, then stopped herself with comical abruptness. "I don't mean—well, I'm sure in *your* case—I mean, it must be so great to have this—er—I mean, babies love you unconditionally, right? I can see that must be—nice . . ." She trailed off awkwardly. I opened my mouth, closed it, took a thoughtless sip of vodka that someone had put into my hand, and choked.

Several of the other young women in the room had come up behind me, I noticed suddenly, and were peering at me curiously. "I heard you just had a baby," one of them remarked abruptly; wiping streaming red eyes, I nodded, and turned around to face her.

"Yes. I have a little boy called Samuel, he's five weeks," I explained. The woman, thin and pale and dressed in a wide-necked red dress, raised delicately arched eyebrows. "Wow. That's, like, so *grown-up!*"

Everybody laughed. "I can hardly look after myself," she went on, grinning, accepting the joke, "*seriously.* I can't even imagine looking after a kid."

"I can't believe it myself, sometimes," I admitted. "I hear Samuel cry, it can take me a moment to realize he's mine—my child, my responsibility."

Six or seven women had collected around us now; people began asking me questions, and actually listening to the answers. Caroline watched for a moment or two, then surged over and cut in. "What are we talking about?" she inquired, assuming a position at the epicenter of the group with a little shimmy of her sleek black hips.

"Motherhood," I replied. A cloud passed over her brow.

"Really." Her lips twitched; her eyes sought out Michael's, but he was plunged back in conversation with yet another nervy, obviously sleep-deprived associate.

"Different people make different choices," Caroline said after a moment, blandly. "I mean, if you ask *me*, the thought of being covered in someone else's shit makes dealing with a recession look good!" The other women laughed, although not particularly comfortably. "But tell me," she went on, dismissing me with her shoulder, "*what* are we all doing for the rest of the summer?"

Immediately, the tone of the discussion changed again, as everyone began the struggle to outdo everyone else with ever-more elegant, exclusive social fixtures. (Never show weakness; I could see the old office culture was still thriving.) Other people were soon sucked in; a handsome, very young associate mentioned surfing with an X Games gold-medalist friend in Puerto Escondido but was quickly trumped by an invitation to a Kennedy wedding. Caroline listed the balls she'd be attending, then struggled to maintain her composure when Michael flaunted the giant yacht he was chartering around Hawaii in July. "I mean, it helps that I saw the crash coming, and shifted seventy percent of my holdings to cash . . ."

Clearly irritated, looking for someone to scratch, Caroline turned at last to me. "You'll just be at home with the baby, I suppose?" she said, narrowed eyes like shards of glass; there was a little movement in the group, as if everybody was thinking, well, I might not be going to Hyannis next month, my 401k's a joke, but at least I'm doing better than *that*. "I seem to remember your husband Tom was into white-water kayaking and paragliding. I suppose all that's in the past now . . ."

"Actually, no, we'll be staying in Paul Dupont's house this summer," I said abruptly, before I could think properly, and was rewarded by an audible gasp of astonishment. "Paul Dupont?" ejaculated Julie, beside me, "the superstar partner at Prince and Cohen? You're not serious! I didn't know you even *knew* him."

Caroline's expression was all I needed to keep going. For a moment, she looked quite old. "Oh yes, he and Tom are good friends from Paul's days at Crimpson Thwaite," I explained cheerfully. "My husband's firm, you know. Paul offered us his house for the summer, and we've decided to accept." I crossed my fingers behind my back.

"I'd forgotten he was at Crimpson until Prince head-hunted him," remarked one of the senior partners, a quiet man named Alvin, who had just joined the group. "Paul Dupont is a brilliant lawyer, and a man of excellent taste."

"And didn't he date—well, you know," squeaked one of the youngest girls, who looked to me like a summer associate. She was teetering giddily on six-inch heels, shirt split open almost to the waist. "I saw him at the Four Seasons last week, I recognized him from that piece last year in *GQ*. He's, like, I mean—he's totally *hot* . . . ." The other women, who were all clearly thinking the same thing, rolled their eyes; Caroline murmured something just audible about "chicks in heat." Mortification spread across the squeaky girl's face like paint through water.

I smiled kindly. "He's a very nice man, you know. And his house is beautiful," I went on cheerfully. "Tom and I are excited to spend time there this summer, with Samuel; hopefully we can find time for some serious sailing."

"He's friends with that dot-com mogul, Adjile Olawe, right?" whispered another young summer associate, with a nervous side-glance at Caroline. "I heard they were neighbors. He's supposed to be a real recluse, but people say he has a mansion built on the rocks. And apparently he saw through Madoff . . ."

I smiled expansively as I picked up my purse. It was obviously time to leave; everybody's eyes were glued upon me. "So I hear," I affirmed, leaning forward to kiss my hostess's cold white cheek. "Yes, we're planning to visit him as well, while we're up there. There were some great photographs of Adjile's place in that piece in the *Times* last year about 'Defining Architecture of the Millennium,' did you see? Anyway; thanks for a wonderful party, Caroline. I doubt I'll see you for a while, because we'll be at Paul's, but do enjoy your—I'm sorry, I don't recall what it was you said you were doing—your vacation this summer, won't you?"

As I walked out past the wall of faces through the hall, and swung open the heavy front door, the summer air met me in a warm wave of fine, dusty pollen. I grinned at nothing in particular as I set off down the stoop, red hair fighting its way successfully at last out of its tortoiseshell comb and flying off in all directions. The street was quieter now; a lone Volvo was nosing its way into a parking space as I passed beneath the leering gargoyles, then off along the root-cracked sidewalk to the subway. The unbroken line of brownstones reared above me like an indifferent army. But inside the houses I heard the familiar sounds of families settling in for the night: children playing last games before bedtime; mothers shouting up and down the stairs; fathers whispering a tender "I missed you."

I quickened my step. I couldn't wait to get home.

2

~

Jeanie

London

I probably shouldn't have picked up the bowl. It was the only one I had without a crack so big the milk flows out of it faster than you can spoon the cereal into your mouth. But it was the first thing that came to my hand.

"Take that, you bastard." Dave ducked. It hit the wall. No more cereal for me.

"And that." This time it was a mug. I think my mother gave it to me. No loss there. It had itsy-bitsy sprigs of lavender on the outside and an indelible brown tea-stain on the inside.

"If you'll just listen to me—"

"And that—" An egg-cup. My flatmate's. Turns out this is surprisingly painful if it hits the right spot. Dave yowled. "You loon!" he yelled, dancing about clutching his groin when he was finally able to draw breath. "I—didn't—touch—her!"

"No, but you were thinking about it," I shouted, aiming a toasting fork at his foot.

He skipped out of the way. "I wasn't!"

"You were." I was running out of things to throw.

"I *wasn't*!"

"You were staring at her cleavage the whole time. I *saw* you crane to get a better look! And I think you dropped your napkin deliberately so you could get a better look at her chubby legs under the table." I found a teaspoon in the sink.

"I didn't," he replied, catching the teaspoon neatly in his hand and putting it down on the table.

"You did," I said, making for the teaspoon again.

Dave grabbed my hand deliberately as I entered his orbit and twisted it firmly behind my back. "Stop it, stop it, *stop it*, Jeanie. You've gone bonkers. Okay, I'll admit it. *If* you stop throwing things. I did—sort of—maybe a little bit—look at—some bits. Of her. It was hard not to. C'mon Jeanie, they were so—available . . . owwwww" (as I wrenched myself free and thumped his shoulder). "No wait," and somehow his arms were around my arms again, and I was held fast. "I looked. I didn't touch. I'm not going to touch. Ever. I *promise*."

I twisted around to look up into his earnest, stubbly face. He's not exactly handsome, my boyfriend, but he does have nice gray eyes, and his features—well, you wouldn't say chiseled, I suppose, but I've never really known what that means anyway. "I'm going to be away from London for *months*, Dave. How do I know you're not going to chase after Ellen the moment my plane leaves the ground? You're going to see her every time you go to visit your mum. I can see it now, you'll be spiritually drawn to the woman who is tending your ailing mother, you won't be able to help yourself, and then she'll bend over to change a bedpan and you'll catch a glimpse of her pink suspenders, and—"

"Jeanie, I won't. I promise. She isn't—I mean, this is cloud cuckoo-land! Really. Have I ever been unfaithful to you? No. Right. And anyway whose decision was it to go halfway round the world for months on end? Seems to me if anyone should be doing the plate-hurling round here, it's me, love." I heard the little vibration deep in his voice.

I stopped struggling and stood still, allowing my head to subside on his hard chest. There was something in his argument.

"All I did was get a little look at—well, what was on offer. You name a man who wouldn't have done the same," he said, reaching out to curl a strand of my brown hair around his finger, then tilting my face up to his. He wiped an imaginary tear from my lashes. "But it doesn't mean I'll touch her, love. I might look, but I'll never touch. I'll be waiting here for you to come back. While you're with your sister and the baby in New York, I'll be here, same old Dave, just like always. Come on Jeanie—" he whispered into my ear, his hands moving down to my tight pink T-shirt, pulling my body roughly into the contours of his jeans, "why don't you show me a bit of what *you* have on offer tonight, eh? Then I'll never think of Ellen again, I promise you . . ."

The truth was—I thought to myself, a couple of hours later, hair tied up in a high ponytail, working my way through six sizzling rashers of bacon and a large glass of wine—I felt guilty about Dave. He'd a perfect right to be upset with me. We'd been together for a whole year, now I was going away for four months to America to help my sister, leaving him in London all by himself to cope with his mum's Alzheimer's, his dad's depression, his own job struggles. It was a lot to ask of a boyfriend, no question about it. Why shouldn't he have a little goggle at Ellen now and again? I was getting to live in New York, he was getting an eyeful of Ellen's plump thighs. In a sense, it seemed a fair exchange.

My flatmate Una crashed in about eleven, which was early for her, accompanied by a very tall man called Holly or Solly or something. Three days before she'd had her dark hair cut razor short on a dare; now she looked a bit like an army recruit, although less so in a leather skirt that only just skimmed her ass. She let the strange man feel her up while I explained earnestly why half the kitchen was in pieces on the floor. "To be quite honest, I don't give a shit," she said at last, after a cursory examination of the shattered bits, helping herself to a slug of wine straight from my bottle and a rasher of dripping bacon from the grill pan. She was incredibly skinny and ate terribly, grazing most days on leftovers and fast food. "Smash the whole place up if you want. And as for Dave, I think you should just dump him," she added, somewhat irrelevantly I felt. "Don't content yourself with maiming the bastard. Kick him out." The unknown man's right hand was now inside her black lace top, and for a moment or two our conversation was halted by the fact that his tongue was sloshing around in her mouth. I waited patiently for her to come up for air.

"That's just because you don't like Dave," I said, when the unknown man paused for a gulp of beer from his bottle. "Because he doesn't have the hots for you, most likely. I'm not going to dump him for *that*."

"Don't be silly," Una replied, irritably, investigating the fridge, carelessly exposing the leaf-green seat of her undies. "I don't like him because he lectures me about recycling yoghurt pots. Because he's *boring*. Because he thinks he's better than me. Like that sister of yours. You should dump him and find yourself an American rock star, that's what I think. Or a tortured actor. Or alternatively one of those enormously sexy, ve-ry hot" (this slowly and meaningfully) "ve-ry *fuckable* basketball players . . ." At this point, the unknown man of great tallness half-laughed, half-moaned, grabbed her from behind, and started dragging her out of the kitchen, down the corridor, and into the bedroom. Gales of giggling and some screaming ensued, plus a lot of furniture rearranging. I shoved my fingers deep in my ears as the noise crescendoed, discovered that that didn't help, then grabbed my bag and denim jacket, slipped my toes into bright orange flip-flops, and swung out of the door, down the steep stairs, and into the summer darkness.

On the whole, I decided, as I flipped and flopped softly along the pavement beside the long row of tall Victorian terraced houses that peered loftily down at me, I regretted the decision to move in with Una a year ago. I answered an advertisement in *Loot* when I was accepted into my Master's in Social Work at Kingsbury College, London: "fun chick needed for spacious two-bedroom." I was a fun chick, I needed a spacious two-bedroom. Check! What could go wrong? What went wrong was that Una's idea of "fun" turned out to be incompatible with even part-time, half-hearted studying. Every time I opened a book, or (heaven forfend) switched on my aged computer to do anything other than surf porn sites, she grumped furiously that I was "bringing her down." She was technically enrolled in a fashion course in south London, but was enraged if her teachers so much as asked her to come in for a seminar ("who the fuck do these people think they are?"). I actually resorted to working in a library. She failed everything, and didn't give a damn; I just about scraped through, and wished I could do better.

But a year after moving in, my course was finished, the last piece of course work submitted, when Q offered to pay for me to go out and help with the new baby. When I got back from New York, I determined, I would move out from Una's hell-hole. I didn't know where; I didn't even know how I was going to afford to live anywhere else (the place was heavily subsidized by my flatmate's surprisingly wealthy, almost invisible father). And I could only hope I'd done enough to get the degree, and that I'd actually be able to find a job. Social workers are both very much needed when the economy goes up in smoke, and horribly susceptible to "cuts."

I sat down on a long wooden bench, erected in loving memory of some much-beloved grandma, and got out my mobile phone to ring my middle sister. The brick buildings radiated back the day's warmth, but there was a cool night breeze prickling my face. I waited three rings; there was a click, and the line opened up into my sister's elegant white Pimlico villa. I could hear the discreet methodical ticking of the heirloom grandfather clock in the hallway. "What—?" She sounded half-asleep. "Oh, Jeanie, it's you—"

"Listen," I breathed into the phone, "I had to tell you. I just *had* to. You've been right all along. I see it all now. Really. I've got to change . . ."

3

Q

My sister Alison—the one squeezed uncomfortably between Jeanie and me—became, in her early twenties, offensively elegant. Tall, but not too tall, she was slim but not bony, and her wardrobe spanned every shade from beige to taupe. She had flawless mid-length bronze nails, glossy mid-length hair, and inexorably mid-length hemlines. She married a minor aristocrat straight out of college, which surprised none of us. If my mother didn't have a plausibly precise story of pregnancy and giving birth, Jeanie and I would assume a mischievous cuckoo placed her in our family of long-faced, big-boned women—just to show us up.

"My darling, I'm just phoning to see how dear Samuel is doing," Alison announced superbly one morning, a week or so after Caroline's party. I was, at the time, trying to force a pick through a big clump of hair matted with something indescribable. (Some people have hair that inspires words like "shiny" and "sleek." Unless I put half the contents of CVS on my head, my thick red frizz could reasonably accommodate a family of goslings.) "And I also wanted to see how you are coping with motherhood," she went on, as an apparent afterthought. Of course, I saw her agenda immediately. "Thank you, Alison. Samuel is doing extremely well, as it happens, and I've taken to motherhood like a duck to water." (Pace a little too quick, but in other ways quite good.) One tine of the pick snapped off in the goo; I opened my mouth to swear, but caught myself just in time.

Pause. "Well, I'm very happy to hear that," Alison replied crossly. "If there are any problems, dear, I hope you know you can always pick up the telephone and ask my advice. After all, I *do* have two children of my own. I'm a very experienced mother."

Alison was indeed the first in our family to procreate, and she never let any of us forget it. Serena and Geoffrey were the kind of children you longed to see covered in paint and mud tumbling backward through a hedge. As things stood, their hair seemed stuck to their little white foreheads, their matching outfits were pressed, their socks clung grimly to knees that seemed unnaturally scrubbed. I'd never seen them with so much as a bruise, and I'd certainly never heard either of them raise a voice—in Alison's presence, that is. It was a different story when Mummy was out of the way. I took the kids to the Natural History Museum once and I swear I saw the animatronic Tyrannosaurus flinch before Geoffrey's vicious vociferous onslaught ("I's goin' to eat it, I's goin' to *kill* it, lemme at it, auntie Q!").

"Thanks for the offer, Alison, but really, motherhood isn't *rocket science!*" I laughed uproariously, and felt the barrier at the other end of the line come satisfactorily ringing down.

"I see," she muttered, sounding mortified.

"But if I *do* have any little problems, Alison, I'll be sure to ask you, never fear," I added earnestly, losing yet another tine somewhere in the midst of the knot. "After all, I know Geoffrey and Serena have given you plenty of practice, Alison dear. Now, I must go, Tom and I need to start packing for our Connecticut trip. Did I mention it? Just a few weeks in Paul Dupont's house . . . *you* know, the one from *GQ* . . ."

I put down the phone, picked up a pair of kitchen shears, hacked off the entire offending lump of hair in a burst of impatience, then dissolved into tears.

It was, in fact, several days after the party before I could bring myself to admit my conversation with Caroline to Tom, my husband, and thus put the plan into action. When my snobbish, superior, all-round-unpleasant in-laws announced their intention to visit, I glimmered the beginnings of an opportunity; time, first, to lay the groundwork. "It will be so delightful to see them!" I said brightly to my husband, and from the moment Peter and Lucille walked in until the second the door banged closed behind them, I was a model of restraint, tolerance, and respect. I affected great interest in Peter's research papers on cardiac surgical procedures and joined in energetically with Lucille's perpetual whines about "those careerist women's libbers." "Motherhood has improved her," I heard Peter concede to his wife as they walked off down the corridor. "Although, my God! What's up with her *grooming*?"

This is not to say it was easy to maintain my sweet-daughter-in-law image during the visit. Peter and Lucille came ostensibly to spend time with the baby and "help out," actually to reinforce the idea that they did everything *right* and we were doing everything *wrong*. "The baby sleeps in a bassinet," Lucille asked, eyebrows disappearing into her expensive blond hairline, "not a crib? It's so tiny! I'd be worried about suffocation myself . . ." And later: "Do you think it's *wise* to use these disposable diapers? Have you thought about chemical—er—*infloration*?" Last was the production of a small box of rice cereal from her bag of "useful things for babies" (none of which were remotely useful for a five-week-old. She clearly viewed Samuel's lack of interest in the spinning-top contraption she produced as evidence of dangerous developmental delay). "Give him two teaspoons of rice cereal for breakfast, lunch, and dinner, and he will sleep through the night," she asserted confidently, opening the box and preparing a bowl of the stuff with cows' milk straight from the fridge. "*Guaranteed*. It's a little trick my mother taught me," she added, smiling beatifically. (She only conceded defeat when he'd smeared half the bowl over her face with a single well-placed kick and thrown up the rest of it into her lap. It was almost worth the visit, I decided, watching puked cereal slowly seeping through the crotch of her beige linen trousers, for *that*.)

Then, as we restored order to the place (Peter was one of those people who seemed to imagine that tiny elves picked up towels off the floor), I casually introduced the idea of a few weeks' vacation away. My tone was as insouciant as I could possibly manage. But for all that, my husband looked at me as if the illusion of a transformed Q was, for him at least, beginning abruptly to fade. "All through your pregnancy you accused me of not spending enough time at home," he said as he stood in the kitchen with a dishcloth in his hand and a painfully aggrieved expression in his sea-green eyes. " 'What will happen when the baby comes?' you said. 'You need to be a better father,' you said. 'You need to watch your son grow up,' you said. Now the baby's here, I've cut back my night hours at Crimpson in spite of the recession, I'm nervous every time there's a knock at my office door, and this is the moment you choose to fly out the door with Samuel and leave me behind . . ."

I protested, sweeping the innards of the newspaper into a box (Peter's strategy is to disembowel the *Times*, section by section, throwing everything he doesn't want on the floor). "It's not that, darling. Hear me out. It's just that after all the hospitals, the worry of pregnancy, it seems a shame to pass up the opportunity of a little bit of time—"

"You seem confident that it *is* an opportunity," Tom cut in acerbically, dark curly hair standing nearly on end as he rubbed furiously, exhaustedly, at his head, "but I should perhaps point out that Paul hasn't offered us his house in a year."

This, I admitted, as I attacked Lucille's lipstick-stained teacups, was indeed a small problem. Last summer Paul was warmly insistent that we should go and stay in his summer place, but at the time we were both working too hard; since my pregnancy, we'd hardly seen him at all (Tom was in his office almost around the clock in order to try to make partner at his firm, while I was confined to my bed).

"Perhaps you could ask him—" I tried not to wheedle.

"Q," Tom snapped, staring at me, green eyes narrowed, "really, I don't understand you!"

There was a muffled yelp from our son, who was sleeping on the sofa, and we both turned hastily to look at him. His mouth was agape, drool spilling gently onto the cushions; he was a little red around the eyes still, from a bout of furious crying that afternoon. He was beautiful; and he was (everyone agreed, from bejeweled old ladies in the street to the plump cashier at the bank) the spitting image of his father. He had a shock of fine dark hair, black eyes that were turning to green, and hamster cheeks. He was warm and floppy in my arms, a little frog with bandy legs and spread-out toes, and somehow the look of too many fingers on his tiny crumpled hands. Sensing his own wrist near his face, he opened his mouth, cracked his eyes ajar, and began furiously sucking. Slowly, his eyelids turned heavy, then drooped, as his body relaxed again in sleep.

My husband and I caught each other's gaze.

"Listen Tom," I went on, walking over and putting my arms around him, his big comfortable chest, his wide warm shoulders, "the truth is, I was thinking. What if you *came too*? What if you said to yourself, forget it, they're not going to partner me—Crimpson made that perfectly clear before Samuel was born—so I'm going to use up all my long-overdue holiday entitlement and go away for a few weeks with my wife?"

My chest thumping now, I stared at the bit of my husband's shoulder in front of my face. It was a very nice bit of shoulder, as it happened, muscly, firm, and covered in starched white cotton. I pleated a bit of it in between my fingers, and waited, hoping.

Tom craned down to look into my face, his warm breath fanning my eyelashes. "You want me to commit suicide at Crimpson?" He sounded incredulous. "In this economy? Q, do you know what's happening out there?"

"I know how it sounds," I admitted. "I know what the partners will say. I know what they'll *think*. But Tom, your position is tenuous no matter what we do. If Luis didn't think you're the world's best lawyer at handling bankruptcies, you'd already be out on your ass. I think *you* should take control now—ask for a few weeks off, which you're entitled to, after all. Luis is bound to support you; he's desperate to keep you around. And then we can use the vacation to really think through the next step."

"I don't want to push Luis too hard, he's still talking about trying to get them to revisit the partner decision," Tom fretted; and then, in response to a lift of my eyebrows, "Yeah, I know. Not realistic. But look, there's my professional reputation at stake, Q. Skipping off for two weeks just isn't *done*."

"People know you in town, Tom, it's not as if you don't have friends and associates in other firms," I said reasonably. "Paul himself, for example. He might be willing to put in a word for you at Prince, or another Wall Street firm for that matter. Not everyone's tanking—people say Mahon and Mackey are actually recruiting; and with your skills—well. You don't need to impress Crimpson anymore. In fact, I think you should view their decision not to promote you as sort of liberating. Otherwise you'd never have risked jumping ship. The stress of being at Crimpson, especially in these circumstances, is really wearing you down, Tom. I can see it in your face. I want to get you out of there. At least for a few weeks."

My husband pulled away, sat on the window seat, and looked out into the evening. The sun was spreading its last colors across the millions of windows outside our own, a sea of orange fire engulfing the office buildings of Manhattan. Samuel sneezed in his sleep.

"We can start again, Tom," I pressed, coming to stand in front of him.

"You were playing me last night," Tom remarked, shaking his head at me, but the corners of his wide mouth were soft, his eyes gentle. "I see it all now. Trying to get on my good side. I *thought* it was too good to be true. 'You're so expert at mothering, Lucille, can you show me that burping position again?' 'Peter, tell me more about minimally invasive coronary bypass procedures.' Very subtle."

I sat beside him. "I want a vacation with you." I took his hand in mine. "And Jeanie—"

"You know *she's* going to want wall-to-wall cocktails and parties and stretch limousines when she gets here, that's why she's coming out to New York."

"Leave Jeanie to me, I can persuade her. And she's not really like that, you know," I murmured reproachfully. Samuel stirred again, and opened his mouth in a cat's yawn; this time, after a second or two, he whimpered and opened his sleep-darkened eyes. I glanced at the clock; it was time for a feed. I picked him up and curved him into the crook of my arm, lifted my T-shirt, and spilled myself into his tiny, insistent mouth. We listened to his gentle suck-swallow, suck-swallow as the window square blackened and the stars appeared to prick out the sky.

"Okay," Tom said slowly, at last. "You win. I'll phone Paul tomorrow."

4

~

Jeanie

I Love New York "(Madonna). "I Feel Safe in New York" (AC/DC). "Summer in the City" (The Lovin' Spoonful). "Skylines and Turnstiles" (My Chemical Romance).

My iPod was brimming with New York–themed music. Before leaving London I spent two days downloading songs and even the occasional album to get myself in the mood, although I hadn't quite gotten around to organizing it all. I'd start nodding off to Paul Simon then get woken up by Busta Rhymes. It was a little bit disorienting.

I've always loved flying. I love the adrenaline rush as the jet speeds down the runway. I love the little dinky dinners in square white boxes. I love sipping gin-and-tonics at eleven in the morning while watching movies of scenically catastrophic destruction. Not that flying is without its downsides, of course: I don't like tucking my knees into my belly button (a necessary feat if someone belonging to the human race is to fit into an economy class seat), and I don't enjoy being told off by gaunt ladies with ugly hats. But there's always the pleasure of needling the ugly ladies through mild acts of rebellion, e.g., reading a magazine four and a half seconds after being asked to put it away. *And* the relief of leaving my problems far, far behind me.

"All the Critics Love U in New York" (Prince). "City of Blinding Lights" (U2). "Streets of New York" (Alicia Keys). "Big Apple Dreamin'" (Alice Cooper).

Somewhere back in Heathrow the morning I flew out, Dave was left yelling at the oil-soaked gaskets and widgets (or whatever they're called) in the engine of "Betty," his Morris Minor, as I soared overhead. I could see him in my mind's eye, fussing under the dented bonnet, rubbing his dirty hands distractedly on his graying T-shirt, swearing furiously at Betty for her remarkable unwillingness to start whenever she's away from home. (Betty was consistent in nothing but this.) Eventually, after an hour or so, after much hammering and yanking and bashing, Betty would (if the past was anything to go by) splutter apologetically back to life, and Dave would hop into the driver's seat and roar back down the North Circular Road into London. Settling back into my seat, I hoped he was all right. I hoped he would manage without me. Perhaps Alison would drop by his flat sometimes, check how he's getting on, I thought to myself, ripping apart my third bag of pretzels. She'd been quite good with him recently.

"Manhattan Skyline" (a-ha). "New York" (Ja Rule). "New York Fever" (The Toasters). "JFK to LAX" (Gang Starr). "I Run New York" (50 Cent).

I saw the skyline unfolding out of the dirty coach window with delight, the mad futuristic buildings thrusting through the yellow-gray haze. The city never looked quite real, more like a Hollywood production. (If you looked carefully I was sure you could see the ticky-tacky tape, holding it all together.) All the way into Manhattan I dreamed about the weeks and months I would spend getting to know the place properly. I would become the sort of person who could go back to England and begin sentences for the rest of her life with the phrase, "When I lived in New York." The sort of person who could throw phrases like "uptown" and "downtown" casually into conversation, and "Broadway" and "Central Park West."

Dave would be fine without me. Really.

"Times Square" (Marianne Faithfull). "To the Five Boroughs" (The Beastie Boys). "Lighters Up (Welcome to Brooklyn)" (Lil' Kim). "Central Park" (Pete Miser). "Manhattan Avenue" (Nellie McKay). "Cabbies on Crack" (Ramones).

I could buy very cool clothes that nobody at home would have. I could take home magazines that nobody I knew had read. I could buy not-very-expensive Christmas presents, write on the label "a little something from New York," and get away with it. I could procure a stunning haircut, then grouse about the fact that "no one styles like that at home." (As long as I could afford the stylist, of course. What, I wondered, could you get for $40 in New York?)

I hoped Dave could hold out until I got back. His mother's Alzheimer's had been advancing fast and his dad's moods had been getting blacker and blacker. Sometimes I wondered how one family could take it all, the illness and the hurt and the loss. If the worst came to the worst, I supposed I could always jump on an airplane and fly home again. I was sure Q would understand. And Dave would be so pleased . . . Perhaps he'd come to meet me at the airport with flowers! I briefly fantasized a reunion involving tears and people clapping, then sighed and shook myself. This was Dave, after all. Dave's idea of a romantic occasion was watching Spurs on the big-screen TV at our local pub—with a glass of wine.

"Englishman in New York" (Sting). "Lonely in New York" (Sophie Milman). "I Can't See New York" (Tori Amos). "Lightning Strikes (Not Once But Twice)" (The Clash).

We need a change of scenery." "We need a break."

Too bad, really; that was what I thought I was getting by going to the States.

Now, I discovered, we were going to Connecticut. I didn't even know where that was. I looked on a map. Turned out it was one of those states so small its name was written out in the Ocean.

"The important thing is that I'm here to see *you*," I said at last, coming to sit beside her, getting my priorities straight, dumping my Top Shop shoulder bag on the floor. My sister and I hugged each other. "It's so long since we've lived in the same house," I added thoughtfully, "and you know, my visa says 'six months.' Now listen, Q, where's this baby of yours? I'm so excited to meet him, I wish you hadn't put him in bed already. Does he look anything like me?"

"A little," Q offered, laughing, and then she described her new son's manifold attractions while I sipped at my hot black tea. Samuel was, I was given to understand, a paragon of a baby, the most beautiful, most advanced, most well-behaved child ever to be born—apart from the fact that he happened not to sleep at night and screamed himself into a fit if she so much as stepped outside the front door. Small flaws, clearly. I cooed in the right places, fingered his tiny clothes, and marveled at the fact that my sister had a child of her very own.

"I've brought a list of clubs and boutiques," I explained, when she finally fell quiet, excitedly producing a well-thumbed page torn from a *Time Out* special on "What's Still Hot in New York." I'd saved it especially; every night, the month before leaving, I'd been reading and rereading it, salivating at the thought that soon I—I!—would actually be beating the streets of New York City. "And—" turning over the page, showing her all the sections—"there's also a section on flea markets. Places where hip young designers flog their stuff. You know, the ones hoping for a lucky break. There'll be plenty of time, when we get back to the city, for us to work our way through them together, won't there Q? It's so nice you're on maternity leave," I went on enthusiastically, in answer to her faint nod, "we can really *do* things together this time. Oh Q, it's going to be lovely!"

She was looking tired, I noticed suddenly—tired, and a bit lumpy.

"You need to get more rest," I said solicitously, touching her thickly tangled auburn hair then hastily letting it go (what was *in* there?). "It's good I'm here, Q. I can really take care of you." Her skin was almost gray; she's one of those people who's sort of pretty when she's plump and sparkly-eyed, but quite plain otherwise. She rested her head on my shoulder. "That would be nice, Jeanie," she said, heaving a big, exhausted sigh, and then she rubbed her face slowly against my shirt, like a fond but knackered pony. "It turns out it takes a while to get used to—all this. Motherhood. You know."

"I know, Alison said you'd be exhausted—" I began, but I swallowed the rest of the sentence when I saw her eyelashes flicker. "Really?" my sister retorted, sitting up straight again, one hand resting defensively on her rounded tummy. (She looked suspiciously as if she were still in maternity clothes.) "Says I can't manage, does she? Typical!"

"I wouldn't say that—"

"Well, I would," Q returned crossly. "You should have heard her on the phone the other day. 'Motherhood doesn't come easily to everyone, Q. For some of us it's second nature, of course. But you mustn't feel it's a comment on your femininity if *you* find it hard . . .'" She mimicked Alison's voice in a scornful high falsetto. "She's just longing for me to fail," she went on. "She wants everyone to think she's the world's best mother and I'm just some careerist freak who can't even change a diaper. Well, I'll bloody well show her—and you, Jeanie," she turned to me owlishly, head swaying, "you can help me by staying on message, okay? Whenever you talk to her, I mean. I deal with Alison on a strictly need-to-know basis, which is a simple enough rule because she doesn't need to know *anything*. But look," she went on, after a moment, snaking her arm around my waist, "let's forget Alison. I try to as often as possible. Let's talk about *you*, dear. Did you manage to finish your course? Your social work degree?"

"Of course I did," I said, nettled (just how disorganized did she think I was?). "So was it useful? Worth the money? What did you learn?" she went on, sounding more like my mother than my mother. "How to speak in words of nineteen syllables," I returned, irritably, draining my cup and setting it down with a bang. That was the one skill I was confident I'd picked up from my master's course, actually. I used to have my friends in stitches at lunchtime, converting every event of the day into social-work-speak: we didn't catch the bus, we "engaged with a broad-spectrum transportation network which facilitated the practice of time-keeping skills and coordinated cross-class collaboration." Instead of cooking dinner we "learned crucial choice-making in a domesticated setting, developing hand-eye coordination and temperature-regulation skills, essential first-order disciplines for all health-care professionals."

Q was clearly half-asleep. "It was—you know, fine," I finished blandly, not feeling inspired to expand in the circumstances. "Really fine." Visibly shaking herself, she opened her mouth to continue the interrogation but fortunately (for my purposes) Samuel began shouting in the other room. I didn't see the child but could attest to the size of his lungs, although why his scream had to be so freakishly high-pitched I couldn't say. That child made some noise! Thankfully, I took the opportunity of Q's absence (she flew off the sofa like a mother duck sighting a fox, wild-eyed and clucking) to slip off for a long, hot shower and some me-time. It had been *such* a long day.

5

~

Q

Don't suppose there will be any baby gear at Paul's house, will there," Tom said doubtfully, as we gazed around at the contents of the bedroom and the sitting room. My heart almost failed me at the thought of all the accoutrements that somehow accompanied Samuel. Was this a good idea? If Tom hadn't talked Paul into offering us his house, and if I hadn't talked it up to Alison on the phone, I think we might have backed out at that point—"holidays in your own place can be so relaxing," I heard Tom muttering disconsolately, eyeing the baby bath, the baby swing, the baby mobile the size of a family car—but who wants to be the kind of parents who get stuck at home, unable to move a step, because of their baby? Tom wrestled three vast suitcases out of the closet.

"I was planning on using the place myself this month," Paul observed, when Tom phoned, deeply embarrassed, to ask "for a favor . . ." But after a pause, he agreed. "If you don't mind sharing with me for a night or two, perhaps a weekend when I come up to work on the boat, I guess it could work." Tom actually viewed this as a plus ("We can catch a game, go fishing—!"). "But what are you doing about work?" was Paul's next, inevitable question, at which point my husband coughed uncomfortably. "I'm thinking of taking an—um—vacation," he said, and you'd have thought he was suggesting crack cocaine. Paul, however, received the information tolerantly. "Great idea," he agreed, "you should spend some time with your new son." Tom relaxed visibly about the whole plan after that; it was as if Paul had given him permission. He marched into Crimpson the very next day and asked for two weeks off. There were some raised eyebrows, but Crimpson still didn't want to think of itself as one of the firms in distress—and Tom had a reputation with the clients as one of the very best bankruptcy lawyers in the city. So the smiles were, for the most part, bland; "Enjoy your vacation," the partners murmured, "and give our best to your wife." Tom's biggest supporter Luis pulled him into his office just as he was leaving (eyes flicking up and down the corridor) for an intense, excitable conversation about "future options at the firm."

We packed the rental car, leaving just enough room for Jeanie to actually sit in—quite an achievement. Glancing back at our trunk of neatly stacked monochrome luggage, I felt strangely clean and pure. No junk, just necessities! We should live like this all the time.

After an energizing argument about the route, and after both of us had checked three times on the harness of Samuel's baby seat (too tight inspires fears of chest constriction, too loose incites images of fearsome automobile accidents), we threw ourselves out into the Manhattan traffic heading out of town for the weekend, lurched over steaming potholes toward the press of the FDR Drive, and dove among the cars heading toward the Triborough Bridge. At the toll, the air shimmered with the heat of a thousand idling engines. Samuel whimpered uncomfortably in his seat; Tom slammed an impatient hand against the wheel, cursed softly, then flicked compulsively through XM radio channels, while Jeanie and I meandered through a desultory conversation about our mother's yoga business back home in England.

But once the barrier finally rose to let us through, a new world opened up. "I-95 New Haven" announced a large green sign above the sweating, smoking asphalt. Picking up speed at last, we skirted the edges of a dozen small commuter cities, curved around the unprepossessing hotel fronts of Stamford, flew across Bridgeport's overpass, and then, as the scattered high-rises and implausible sheer face of New Haven's East Rock glimmered a tantalizing gold and bronze upon our left, sped beyond, around the underarm of the coast, into the deepest part of the state.

When we finally left the highway and struck out into the winding roads of interior Connecticut, we seemed to be in a different country altogether. The roads were narrow, and the houses modest; a few clapboard farms, slightly dilapidated, sat in the midst of open, undulating fields, where cows half-slept and nosed the grass and flicked flies along the banks of thickly rush-edged ponds. And then, quite suddenly, we entered a dark tunnel of pines and maples whose branches met above us. Down headed the road, further and further, sweeping around sharp corners set with low red Capes; until, at the very bottom, as the road traversed a neat triangle of carefully mown green grass, the sea appeared before us, orange and crimson and palest blue in the lights of the setting sun.

Sussex, the town where Paul's summer house lay, hugged a cove notched into the Connecticut coast. The house itself was—we knew from Paul's detailed instructions—located just outside the small center, off a rough, dusty path running perpendicular to the coastal road. Surrounded—almost encased—by trees, the simple white house gleamed in the semidarkness like something out of a fairy tale as we bumped along the drive. "Good size," said Tom thoughtfully, looking up at it. Jeanie, peering through the windshield, seemed rather more uncertain.

But if the home was Quakerish on the outside, the inside had, as we quickly discovered, recently received the loving attention of an expensive interior designer. The wooden floorboards had been evened out and stripped to a gleaming sand color, and ocean-hued silk curtains tickled the floor in the breeze. Nautical-themed carpets and pillows were thrown next to pure white armchairs and sofas. A large modern canvas splattered with lines in declining shades of ochre stared down from the gloss-painted mantelpiece. The table and dining chairs were polished teak slabs, as were the kitchen cupboards. The oven alone was the size of a New York City apartment.

Upstairs were two enormous bedrooms with en suite dressing rooms and vast, echoing bathrooms, equipped with claw-footed iron tubs and rain showers. Fawn-colored glass tiles turned rich gold with a flick of the light switch; amber-colored towels as thick as a woman's arm lay neatly folded on silver rails (Paul employs a housekeeper to come in and clean once a week, and to set up the house for him and his guests). It was—we realized, as we ran from room to room, exclaiming at the size, the space, the coolness—like something out of a tourist magazine, *Martha Stewart Living* at the very least; a fantasy come to life, a dream of secluded quiet, a cloistered retreat equipped with swansdown and a dizzyingly expensive entertainment system.

Jeanie was, in spite of herself, deeply impressed. "Blimey," she said, staring wide-eyed at the expanse of opulent minimalism. "How much d'you think all this stuff cost? How can he afford it?" After dinner (pasta thrown together from packets), she curled up on the sofa, tapping out e-mails to her friends in which she described the place in precise, intimate detail. Dave, she said, would be particularly intrigued. "He just wouldn't believe it," she said, looking up for a moment with a grin between gulps of iced Chardonnay. "All these rooms! The space! The huge bathrooms! The weirdo art! Although—" her excited smile slipped down her face a bit—"he might not approve . . ." She took another sip of wine, looking thoughtful. "He's very into the environment these days, he might sniff about the 'carbon footprint' of the house." She shook her head a little, then started tapping again. "But I've *got* to tell him about the kitchen and the bathrooms, he'll be simply amazed . . ."

Tom and I left her to it, and took ourselves upstairs to our room. A vast downy quilt and floaty white pillows were piled on top of an iron four-poster in the middle of the room. At the bottom of the bed, on a painted ship's chest, stood an enormous display of lilies and ferns with a card from Paul that said, simply, "Enjoy."

We'd put Samuel to bed in his bassinet before dinner; I picked him up now with cautious, gentle hands, nursed him while he slept, and levered myself into the cool sheets without making a sound. Tom, who had been anxiously watching the whole careful dance, produced a big thumbs-up gesture in the darkness and we settled down with matching sighs of relief. For ten minutes, Samuel slept the heavy, dreamless sleep of the innocent. I drifted off listening to his thin, even moth-breaths. Then, a few moments after I'd lost consciousness, just as I was walking into a dreamland of warm black velvet and soft white down, I was woken by an ear-splitting shriek, a sound to tear body from soul.

"What the—"

Maybe it was because of the trip, maybe the change of surroundings, but the night that unfolded was nightmarish. Samuel was up at midnight, then again at two a.m., three thirty a.m., four a.m., five fifteen a.m., and finally for good, chirruping hopefully, at six a.m. "Can't you *do* anything?" Tom said raggedly, somewhere about four a.m., but by this point our son was acting as if nursing, cuddling, and singing were all activities approximately akin to torture. "Oh, right, I'll just switch the 'off' button, silly me, why didn't I think of that before," I told my husband, and I think I even hit him at one point.

We fell down the stairs together just as the first rays of sunshine were filtering through the window blinds in the kitchen, cheeks flushed, eyes hollowed. I had the oddest sensation of having lost the fluid in my brain. "Obviously, it was just a one-off," Tom remarked in a ghastly voice, turning pancakes on the stove with shaking white fingers, as the room brightened quickly to day. I nodded. (I think I actually heard my brain rattle.) "Once he gets used to the place, it'll be different," he went on, slapping a syrupy mess of half-cooked pancakes in front of me. "We can work on getting him into a *routine* while we're here, Q," he added, sitting down on the stool opposite me with the stiff, jerky gait of a very aged man. "Then when we go back to work, at the end of our holiday, he'll be sleeping reliably throughout the night. We'll be *totally* in control by then."

Outside, the pines stirred in the morning breeze, and the waves dragged shells in and out of the empty shore. Tom and I picked up our forks, and set about our breakfast in silence; Samuel had gone back to sleep. The house was utterly quiet.

6

~

Jeanie

On our third day in Connecticut, we took a long walk around the town of Sussex. (Personally I'd call it a village, but that bit of Frenchery seemed not to have made it across the Atlantic.) The center was basically one long street that fell into water at the end; the main road turned into a footpath which became a boardwalk, and then finally the river. A few miles south the river opened out into the sea, and in my mind's eye the route continued— across the Atlantic, around Ireland's choppy bottom, to England. You could see signs of English heritage everywhere, from the name of the town to the small village green, halfway along the street, to the shape of the houses (simple and square). But those New Englanders had brought their own twist, since everything—houses, barns, garages, shops—was made of wood. Walls, roofs, doors, you name it; wood, wood, wood, not a brick in sight. I couldn't help eyeing the wooden boxes and their wooden lids with an Englishwoman's inevitable bewilderment. "They don't look safe to me," I said suspiciously to Q, standing staring at one from the middle of the long narrow street. "How come they don't rot or burn down? What happens when your neighbor lights up the barbecue?"

The place was nice enough, but perhaps not quite as beautiful as it had been in its heyday; the paint on the houses was peeling, I noticed, the gardens were chock-full of weeds, and the chimneys were tipping slightly to the side, like women who'd taken to drink. The ships in the docks that fanned out around the coastline seemed to bring wrinkly-brown pleasure cruisers instead of roaring trade, and most of them stopped for an hour or two at most, sampling microwaved French onion soup in small restaurants with names like Kat's Kozy Korner. Chain chemists and banks lurked down side streets in concrete bunkers marooned in asphalt. Q told me that Sussex was chiefly popular for its proximity to a very large "outlet mall" (a place where you could wrestle comrades to the ground for a cheapie pair of Calvin Klein knickers, apparently). Tourists generally preferred the charms of places farther along the coast (with more English names—Essex, Norwich, Old Lyme), towns that had a similar shape but more original buildings and more zealous old people committed to preserving them.

Paul, the man who owned our house, was apparently left it by an aged uncle, and I gathered he more or less ignored the town, focusing instead on his expansive dock. He also owned a place in somewhere called "the Hamptons." I didn't know what this was, or why it was plural, but Q and Tom discussed it with a slight air of consciousness, as if even mentioning the Hamptons in conversation gave you an "in" to polite society. (I imagined an Edith Wharton novel, a place of tall white mansions reaching down to the sea, of conservatories filled with yellow roses lapped in eternal sunlight.)

We strolled down Sussex's long main street, pushing Samuel, whose screams echoed up and down the narrow sidewalk. When he'd finally yelled himself into purple silence, we bumped the buggy up to a small coffee shop with cheery cotton curtains at the window, round wooden tables on a plain wood floor, and shelves piled high with model sailboats in full rig, and drank our cups of coffee in welcome peace. Q kept touching Samuel to check he was breathing until Tom impatiently slapped her fingers away.

"Jeanie, how are things with Dave?" Q began, glowering beneath her frizz across the table at Tom. "We were—uh—sorry he couldn't come out with you, but it's great he let you come for such a nice long stay." She dropped a brown knobbly cube of sugar into her mug and vigorously stirred it with a plastic swizzle stick, then surreptitiously touched Samuel's cheek when Tom wasn't looking.

"Yeah—good thanks," I replied cheerfully, "thanks for asking. Dave's still having problems holding down a job, but it's hardly surprising, given how much time he spends with his mum. She barely knows where she is most days."

"And he's very into the environment now, you said."

"Mmm. It's his latest thing. It was his flatmate Badger who got him onto it—"

"Badger?"

"Yup. He has a shock of white hair down the center of his head."

"I see. Makes perfect sense."

Tom seemed to be watching a game of rounders played with helmets on the green outside the window.

"And Badger is an eco-warrior, is he?" Q went on a few moments later (she was now holding Samuel's tiny hand under the table).

"Something like that. He's had a big effect on Dave. When we first got together, Dave was a tabloid reader, *Sunday Sport, News of the World*, that sort of thing. Cigarette propped permanently over his ear. Favorite way to spend the weekend was down the pub. But over the past year he's been taking a lot more responsibility for his mum, and Badger's got him demonstrating against global warming and globalization. It's quite sweet really. I'm not sure he always knows quite what he's demonstrating against, but he does love a nice walk through Hyde Park with Badger."

"Well, who wouldn't," Q murmured neutrally. She'd never been particularly fond of my boyfriends. "And you're still getting on well, the pair of you? Is he—er—reliable, and trustworthy, and—"

"Faithful," Tom supplied, still looking out of the window. I scowled at the back of his head.

"Of course," I said crossly. "All of those things. And more."

"More—?"

I expatiated further on Dave's many, many virtues. "These last few months he's been giving his dad every penny he has to help get the best care for his mum," I explained earnestly, "even if it means he doesn't have enough to pay his own bills. His sister's always telling me he's the best big brother in the world, and his dad depends on him. He would have been an amazing social worker, if he could've afforded to complete our course. He's really *strong!*" I banged my hand on the table for emphasis; the cold dregs of our coffee jumped and shuddered in their corrugated plastic pots.

"Impressive," Q admitted; I was proud.

"And he was happy for you to come out here for four months, was he?" Tom suddenly turned and looked me full in the face, green eyes sharp as glass. "I mean, it seems like a long separation," he went on. "I'm surprised he was okay with that. Dave, I mean. You too."

I picked up my tepid coffee and dashed a gulp down my throat. *I can't believe you're doing this*, were Dave's actual words, as I recall, when I first outlined the plan. We were in our local at the time. He thumped his fist on the table until the beans-and-sausages shook and the barmaid appeared with a wary look in her eye. "A crook of the finger and you're off! One day it's Alison, the next Q in America . . . And I don't understand why, Jeanie, because they don't really need you, but *I* need you. Your mother claims they need help with this baby, but as far as I can tell they've got plenty of money to get a nanny—a whole fleet of them if necessary. What happened to togetherness? What happened to *us*? How do you imagine we're going to have a relationship on two different continents?"

"Dave," I began miserably, reaching across the rough, knotty pine table for his hand, "see it from my perspective. This is my one opportunity to live abroad. My course will be finished, I won't have a job, it's the one time in my life I'll be free to travel. And it's my one chance to get to know Q's little baby . . ."

"It's your one chance to spend these four months with me," he growled. "We won't get this time back again, Jeanie. What's passed is passed. And you just expect me to sit around waiting for you, do you?" he continued suddenly, with an awkward rasp in his voice. I felt my bottom lip wobble. "You think I'll just be hanging around for you, good old Dave, waiting like a patient dog for when you've finished your travels?"

"Well, I can't insist, but I was definitely *hoping* you would . . ." I replied miserably. "I mean, I'll understand if you don't want to, Dave, but I—I will be waiting for you—"

"And so will I, but the bloody difference is, I don't have a choice," he said angrily, and stood up to order another couple of pints. He sniffed loudly as he went, rubbing his arm across his nose in a single, characteristic gesture. I watched him lope across the bar floor, navigating the yelling, laughing crowds, the heaped coats and duffel bags, the strewn bar-stools, with practiced ease. I really like Dave, I thought to myself suddenly, and he is my boyfriend, but I can't help wanting to see a bit more of the world than the inside of a London pub.

Q, I suddenly realized, was talking. "I don't want you to worry about the cost of speaking with Dave; use our phone while you're here," she offered. "If Dave can't afford to ring you, just call him. We'll pay. It's the least we can do. Here's the thing, Jeanie," she continued, leaning across the table, "I know I was a bit negative about Dave when you first got together, but if he makes you happy—if he recognizes what he's got—then that's all that counts. I don't care that he doesn't have money—"

"Or a job," contributed Tom, sotto voce; Q rolled her eyes. "There are lots of ways of working, I understand that," she said firmly, as if she'd made up her mind about something. "Seriously, I do. Dave's work isn't the conventional sort, but it's extremely valuable. Saving the environment—I don't know what's more important than that these days." She smiled in what I'm sure she hoped was an understanding way. "Tom and I were talking about this. If Dave would like to come out and visit you once we get back to New York, we'll cover the cost of his flight too. It'll be tight in the apartment, the five of us, but we can manage."

"Thanks," I said, imagining Dave's face. A trip to New York—! "That's really kind of you, I don't know what he'll say—it'll depend on his mother's health, obviously. Plus there's a beluga whale press release to complete, a new project of Badger's," I added importantly. And then, in response to a raised, delicately skeptical eyebrow from Tom, "Well, not just belugas, but all toothed whales; you have to think of the bigger picture, the full marine spectrum, obviously . . ."

"*Obviously*," Tom echoed, and then he sharply twitched Samuel's blanket out of Q's hand with a muffled exclamation. He went back to watching the funny rounders game out of the window, while Q moved her hand millimeter by millimeter closer to Samuel's slumbering form.

7

Q

Paul is coming to stay this weekend!" Tom announced delightedly, flicking his cell phone closed, and I struggled to produce an expression of appropriate joy. "Paul! Wow. That's so great," I said enthusiastically. "I'm pleased. In fact I'm *thrilled*! I can't wait. Paul. Way-hey!"

My husband stared. "D'you have a crush on him or something?"

The truth was, I wasn't making much sense anymore; I seemed to have the brain power of a flickering candle. After three nights of no sleep I was not actually a human being, but rather some sort of nonsentient lower organism. Something from the bottom of a pond, perhaps. Something without arms and legs that lies still and senses currents.

Samuel had given up sleeping and taken to crying instead. He'd had three screaming fits so far that day, each worse than the last. They came from what seemed like nowhere: one moment he was staring into blank nothingness, the next his face folded in upon itself, his mouth puckered up, his skin turned a mottled, blotchy red, and he began to yell.

The day didn't start out too badly; for the first half hour or so after he woke up, Samuel was quiet—peaceful, even happy, snuggling into my shoulder, his round plump bottom tucked into my hand. In spite of my tiredness I tickled his toes, and laughed with him as he kicked and bounced, bounced and kicked, then reached hopefully toward my face with stubby, interested, exploring hands. But then, just as I settled down for breakfast, everything changed; gurgles became whimpers, which became, in a fraction of a second, in the lapse of a heartbeat, a scream. The pitch of his shriek seemed to settle just under my ears and then, drill-like, bored its way up into the deep inner lobes of my brain. Everything turned cavernous, orange; the world dwindled to one child, one head, one mouth, one scream.

"Tom," I said hesitantly to my husband, remembering all this, "d'you think Paul is going to want to spend a weekend with Samuel when he's like—er—the way he is?"

"Don't be ridiculous, Q," my husband scoffed, "all this screaming will be over by the weekend. *Obviously*. His crying jag is just a short-term thing. *Short-term*. Blink of an eye, it'll be gone. Done. Over with." (By which I realized that he too was losing the ability to construct grammatical sentences.)

I could only hope he was right, and that Samuel's behavior would improve, because otherwise Paul would arrive here to find the three of us laid out cold. Either I would kill us all, or Tom would, or Jeanie. The poor girl didn't sign on for this, and she was certainly not enjoying it. She'd rushed into the kitchen at eleven o'clock that morning to find me covered in sweat and shaking, Samuel writhing in my grasp like an armful of smoking serpents. "What's going on?" she asked, confused, eyes still droopy, clutching her robe around her; Tom was out collecting bread for lunch (read: beating his head against a brick wall). "I don't know," I said, then repeated the words three times to make myself heard. "Can I do anything?" she yelled, uncertainly, shrinking away from me and the baby; I shook my head and shooed her out of the room. Alone with my son once more, I took a deep breath, a gulp of water, mentally shook myself, and tried a pacifier, but Samuel beat me off as if what I was actually trying to do was torment him with tiny red-hot needles dipped in acid.

"Anyway," Tom went on, thoughtfully, peering down at Samuel, who was briefly asleep, "it's probably louder than we think it is, right? The crying, I mean. He's our son, we're hyper-conscious of him. I'm sure other people will sort of—er—tune him out . . ."

We had the opportunity to test this interesting theory out half an hour later, when the doorbell rang, and a local fisherman's wife named Marie arrived with an order of sturgeon.

I went to answer the door, noticing the swirls of purplish gray that now loomed on the very edges of my vision. The ground was pulling me into its force with a gentle tug upon the bottom of my eyebrows; my knees were stuffed with floaty puffs of cotton wool—

Marie's bright cheerful voice lifted me out of my stupor. "Hi, you people, how're you settling in?" She was a familiar type of the area, big hipped with coiffed hair and large stately glasses; a connoisseur of Hollywood gossip but utterly happy in a small town; a devoted reader of fashion magazines while comfortably unfashionable herself. "Ooof—that's some yell," she observed, walking into the kitchen, as Samuel opened his lungs.

Three minutes later, she actually had her fingers in her ears. "Kid has volume!" she said, retreating to the door, having plopped the quivering wet package down on the table. "Colic, huh? My eldest had it too. Gave us a crazy time."

We stared at her. What?

"And the worst thing is," she went on cheerfully, having achieved the comparative quiet of the front hall, "there's nothing you can do. Just got to wait it out. Of course, it seems never-ending at the time. I don't envy you . . ."

I stood with my hand clutching the door, waving her a faint farewell as she heaved herself into her truck and swept out of the driveway. Colic? What exactly *is* that? I vaguely remembered something about sweating colts in some James Herriot novel I read when I was ten . . .

I dragged myself into the bedroom and feverishly unearthed (from beneath Tom's tottering pile of gold-embossed thrillers) *After Birth: Surviving the First Year*, a book I slung into our overstuffed suitcase when Tom was not looking. The cover was adorned with an image of peaceful, fulfilled maternity: a slumbering naked child slung over a serene woman's shoulder. No one was screaming.

After Birth had a whole section on "Colic," I discovered, looking in the index, complete with subsections on "Remedies," "Possible Causes," and "The Myths." I was briefly euphoric; I hadn't had much recourse to *After Birth*, but whenever I'd used it, it had concrete, useable answers. What to do when the umbilical cord gets icky: keep clean, use alcohol wipes, don't worry. What to do with a scurfy head: use oil at bath time, wash off, don't worry. A hundred other small but equally useful pieces of information bristled in its pages: use rectal thermometers for a really accurate reading; remember to keep blind cords away from your baby's crib; take your baby to the hospital if his fever tops 103. It was a how-to guide to motherhood, and it had never failed me.

Colic was a term "for sustained infant crying," I learned in its pages. But there was something missing here, some crucial gap between word and meaning, since presumably all children with colic cry but not all children who cry have colic. What is it? According to Nurse Barbara Trimblethwaite, illustrious author of *After Birth* (over a million copies sold), no one really knows. However, she lit upon a comforting fact: colic was not "serious," she claimed (unless you call screaming for hours on end "serious," of course), and it gradually subsides by week twelve.

I slumped onto the floor, raking my hands through my disheveled hair. Paul Dupont, one of New York's most dashing, brilliant, erudite men was arriving in three days' time, and would surely find his house possessed by a monster. A six-week-old tiny pink banshee who could clear a stadium on Super Bowl night. Would he ask us to leave? Could we possibly put him off until week twelve, when the spectral possession would apparently pass from the body of my once-perfect child?

"No chance, Q." This, sadly, was Tom's opinion. "He's got to get a boat ready for a regatta down in Florida in a couple of weeks. Look, there's no point in worrying about this, we'll just have to explain what's going on" (he set his shoulders manfully). "Paul has handled the Supreme Court. Of course he can take the crying of a little new-born baby . . ."

"You know, Q," he continued in a whisper half an hour later, when we were both laid flat out on the floor, Samuel slumped between us, "I thought when we had a child—well, I thought he'd just sleep and play, and cry a bit when he was hungry, you know? But this colic thing, if that's what it is—I mean, he cries *for what seems like no reason at all*. Did you know that could even happen?"

I didn't, of course. I wasn't quite sure what I'd expected mothering to be, but it wasn't this. It didn't have to be perfect, I didn't expect miracles. *But could somebody please explain*, I said to myself, hot tears sliding down my cheeks, *why it has to be like this*?

8

~

Jeanie

The ghosts ate, but I wasn't sure when; they ate in the middle of the night—in the middle of the morning—whenever Samuel happened to give them five minutes of peace. I made sandwiches and left them in the fridge, and usually the next time I checked they'd disappeared.

"Alison," I whispered into the phone one morning, *"it's not as much fun as I thought it would be."* Alison clicked her tongue at me. "Darling, who ever said it would be fun? You're not there to have fun, you're there to help. So the baby cries a lot, does he?" She was obviously very interested. "What's wrong, do you think? Is Tom helpful? Is Q coping?"

I had to describe Samuel's screeching fits while she clucked and muttered worriedly on the other end of the phone. "It sounds like colic, you know. You should tell her to contact me, I can help," she added confidently. "I expect he's having gastrointestinal troubles, perhaps caused by her milk composition, I think—" I switched off while she gabbled on about digestive matters. Parents!

But then she had to run off to collect her son from school. Feeling rather lonely, I turned to my computer for support, locating a wireless signal in the bathroom. I opened my inbox, where twelve new e-mails awaited. Seven were from Dave ("I LOVE YOU, YOU OLD BAG"); three were from my mother ("Just when *are* you coming home?"); one, strangely medieval, offered me the opportunity to improve my peniss lenght and enhance my ladys plcsure. One, from college, three days old, contained news that caused a profound darkening in my mood.

"Dear Jean Boothroyd," it opened, and you know you have to worry when the writer drags in your last name at the beginning. "We still have not received your" (big gap, text continues on next line) "coursework for the independent study module (SW415)" (big gap, text continues three lines down) "and we regret to inform you that you have not therefore fulfilled the requirements for the Master's Degree in Social Work and Social Policy. Yours sincerely, Ann Dougins (secretary to Professor Sibelius Mordaunt, Dept. of SW&SP, Kingsbury College)."

This was something of a downer, since the day before I left England I submitted an application for a job in which I claimed—and I guessed this part really mattered—that I was about to receive my master's degree in social work. It was also quite bewildering, since I'd given a large, bound copy of my final coursework (SW415) three days before that to the very same Ann Dougins, who was (I believed) cohabiting with Professor Sibelius Mordaunt and thus had ample opportunity to deliver said manuscript into his plumply wrinkled blue-white hands. In other words, the whole thing was a typical bureaucratic fuck-up of collegiate life, but one of those things that is nightmarishly hard to resolve when you are three-and-a-half thousand miles away from London, in a small American seaside town.

I finally got through to Professor Mordaunt, who did a very good job of acting as though he hadn't the faintest idea who I was (even though I'd been sweating through his wretchedly tedious classes for months). "Jean? Jean?" he said fretfully (I'd clearly disturbed him in the midst of his mid-afternoon milky drink). "Boothroyd?" he added, as though the name itself was an offense. "Yes," I explained patiently. "Boothroyd. With a B. And a Y. And an—er—double O in the middle . . ." I discovered I was doing a simply horrible job of spelling my name, and stopped.

"And you've completed this coursework, you say?" he asked, with evident suspicion. "You've actually submitted it to Ann—to Miss Dougins?"

"Yes. Weeks ago. It's bound and everything," I said, as if this was the important part. "It's about the impact of short-term separations on families," I explained, hurrying on into the meat of the subject, "especially children aged between seven and twelve. Prison, family members serving as carers in other parts of the country, job relocations, that sort of thing. I worked with families in south London, placement in Brixton . . ."

"Wait a minute, yes, yes, I remember now . . ." Professor Mordaunt began, slowly, "but it's *Jean* Boothroyd, I think?" he shot at me suddenly, as if I'd been masquerading all this time as Cheryl or Amy or something.

"That's what I said," I replied, starting to lose a scrap of my patience. "You see—"

"Of course I read your thesis," he went on cheerfully, "it's all coming back to me now. I wondered why you *will* keep working on children, clearly not your greatest strength. You just don't have a real feel for family issues, do you?" he continued, without waiting for an answer (which was a good thing, on the whole, since I was temporarily bereft of the means of providing one). "It was fine, not great; think I gave it a B -. Or maybe I felt generous and bumped you up to a B, I'm not sure. Not that it matters, really, eh? B, B -, all a bit of a fiction. Depends which way the wind's blowing, eh? Oh Lord, the thing must be around here somewhere, I wonder what happened. Yes, yes, I'll speak to Ann—Miss Dougins—and make sure the examination office is informed before graduation week that you've done every thing you were supposed to, good little girl stuff, eh? If you haven't had the letter in a week or two let me know, though. Eh?"

I put the phone down and pounded some pillows for a bit, imagining Professor Mordaunt's puffy white face (and Ann Dougins's equally puffy, and probably equally white, buttocks) were in fact receiving my blows. First they lost the work drenched in my heart's blood. Then they told me I couldn't graduate. And then, to cap it all, here was Professor "I'll Sleep With Anything That Moves" Mordaunt telling me I'd "no feel for family issues" *just* as I was about to move into a life dealing with, well, family issues. I stared at a photocopy of the application I'd just submitted for a job in Cumbria, supporting the children of imprisoned parents. Oh dear.

Why didn't I have a feel for family issues? I pondered, anguished; what did that even *mean*? Why did he wait till now to tell me about it? Did I perhaps have a feel for something *else*? Did I get a B or a B -? Who knew?

I phoned Alison back, to ask her what she thought. She was home by this point; I could hear the kids in the background. "Darling, you can't let some professor make your mind up for you, you have to do that yourself," she chided, and I explained disconsolately that after a full year of study, I still had no idea which area of my field interested me most. The course was quite long, and there were so many different subjects! "Well, what does Q think?" Alison asked at last, quite sensibly, and I had to explain I hadn't mentioned a word of this to our sister. "They don't have time to talk to me *at all*, you know," I said sadly. "Not anymore."

9

Q

When you go to work, no one sits on your shoulder and screams until your eardrum implodes.

When you go to work, you get to wear clothes that don't have spit-up, vomit, and poo on them. When you go to work, you have coffee breaks, and you're allowed to eat lunch without a squirming ten-pound weight in your arms. When you go to work, even the most evil, obsessive, work-addicted partner believes that you have a right to four consecutive hours of rest at night.

One night, about a week after we arrived in Sussex, I had an intense dream in which I took on Caroline. It was a real humdinger, sort of *Working Girl* meets *The Bionic Woman* meets *Crouching Tiger, Hidden Dragon*. Lots of impressive fight moves on my part and some pathetic gibbering on hers. "What kind of a weakling are you?" I shouted, arms akimbo, laughing loudly with impeccable red lipstick and glossy hair blowing wild in the breeze. "You *just* work? I can juggle a small child in one arm while wrestling a fresh-killed deer into the freezer with the other and looking up cases on Westlaw with a pencil stuck in my teeth." To demonstrate my general superiority, I turned cartwheels, produced ten-inch knife blades from my elbows, and finally punched her in the gut with my stiletto heels. It ended with her begging me on her knees to return to Schuster—"with a raise." Very satisfying.

The truth was, I couldn't imagine how I was going to go back to the office in three weeks when I was unable to lift a cup of tea to my lips without spilling the whole lot on the floor. I would have to be able to brush my teeth, walk in a straight line, and speak in full sentences at Schuster. These seemed, quite frankly, unimaginable feats.

Still, cornered by Tom, I phoned the small, pristine daycare center we were inspired to choose by the wife of one of Tom's colleagues ("They have care-cams!") and arranged a preliminary visit to help Samuel acclimatize to the place. Schuster was allowing me to go back part-time for the first month—a ludicrously humane decision for a Wall Street firm, particularly in a recession—so we could ease ourselves slowly into our new life.

That was the plan, anyway.

My mother-in-law was, of course, horrified at the thought of what she called "group child-care arrangements" ("Won't he become terribly *aggressive*?") and disgusted by my sordid careerism. She also made it quite clear to me, when she phoned to speak to "my son Tom," that I was basely dragging him down.

I could hear the disapproval flowing down the line as soon as I answered the phone; I knew the speech that was forming in her mind as I sketched our days in Connecticut. "My husband never had to change a single diaper," Lucille would say, if she could. "*I* took care of the family so *he* could take care of his career. And what has he got now? A world-class reputation. What have I got? More Tiffany jewelry than my bony neck can possibly support, and the self-satisfaction of a woman who knows she's done everything that could possibly be expected of her."

She restrained herself, however, and got straight to the point: "I have good news." (I'd managed quite successfully in the past to hint that access to her grandson depended on a good relationship between the two of us. And a good relationship depended on her keeping her views about my domestic arrangements to herself.) "*Very* good news. Tom will be delighted. A friend of his father's has a wonderful job opportunity, very solid income, excellent prospects. For when he leaves Crimpson, I mean. It would mean moving to DC, but . . ."

"Thanks, Lucille," I cut in brightly, "thanks a lot, but I don't think Tom will be interested. He doesn't like Washington at all."

Lucille tsk'd. "I know you think you know everything about Tom, Q," she returned icily, "but I should perhaps mention that I've known him longer than you. And if I know anything about my son, it's that he needs *professional challenges*. This job of Peter's will get him in the eye of people in the administration. It could open up real *political opportunities*! Maybe a future on Capitol Hill! I think you should support and encourage him, Quinn dear. I think—"

"Lucille, Tom doesn't have the remotest interest in a political career, as you well know, and frankly *I* think," I began, but at that moment Tom himself appeared in the doorway. He looked over at me quizzically, then—when I mouthed "your mom" unwillingly at him—reached out and almost snatched the phone from my hand. "Oh, hi, it's you," he said, glaring; I flushed. He turned his back as he sat down and, as I let myself out of the room, I could hear him embarking on conciliatory efforts. "No, that's not what Q *meant*," he assured her. "What she meant to say, I'm sure, is . . ."

I sat and stewed downstairs, snuggling Samuel while moving plates pointlessly around the kitchen, until Tom reappeared. "Q, Mom was just trying to help," he began irritably. "She's obviously concerned about me, which is reasonable under the circumstances."

"Tom, she's not just worried, she's got fantasies of having a senator son, and she wants me to be a quiet lady in pearls who stares adoringly up at you while you kiss babies," I returned sourly. My exhausted brain seemed to be trying to sneak out my ears. "She thinks I emasculate you."

"She's just from a different generation. She was a good mom and she's a good wife. I can't understand you sometimes," he went on boldly, back stiff and poker-straight. "Let's face it, she's quite right that I need a—well, some kind of a career plan."

"You should have heard her on the phone just now, Tom! I knew what she was thinking to herself, what she says to all her posh lady friends . . ."

Tom was looking at me with an unreadable expression on his face. "Q, she told me what you talked about, and she's right. I need a new challenge. And I don't like changing diapers," he added abruptly, flopping down on a chair. "I'm bored. I don't like sitting around here all day. Samuel doesn't *do* anything yet, except cry and need changing. Whenever I bathe him I half-drown him, and whenever I dress him I snap his fingers backward or get the poor kid's skin stuck in those clippie things. It's a nightmare. I'd rather be at work, frankly."

I gazed. "Do you think *I'm* enjoying this? Do you think I'm having fun?"

"I don't know what you're feeling, to be honest," he snapped. "You're a mystery. You don't seem particularly happy when you're with Samuel, no. But every time I suggest going out, or leaving him with Jeanie, you act like I've hit you. 'I can't leave my son,' you say, and 'He'll cry without me.' And sometimes: 'He'll think we've abandoned him.' Honestly, Q, if I hadn't seen the surgeon cut the umbilical cord, I'd think you two were still attached."

"That's ridiculous!" I scoffed, but there was enough truth in it that I agreed, eventually, to go out with Tom for dinner the next evening, before Paul arrived. Jeanie could babysit. It would be good for us, I knew; we'd hardly had a moment to ourselves since Samuel was born—so silly, when we had Jeanie to help look after him. But some deep, instinctual part of me worried that Jeanie might snap, that only a mother could withstand the terrible tearing, tortured sound of his screams. "That's ridiculous," my sister asserted, her long, honest, pretty face genuinely horrified when at last I managed to feel out this thought. "I won't say it'll be easy, being alone with Samuel if he gets into one of his—y'know, fits, but if things get too awful I'll put him in his bed, take a deep breath, and phone you. All right?"

And that, it seemed, was the best we could do. "Besides, Q, you're going to have to get used to it—leaving him, I mean," Tom pointed out, catching my hands. "After all, in just three weeks' time, you'll be leaving him with somebody else *all day*."

I smiled brightly, nodded, and pushed his words into a corner in the back of a box in the very farthest recesses of my mind.

10

Jeanie

t long last they went ("Are you sure—do you think you can—
what about if we—").

Paul Dupont was due to arrive approximately five hours
later, between midnight and two a.m. Since there were only two
rooms upstairs, I'd had to move my belongings out of the enormous double bedroom I'd been sleeping in so far into a wardrobe
off the living room stuffed with a jumble of graying mops, rags, and
a Hoover. I remade the bed for him (with matching sheets) then
folded out the green sofa and made it up for me, working very hard
not to mind the loss of my lovely room. Then I put Samuel on the
floor beside me in his bassinet; he was blessedly asleep.

It was quiet as a church in the house; a striking relief from the
madness of the day. Q was winding everybody up and radiating
stress; it was crackling like electricity in the air. Thank goodness
she's gone out, I thought to myself, pouring out a very large glass
of wine. Then I pattered upstairs to the bathroom with it and filled
up the tub to the brim, relaxing with a sigh into the water. I left the
baby monitor out in the hallway. It was *so* lovely to be alone for a
change!

∞

Now frankly, I blame the glass of wine. Or, no, maybe it was the order of things; I should have had the bath first and *then* the wine. As it was, with a heavy dose of Chardonnay thickening my brain, it seemed a perfectly good idea to leave my clothes off after the bath and stretch languorously along the sofa, hair loose, with magazines and a simple but rather fabulous meal of fresh fish, olives, bread, and cheese. Samuel was still sleeping.

I looked up at half past eight, conscious of a sudden change in the air temperature, to find the front door open and a tall man in a suit staring wide-eyed at my utterly, entirely, inarguably naked bottom. I did what I suspect any woman would do, yelped and started violently, at which point I unfortunately knocked my plate off the sofa-bed and on top of Samuel's bassinet. Waking with a start, he began to scream as if his head had been bashed in, and I was in the unfortunate position of deciding whether to rush off the bed and pick him up, thereby giving the strange man an even better look at my naked body, or to cover myself with a sheet, which would have the unfortunate appearance of heartlessness and which might leave Samuel in a state of injury for longer than strictly necessary. My better self came to the surface and I hurled myself off the green sofa-bed, shouting "look away, you git!" before scooping Samuel up; he—thank God—was entirely unmarked. However, he continued to scream with such passion and intensity that, in something of a panic, I frantically pulled his eyelids apart with my thumb and forefinger, trying to remember if his pupils should be *large* or *small* after a blow to the head. At which point the very superior man staring, with fascinated brown eyes, at my bosom looked up and said, for Christ's sake, naked lady, why are you torturing that poor child? Summoning up a haughtiness I didn't know I possessed, I drew myself up as tall as I could and (struggling to cover myself with my right hand while clasping Samuel against my breast with my left) asked him who *he* was and what he was doing in *our* house?

The supercilious man casually dropped a black duffel on the floor, pulled his flamboyant red-and-gold tie loose, then said that since it was his house he supposed he could come into it whenever he liked.

Fair point, I suppose. It suddenly struck me that my fig leaf (so to speak) was rooting around at my breasts, trying to suck milk out of my nipples. The lack of milk in the expected place was clearly beginning to bother Samuel, and his cries redoubled in intensity; I held him away from my body, from my resolutely unmaternal breasts, and he began to cry even harder. As embarrassing moments go, this was probably the most memorable one of my life. There was that time with my ex Theo when the next-door neighbor called the police because he heard—no, no, this one takes the biscuit.

After a few mortifying seconds, the horrible man with cheek-bones (Paul, I suppose I should call him) remarked calmly, over the din of Samuel's screams, that he didn't know Tom was hosting a colony of naturists, but that I should feel completely free to pursue my interests in his house in future.

I threw him a withering gaze (although there wasn't any marked withering on his part, I have to say. If anything, I'd say his lips twitched). "Please turn your back," I told him coldly. "I'll put on some clothes and then I can deal with this poor child."

"Well, all right then," he returned with equal coolness. "I will, but frankly I think I've seen what there is to see."

It was starting to feel like something out of a bad farce—or, worse, a porn movie, according to whose script I should suddenly appear, for no clear reason, to be overwhelmed by the need to drop to my knees and—well, you get the point. Obviously I wasn't anything of the sort, although there was a look in his eye that suggested he might be familiar with the script, and ever so slightly wondering if the fantasy of a dark moment was about to be realized. Pah. I waved Samuel in front of his face to remind him of the baby's presence, since I have long observed that infants are a reliable passion-killer. It might have been the waving, or it might have been Samuel's hysterical efforts on my behalf, but either way Paul silently handed me my pajamas, which were mixed up with a damp towel on an armchair, then turned his dark head and presented his back. I put the hysterical Samuel down in his bassinet for two seconds, hastily pulled on the pajamas, then began the long, long business of calming him down.

When, eventually, he had hiccoughed and burped himself into a state of relative calm, I looked up to find that Tom's ghastly friend had vanished. Thank God, I thought to myself, relieved; with any luck he's gone to bed. Or, even better, gone out. To kiss his boat goodnight, or whatever it is rich people like him do. I was trying cautiously to loop my hair out of my eyes without waking Samuel when I heard the sound of voices in the kitchen: Q and Tom were back.

Q rushed into the sitting room in a vast, clucky panic. "Samuel— is he okay? Jeanie? How did you get on?" she asked hurriedly, peering down at the moist bundle in my arms.

I conjured up my most confident smile. "He was—um, ah—fine," I told her, passing the baby off as gently as possible. "He slept a bit, cried a bit, you know, the usual stuff, nothing to worry about."

"Really?" she asked, relief lightening her eyes as she looked down at the baby, "he was okay?"

"Of course—" I began, but then I stopped because the horrible man suddenly appeared in the hallway, bowing his head slightly to fit through the door. Q and Tom turned in surprise at the sound of his footfall. *"Paul!"* cried Tom. "We didn't expect you for hours!"

Paul, who had now changed out of his work clothes and into a pair of black jogging pants and a black T-shirt, strode forward and shook hands with Tom and Q. "I met my deadline early, so I got a head start on the Friday-night traffic leaving Manhattan," he explained sweetly, scratching at his emerging stubble. "I arrived to find your friend—oh, sister-in-law, I see—tending a peacefully sleeping kid," he went on calmly. "Quiet as a mouse."

Q beamed at me, Tom threw me a look of purest gratitude. Behind their backs, Paul looked over at me, brown eyes alight with amusement, and grinned a slow, fiendish grin.

No embarrassment at his earlier behavior, my God! He should clearly have backed out of the room as soon as he saw me in my buck nakedness, then kicked over a few buckets before clunking up the front steps, swearing loudly. He should have sworn blind, if asked, that he didn't see a *thing*. Abject dishonesty was the only honorable course available to him. What an awful man! Of course it made me miss Dave even *more*.

11

~

Q

Tom and I were on our very best behavior the night of our first post-Samuel date. We avoided the topic of parents entirely, concentrating on less contentious subjects: holidays of the past, for instance, and Samuel's undoubted superiority to all other children. We licked butter from oysters and gorged ourselves on hot, plump fries while gazing across the expanse of the Sound, which glittered like a pale opal in the fuchsia lights of the setting sun. We drank cold white Chilean wine, purchased from Sam's Package Store, in plastic water cups until the sea seemed somehow to become a part of my head. We swayed home, warm and together, Tom and Q, a couple again.

"He's a good kid really," Tom said, chuckling, picking up on our earlier conversation as we wound our way slowly along the dark driveway. Tall pines reared up all around us, black and still; beneath them, in the red earth, lay pine cones sticky with sap. Before us, at the end of the winding dirt path, surrounded by maples, the house glowed like a giant pearl in the moonlight. "And he seems so much more alert than he used to be—"

"Did you notice how his eyes swiveled when you came into the room this evening?" I asked proudly, resting my head briefly on Tom's shoulder.

"Yes. And I really think he heard that gull on the deck this morning. Did you see how his eyes turned?"

After sharing a few more moments of equally dizzying brilliance from Samuel's short life, we fell into contented silence. Sometimes it is easier to see your infant's perfections when he is not right in front of you.

"*Have* you thought about what you want to do after Crimpson?" I asked suddenly.

"N-no," Tom replied slowly. "That is—no."

"What does that mean?"

"It means—it means I can't make any decisions until I know what you're going to do." His face was hard to read in the darkness.

I blinked. "Come again?"

Tom stopped, and looked down; I could just see the gleam of the white part of his eyes. His breath was warm on my face. "Just what I said. Are you going back to Schuster? Or—not?"

There is such a noise and a jostle in the forest on a summer night; when you stand still it seems as though every leaf, every patch of undergrowth, is bursting with life. There was a rustling somewhere behind me, and I turned a little nervously to look; a skunk ambled unhurriedly from between two trees, stopped and gazed at us for a moment, then resumed his course, his white stripe sharply defined in the moonlight. Other, smaller animals scurried as mere shadows beneath the lowest boughs of the pines. High above, we heard an owl's jubilant call, then the desperate squawk of some little animal. An acre away, a dog clinked his chain, and someone's screen door opened and closed.

"You think I'm *not* going back?" I countered at last.

Tom shrugged. (I heard the fabric stretch and move across his shoulders.) "I can't see it, quite frankly, Q. You've been losing interest in corporate law for months, if not years. You hate half the people you work with. You can't bear to leave Samuel for twenty-five minutes. Why on earth would you go back?"

"Because—because—they've paid my maternity leave," I returned helplessly. "Because it's my job. Because jobs are hard to find these days. Because I don't know what else I would do."

Tom half-laughed, and put his lips to my hair. "I'm the one whose job's on the line, but you're the one who most needs to quit, Q. Least, that's how it looks to me. When you were on bed rest I was frightened by how quickly you forgot your working life. The moment you walked out of the office it was as if the whole place slipped straight out of your mind."

"That's not *quite* true—" I was defensive.

"No, but almost. What do you *want* to do? If you could do anything in the world, I mean? If we weren't in a recession? Save gorillas? Teach high school? What?"

We had begun walking along the driveway again, and at this moment we rounded the final corner to see . . . an unknown car parked in the driveway. I'd opened my mouth to answer Tom, but as soon as I saw the car I forgot everything: for about three minutes, as I charged breathlessly up to the door, heart thumping, hands shaking, I thought of nothing but our son: was this a doctor? But no, no, of course not; it was only Paul, who had arrived a few hours early from New York. As soon as he walked into the sitting room, he was like a refreshing spirit from another life, his thoughts full of work and gossip, of boats and sailing, of sports drafts and deals and rookies and the new season. Tom's face lit up immediately. "I'm so glad to see you!" he said happily, and the two of them went out onto the deck.

I fetched a bag of tortilla chips the size of a pillow case for them, then took myself off to bed with Samuel. As I lay in the darkness, I could hear their laughter echoing around the silent, watchful ranks of moonlit pines. All too soon, my son's wails joined in.

12

⁓

Jeanie

O f course, I made it quite clear to Paul that his Harvard-University-*GQ*-spread charms wouldn't work on *me*.

I heard him with Tom outside the first night, the night of his arrival. He was talking about dining with some Supreme Court judge, about going to Washington to meet with White House lawyer-types, about being asked by Bill Gates to advise on some charitable committee ("I said, Bill, sorry, just don't think I have the time . . ."). Tom was clearly impressed. It sounded like humbug to me.

He came inside to fetch some ice just as I was about to go to bed; I was standing by the kitchen sink, filling a glass with water. I stiffened as I caught sight of him. "Hey, Jeanie," he said softly, coming up behind me and standing a *little* too close (I felt his breath in the hairs of my neck, just beneath my ponytail). "I'm sorry about earlier. Really. I was a bit—um—surprised when I walked in."

I moved away, and stared him down. "You behaved *despicably*," I told him. (Actually I stumbled a bit, added a syllable, and came out with "despicabibly," but I think he got the point; *note to self:* avoid polysyllabic words in moments of high drama.) "We have to live in the same house for the next few days, I realize," I went on, reaching for the tones of an English grande dame, Peggy Ashcroft perhaps, or Maggie Smith as an E. M. Forster Edwardian; "but I can *assure* you I shall avoid you as much as I possibly can." We looked at each other for a moment, then I turned on my heel and left the room with the fuck-you poise of one dressed in rustling silks. (It's unfortunate that I was wearing my bunny slippers at the time, but I'm fairly sure my cool demeanor overcame the effect of the pink floppy ears.)

Frankly I felt he had an ulterior motive. He clearly imagined a few polite words and a cocked half-smile would be enough to win me over, most likely into his bed. He was about to learn that English girls were more discerning.

Americans seemed to think the British were uptight, but I'd yet to meet an English lad half as uptight as these American city types. Work was what defined them. I couldn't quite tell what they did for kicks, or if they even liked having fun. While other Americans were busy pursuing happiness, to these men it seemed almost incidental. They were so busy working they'd forgotten how to enjoy life.

Take Paul, for example, I mused, as I brushed my teeth. Oh, he had muscles—but not the muscles of a man who spent his life in the hot oily place under a car. Paul had the small, tight, well-defined, perfectly proportioned biceps of a man who attended a sleek white gym in Manhattan. Who'd sweat discreetly while sliding polished shiny dumbbells up and down a polished shiny rack. I can see him now, I thought irritably, sliding into the sofa-bed; I can see him, wiping three drops of rogue perspiration off his forehead with a fluffy white towel slung casually around his neck. Because he won't want to get his high-thread-count organic cotton T-shirt dirty, will he? Certainly not! He's got a certain standard of personal grooming to maintain. He finishes his circuit then pops into the sauna to open his pores, and before he heads back to the office he slips a comb of citrus gel through his hair.

Paul wasn't the kind of man who'd pull a sickie to take you to the zoo. He obviously spent eighteen hours a day at work, got home at midnight, gave his slumbering wife a chaste kiss, then leaped out of bed at five a.m. to face another exciting day of contract negotiations (I laughed scornfully as I kicked off my slippers). His idea of living was presumably counting the zeros in his bank account. Meanwhile his wife was shagging the doorman and his children were snorting cocaine to get over the unbelievable, ineffable *boredom* of life. This was not the kind of man to appeal to *me* (I switched off the light and pulled the covers up to my chin). And I'd made that completely clear to him.

I lay in the dark, thinking about my boyfriend, who was a different story entirely. "When d'you want me to come over to America to see you?" he'd asked me excitedly on the phone that morning.

"You can come out any time you want," I replied, wondering briefly what Dave would make of this home of rich, elegant whiteness. He was a T-shirts, work-boots, and newspapers-on-the-table sort of man—the real deal. "But I think you should aim for sometime next month; go for halfway through my trip to split the difference. Limit the amount of time we're apart."

"Good idea, I'll look into tickets. And you said your sister will help with the cost, right? Bloody marvelous, tell her 'thank you' from me. I can't wait to see you, Jeanie. I can't stop thinking about you, to be honest. The bed seems so cold without you.

"I'll feel like a bit of a hypocrite, though, going to Heathrow," he went on, earnestly. "Badger's mate Ranger has been telling me all about the environmental impact of air travel. He's, y'know, an expert; he spent two weeks last year kipping on a runway to demonstrate against Terminal 5. He's seriously *hard-core*. Did you ever think about how many gallons of fuel are used over three-and-a-half thousand miles, Jeanie? And the *injurious* effects of it all go *straight* up into the atmosphere! Still, there's no other way I can get there, I suppose, and I can't wait four bloody months to see you . . ."

I could see him in my mind's eye, biting his jagged, worn-down fingernails. "Dave, I'll have to leave that decision to you," I told him a little impatiently, "but personally I think politics have to yield to practicality sometimes." That sounded rather good, so I said it again. "And anyway, there's bound to be some research you can do out here— you might gain a whole fresh perspective on—on—on the Kyoto Agreement," I finished inspirationally. "True, true . . ." I could tell he was impressed by my argument.

"Well, I'll see what it'll cost, and perhaps I'll ask Ranger to look into the number of gallons an airplane really uses on a long-haul flight, then I can make an *informed* decision. Or—" he thought for a moment—"maybe I'll just say 'bugger it' and come over, what do you think?"

I laughed, and told him that sounded like the best plan.

It was ages before Tom and Paul went to bed.

13

⁓

Q

Q, are you awake?" (I pulled the covers over my head and pretended not to hear.)

"Sweetheart, it's eleven o'clock. And it's a beautiful day." My husband had tiptoed into the room and was peering hopefully into the duvet. "Paul has a suggestion . . ."

I half-opened my eyes. "What is it?" I growled.

"You don't have to come—I think Jeanie would stay home with you, if you want. So don't feel—I mean—" I groaned, clutching my forehead. I had the strangest sensation of having a metal sword lodged inside my brain after the night's terrible screaming. *What?*

"Well, Paul has to take a boat to his friend's house this morning, further along the coast, he's going to help him replace some rotten wood in the stringers. His name's Adjile—did you ever meet him? Ex-CEO of G-Metrix dot-com? Well, anyway, he's offered to take us all sailing—that is, Adjile's offered to lend Paul a boat for the afternoon so he can get some time on the waves. We could all go. But only if you want, of course."

I thought about this for a moment. Adjile Olawe . . . "The baby needs more time outside," I said, at last, throwing back the covers. "Vitamin D and all that. We should go, it'll be fun. And I'd *love* to try sailing, I don't really know how to do it, but perhaps you can show me?"

Tom's face was transfigured.

I dressed myself quietly in my capacious jeans and XL green button-down shirt—Samuel was miraculously sleeping—and went downstairs to find Paul and Jeanie sitting silent, side by side, in the kitchen. Paul was leaning backward in a chair, reading the property pages; Jeanie was working her way through a tottering stack of waffles, dressed in a tight plum-colored T-shirt and skimpy denim shorts. "So. Are you going to come with us today, Jeanie, or not?" I asked, observing her get-up dourly.

Jeanie looked up, her face smeared in syrup. She was rather taken with American breakfasts. "Wha—? Oh, you mean this sailing business," she said, through a full mouth. "Well, really" (swallowing hard), "I suppose I should, but I've always thought boats were just big toys for men with too much money," she added airily, as if she'd been giving the matter a great deal of thought over the course of a very long life. I stared at her. "Yes, the consumption of resources—and the—er—damage to marine ecosystems from the—um—rudders is positively shocking," she finished triumphantly. She launched into another waffle.

"Well, we'll all understand it if your political principles prevent you from coming." Paul put down his newspaper. "I wouldn't want you to do anything that makes you *uncomfortable*, Jeanie. I'm sure between us we can help Tom and Q with Samuel, so why don't you just stay here? We'll spend the day sailing on the Atlantic, enjoying the views of the house from the sea (it just won another design award, Q, did you hear?) and you can work on that press release on—what was it you were telling me about? Oh yes, whales' dental cavities, instead."

Jeanie choked slightly. "Well, obviously I would under normal circumstances," she explained carefully, "but Samuel has been tricky recently, I wouldn't want—"

"No!" Paul interrupted. "Certainly not. You stay here. Adjile and Lily aren't your kind of people anyway, from what I can tell you'd be shocked by their way of life. They have a personal chef. The desserts are phenomenal, I had this thing with iced chocolate last time that was beyond description. Amazing fish too, fresh-caught in the Atlantic. Plus Adjile has a world-class wine cellar, the quality of his champagne beats anything I've had in New York; he sponsors a small family operation in Epernay. All that consumption would make you sick, Jeanie. Much better to stay away. Have lunch by yourself. I think I saw some brown sliced bread in the fridge."

He went back behind his newspaper. Jeanie put down her waffle carefully, and turned to me.

"Q, love, I think I will come today, in spite of everything, because you look very tired, and I came here to help." She wiped her sticky mouth on a napkin, and smiled virtuously at me. "And I promise you I will keep all my *deeply held* political ideas to myself today, you don't need to worry. I would *never* embarrass you with your friends."

I thanked her faintly as I slithered into a chair and helped myself to some breakfast. Paul glanced up over his newspaper, folded down a corner, and looked at her with his head on one side. I wondered what he was going to say, but then—"you've got some syrup on your face still," was all he remarked, coolly, and, reaching out, he wiped Jeanie's cheek with a deliberate finger.

14

~

Jeanie

I love sailing. I am *brilliant* at sailing. Paul told me so.

Dave would probably have been horrified if he'd seen me speeding across the Atlantic with a man who wore a gold signet ring on his pinky and designer linen shorts. But Dave wasn't there, and I felt I was allowed some fantasy time before I settled into life as an eco-warrior's spouse.

It was a fantasy day. I could almost believe I'd imagined it, except for the sunburn on my shoulders and the fact that the sitting room was rocking beneath my feet for hours.

Q turned out to be surprisingly amenable to the idea of a trip along the coast followed by a sail ("Don't know what Samuel will make of it but I'm bored to death of sitting in the dark"), so at eleven a.m. we bundled ourselves into Paul's huge olive-green SUV, a boat attached to the back, and drove fifteen miles along the coast to a small peninsula. Just as the road seemed set to end in the Atlantic Ocean itself, Paul took a winding, pitted dirt track that led across rocky ground, past clusters of sparse pine trees, to a set of stone gateposts; at the end of a short driveway a huge modern house reared up against the rock, with vast glass windows overlooking the ocean. Adjile (made millions in his dot-com start-up, retired at twenty-nine) greeted us at the front of the house, dressed in oil-stained clothes with a very charming smudge on his nose and fabulous manners. Mrs. Adjile (her name's actually Lily) emerged after a few minutes dressed in similarly stained shorts and a tight ruby-colored tank-top. "I'll get onto Ricky about ordering new spinlocks," she told Adjile briefly, before reaching up to give Paul a big hug. As she turned to us with a warm smile, I discovered with a sense of shock that she had *gold eyes*—literally, gold eyes, set beneath high-arched brows. Other than that she was quite normal-looking—tanned skin, muscly legs, narrow shoulders, and a wide chin—but still, *gold eyes*! Paul, Tom, and Adjile vanished off to attend to Paul's boat while Lily offered us lunch on a long, hot cedar deck strung across the rocks. We watched the green waves bubbling beneath us while slurping seafood with wholegrain bread and fresh white butter served on ice. Tom and his friends reappeared after an hour or so with the satisfied air of men who have wrestled with machinery and won.

I'm a practical English girl, but I was in serious danger of losing my head. If only Una could see me now, I thought, as I flicked out my white damask napkin and sipped at my flute of sparkling rose-colored wine.

After lunch, Adjile and Lily took us down a steep rocky path, then across the beach to their dock, a long wooden walkway with eight boats bobbing gracefully beside. The air was filled with the noise of their creaking and flexing as the water flopped lazily against the barnacled posts of the dock. The boats were a range of sizes and shapes, and Tom and Paul spent a few minutes exclaiming excitedly over Adjile's new purchase, a "Tornado catamaran" (which looked nothing like a boat to me, but still). Adjile, Lily, and Paul had a quick discussion about which "craft" Paul should take, finally settling on something called a Flying Dutchman. I was pleased because it was, in my opinion, by far the prettiest, a picture postcard of a sailing boat with a gleaming mahogany deck and bottom and a long, attenuated prow. Adjile unlooped the boat's mooring rope from around a big cotton reel affair while Paul rummaged about in a wooden chest on the dock for life vests. "Who's coming first?" he asked, when he finally emerged, laden with fluorescent padding.

Tom grinned, bursting with childlike pleasure, and raised his arm. "Me, me, pick me!"

Paul laughed. "Okay, of course you'll come, Tom, but I can take one more—"

"Go, Q, go," I said, smiling, "I'll take Samuel," and I pushed her gently toward the boat. She looked back at me. "If you're sure . . ." she said, with a tiny show of reluctance. "Of course I am," I replied briskly, removing the wriggling bundle from her arms. "Samuel will be fine with me. Have a wonderful time!"

It seemed suddenly perfect, this golden day in the golden light of the hot wooden dock, my tummy full of pink wine and fresh bread and salty fish. Samuel blinked and lifted his head unsteadily as I pulled him toward me, then settled down on my chest with a long sigh. The water began to lap vigorously against the dock as Paul sprang onto the boat. Tom and Q strapped themselves into their life vests, then Tom helped Q maneuver herself gingerly onto the deck to join Paul. After a quick conversation about who should steer ("You wanna go first?" "No, that's okay, I'll take us home"), Paul settled himself at the stern and took the tiller while Tom started winding and pulling at things energetically; three blinding white sails flew up the masts. They flapped and cracked excitedly in the warm, sandy wind; Tom tugged on something blue, and obediently the sails smoothed into an elegant curve. The boat slipped away from the dock in a frothy emerald-green trail.

We watched them go, then Lily turned to me with a smile. "Would you rather come up to the house or wait on the beach for your sister?" she asked, shading her sparkling golden eyes against the sunshine. "You're welcome to come inside if you'd like, and we can help you with Samuel, if there's anything we can do for you—"

Now, I rather fancied poking about in their architect-designed house, but in the end I decided to wait on the beach. A private beach, of course. Officially, I disapprove of private beaches. Natural phenomena should be for everybody to enjoy. Unofficially—don't tell Badger!—they're rather nice. So I followed Lily back along the dock, down a small flight of uneven stone steps and along the beach to a pair of brightly striped and padded chaise lounges beneath a pink beach umbrella. Lily disappeared, then came tripping through the dunes a few minutes later armed with a bowl of warmed pistachios and a glass of something orangey with lots of ice in it and a large slice of mango. It might or might not have had alcohol at the bottom. I sipped at it while Samuel investigated my necklace, and watched the bright white boat slipping simply and easily through the greenish-gray crests of the ocean.

They were out for over an hour, during which time Samuel dozed, pulled my hair, filled his nappy, and generally behaved himself remarkably well. Then, just as he was starting to whimper and root hopefully at my breast, I discovered I could see Tom's shock of dark hair and Q's auburn curls. The boat was getting closer; Tom was bringing them in.

I crunched back along the sand and arrived in time to see Paul helping Q jump over the side of the boat at the end of the dock. She tumbled out laughing; it had been years since I'd seen her so happy. She took Samuel with a broad smile on her face and a little bit of sunny warmth in her skin, freckles popping on her cheeks and arms. "You had a nice time, I take it?" I asked her with a grin.

"It was *fantastic*—so much fun. You go out now, Jeanie," she said breathlessly, nodding back at the boat. Paul was waiting with the sails lowered, holding on to a boat hook thrown onto the dock. "Yup, it's your turn," Tom agreed. Like Q's, his clothes were drenched. "We'll take Samuel, have a great time!" he added, brushing the fine sandy grit from his legs.

I looked at them uncertainly. "But Tom, you can go out again, or at least come with us," I began, thinking, oh God, me and Paul on our own on the sea, how embarrassing, I barely know him, I've hardly made eye contact since he saw me posed like something out of a Degas painting. What on earth would we find to talk about? "You love sailing!"

"I've had my fix for today," Tom explained peaceably, watching Samuel nuzzling at Q's breast. "And Adjile has invited me to come up here any time I want to sail. I think I might take him up on the offer."

"So it'll be nice for us to have some time to ourselves now," Q added cheerfully, setting off toward the beach. "Wait; no that sounds awful, I don't mean—" She stopped and turned around, looking confused. "Oh God, I'm sorry, Jeanie, if you really want one of us to come of course we will . . ."

"No, no, it's fine," I said hastily, picking up Q's abandoned life-jacket from the wood planks. I took a deep breath. Fine, I thought, strapping myself into the slab of purple and lime-green, I can do this. I can sail a boat. I can spend an hour with pig-man Paul on my own.

Paul watched me as I approached. "Just you this time, is it? Okay," he called coolly. "I think we can manage. Climb aboard."

Now that I was actually about to get into the boat, it looked unexpectedly large; I could swear it had grown. For the first time, too, I noticed all the baffling ropes in every hue from cherry to sunflower-yellow, not to mention the clamps and hooks and other strange instruments dotting the boat. What on earth did they all do? Was I supposed to know? I investigated the bobbing surface of the deck dubiously, then, holding onto a dock post, reached out a cautious leg.

At that moment the sea seemed to sort of suck the boat down and away. There was a loud *flub* sound; the boat creaked protestingly, and my leg landed in space. I threw my weight back onto the post, and looked distrustfully at Paul. "Sorry, sorry, I'm *trying* to hold it," he said, grinning, the muscles in his forearm flexing. "Come on, hurry up!"

Holding on even tighter to the post, I reached my leg out again and then, half-closing my eyes, threw myself into the boat. I landed on the deck in an ungainly red heap, limbs sprawling, one foot in a bucket, and my face (why, God, why?) smooshed into his lap. "Well, that's one way to do it," a voice murmured above me. I felt a wet, gloved hand in my armpit, and Paul hoisted me up; his soft gray T-shirt smelled of salt and sun. "All right?" he asked, and I nodded, the blood filling my cheeks. "Okay, good," he said, as if ladies precipitated themselves into his lap on a regular basis. "Sit over there on the starboard, that's right, a little further back, ass over the side—perfect," he explained, releasing the boat hook, and immediately water opened up between us and the dock. "Now, look up there. Do you see that triangular-shaped thing above your head? Hang on to that as we go. I'll do the rest." His muscular legs were burned dark, I noticed, as he arranged himself at the tiller once more.

He pulled on some ropes, the sails rose and swelled, and suddenly the boat was moving; I barely had time to make myself comfortable before we began to really pick up the pace. I hung on to the triangular handle nervously, my shoulder tight and strained. A sudden spray filled my nose and my eyes; the boat was thumping across the water now, speeding out to sea in an exhilarating fizz of salt water and wind.

"Ready to come about?" he called after a few minutes, craning forward, brown eyes glinting in the sun, to make sure I could hear above the noise of the sails. I looked back at him, doubtfully. "We need to turn the boat all the way through the wind, make a ninety-degree turn. I'll say 'prepare to come about,' then you duck right down, keeping your head clear of the boom—this thing—and get over onto the other side of the boat, same position as you're in now, okay? Prepare to come about—*About!*"

I ducked my head down beneath the boom as it swung sharply over, then (as elegantly as I could) scrambled up onto the opposite side of the boat. I'm not quite sure what was happening while I was tangled up on the gritty bottom of the boat but suddenly we were setting off in a completely different direction, out toward the open sea (on the first tack, we'd been heading toward a cluster of small islands a few miles off shore). Getting comfortable on my new perch, I peered under the taut white sail. There was nothing out there, no boats, no islands, nothing at all; just sea, sea, sea. The horizon stretched before me, endless blue passing into endless blue.

"It's beautiful out here, isn't it?" he called suddenly to me, and, forgetting everything, I nodded, laughing for sheer delight as the wind whipped my hair out of its ponytail. "This is my favorite way to spend a weekend, just me, the boat, the sea . . . cheesy but true," he explained, leaning through the breeze toward me. "I'm a stereotype from a Hemingway novel, I know. But I love the views, the sound of the boat, figuring out how to use the wind. What do you think?"

"I love it. I just love it!" I admitted, and he grinned, satisfied.

The water had an extraordinary effect on us. We sailed for another forty minutes, chatting about—I'm not sure really; things we like to do on weekends, countries we want to visit in the future, that sort of thing. The kind of conversation you have with a stranger when you sketch your personality for them, with a little bit of innocent exaggeration and some judicious gaps. Jeanie: fun-loving twenty-four-year-old. Paul: adventurous thirty-year-old. Speeding through the waves, watching the wind in the sails, neither of us made the slightest effort to tell the other one anything more. But we laughed a lot.

After a while Paul asked me if I wanted to take on some of the real work of the boat, keeping the sail taut in the wind, for example, by manipulating one of the cherry-and-white-colored ropes. And then (for ten glorious minutes) he let me take the tiller as well. I don't think I've ever felt so powerful. The boat was quick and responsive in the water, sensitive to the slightest movement. At one point I was distracted by a swift gust of wind and tightened the rope in my hands; for a second, I found us up in the air, the sail almost horizontal beneath us, and I wondered for a shocking moment if we were about to go over. Almost by instinct, I let go of the rope and felt the boat lurch back down to the swelling surface of the sea. A great rush of water splashed over the boat; I tasted salt on my lips, and pushed the dripping dark hair out of my eyes. I realized I was laughing, and Paul was laughing up at me too, although with a faintly quizzical expression. "A bit close that one, Jeanie, not too close, but still—" he yelled above the wind. "Just pull the sail in enough so it stops flapping, okay? I wouldn't enjoy telling Adjile we've capsized the thing, and it's a long swim home."

He nodded back behind us. I looked over my shoulder; the coast seemed miles away, a thin silver strip already far in the distance. It was, indeed, a long swim home. I shivered.

Paul was watching me. "It's been about an hour, we should probably go back, I'll take us home, okay?" he said gently, and he came over to me, nudging my damp body aside. Feeling suddenly very conscious of my arms and legs, not to mention my soaked top and shorts, I surrendered my position and slithered over to my old spot on the side of the boat and grabbed for the triangular hook. We sailed quietly home, watching the gray-green water thump-thump-thumping past us.

Q and Tom were sitting with Adjile and Lily on the beach. As Paul and I approached, we could hear them laughing. Samuel was half-lying, half-sitting on Q's lap, in a mercifully good mood. I could hear him burbling as he lifted his head like a curious tortoise at the spinning gulls in the blue sky.

Paul steered us toward the dock, lowering the sails to slow down the boat. Adjile had strolled over and was waiting; as we drew level with him, he reached over and guided us in. "Enjoy yourself?" he asked, tying off the hitches, and I nodded.

"It was just—*amazing*," I said happily, and he and Paul laughed. "Thanks," I said to Paul, as he helped me out, "thanks for showing me what to do. I had such a lovely time." And then I turned around, biting my lip, embarrassed all over again—I sounded like an awkward English schoolgirl, for God's sake . . . I was also painfully conscious of the imprint of his wet, gloved hand on my arm.

"Hey, Jeanie, wait up—" he called softly as I walked away from him, wringing the water out of my hair. I turned around. He was unfastening his sailing gloves and stripping off his life-vest. "You're a good sailor," he went on, grinning. "You've got good intuitions, you know?"

"*Have* I?" I started to say, eagerly, then flubbed it, stumbled over the words, and blushed again and again in spite of myself.

All in all (as I explained to Alison, in a hastily dashed-off e-mail when we arrived home, the words flying out of my fingers), it's a good thing he showed his *true* colors on the way home. Really, a very good thing indeed. Or who knows *where* things might have ended up!

15

~

Q

ey, dude, I'll catch you later." Paul shook hands with Adjile; his lips touched Lily's smooth brown cheek. "Thanks, guys. That was a great day."

"Always welcome," Lily replied, laughing, and then she turned toward me, her extraordinary eyes sparkling. "And it was so nice to meet you and your sister. I'm always *amazed* when I meet sisters who actually get along. My sister and I hated each other when we were children. To be quite honest, I don't think much of her now, either! Such a catty little thing . . ."

We walked toward Paul's car, her light arm linked through mine. "Have you two always been friends?" she asked curiously. I was acutely conscious of the smallness of her body as we walked, her narrow waist, her tiny feet, her lustrous hair gleaming in the late-afternoon sunshine. She seemed almost to fly over the rocks. I had to work not to stumble.

I looked over toward Jeanie, and grinned, a little embarrassed. "I think we united against a common enemy as children: Alison, our other sister," I explained. Alison is hard to describe to new people; I thought carefully for a moment about how to characterize her. "She's the middle one. Always too self-confident. Married a minor aristocrat, so now she gets to throw a bit of mud at a wall and call it 'art.' No one likes to challenge her, of course, so she's become very—well, smug as an adult. Even more superior. She's competitive as well, although she hides that part of herself from everyone but us."

"Really? So there's a third. How funny," Lily remarked. She looked up. "Isn't she terribly jealous right now?"

Funnily enough, this view of things had never occurred to me. "I don't think so," I said. "No, not really. Alison has far more important things to do than think about us. Great Sculpture to complete, for one thing. Of course, her stuff is *terrible*, isn't it Jeanie? Just terrible!"

"Now you sound more like a sister!" Lily laughed, handing me into the car. "Sisters see through each other like—like tigers through smoked glass. I think I heard that somewhere. Okay, so I get it now. Alison's the odd one out. Well, I hope to meet her one day. Finish the puzzle. Put all the pieces together."

"Not likely," I returned laughing, still trying to exchange glances with Jeanie, who had her back to me and was fiddling awkwardly with something under her nails. There was a strange flush on her cheeks. "Alison came out to see me a few months ago, while I was pregnant, and she made it very clear she'd have better things to do for the next decade than visit again. Jeanie and I don't get on with her terribly well, so we don't really care."

Tom passed Samuel in to me while Paul, now changed into a pale linen shirt and trousers, helped Jeanie into the front seat. "I can manage, thank you," she said, sounding slightly pent up, as he slid his hand beneath her elbow; Paul shrugged.

"Of course. Whatever," he returned, coldly brusque, pouring himself into the front seat.

It was a small moment, but such is the strange chemistry of conversation that it somehow seemed to poison what followed. There was nothing I could put my finger on, but once the final good-byes had been waved, and our hosts, arms around each other, had receded into the darkness of the starry evening, the good mood receded too. Jeanie, edgy and agitated, seemed primed for a fight, and every conversational topic seemed to find her and Paul on different sides. Paul admired a house set high upon a bank, Jeanie thought it far too big. Jeanie liked a song on the radio, Paul called it "sentimental." Paul mentioned that he loved to drive, Jeanie hissed about environmental damage. Jeanie sympathized with the travails of a famous popstrel who had recently lost custody of her children, Paul declared her a lunatic. Jeanie said London had the best food in the world, Paul shook his head and asked if she'd ever been to Hong Kong. And so it went on, and on. Jeanie: thrillers; Paul: detective fiction. Jeanie: musicals; Paul: theater. Soon their arguments were beginning to get personal. "I can't *think* why you—" "Oh shut up, Paul, that's plainly *ridiculous* . . ."

By the time we pulled into the driveway, Jeanie was sunk into her seat with her arms tightly crossed around her breasts, radiating cold fury. Paul was sitting beside her with an air of insolent ease, one hand on the wheel, the other arm lying negligently across the top of her seat, holding forth on the merits of basketball (Jeanie having indicated initially that she preferred tennis). We unpacked our-selves and the baby in silence. Jeanie stalked into the house without unfolding her body, without saying a friendly "good-bye" or "thank you" to Paul, without even talking to *me*.

"Nice end to the day," Tom said, weary and rueful, as we stumbled into our room. "*That* was fun. Not the day, I mean; the trip home. What was *up* with her? She can be really immature sometimes. You can tell she's twenty-four, can't you? *Crazy* behavior." He shrugged his wide shoulders. "One minute everything seems fine. The next, for no reason at all, she starts scratching at Paul." He yawned, pull-ing off his T-shirt and throwing it onto a chair.

Of course I was moved to defend her ("You were twenty-four yourself not so long ago," I reminded him tartly), but I took some-thing of his point. "Do you think they're going to keep this up all weekend?" I whispered, as we got into bed. "I hope not!"

Tom opened his mouth to reply, but his words were drowned out by—what else?—the sound of a very unhappy, very hungry, and very awake small baby.

I was starting to think there was some great ledger in the sky, and that every moment of pleasure was balanced out by a wail from our miserable son. Oh look, said some awful malignant deity, peering down at us. Tom and Q have managed three minutes of happiness, time to poke a stick in that child's innards to make him scream.

"Are we nearly at twelve weeks yet?" my husband moaned in the cold white gray of five a.m.

16

⌐

Jeanie

One distinct problem of sleeping in the sitting room was you couldn't lie in. I longed for my pretty bedroom with its thick mattress and luxurious en suite—but, of course, I'd had to give it all up to Paul. I heard Q and Tom and the baby squalling in the kitchen the morning after our sailing trip at seven; my head was pounding. After trying to ignore them for twenty minutes, I gave up and reluctantly presented myself. Ten minutes later, Paul himself emerged, showered, pressed, and polished in smart linen trousers with a silky cotton shirt. Q and Tom suddenly discovered pressing reasons to take the baby outside, which left the two of us glowering at each other over the breakfast table. Looking at his elegant get-up, I wished I was armored in something more than just my pink gingham M&S pajamas. I was always underdressed around this man.

He lost no time in getting straight to the point. "You talk a lot of crap," he said airily, "but I like the fact that you have opinions."

This caused me, briefly, to lose my footing. "Well, yes," I said vaguely. "Of course I do. *Lots* of them, actually."

This didn't seem to be my strongest point, so I stopped and paid a great deal of attention to my mug, watching the tea-bag globe swirl a trail of brown through the milk. Paul cut himself a slice of bread, which he covered in a thin, even film of blackcurrant jam. "So Jeanie," he went on. "I know about your family. I know where you

like to take holidays. And I know all about your flatmate, the terrible Una. But what do you actually do for a living? How come you're
here for six months?" Watching me, he set his perfect teeth into the
sandwich.

Now let's make this clear: it was a little after seven thirty on a
Sunday morning—not a time, you might think, for virtual strangers
to start quizzing a girl on her life and career path. "I'm going to be
a social worker," I said. "You know, to help people. Think about the
needs of others. Devote myself to—um—social well-being."

"Oh, I see. You've just finished the training, then?"

"Yes. I have a master's degree." Well, almost.

Paul looked interested. "Really? So what kind of social work do
you do? What do you specialize in?"

"Family issues," I blurted, and then felt myself turn four shades
of puce. "That is, I think so. Possibly. If I—that is, if I—"

"If you—?" he prompted.

"It's very complex," I said seriously. "Government funding. Limited opportunities. Decline in welfare state. Recession. It's not easy
to know what you're best at. Course only one year long. And—I'm
only twenty-four," I finished snappishly, detecting a faintly derisive
glint in his eyes. "I don't have to have everything sorted out yet, you
know!"

"No, of course not," Paul returned thoughtfully, collecting
crumbs from the plate with his last morsel of bread. "So you're done
with your course, but you don't actually know what interests you. I
see. Perhaps—" tones very polite—"you'll find out exactly what your
focus is while you're here?"

"What's that supposed to mean?"

Paul looked absolute innocence. "While you're visiting Q, I mean.
Perhaps you'll have some sort of epiphany, a magical moment, and
realize what it is you want to do. Since I assume—" he paused ("Go
on," I growled at him)—"given the state of the economy, you're not
just out here treading water. I assume you're applying for jobs."

"I applied for one in Cumbria a few weeks ago," I said a little desperately, and Paul arched his eyebrows. "Did you, indeed? In what town?"

I swallowed. "Small place, you wouldn't have heard of it."

"Try me. I know Cumbria quite well as it happens; I have an aunt from Kendal. I spent much of my childhood boating on Lake Windermere, pretending to be in an Arthur Ransome novel. Beautiful part of the country! Has there been much immigration in the area recently? What's the demographic these days?" He sat forward.

There was that lecture on "preparing for job interviews" held beneath the flickering lightbulb of Wolsey Hall 103, of course, but I slept my way straight through it. Una and I had hosted a particularly raucous party the night before (the police were called, but then, as Una said, if they *don't* thump the door down the music isn't loud enough). I woke up at one point to hear Professor Simscod talking about "demographic surveys" for interview research, then slumped under the chair and went back to sleep with my head propped on my ring-binder.

"Cumbria is an—er—rural community," I asserted now, hopefully. "Cumbria is in the Lake District Cumbria is known for two things, lakes and hills." (*Think of something, think of something*—)

And then (it was as if a light had gone on in my head): "You know, there are some really interesting parallels between Cumbria and Connecticut," I continued, determinedly wrestling my serpentine adversary. "That is to say, youth centered in urban areas, older people in the countryside. I think there are fascinating opportunities for research, actually. For an—um—*comparative investigation*. In fact I'm hoping to get more *perspective* on those *compelling* cross-cultural issues by doing some volunteer work here in Connecticut next week."

Paul looked definitely impressed. "Really? That's fascinating. Where will you be working?"

There was a small card in a shop window the day Q and Tom and

I first went into Sussex. "Summer Volunteer Wanted, Ten Hours a Week"—

"I'm going to work as a volunteer assistant at the Quiet Lanes Elder Care Home in Sussex," I announced superbly. "I'm very much looking forward to it. I'm intrigued to see how geriatric care—um—happens in Connecticut. Cumbria, Connecticut, I think the similarity is more than just beginning with C, you know? I think there's a potential research paper here. I'm going to look after Samuel and help Q in the mornings, then work at the Home in the afternoons, and in the evenings—I've got a political blog to write!"

Paul wiped his mouth carefully, took a last sip of his coffee, and stood up. "Then you are a very energetic young woman. What's your blog about?"

"Oh, it's an activist thing," I said airily. "You wouldn't be interested. Right now I'm writing a piece about ships' fuel. And—um—clouds. Big dark clouds. With rain in them. Oh, you can't just sit around anymore these days, waiting for jobs to come to you, you know! You've got to take the initiative. In fact, I need to get back to work on that blog, as it happens, so if you'll excuse me . . . *thank* you . . ."

I stood up and stalked past him out of the kitchen, leaning up against the wall in the hallway once I was out of sight.

Safe. As long as he didn't ask me for the Web address of my blog, of course. (If the worst came to the worst, I decided, I'd direct him to Badger's www.ecowarriorsunite.blogspot.com, although then he'd probably think me insane. Badger's stated goal, in big black type across the banner head, was to "smash a fist in the ugly face of the Industrial Revolution." He had several postings on the evil threat to world peace posed by electricity.) And I also had to hope Paul wouldn't come back next week and ask why I wasn't down at Quiet Lanes, washing old dears.

After wiping my face and splashing water into my eyes, I went outside barefoot; the deck was wonderfully warm on my soles. "Are you and Paul on better terms yet?" Q hissed at me anxiously, suddenly appearing from the garden with Samuel strewn over her shoulder. Her sun hat had slipped down rakishly over one eye, as had his; they looked oddly twin. "We thought we'd leave you two to sort it all out. The sparks were flying last night, my goodness . . ."

I was just beginning to scoff at the idea of *sparks* (the man is as boring as a drill bit, really) when I heard his voice unexpectedly close behind me. "I wanted to find you," he said coolly to Q. I slipped myself into the hammock on the deck—I didn't care if he'd heard!— armed with a fat, fragrant copy of *Vogue* and a free sample of some very appealing pink nail polish.

"I wonder if you and Tom could spare me a moment?" Paul went on politely. "I have a proposition to put to you both."

Q, looking surprised, explained that Tom had gone on ahead to the beach. "Let's walk on together and find him, then," Paul said, gesturing with his hand for my sister to precede him down the steps. "You see, I've recently heard of a job opportunity that—it's just possible—may interest you *both*."

When they'd gone, and while the first coat of "Amour En Rose" was drying on my dusty toes, I called Alison to tell her everything. "He sounds awful," she agreed (I could hear Geoffrey pulling the cat's tail in the background). "What an awful man, Jeanie. So snide, so condescending! Why do you think Tom is even *friends* with some- one like that? How can Q possibly put up with him?"

17

Q

I've got an idea: hear me out, okay?" Paul began, smiling. We were walking together along the seashore to find Tom, Samuel tucked into a baby carrier attached to my chest. The waves were a bright sparkling green; the gulls were wheeling smoothly in the warm air above us, and the sea was dotted with white sailboats as we crunched along the shells.

"A friend of my father's owns a small law practice in Cheasford, a town just along the coast a few miles from here. Kenton Tyler—that's his name—is looking for someone to take it over so he can retire. He's hoping to find one lawyer—or a couple, ideally—willing to work with him for a few months, get the ropes and the feel of the place, help him put a bit more money aside, and then when the clients are comfortable with the transition he'll pull out and let the new people take over the practice."

I stared. "You don't mean—you *do* mean—wait, Paul, do you mean *us*, taking over a law practice, here? Tom and me? *Here*?"

Paul glanced down at me, and rubbed his jaw thoughtfully. "Not what you were expecting to hear, I guess. But Tom told me the other day he was tempted to consider a serious change of career path. He says he can't hack hundred-hour weeks anymore. And firm work isn't going to get any better in these economic times."

"That's true—"

"You know, there's a lot to recommend life up here, Q. Cheaper real estate, more square footage, not to mention good, safe public schooling. The usual benefits of suburban life. Didn't you grow up in the countryside? Ah—there's Tom—"

We saw him just ahead, skipping stones across the surface of the water. My husband was bent down, knees almost in the damp sand, with a small pile of rounded rocks collected beside him. As he let the stones fly, with a practiced flick of the wrist, there was an expression of intense concentration on his face.

"Hey, Tom—walk with us," Paul suggested, and Tom, glancing up, dropped the stone in his hand. It fell with a soft *tink* on the pile he had amassed. We set off along the edge of the waves.

Tom listened respectfully to Paul's account of the firm, its client base, its advantages and disadvantages, and Kenton's own personality ("Kinda eccentric, but a good old-fashioned lawyer"), then caught my eye behind his back.

"You should go and meet him," Paul was saying seriously. "You wouldn't have to make a commitment up front. You could live here, in this house, for as long as you need, and spend a few months with Kenton to get the feel of a rural practice. Of course it would mean resigning from Crimpson . . ."

I recognized the look on Tom's face. "Well, quite. But look, Paul, when Q and I said we were thinking of a change I don't think we meant anything quite as dramatic as *that*." He pulled his ear a little helplessly. "We were thinking of another pair of firm jobs, or perhaps Q could take some time off for a few years, until Samuel's in school—"

"Another firm job? Get real." Paul picked up a large rock now and threw it overarm, hard, into the sea. There was a pause, then a sharp answering *plop* in the deeper, cooler part of the sea, fifty yards out from the shore. "If you take a job at a less prestigious firm you'll work fractionally shorter hours for substantially less interesting work, Tom. And if Q takes much more time off, she'll not only lose her job at Schuster she'll effectively quit the field. Law partners don't take kindly to 'mommy breaks.' They're looking for any and every excuse to hack out 'dead wood' at the moment."

Again, for a split second, Tom and I exchanged looks.

"Seems to me you haven't fully grasped the reality of your situation," Paul was saying, picking up another rock and letting it fly off into the sea. The water splashed; a surprised gull leaped into the air. "Lawyers don't work flexi-time, not in a Wall Street firm, and certainly not now. The pressure out there is intense. It's time for you guys to face facts."

"Paul," Tom replied, assuming reasonable tones, "that's obviously true, but Q and I are overqualified for a rural practice. Just because we're parents now doesn't mean we want to spend our days drawing up wills and divorces, you know! There's got to be a job that will let us work flexible hours, but that we'll still find interesting, challenging . . ."

"Name it," Paul said coolly. "And as for Kent's job: you think you're overqualified to work here? You think rural practice is boring? Okay, if that's what you think: go and meet Kent, I dare you," he added. "See what his practice has to offer, then do a cost-benefit analysis. Don't reject the idea out of hand.

"But look, obviously I have other suggestions," he went on. "Justin Van der Bossche at Prince was always a fan of yours, Tom; so if you want to go back to 'big firm' law, I'm sure he'd be willing to interview you."

Tom looked up sharply; I could tell he was flattered. "Justin? Really?" he asked, surprised, and Paul nodded.

"He was very impressed by the way you handled the Maccabee Brothers a few years back. Oh, and in the meantime, I can suggest some consulting work; I have useful connections at DeVelt which might help you span the transition from Crimpson. For when you actually—resign."

Tom and Paul walked on along the beach, two tall figures with hands thrust deep in their pockets, while I settled myself down to nurse Samuel, who was beginning to wail. I looked out to sea, thinking about a return to late nights and early mornings, a return to seeing each other on weekends, of packing my overflowing mother-love into a rushed kiss over breakfast toast. I was due to go back to Schuster in less than three weeks. Tom's holiday from Crimpson would be over next week.

If he still had a job to go back to, of course.

"Of course it's—y'know, insane," I offered, trying to laugh, when Tom finally came to sit beside me. Paul had taken himself off to give us time to talk. Tom nodded, gentling our son with tender fingers, as the gulls shrieked and cackled and fluttered in a great white whirl-wind at the sound of poor Samuel's wails. "We can do better than small-town law," I went on firmly. "I mean, what kind of a life could we have *here*? The whole idea is simply ridiculous!"

18

Jeanie

Dave phoned to say he'd found a cheap flight, and was coming out in five days' time. "It's a bit sooner than we planned, ob-viously, but it's a special offer. This week only," he explained, his voice brimming with excitement. "Plus Ranger says this airline is investing in researching cleaner fuel options," he added virtu-ously. He paused. "Although, to be honest, I'd have bought the ticket even if they weren't. Bugger the environment. I can't *wait* to see you, Jeanie, I miss you so much. Gotta get my hands on that body . . ."

"My boyfriend is flying out to see me," I told Paul airily. "This weekend."

"I'm pleased for you," he replied calmly, and I flushed.

"He is an environmental warrior," I went on severely. "He's very hard-core. We'll probably go and demonstrate in Washington against—" I frantically rifled the back-pages of my mind for something to demonstrate against.

"Air travel?" Paul offered innocently. I scowled.

I was already a little overwrought because I'd had to spend several hours with Paul by myself while Q and Tom went out to do shopping. Extraordinarily, Paul's office was actually able to do without him for a *whole Monday*. "Are you sure you can hack it, sitting around here with me, doing nothing?" I asked him once the sound of the car had receded. "I mean, don't forget the brevity of life!" I went on sarcastically. "A day sitting lazing in Connecticut is a day you have failed to earn a million dollars on the stock market. Did you think about that?"

Paul looked up at me over his paper. He was sprawled comfortably on the window bench in the kitchen at the time. "Thanks for worrying about me, but I have a well-diversified stock portfolio," he said calmly, sipping at his small white cup of espresso. "I assume you also have your savings safely invested?"

"Of course," I returned coldly, wondering frantically whether I'd ever actually got around to filling in that retirement-sheet thingie the bank gave me when I graduated. I mentally cast an eye over my current financial position. One current account, overdrawn to the tune of £562.47 (last time I checked); student loans totaling £16,902; contents of Abbey Savings Account (established for me by my parents when I was born, and regularly rifled since for stereo/bike/shoes/booze/cruises): £123.89. I couldn't honestly say my money was "working hard" for me, since it barely existed. I gulped and threw him a discouraging look before leaving the room for the washing machine in the small laundry area just off the kitchen.

"Do you want me to hold the baby while you do that?" He was standing just behind me, I realized, in the door to the laundry room, and was watching me clutch Samuel in one hand while attempting to fold clothes with the other. We'd had washing piling up for days now; Q was managing to get it all into the machine but then lost the plot when it came time for the sorting. (I'd actually found her in tears over the socks. "So many of them! And they never match! And half of Samuel's simply evaporate into thin air!" I'd promised her I'd get on top of it all, although I was increasingly inclined to agree with her that the washing machine subsisted on a nourishing diet of baby booties.)

"Of course not, I'm managing perfectly well," I said testily to Paul's outstretched arms. "You go back to your serious newspaper reading. I wouldn't want to disturb you." I put Samuel down on the floor on a soft bed of towels and went back to my folding.

Paul sat down on the tiles beside me with a pile of washing in his arms, "It's fine, I'm happy to do it. I'll start work on this," he said calmly. "I'm pretty good at folding. Although—"

He plucked something out of the tumble of clothes. It was my knickers, of course, and it had to be the pink ones, didn't it, the ones my flatmate Una gave me the previous year, with the words "Access All Areas" in white fluff on the front. The ones I wore when everything else was in the basket. I blushed three shades deeper than the undies and snatched them out of his hands. "I don't think there's enough here to fold," he said, all innocent bewilderment, and as he was holding on tight to them, they sort of *ping*ed as I pulled. I turned magenta.

"Get off," I muttered furiously, scrunching the offending undies into a package roughly the size of a postage stamp.

"Sorry, I apologize," he said, sweetly, picking up a large gray T-shirt instead. "How about I do Tom's clothes? That seems safer. You do the rest."

We sat in silence, folding. There is something indescribably embarrassing about sitting next to a man with your underwear accumulating in small piles between you. He walked around my lacy bras with an excessive carefulness that simply drew my attention to the fact that he was, in fact, very conscious of them indeed. Look as much as you want, I told him scornfully, with my eyes, because you ain't going to see me *in* this stuff.

"Must be almost lunchtime," he said with a yawn, when the laundry was organized at last into four separate neat piles—plus a selection of lone baby boots in fifteen hues of blue. "Why don't we walk into town? We'll pick up sandwiches for everyone, there's a new little gourmet place I've found. And you can show me the place where you'll be working."

I secretly thanked the heavens that I'd thought to telephone Quiet Lanes Elder Care Home the previous night—I excused myself when everybody else was eating, correctly anticipating from further experience of Paul that I might need corroborative information. I told the woman who answered I wanted to ask about the position, only it turned out you didn't need to do anything so formal as submitting a form, because the job was unpaid and thankless, and basically involved emptying bedpans and singing "America the Beautiful" and helping with knitting. "Gee, this is just *wunnerful*," Mrs. Forrest (manager of Quiet Lanes) said, when I explained my background. "We usually just get sixteen-year-old girls who can't tell a knife from a fork. They do their best, but they keep trying to talk about iPods, y'know? I'll tell the old folks today you might be coming, they're going to be *psyched* . . ."

I was left with the uncomfortable suspicion that by leaving my name, age, and telephone number with the said Mrs. Forrest, I had not only applied for but been given the job.

"In fact," Paul went on cheerfully, "if you want, we can go in and meet the old folks; I bet they'll be thrilled to see a baby. My grandmother was always transformed by the sight of children. My sister

Jenna's little boy used to have an extraordinary effect." We both looked at Samuel, who was just embarking upon one of his fits, purple and thrashing. "Well, maybe not today," he conceded after a moment "But the walk will do him good at least," he added. Five minutes later I found myself walking, Samuel dressed and strapped into his buggy, down the driveway, along the road, and into Sussex. Paul, I reflected, achieved an awful lot through sheer force of will.

The sidewalk was narrow; Paul's arm was pressed close to my shoulder. Cars whizzed past us. I was conscious of Paul glancing several times down into my face.

"So tell me more about your boyfriend, Jeanie," he said, at last, when Samuel had mercifully slipped back into sleep, his poor tiny face streaked with tears.

"What do you want to know?"

"Are you serious about him?"

"I—yes," I said. "I mean, he's very kind, and he loves me, and we have fun together. I know you think I have to have everything worked out at twenty-four, but I don't, and for the time being at least, fun and laughter are enough for me."

Paul laughed. "Point taken. Actually, fun and laughter sound more than enough, they sound positively good. I didn't have anything like that at your age."

"Perhaps you were too busy working."

"Perhaps."

"So what about you?" I asked suddenly, looking up at him, smiling roguishly. "Is there anyone special in your life?"

"Yes, there is. She's called Tina. She's a musicians' agent."

"I see. And why didn't she come with you this weekend?"

"Because she's speaking at a conference in LA."

"Oh. Is she very important?"

"Very."

"Is she very beautiful?"

"Very."

"Oh." I'd sort of imagined a different reply, something along the lines of "no, she's not very pretty, just terribly competent." Now I felt crestfallen, outdone by the absent Tina and her manifold talents and charms. She was obviously very glamorous. I sneaked another quick look at him, at his elegant clothes, his handsome face, his heavy brows, his pronounced cheekbones, his long eyelashes. Of course his girlfriend would be stunning. Of course she would be successful. "Are you going to get married?" I asked disconsolately.

For the first time since I'd met him, Paul looked confused, even wrong-footed. He coughed. "Uh—well, you're not the first person to ask me that question, let's put it that way," he said at last, with a slightly strangled laugh. "It's—nothing's fixed."

"I see." I didn't really. Was the gorgeous Tina less committed to him than he was to her? Or the other way around?

He had paused for a moment, and was standing by a wooden fence overlooking the sea; I retraced my steps, reversing the buggy, and went back to join him. On the beach below, a sun-wizened man was just hauling in a catch of opalescent fish. We watched the bloody, slippery bodies tumbling out of his net onto the wooden deck. "Actually—" he began, but at that highly interesting moment, a horn beeped loudly behind us, and the car that had just passed stopped, reversed, and metamorphosed into Tom and Q. "Where are you going?" Q shouted, falling out of the passenger seat in her haste to see Samuel. "What's going on, is he all right, how has he been doing, is he hungry, why's he wearing new clothes, what happened to his bunny, oh there it is . . ."

Paul and I exchanged amused glances for a fraction of a second— did she think we couldn't take care of a child, how silly—and then I busied myself explaining everything that was needful to Q. She decided she wanted to walk the buggy back to the house, to give Samuel more time to sleep, and suggested I take the car home with Tom.

My brother-in-law's face was cold and cross; they'd clearly been arguing. Q was barely looking at him. Paul, after a second's pause, offered to walk home with my sister. There was no room for three-abreast on the pavement, so, feeling vaguely cheated, I opened the front door of the car and got in beside Tom.

"What's going on, then?" I asked him, as we pulled off. The air conditioning was on high; I shivered. Tom kept his green gaze firmly fixed on the narrow bending road.

"Nothing much," he replied shortly. There was a pause. And then, keeping his eyes straight ahead: "I love my son, but God Jeanie, I need a change of scenery," he blurted. He rubbed a hand over his face, his pale sunken cheeks. "I don't know how much lon-ger I can take this, to be honest. I have to get out of the damn house, have something else to think about. I mean, what does she think I am? Does she think I can take this—the screaming, the yelling, no sleep—indefinitely? Some days I think I'll just go back to Crimpson and be done with it . . ."

He stopped himself, biting his lip, then glanced down at me for a second. "Forget it, Jeanie, this isn't your problem," he went on, in a tight voice, "Obviously we'll work something out soon, I mean, she understands, right? She understands I need challenges in my pro-fessional life. *Obviously*."

We drove on in silence. I couldn't quite think what to say.

19

~

Q

So you are enjoying motherhood, then, darling?"

Alison's tones were silkily insinuating. In my mind's eye I could see her, sitting at her burnished eighteenth-century desk in the sunny alcove of her expansive study, overlooking a discreet south London garden. A huge oak nods in at the window. The carpet beneath her feet is spotless deep-pile white—the sort that swallows every sound—and as she leans back in her chair, the cable of her old white telephone flexes gently. There are homemade sugar biscuits on a plate of thin bone china at her elbow, a cup of pale tea idling in her hand, and a smile of deep self-satisfaction on her lips.

At this unfortunate moment in the conversation, just as I was summoning up a particularly breezy account of my life and capabilities as a mother, Samuel, resting in my lap, began to cry—loudly. This put me in a tricky position, not least because the phone kept willfully flinging itself away from my hot, sweaty grasp. "He—er—he has his *moments*, of course, but generally he is an—er—easy—did you hear me? *Easy*, I said . . . A very easy child—"

Alison listened to the yells in silence for a while, then decided to start diagnosing his distress from her lofty perch three and a half thousand miles away. ("I was an unusually attentive mother, I could just *feel* what my children needed, I think it was a gift.") "He sounds tired," she asserted, at which point I almost hung up the phone on her because he'd only just woken up. When she heard this, she switched tack and went down the usual list of causes of baby crying—which, as I pointed out, in a voice that was testy in spite of my very best efforts—I was perfectly capable of doing myself.

"Well, that is strange," she conceded at last, sounding unusually unsure of her ground; "quite peculiar!" And then (I could hear self-confidence flooding back into her voice): "in that case, Q, are you sure there's nothing *wrong* with him?"

I spluttered wrathfully in response to this; I did not tell her, of course, that only the night before we took Samuel to the hospital, that Tom and I had been worrying for days, weeks now, that something was really wrong with our son. "Alison, don't be so ridiculous," I said instead, as forcefully as I could. "Something wrong—just because a baby cries! Hahahaha! Which one of us is the first-timer here, hmm?"

I won that battle, I suppose, but I put the phone down sweating and disgusted with myself. I didn't mind snapping at Alison's heels over clothes, money, Mum, Jeanie—the usual territory of sisterhood, in other words, but I didn't want to drag maternity into the mix. There was something particularly horrible about using children as soccer balls, bouncing them backward and forward from one side to the other. Still, Alison brought out the worst side of me; she always had.

It was at nine o'clock the previous night that we heard the first yell from the bedroom. At half past midnight, Tom strapped Samuel into the car and drove him around winding lanes while Jeanie and I collapsed in the kitchen with a bottle of wine, feeling hellish. At one forty-five a.m. Tom arrived back with—we heard the yells before the car door even opened—a child in a truly frantic state. His face was covered with a sheen of saliva and snot, and he seemed to have developed some sort of rash around his eyes. His legs were drawn tightly up to his chest, and his yell was a horrible monotone.

Tom handed Samuel to me with a gray face. "We must take him

to the emergency room, Q," he said, and his voice was clipped, the tones of a man on the edge. "It's been five hours now; he cried the *whole* time we were away. I stopped and cuddled him, I put music on, I drove with the windows open, I took him to listen to the sea, I hummed in his ear like a giant frigging bumblebee, nothing helped. We have to take him up to the hospital, Q; this *can't* be normal. Let me just change my shirt (he threw up all over this one. Twice)."

I sent Jeanie to bed and stepped out into the cool night air with our poor suffering child. The thought of setting foot in a hospital with Samuel was horrific . . . tests, needles, wires, and IVs . . . but on the other hand, maybe someone could *help*. . .

We strapped him back into the car seat and drove to the nearest hospital, a brick box building fifteen miles away, humming with low-level night-light. The entrance to the emergency room yawned like a giant neon mouth atop a dark circular driveway. Tom parked while I ran in and delivered our details to the strained-looking triage nurse through a cacophony of yells ("He won't stop crying." "I can see that."). The bunch of drunks in the waiting area took one look at us, then moved as a man to the other side of the room.

I stood in the blue-carpeted sea of the waiting room, swaying slowly backward and forward, rocking Samuel in my arms—my beautiful, perfect child. The only time I'd ever been in an emergency room before was when I was thirteen and smashed my finger playing netball at school. I was torn then between the novelty of the experience (an X-ray! Maybe I'd even get a cast!) and the fact that my finger hurt like hell. Plus until my mother arrived I was attended by Mrs. Gilbert, the games teacher, who wouldn't stop grousing about the fact that Priscilla, her shaggy golden retriever mix, needed to be let out for a pee.

"What did you do?"

I heard a whisper behind me, and turned to see Tom, clad in a fresh T-shirt, Samuel's diaper bag slung over his shoulder, staring at me open-mouthed. Following Tom's gaze, I looked down to discover Samuel sleeping quietly at my breast. The hospital's harsh white light showed every blotch on his pale, tired skin, but already we could see that the dark red clouds around his eyes were passing.

"How in God's name did you do that?"

Samuel muttered slightly, stretched, and snuggled more closely into my breast. I blinked dry eyes. "I've no idea!"

Tom drew me carefully to the hard metal chairs, and we sat together, staring in profound silence at our sleeping son. "Should we wait to see a doctor or—go home?" I whispered, eventually, while Tom shook his head slowly from side to side. He was shaking.

"I truly thought he'd *never* stop," he intoned. "Never, ever, ever. Never." (The woman next to us glanced at him, drew her jacket fractionally away, and muttered something distastefully about "getting all types in here." Since she was garlanded in green toilet paper, I thought this not entirely fair.)

Both of us were utterly beyond the point of decision-making. We sat for another half hour, staring at Samuel, making half-hearted efforts to stand up, failing, stumbling back down— at which point we were called, fortunately enough, to see a sympathetic young doctor perched on a trolley in the corridor. "No fever, heart rate's good, blood oxygen is good," he told us briefly, "and Samuel's not crying now. Colic. Bound to be. But check with your own doctor if you need reassurance." He waved at us cheerfully before rushing off to deal with a woman who had half a wine glass sticking out of her face.

"Q, gotta do it, gotta call th'doctor in the morning," Tom pointed out numbly, as we dragged ourselves into bed at long, long last, an hour later. "Describe it all, what's been happening. Appointment. Arrange appointment for when we go back to the city. Checkup."

"Tom," I said, pausing with one leg on the bed, one on the floor, "*are* we going back to the city after next week? For good, I mean?"

Silence. And then: "Whaddya saying?"

"Just what I said. Are we really going back?"

"What else?"

"Stay here."

"Stay here?"

"Yes." There, I'd said it.

"Christ. For—how long?"

"I don't know."

This time, a very long silence. "Q—" chewing his lip—"We both know I *can't* take more time off. No one takes a three-week vacation, not at Crimpson. Not even for a honeymoon. They'll fire me."

"So let them."

"And then?"

I didn't reply as I levered myself into bed, just contented myself with a vague "I don't know" as Tom, in the middle of a thought, collapsed into exhausted, unsettled unconsciousness. All I knew was, I couldn't do it, I just couldn't do it; I couldn't go back to the office, couldn't reenter that world of hysterical, overhyped boredom. But if I didn't, and if Tom didn't, what on earth were we going to do?

Of course I said nothing of this to Alison, when she called; nothing about the storms of crying, the hospital, or our strange, lengthening holiday. Alison is one of those people who glide through life unaffected by trauma or crisis, someone who never seemed called upon to wrestle big decisions. She couldn't possibly help me; she didn't need to know.

20

*

Jeanie

I can't tell you how pleased I am to hear about that volunteer work you'll be doing," Paul said on the Monday night, just as he was heading out of the door. Tom and Q were clustered behind him, thanking him for his hospitality, his house, etc., etc., when he paused and turned to me. "In the retirement home on Quiet Lanes. It's so great to think that you'll be giving something to this community." Tom's mouth had fallen open; Q looked bewildered.

"Didn't you know?" he asked, with apparent surprise. "Jeanie's going to be helping out with our senior citizens at Quiet Lanes. It's a great place. She has a wonderful idea for a research project, don't you, Jeanie? Well, good-bye then," he finished, flashing me a smile as big and sparkling as the Koh-i-Noor as he put out his hand (I felt the hard gold of his signet ring against my little finger). "It was so nice to meet you! Good luck on the comparative study. And I hope your boyfriend has a wonderful visit."

Tom stared at the door as it closed behind him. "What the—?"

"*What* are you going to do, Jeanie?" Q asked in bafflement, and of course I was stuck, wasn't I, with having to agree with the preposterous story.

"I—er—yes, well, nothing's definite, but I've given them a ring, they've suggested I go for an initial visit, so—maybe—"

My incoherent wafflings were cut off by Q, who turned to me with an unexpectedly positive face. "I think that's a *fantastic* idea," she said firmly. "You can't spend all day listening to Samuel wail, it's too much for anyone. You need a break from it. And since you haven't got a work visa, volunteer work is a great way to get out of the house." She smiled kindly. "I'm so glad, Jeanie. Plus it will be a wonderful opportunity for you to get more experience of caring and welfare, and it'll look good on your CV when you get back."

"And I don't feel so guilty about keeping you in Connecticut, now you have this job," she added in the morning, when she outlined a new plan to keep us all up in Sussex for a further week at least (she was going to try to persuade both her firm and Tom's that they needed more time off on medical grounds—in other words, because of Samuel). "If it wasn't for the job I would feel terrible, but it's wonderful to think you're making a place for yourself here. It's bound to impress future employers in the UK."

"Bedpans here I come," I muttered ruefully to myself, when the door closed behind her.

Then I began sketching out some questions to be addressed in a comparative study of Cumbria and Connecticut, just *in case* Paul ever appeared in Connecticut again:

1. Compare contributions from government versus contributions from patients' families as percentage of total cost in homes in the two places. (I copied this question from a course paper, and I felt it sounded quite impressive.)
2. Compare job descriptions of care managers. How much caring?
3. Compare roles of nursing staff. How much nursing?
4. Compare facilities. Size of televisions, etc.
5. Compare numbers of patients in total, and
6. Number of patients on average in homes across the two regions. (I wasn't sure my math was up to this, actually. I

thought wistfully about the years I spent sucking licorice all-
sorts under the desk instead of paying attention to the dour
Mrs. Grindley at school.)

Right, time to start digging about on the Web, I thought to myself; I could even go to the library, that way if Paul came to stay—just
to be on the safe side—I would have concrete facts to draw upon airily in conversation. "Yes," I could say brightly, "I have discovered
that only point-four percent (factoring in the cost of living, taking
the rate of inflation into consideration) of geriatric care is admin-
istered locally, demographically speaking." And maybe, I pondered,
I could call that lady who ran Quiet Lanes and ask her; maybe she'd
fill in a questionnaire!

Alison was very impressed when I phoned her to tell her all about
it, although we ended up spending rather a lot of time talking about
Samuel and Q. She was really worried when I told her all about the
hospital trip, and made me describe in achingly minute detail exactly what the doctor said and how Tom was behaving ("Do you think
their marriage will survive?"). But she thought I was doing a marvelous job finding a way to set myself apart from other candidates at
the interview stage, and even suggested her husband might be able
to pull a few strings for me in the government. She could be a very
handy sister sometimes.

21

Q

Paul set up a meeting for us with Kenton Tyler, the friend of his father's from law school, the day he left. Tom authorized the call, but Paul saw immediately he wasn't entirely happy about it. "Look, you're not making any kind of a commitment by going," he reminded us, slipping his phone back into his pocket. "It'll just give you a sense of how small-town law compares to big-firm life. You can weigh up the benefits and see how the job meshes with your new priorities. And if it's not something that interests you—if you don't think the firm has good enough prospects—there's no harm done."

We gathered the strangest collection of oddments, baffling fragments, about the old lawyer over the next few days. "Old man Tyler?" Marie, the fisherman's wife, said, when we bumped into each other at the farm stand. "He's—let's just say he's a character. A particular—*type*—of character." The lady in the general store gave us a searching look as soon as I mentioned his name, and muttered something about Jose Cuervo. The girl who pumped our gas at the local station giggled, told us her mother knew him, then blushed ferociously. The state trooper's face tightened into blankness (we got talking to him at the pizza truck). "Kenton Tyler is connected with half the people in the state, *one* way or *another*," he said severely, before stalking off, jumbo slice in hand, down the street.

In spite of some misgivings, and my exhaustion, dressing for the meeting was oddly fun. I stripped off my stained T-shirt and Gap shorts and kicked off my gray sneakers. Then I slipped into an outfit I purchased, optimistically, the week after the baby's birth—a pressed linen skirt and a white cotton shirt, two sizes bigger than my normal size but not—blessedly, not!—maternity wear. I looked at myself in the mirror. I looked bigger than normal but, well, not too bad (I sucked in my stomach). After a good deal of thought, I also donned a pair of heels. Then I brushed my hair, pulling out the worst of the tangles, and twisting what remained into a plausible chignon. I rubbed my cheeks with foundation, brightened my eyes with mascara, and—from the depths of my makeup bag produced some lipstick to give my gray face some color. Then I added a pair of earrings, a purse—instead of a diaper bag . . . Tom looked me up and down as I entered the kitchen, feeling intensely self-conscious. He smiled, but didn't say a word.

Samuel was restless and distressed before we left. I was sure he could sense something unusual was happening. "Shut up and don't worry," Jeanie admonished me severely, as she wrestled my wailing son out of my arms. "Of course you can leave him with me. I'm sure he's just a bit windy. Now get out before he throws up all over that shirt!"

I watched her in the side mirror as we pulled out of the drive-way, competently hitching Samuel over her shoulder, her hand carefully guarding his still-shaky neck, then settled back against the seat with a sigh. Jeanie was right. I needed to switch off my mommy radar—my madar, as I called it to myself—for a few hours.

Our journey to Kenton Tyler's office took us several miles along thickly wooded roads. Clapboard houses flashed past, some old but many new, set on manicured green lots with purplish shrubs lined beneath the windows. Enormous cars sat hot and shining in the sunshine. Children thumped basketballs against asphalt, dogs panted in the cool on the edge of their yards, where clipped grass gave way to thicketed wetlands veined with brooks. Every few miles we glimpsed small lakes glinting through the trees. Dilapidated farm stands offered tomatoes and cucumbers for sale, and bunches of flowers, wilting gently in the damp, warm morning heat.

"There's a good French restaurant a few miles away," Tom told me, turning left at a small triangle of yellowing grass. "At least, I drove past it last week, and it looked okay. Everyone around here raves about it."

A sign outside a gas station announced that we were entering Cheasford, a small town sprawling around a simple old white church and a thriving general store. Half a mile on, we passed the large wooden general store in the center of town, turned right, then pulled into a small apron-shaped strip with a pizza joint, a brake specialist, and a dry-cleaners fronting the parking lot. In the distance, just visible through the large back windows of the restaurant, was the ocean.

In the corner of the strip stood a squat, square, three-floor building with a small weather-beaten sign outside the door and a thin row of hot-pink impatiens peering uncomfortably through a heavy carpet of red cedar mulch. The first floor, we learned from the sign, were the offices of Luna Lilly, Reiki Specialist. Julie's Hair Emporium occupied the second (a thick draft of hairspray and singed hair wafted down from her windows as Tom opened the car door). The third floor housed the law offices of Kenton Tyler and Associates, LLC.

"This is it, then," said Tom bracingly.

The building's painted aluminum door was white and peeling, with a large clear glass panel in the center. Inside we could see a small, square, anonymous blue hallway, adorned with anonymous plastic flowers in an anonymous glass vase. On the right side of the hallway was another door, on the left a flight of stairs.

There didn't seem to be a buzzer, so Tom knocked. Nothing happened. He knocked again.

The door on the right slowly opened. A face appeared, followed by the body of a short but lugubrious-looking woman in her fifties with suspiciously blond hair restrained by a velvet Alice-band. She observed us for a second or two, then opened the front door. "May I help you?" she asked in honeyed tones, blinking in the daylight. A heady scent of sandalwood swirled around her loose purple cotton robes and silver-fringed shawl.

"Thanks; we're here to see Kenton, the lawyer on the top floor," Tom explained. "May we come in?"

The woman rolled her eyes. "I s'pose I'll have to let you, because he never opens the door. The stupid old FART," she yelled suddenly. "Thinks I'm his fucking SLAVE, the crazy drunk BASTARD." Luna Lilly jerked her head in the direction of the upper floors. "He can HEAR ME, I know he's fucking LISTENING TO THIS, pretends he doesn't hear the door, the lazy ASSHOLE!" She was now standing at the bottom of the staircase, holding onto the banister and craning her head up the stairs. "You hear me, I KNOW you do!" she yelled furiously, shaking her fist, "and you might as well know this, you old fucker, don't come running to me with a bottle of Kahlúa the next time your ex-wife calls, I'm not doing it again, you bastard, last night was the last time, y'understand? You hear me up there? NEVER AGAIN!"

She turned round, fixed us with a disapproving gaze, then disappeared in a swoosh of purple print and heavy perfume. Somewhere above us, we heard the click of a door opening. *"Is she gone?"* a low voice called.

Tom gave me the kind of look a man gives the woman he's sent, purely by accident, to the guillotine. "Umm—"

"Mr. Tyler, is that you? We're friends of Paul's," I called, setting off up the stairs. "We're here to talk to you about your practice—ah! Hello." I shook hands with a short man with impish blue eyes and a long white ponytail, who was hiding, quite unashamedly, behind the third-floor door.

"Hey—good to meet you, come on in," he said, grinning, pushing a strand of long white hair behind his ear. "Sorry about that" (with a nod down the stairs), "we have a sort of—er—love/hate relationship, we're in the hate phase today, it'll pass, but I sort of keep out of her way until it does." He beckoned us into a small square office thick with stale cigarette smoke. We could virtually see the nicotine curling and expanding, yellowly, in the dark, dusty air.

Tom retched. Kenton peered round me to look. "You all right, young fella?" he asked concernedly; Tom waved his hand vaguely. We stumbled into the middle of the room like children in a fairy tale, our eyes slowly getting accustomed to the gloom.

The office was lined with about fifteen tottering bookcases from which law books and trial transcripts spilled. Toward the window, on the right side of the room, stood a heavy, overcrowded desk, behind which Kent was now sitting; in the middle of the room stood two red, threadbare velour armchairs. Through a door in the middle of the opposite wall we could see a brown metal desk, an orange-cushioned metal office chair, and an old computer; this, presumably, was the secretary's office, although there was no secretary anywhere to be seen. A clock ticked loudly by the window. It was twenty minutes slow.

"Sit down, sit down," Kenton said, cheerily, waving at the red chairs. Both were covered in books, ashtrays, yellowing newspapers, and—most extraordinary of all—socks. We stared speechlessly at what looked like a month's collection of them, dirty and unmatched, spilling over the arms of the chairs and onto the floor, falling out of every crevice like so many maggots.

Tom seemed to have lost all power of speech. I swept the socks casually off the chair onto the floor, lowered myself down, and looked expectantly at Kenton.

Comfortably ensconced behind his heavy wooden desk, he was nodding and smiling approvingly at me. Tom subsided into the second armchair.

Kenton picked up a smooshed pack of Marlboros from the table, slid out a cigarette, and lit it with a flamboyant *swish* of a match. "Now then, you two," he said, after a long drag (and a pause for a luxurious exhale), "I'm meeting you because young Paul suggested I should. I wouldn't normally waste my time on a couple city lawyers, frankly. Still. Why don't you start by going through your experience?"

It suddenly struck me, from the attentive look in his eyes, that this was a job interview.

Tom was staring at Kenton with the fascinated look of one confronting a lunatic. I knew what he was thinking. Kenton interviewing *us*? Kenton investigating *our* credentials? Shouldn't he be down on his knees, thanking us for considering taking on this nowheres-ville practice of his? Us—us! With our degrees from Oxford and Harvard, our years of London and New York City experience . . .

"It's a pretty challenging job, this one, make no mistake," Kenton was saying judiciously, leaning back in his chair with his fingertips lightly together, cigarette stuck to his lower lip. There was suddenly an enormous snapping sound and the chair pitched backward, smacking his head into the windowsill behind the desk. We caught a glimpse of a pair of bony ankles above yellow checked socks as the seat flew into the air. Moments later, Kenton's face reappeared as, with a practiced tug on the underside of his desk, he righted himself. "Must get that fixed," he explained coolly, clicking the seat back into place. Cigarette still glued miraculously to his lip, he tucked a few loose strands of hair back behind his ears with yellowed fingers. "It may look easy to you, but there are challenges a country lawyer faces that'd make you city types blench. Frankly, I'm not sure you'd be up to it," he went on severely. "Do you have your résumés with you?"

Tom made an odd gurgling sound.

"Well, no, we don't," I explained sweetly. "Truthfully," I went on, "we're not sure if this is a life for us or not. We don't feel ready to apply for your—ah—very interesting position just yet. Perhaps you could describe an average day here at the practice first?"

Kenton nodded. "Makes a lot of sense, a lot of sense," he said judiciously. "Well" (locking his hands behind his head), "we get some pretty tricky divorce cases, and there're probate problems to be worked through, figuring out how to divide up money between taxes and all the members of a family; some you know about some you don't—heh heh . . ." He took another long drag on his cigarette.

Tom and I exchanged glances. The odd messy divorce and a trip to probate court once in a while . . . it sounded like a lifetime of soul-crunching boredom or an easy way to earn a buck, you could take your pick which way to look at it.

Kenton's face, I suddenly realized, had developed an unexpectedly knowing leer. "Think it sounds pretty easy, don't you?" he said, leaning forward, toward us, "*I* know what you're thinking, you two! And there's something in it, I suppose; you won't be dealing with multimillion-dollar mergers up here, it's true. But you need something else to practice in these parts, something I don't think—I could be wrong—you two actually have."

Tom was alert now, sitting upright. I knew what he was thinking, of course. Half of him was frankly disbelieving. The other half was thinking: A hoop I'm being told I cannot jump through! I *must* prove I can jump through that hoop . . .

"What's that, Mr. Tyler?" he asked. "What's that?"

Kenton stuck his cigarette in his mouth and took a long drag. "D'you know, young man, I don't know if I feel like telling you," he said slowly; and then, his face splitting into a grin that would not have shamed a Cheshire cat, "in fact, I've thought about it, and I'm sure I don't!"

22

⌒

Jeanie

I'm going to hitch down to Heathrow," Dave informed me seriously, "to minimize my carbon footprint. Ranger's idea. And then I'll hitch up to Connecticut from New York."

"Dave, I don't think you can hitch in America," I said faintly. "Everyone'll think you're a psychotic killer. You'll probably get *arrested*."

"Then I'll try to persuade the policeman to give me a lift the rest of the way," he returned cheerfully, and I gulped a bit, because I couldn't imagine any of the heavyset men with guns and crew-cut hair I'd seen around Connecticut consenting to chauffeur a loony Englishman.

"Dave, honestly, I think you're more likely to get chucked in jail," I explained nervously. "And when you come into the country, for goodness sake, please don't wear your FUCK AUTHORITY T-shirt, I just don't think it's a good idea, they have all these cameras in the immigration area . . ."

"Oh, Jeanie, don't be such an old woman," he said impatiently. "I think they have something called freedom of speech over there, right? Honestly, love," he went on, "don't worry about me, I'll be fine. I'm really looking forward to it, they give you free drinks on the plane, right? And you can show me around the area. I've never been to America before, never been out of Europe. Only time I ever travel is when England is playing away! Ha! Perhaps we can do some trips—if it's all right with you, of course. And if we can lever ourselves out of bed, which I'm not at all sure about. God, Jeanie, every time I think about . . ."

"I have things to do, Dave, I'm about to start volunteering at a geriatric home," I cut in, feeling suddenly rather uptight. "I can't just—I mean, of course I'll show you around, but I do have to help Q. Remember I have responsibilities here."

"I know, I know. And I can help as well," he said earnestly. "I like kids. Funny little scraps. But I really want to enjoy this holiday, Jeanie. I've spent the last three days dealing with my mum, y'know, full-time. Poor old sod, she's been very demanding. Yelling the place down, most days. Dad needed a break, so I've been doing it all on my own—apart from Ellen, of course. Thank Christ for her. If she wasn't there to help I don't know *what* I'd have done—"

"Really," I answered, not rising to the bait.

"Yup. She's such a helpful lass, so—so warm an' understanding."

"Really," I repeated. I could hear Dave's irritation grow.

"Mmm. She's been a rock for our family, and she's a pleasant sight at the lunch table n'all. 'A good-looking, strapping sort of girl,' as Dad puts it."

"Well, isn't that nice. You can *all* ogle her over the meatloaf."

"Is there something wrong?" Dave exploded at last.

"Of course not," I said, feeling tetchy.

"I mean, are you getting your period or something? Because you're being really difficult at the moment."

"What, because I refuse to ask you what color Ellen's stockings are this week?"

"No, because—because—I don't know why, but you just *are*."

By the time we put the phone down on each other ten minutes later, we were thoroughly out of sorts; we barely said good-bye, just sort of harrumphed at each other. It'd been a little while since I saw Dave, and surely it wasn't surprising we weren't rubbing along as well as we normally did. There'd been so much going on in my life in Connecticut. It's going to take us a while to get back into the swing of things when he arrives, I thought to myself. You have to expect a difficult transition.

In spite of that, I was really looking forward to seeing him. He'd promised to stop off at Una's and pick up my favorite red dress, for a start.

23

Q

The young woman was short but lean, her pale yellow hair tucked untidily behind her ears. She was dressed in faded jeans and a baggy pink-stripe T-shirt that bore the signs of many meals' cooking. On her feet were a pair of scuffed flip-flops; a pair of large gold hoops dangled from her ears. A scar like a sideways T ran across her nose from one cheek to the other. The nails on her left hand, I noticed, were bitten down to the quick.

It was the Thursday afternoon after our visit to see Kent, and I'd left Samuel with Tom while I went to pick up some groceries. I saw the yellow-haired woman standing in front of me in the queue at the general store, grabbing onto the wrist of a little boy of about four. His dark brown hair was cut short, and he was wearing a pair of green army pants and a Spider-Man T-shirt. Sticking out of his pocket was a rough, faded, well-worn scrap of blanket. He was pulling away from her, trying to pry her fingers off his wrist, while she simultaneously hunted with her free hand through an open bag slung over her shoulder. "I swear I don't know what's happened, Katie, I had more coupons somewhere . . . Paulie, stay *still* . . . !"

The young woman behind the cash desk shrugged. "Forget it, Emmie. I'll put the milk on the tab this week, okay? You can bring in the coupons next week." She got out a black notebook from under the cash register, and wrote down the new entry. I knew Katie reasonably well; she was the daughter of the general store's owner, a kind, efficient woman named Liz. Katie was about twenty-four, I guessed; maybe two or three years older than the struggling young mother.

Emmie nodded gratefully, produced a few dollar bills to pay for her bread and cans of Spaghetti-Os, then ran after Paulie, who had finally broken free and was now attacking the cereal display in the window, which was wobbling precariously. "Paulie, I swear, if you don't get your ass over here, there'll be no more lollipops this week, *this whole week,* d'you hear me?" she warned. "Not one!"

Faced with this serious threat, Paulie shrugged, gave the stack of boxes one more push for luck, then slipped his hand obediently into his mother's. Emmie, bustling back to the cash desk with the boy in tow, suddenly stopped and swore softly. "I forgot to get soap . . ." she said apologetically, lifting up a small cardboard box from a nearby shelf.

Katie shook her head, laughing, and offered to put the soap on the tab too. In the middle of writing the new item down (and while Emmie was informing Paulie what his gramps would say when he heard about this), Katie looked up with a searching glance.

"You kicked that worthless son of a bitch out yet? For good, I mean?"

Emmie flushed, tightened her lips, then nodded down meaningfully at Paulie, who was now sitting on the floor, peeling bits of crackling skin off a large shiny red onion. Katie rolled her eyes. "Whatever. Did you?"

Emmie nodded shortly. "Yeah. I did, as it happens. But—" She glanced down at Paulie, then looked carefully around the shop; I hastily dropped my eyes and pretended to be paying a great deal of attention to a box of plastic sunflower pins being sold to raise money for some local charity. It was none of my business, after all. "Jeez, Katie, it's, like, a nightmare. He says he's going to take Paulie away." The last words were a miserable whisper.

"He does?" (Katie sounded shocked; I chanced a glance up.) "How come?"

Emmie shrugged. "You know what he's like," was all she said, still keeping a careful eye on her son. He was now investigating the fruit display, but like Emmie, I thought he was listening. There was something quietly alert about him.

Katie rang up the soap, then slipped it and a strawberry lollipop into the top of Emmie's brown bag. "You don't need to worry," she remarked evenly, closing the little book and sliding it back under the register. "He can't beat the crap out of you for three years—oh shut up, Emmie—then suddenly claim World's Best Dad award. It just isn't going to fly. No judge in the state is going to listen to him. I'd forget about it, if I was you. Don't let it bother you."

Emmie stood, hands on her brown bag. Then she leaned forward. "It isn't that simple," she whispered across the conveyor belt. Paulie had found himself an apple and was taking big, juicy, unnoticed bites. "I wish it *was*, Katie. But he says stuff. He's—starting telling people things. Things that aren't true. Plus he's the one with the job still. I'm worried, Katie, real worried. You know what people think—about me."

Katie rolled her eyes ("It wasn't your fault Brigster's went bust"); the mother picked up the bag of shopping. "You *know* I'm right, Katie. It's just the way it is." She turned around and reached for Paulie's hand; dropping his apple, the little boy scampered to join her.

As Emmie maneuvered herself and her son carefully to the door, I caught sight of her face, the scar pinched tight against her white skin. "Good-bye," Katie called after her; we heard a faint "U-huh!" as the bell on the door jingled sharply.

Katie moved onto my groceries with a preoccupied face. Tins of tomatoes and packets of fettuccine, bags of cookies and pots of yoghurt, all sailed toward her, and were swept through the scanner with rough, unconscious hands. It was only when she'd finished, and was announcing the total, that she looked up at me.

Something changed in her face. "You're that woman from the Dupont house, right?" she asked sharply, sliding her fingers into her jeans pockets; when I nodded, she looked thoughtful. "Mom told me you people know Kenton Tyler. That true?"

"Yes, it is," I said, briefly wondering how much fodder our household provided for local gossip. *There's three of them, and a kid. You should hear the screaming* . . . "Not very well, though. We just—I—well, my husband's an old friend of Paul Dupont's," I explained.

Katie took this in, while dropping bricks of tomato puree and quarts of milk on top of the eggs and grapes in the big brown bag. I heard a despairing *smoosh* as a quart of orange juice landed on a plump juicy peach that had manfully fought loose from its box. "People say Kenton Tyler is the one lawyer around here that isn't too picky about getting paid. Is that right?" she asked at last, when everything was packed, standing with my credit card held fast in her hand.

I was in the middle of rearranging the shopping and mourning the peach, whose yellow flesh was now spattering the inside of the bag, but as she spoke I began to see where this was going. "I—to be quite honest, I can't tell you," I said feebly. "I mean—I take it you are talking about—I couldn't help overhearing—the young—er—Emmie, I think was her name—"

I reached out my hand; Katie was holding my card in a most ferocious grip. "I've known Emmie since pre-K," she asserted, a battle-light in her eye. She wasn't giving up the card. "She's got herself in trouble a few times, I guess, but she's a good mom. That Ryan's an asshole—everybody knew it, but nobody stepped in when she was stupid enough to get herself hitched to him. Landed her in a hospital more than once, not that *she* would tell the cops what happened—it's the old story, y'know?"

I nodded.

"She never drinks when Paulie's around, just to let her hair down once in a while, and when a girl's got bruises the color of pomegranate all over her chest, why the hell not? Now look," she went on, a note of wheedling entering her voice, "maybe *you* could talk to Mr. Tyler? See if he'd be willing to take on Emmie. Because that girl hasn't a dime—"

This was awful. "Katie, I can't help you, I have no influence over Mr. Tyler, and it's really his choice who he takes on," I explained firmly. "Emmie can go and see him, of course, but that's up to her. Now—can I have my credit card please?"

Katie reluctantly handed it over. "I guess," she said dourly. "But if—if! You happen to see him, would you do me a favor and mention her name? It's a small thing, just a small thing to ask. We're a community here. We try to help each other. You understand?"

By the time I got outside, bags sticking uncomfortably into my armpits, Emmie had just finished strapping Paulie into his seat and was slipping herself into the front of her battered white car. Hanging baskets of trailing ivy and sweet jasmine were festooned along the roofline of the little store's porch; the rich, warm smell came wafting toward me as I walked down the wooden steps in the afternoon sunshine. I watched as Emmie turned around to reply to something Paulie said; he made a funny little gesture in the air, and I could see her laughing in response. She reached over and tweaked his nose. He stretched both arms forward, and I could even hear the shouted words: "Cuddle, cuddle . . ."

Impulsively, I walked over to the car and tapped on the window.

Emmie's pinched face looked startled, but after a moment she rolled it down. A smell of melted candies and Play-Doh poured out of the interior. "Yeah? Can I help you?"

"Emmie, your friend Katie told me you might want a lawyer," I said quickly. "This man" (I scribbled Kent's number onto a card of my own, then gave it to her) "might be able to help you. Okay?"

She looked down at the card, then up at me, her brow furrowed. "I—okay—thanks—"

I nodded perfunctorily, then walked away and started loading my own car, telling myself I'd done all I could. By the time I'd finished battering paper bags into the crevices left between the baby buggy and car seat frame in the back of the car, Emmie and her young son were gone.

24

~

Jeanie

Quiet Lanes Elder Care Home was pink—very, very pink. The paint was pink, the doors were pink, the sign that announced WELCOME!!!! was pink. The bed-heads were covered in pink velour. The bedspreads (comforters, they call them in America) were a glut of pink roses, and smelled strongly of hospital-grade stain remover. In every room dangled pink ruched lampshades, and pink plastic flowers reposed in a—yes—pink glass vase in the silent, pink-carpeted entrance hall.

You might suspect that only old people who liked pink came to Quiet Lanes, but there was a settled expression on every face that suggested that personal inclination had little to do with becoming an inmate. The old people were clean, and the staff were cheerful enough, but there was an inescapably institutional feel to the place.

"Hello—you must be Jeanie—gee, we are just so *excited* to have you here," gushed Mrs. Forrest, an unexpectedly tiny woman of about forty with eyes like a sparrow's, short blond hair, and massively strong calf muscles, when I hesitatingly walked into her office. A scarf of vibrant fuchsia was coiled around her neck. She put her hands up to her face and stared at me with a look of deepest admiration, as if meeting me was pretty much the most exciting thing that had ever happened to her. "Your experience! Your qualifications! I have, like, a whole *file* of stuff here on you!" she added, waving a (you guessed it) pink envelope file in my face, which appeared to house my one-page CV and a lone faxed letter of reference from college. I wondered what earlier volunteers had proffered.

"Come in, come in, everyone is *crazy* to meet you!" she added, leading the way out of the office and beckoning me energetically toward the day room. I followed awkwardly behind her, down a corridor of badly painted portraits and framed poetry ("Quiet Lanes is the place to be / If you're old and like the sea").

Twenty pairs of eyes looked up as I entered; twenty faces registered a degree of vague interest that Mrs. Forrest interpreted as body-shaking delight. "I *told* you!" she said, laughing deeply, as she looked appreciatively around the room. "Crazy! And here is—Jeanie Boothroyd!" she announced to the assembled company, as if I were a rabbit she had just produced from a silk top hat. She even did a little mime of a drumroll as she spoke (completing, for me, the likeness between her and the Energizer bunny). Clearly, Mrs. Forrest was a lady who liked to use her arms.

I smiled awkwardly both then and repeatedly over the course of the next half hour, as Mrs. Forrest introduced me painstakingly to every person in the room ("This is Teddy, he's got Parkinson's, his wife died last year, he has a catheter; this is Sue-Ellen, she's had three husbands, she does fortune-telling, her daughter is a federal prosecutor—isn't that *wunnerful?*—and she just had a mastectomy. This is Tim, he does yoga, you must come and watch sometime, we have to take him for a colonoscopy tomorrow. This is . . .").

I was just about to begin a tortuous explanation of how I was unlikely to be able to come ever again (tremendously important obligations requiring my immediate presence elsewhere) when I caught sight of two of the inmates exchanging sly glances behind Mrs. Forrest's back. The look said, as clear as day, "Oh Lord, here she goes *again,*" and it gave me pause. The two ladies caught sight of me looking at them, and one—the woman called Sue-Ellen, a lady of faded majesty with a bouffant haircut—raised her delicately penciled right eyebrow a millimeter upward. It was a tiny but unmistakable gesture of camaraderie.

I allowed myself to be ushered onward by Mrs. Forrest toward the tea-urns, then began to locate lost magazines, slippers, and letters, while dodging a million questions. Everybody was very curious about me, it seemed—about who I was, what kind of family I had, what the weather's like in England ("How *do* you tolerate that rain?"), and, most important of all, what I thought of America. I was just about managing to keep them at bay when a cool, questioning Southern voice brought me up sharp. "Did I hear you say you're one of three, my dear?" asked the lady called Sue-Ellen, keeping her foot squarely on a copy of some old-lady magazine I was trying to retrieve. I stood up. The foot, encased in an impeccably white sneaker, was down flat and hard. "That's right," I said, smiling politely. "Like Macbeth. We're the three weird sisters."

"Hand in hand, hmm?"

"Something like that."

She slowly moved her foot off the magazine; I picked it up, then returned it to its rightful owner on the other side of the day room, conscious all the time that Sue Ellen's blue gaze was fixed upon me. When I finally caught her eye, she beckoned me over with a little flick of her forefinger. "Three English sisters. Sounds less like Macbeth than Jane Austen to me, actually," she began, making room for me beside her on the sofa, then patting the open space. Each fingertip was finished with perfect salmon pink polish. "Tell me, my dear: do y'all compete over beaux?"

I burst out laughing—suddenly we were in *Gone with the Wind*—and, surrendering, sat down. "Hardly. My two older sisters are married, and I can't say I fancied either of their husbands."

"Really? What was wrong with them?"

I shook my head at her. "Nothing's wrong with them. Just not my type."

"So what is your type?" Her china-blue eyes were disconcertingly wide.

"My boyfriend is called Dave," I explained carefully, "and he is—he is—oh, I don't know. Hard to explain, really. Very friendly. Fun to hang out with."

"And your sisters' husbands aren't either of those things, I suppose?"

This old woman was quite exasperating! "I didn't say that," I returned awkwardly. "That's not what I meant. But my older sister's husband is too work-obsessed, too ambitious for my taste, and my middle sister's husband is—very solid. Dependable. Boring, to be frank."

"I see. So you like men who can't keep a job and aren't reliable. Do I have that right?" Her wrinkled face was politely bland.

"I wouldn't put it like that—I didn't mean—I just—oh, I'm only twenty-four!" I said, realizing as I spoke that I'd given the same answer to someone else not so long ago. I felt my face flush; Sue-Ellen put her head on one side, looking for all the world like a bright little bird with golden plumage.

"I'm sorry, my dear, I'm just teasing you," she remarked after a moment or two, laughing a little as she took my hand in hers. "I was the youngest of three myself, you see, and we *did* compete over beaux. You should have seen me! I was just dreadful! Whenever one of my sisters brought home a young man, I couldn't stop myself, I just *had* to have him. Or his older brother. Well, you know how it is . . . And I didn't feel bad, because the other two did just the same thing. It's a miracle straight from the Lord that we got married at all—but we all did, you know. In fact, I was married three times."

"And your sisters? Did they get married too, or did you steal their husbands away?"

"No, my dear, certainly not," she replied seriously, "once God had joined them together, it was a different matter entirely. I wouldn't have dreamed of getting between them. Tilly was married twice, and Grace—that's the oldest—has been married for fifty-five years. So you see, my dear, we were terrible teenagers, but quite respectable once we were grown-up. Although—"

"Can you believe it? Time just *flies by* here!" Mrs. Forrester trilled suddenly, dropping her hand on my shoulder, her fuchsia scarf vibrant in the sunshine. She smiled down at me kindly, mouth wide, perfect white teeth sparkling. Sue-Ellen shrugged, and allowed me to be steered gently to the door, past the little chattering groups of bridge-players and crocheters, all of whom waved as I passed. I stole a cookie from the kitchen, then let myself out of the building and walked back along the coastal road (the one Paul and I walked along a few days earlier), feeling thoughtful. Quiet Lanes was, in some sense, worse than expected—more claustrophobic, more smelly, and definitely more pink. But the job itself wasn't too bad, I thought to myself, as I let myself back into the house.

It was just a shame (as I explained to Alison, an hour or two later) that it would prevent me from spending time with Dave. I'd be away most afternoons during his visit, helping out at Quiet Lanes. "I wouldn't worry about that, darling," Alison replied earnestly across the vast crackling distance between us. "He'll be delighted to see you engaged in geriatric care, I'm sure. After all, someone placed as he is—the situation with his mother—will be extra-sensitive to the need for *quality* volunteer work in elder homes. Don't you think?"

Which was really an excellent point, one I determined to make to Dave himself if he got uppity about my working when he actually arrived.

25

Q

My cell phone thrummed and jigged on the breakfast table. It was Fay, the partner from Schuster and Marks. I hadn't heard from her—or from anyone at work—since Caroline's party.

Her voice on the other end of the phone was like an echo from another life, rising thinly, almost inaudibly, through vestigial soup. "Hello, hello? Where the fuck are you, Q—you sound as if you're on the moon. *Where*—? Fuck, you might as well be. What are you doing in . . . none of my business, I suppose. Look, I'm calling because you'll be back from maternity leave in two weeks, and things are happening fast these days. I wanted to bring you up to date on the cases you'll be taking over—we've got, like, zero time to prepare the Mingge Brothers case, and then there's the Castle One Properties merger we agreed you'd take over, and I want to run through the details of *Alliance Construction v. Gettysfield Industries*. So it might be easiest if we meet up, you can get right up to speed, hit the ground running the day you return. Are you going to be available any time in the next week?"

I fought down the panic. Actually we were thinking of coming to the city in a few days, as it happens, I told her faintly. I'll come into the office Friday and we can talk then. I let her think we'd be just chatting about cases, there was no need (I decided) to hint at Any Other Subject just yet, so I walked carefully around the holes in my words and jogged determinedly onto the safer ground available to women and colleagues (how's Arlene, when's Chris getting married, what's up with Susan's house—*no*! It didn't! She *didn't*!). At the end of the conversation I hung up the phone, then stared at it.

What had people been saying about me behind my back? The thought of the complicated office politics, of what my colleagues say about women who begin the long slither *down* the greasy pole, made me feel briefly sick. I thought of Caroline's eyes, sharp as glass, of Michael's supercilious blandness. I thought of the fraught clients, the mind-numbing hum of the air-conditioning, the freaked-out terror of the junior associates, the nervy behind-closed-doors jockeying of the partners . . . And then I thought of the bigger gossip network, of the two-way flow of news from Crimpson out into the legal community. Tom had already put in a request for another week's leave on the grounds of Samuel's ill health. People were bound to be talking.

But how impossible it would be now to leave my son, to hand his small, frail body over for someone else to hug and smell and love twelve hours a day, to unclip my bra in the office and spill my breasts into plastic cups and bottles. Impossible to deal with the second-by-second crises of a firm struggling in a recession, while thinking every second only of *him*. . .

I saw, in a single moment of absolute clarity, the conversation I must have with Fay.

We were going down to the city on Tuesday—in four days' time. Our time there would be busy; apart from my meeting at Schuster, and Tom's emergency rendezvous with Luis at Crimpson, Lucille and Peter were planning to come and "see how you folks are doing." And we had lunches penciled in with our friends Brianna and Mark, while Paul said he wanted to bring us dinner one night.

Jeanie stared at us in frank bewilderment when we told her about the trip. "You're leaving me here?" she asked incredulously. "*All alone* in Connecticut?"

I wrinkled my forehead at her. "No, you'll have Dave," I replied, surprised, and her mouth hung open.

"But you said you wanted to see more of him . . ." she began accusingly.

"I know, I know," I returned apologetically, "but we have to go into work, there are—well, good reasons I promise, and we also have an appointment for Samuel at the doctor's. I would suggest you come with us, but there isn't room for five of us in the apartment, not for a full week, and anyway you have your new job, right? You can't skip that. Plus I can't imagine Dave will want to make the trip up and down from New York *four* times in the course of ten days . . ."

She looked briefly as if she was being strangled. "I see. I see."

"And look, if you want, you could both come at the end of his trip, he could leave for London straight from New York," I went on. "We can squeeze for a night or two in the apartment, I'm sure, and you'll have finished your first stint at the Home by then."

It was sweet, I decided, that she was so desperate for Dave and me to get to know each other. No matter what was going on in my life, I felt I'd have to make a serious effort with him this time.

26

*

Jeanie

'Ello, love," he said, standing on the doorstep, looking strangely out of place against the Connecticut sky.

I looked round his shoulder into the driveway, fully expecting to see a police car and an armed officer grimly waiting, but there was nothing, just a cardinal hopping in the grass and a few gray squirrels scaling the trees. "How did you get here?" I asked suspiciously.

He stared at me. "The heavens opened and put me here. I got in a time machine. How d'you bloody *think* I got here? I flew," he returned crossly. "On the eight a.m. flight, landed at ten thirty New York time. Then I hitched a ride with some bloke who works in insurance up in Hartford. Nice bloke. Didn't even know that planes contributed to the greenhouse effect—can you believe it—he does now—I met him on the flight, we had a nice chat, he says he's going to tell his bosses all about it the next time they want him to fly to Tallahassee. Anyway. Can I come in, or what?"

I stood back silently to let him come into the house, but he stayed still for a moment, staring at me. I gazed back mutely. "Aren't you forgetting something?" he asked impatiently.

"Sorry, I—?"

"A bloody kiss, Lady Muck, I've flown round the world to be here with you," he said, with a catch at the back of his throat, and I flushed, apologized, leaned forward, and brushed my lips against his cheek.

He turned his face, and our mouths met; his arms went around me, and he pulled me close. I'd forgotten the taste of him.

"Now, isn't that nice—oh I'm *sorry* to interrupt—but I just wanted to say how pleased we are to have you here," came Tom's voice from behind me, and he emerged from the sitting room with Samuel clutched and sprawling under one arm. "Dave—it's so *great* you could come," he went on cheerfully, rather overdoing it I thought. "Where are your bags—Christ, is that all you brought, very impressive, I always seem to end up with a dozen garment bags—still, it helps if you don't carry suits, doesn't it—can I help you—yes, and this is Samuel . . ."

Dave peered uncomfortably into Samuel's face, then took a step backward as the baby began to howl. "Don't mind him," Tom continued, "he does this all the time. Now, how about something to drink, Dave? Tea, I presume?"

Q was out shopping, but when she appeared half an hour later she literally threw her arms around his neck. They'd obviously had a conversation up in the privacy of their darkened, muddled bedroom last night about "making him feel welcome," but Dave looked a bit startled, as well he might, since the last time he saw her a year or so previously she was hissing at him like an overwrought cat about how he was "taking advantage" of me and was (I think I have the phrase correctly) "a work-shy, weak-kneed layabout." Now she effectively laid out a red carpet into the bosom of our family. "We're so delighted you've come all this way to see us, you must be exhausted, please don't think about us, if you need to go and sleep, just feel free . . .

"And how is your mother?" she went on, pouring him a third cup of sweet tea and producing some chocolate chip cookies from her shopping bag. "I hear you've been a real rock for her these past few years." She arranged her features into an expression of sympathy and simultaneous admiration. As well she might; Dave was an exemplary son.

"She's not doing so good," Dave explained soberly. "Not good at all. It's no surprise, of course; we've been waiting for this to happen. Alzheimer's—it's a terrible disease."

"When was she first diagnosed?" Tom inquired solicitously.

Dave shrugged. "While I was at Uni in Manchester, but she was mostly all right then," he explained. "She served up a bloody good Christmas meal that year, just a few weeks after the diagnosis: turkey, fifteen trimmings, homemade Christmas pud, brandy butter, you name it. We all thought, maybe she'll be the one to beat it, you know? Maybe it won't *get* her. But it was later that night, while we were still cleaning up the dishes, she forgot Dad's name for the first time, started talking about Stan, some bloke she was engaged to before she met Dad, who died of meningitis." Unused to so much warmth from my family, he was becoming expansive. "Dad was really upset, because he always suspected she loved Stan best. It was horrible—him in tears, Mam's bewildered face above the turkey carcass . . . 'course, it was just the beginning. Dad couldn't handle it, any of it, and neither could m'sister, but thank God Mam's cousin Brenda was willing to move in and help. She's been bloody marvelous, don't know what we'd have done without her, and God knows what Dad's been able to pay her. Her stepdaughter Ellen's been helping these past few years too, when she can. She works in a home for adults with disabilities and comes to help Brenda with Mam on weekends and at nights. You remember Ellen, don't you Jeanie?" He smiled sweetly.

Actually, the first time I saw her I nearly fell off my chair; I'd imagined, from the family description, that she would be a soft-footed, gentle young lady, prompted by an almost spiritual calling to take care of the elderly. She was, in fact, bottle-blond and twenty,

with the kind of plump-cheeked, big-bottomed cuteness remi-
niscent of a 1960s *Carry On* film. " 'Ello, Dave," she said when she
arrived for lunch, kissing him loudly on the cheek, pressing her
D-cup boobs into his chest. She chattered merrily throughout the
meal, forking great loads of fish and chips into her big, round, lav-
ishly lipsticked mouth with appreciative smacks. God knows what
she was saying, I was too busy staring at her cleavage. White shirt
open to her nipples, or thereabouts, and tucked into a short navy
skirt that bulged over a generous tummy. Every time she sat down or
crossed her legs, she exposed the thick tops of a pair of black stockings fastened with pink plastic suspender clips. Dave, exposed to
the sight of these undergarments just as he was trying to serve her a
cup of tea, was so flummoxed he spilled the hot liquid over the table,
which for no reason that I could see required Ellen to peer down her
cleavage and say, "No harm done to these fellas, I'm pleased to say!
Eh? Eh!" and nudge Dave furiously with her elbow.

I muttered something ever-so-faintly sarcastic about how Ellen was "a big-hearted girl," but I don't think Dave heard, he was too
busy being smothered in a blanket of warm sympathy by Q and Tom
("Your poor mother . . . so terrible for you . . . what a tragedy . . .
if there's anything we can do . . ."). Feeling somewhat upstaged by
them, I reached out for Dave's hand and squeezed it sympatheti-
cally. He looked up at me, an expression of tenderness softening his
face. I drew back my hand. "I really have got to get to my new job," I
explained. He stared out of the window at the vibrant green of the
maples against the peacock-blue sky, then turned back. "I understand. What time do you start, then?"

"I should—well, I mean I think—I should probably go now-ish,"
I explained, tying my hair up high into a ponytail. "I have to do ten
hours a week, and we'd arranged that I'd visit today. Such a shame
really—but you can sleep a bit, and when I get back we'll go down to
the beach."

Dave nodded, and stood up too, picking his huge tatty green rucksack up off the floor. "Fine. Show me to our room, Jeanie, and I'll get out of your hair," he said, nodding politely at Tom and Q. I could hear them still clucking enthusiastically behind us ("Anything! Anything at all! Just let us know!") as we walked through the hallway and up the stairs.

Dave, who seemed immune to the opulence of the furnishings in the gorgeous double room I presently introduced him to, settled down with a gusty sigh on the bed, yawned, and stretched himself fully out, muddy trainers flaking dirt all over the white counterpane. "Fantastic, I could do with a kip." He yawned again. "It was a long flight, I'm absolutely shattered." Then he rolled over to face me, stroking the pillow gently with one hand. "You *really* have to go now, love? Or do you want to—well, you know, take a nap with me first? God, I want you Jeanie, I can't wait much longer . . ."

"Dave, that would be *lovely*," I replied earnestly, "but I really *do* have to go—you know how it is—they're all so fond of me—I don't want to keep them—"

Dave sighed, rolled back over, and popped some tea-tree gum out of a silver foil packet from his jeans pocket. "All right, Jeanie," he mouthed, through the hard gray square, "forget it. I understand. One day this week I'll come with you to the old folks' home, I reckon, but now I'll just have a shower and get clean." He kicked himself off the bed, opening the door into the dressing room. "I'll unpack, you go off to your job, I'll keep the bed warm for when you get back." When I walked in a few steps behind him, he was in the middle of rifling through T-shirts and underwear; having found what he needed, he stood up, and started to strip off his clothes. In a second he was naked, standing unembarrassed before me, his travel-stained attire in a small heap before him.

Professor Mordaunt had begrudgingly given up my coursework, it seemed, because when I walked into the kitchen, Q silently handed me an envelope in which I found a certificate telling me I'd been awarded a master's degree by *Kingsbury College* (penned with enough curlicues to satisfy a sovereign) I felt very happy, very relieved, and very apprehensive. "It's time to start applying for jobs," I said slowly to Q, slipping the certificate back into its envelope, and she laughed.

"You've got to grow up sometime," she said, scooping up Samuel, smiling with a hint of a challenge in her eye. "And if you ask me, love, quite honestly it's about time."

27

Q

I mighta been a bit hasty."
Kent Tyler was standing on the front porch, hands plunged in his pockets, a frown creasing his forehead. He was wearing a pressed button-down shirt with his jeans, but there was still something indefinably disreputable about him. "The other day, I mean." He passed his hand anxiously over his head, smoothing down his wispy hair, and pulled awkwardly at his thinning ponytail.

"I'm sorry?"

"A bit hasty." He coughed uncomfortably. "Y'know, when you visited me. Y'want the firm?"

Tom had come up behind me; I felt his warm hand in the small of my back as he stood over my shoulder. "Hello, Mr. Tyler. What can we do for you?"

As he caught sight of my husband, Kent licked his dry lips, then stretched them wide into an oddly misshapen smile. "I was just stopping by to say, y'know, that you passed the test. Congratulations. You did it. When can you start?"

The hand on my back tightened. "Uh—what?"

Kent did a strange sort of jiggly dance, staring down at his toes, and when he looked up his face had changed expression again. "The firm. You can have it. Whenever you want. Like, how about next week?"

A gull sailed toward us, then sat down on the porch rail, moving its feet to get comfortable. It refolded its wings, twice, then put its head on one side and watched us with a bright, interested air.

"Mr. Tyler, that's very kind of you," Tom began carefully. "But I don't think that we—I mean, I thought we made it quite clear that—"

"Look, what's the problem?" Kent interjected sharply. "It's a good firm, you know! A real strong one. Large client base. Good—pretty good—reputation. Offices all paid up for six months. Five months. Four months. Till next week, at least."

"I'm sure they are, Mr. Tyler, but—"

"And you get to live here, in Connecticut!" He gestured broadly around the garden, at the house, and down toward the sea. The gull squawked a bit at Kent's carelessly waving arms, left its perch protestingly, and settled a few feet farther off.

"Lovely views. Big houses, for cheap. Public schools. Fresh vegetables. Mmm! And—er—er—"

"Mr. Tyler, honestly, it's not that . . ."

"I'm telling you—" (this with an emphatic bang on the house's wood siding, which caused the gull to fly up with one final, agitated squawk and sail off into the blue)—"this is the good life, you know? Recession-proof, in a way; people always need their local lawyer. And while running a firm (I'll be honest) is a bit much for one old man, for a young couple it's a dream. You take over my firm, you take on my—er—position in the community. You couldn't get this kind of a client base if you were to set up on your own out here. No one would trust you. But if you take over my name, you'll take on the trust. The trust, you see? I've been building it up for decades. 'Course you might lose one or two of the clients, but mostly they won't bother to look further afield, not in these times at least."

He paused, panting a little from the exertion, his faded blue eyes struggling to focus as he looked from one to the other of us in the sunshine. "Mr. Tyler," I said, taking him by his gnarled hand, smiling a smile I hoped was suitably gentle, "I'm sorry, we're just not really country types, you see? We live in New York; that's who we are. I mean—well, you can't change that in a few months, can you? We'd need much more time. I'm so sorry . . ."

Kent pulled his hand roughly away. "What you talking about, you're sorry?" he scoffed, thrusting out his chest. "I was going to offer you my firm because young Paul said you were to be trusted, but I've got guys up and down the coast *begging* me to let them take it on. Offering to pay me big bucks, too." He slid his fingers together meaningfully. "I don't *need* you; what, are you kidding me? I only put you people to the top of the pile 'cause Paul Dupont vouched for you. Otherwise you wouldn't have stood a chance, I'm telling you. Not a *chance!*"

And with that, he walked off down the steps to his old rusty two-tone pickup, chuckling loudly. He opened the big, heavy door, wincing as he did so.

"Listen—" I felt oddly compelled to continue the conversation and, pulling away from Tom, I walked down the steps after Kent— "we see the advantages, really we do, Mr. Tyler. But if you're a town person—well. And then there's the job itself. When I compare what you do with what we do, it's—it's completely different, you know? Not—" I put out my hand in response to something in his face— "worse, or better; just different. Different kinds of cases, a different spectrum. And different clients."

I hadn't got it right even now; I was irritated with myself. Kent shrugged again. "Like I say, it makes no difference to me," he replied coolly. "Don't have to explain yourself. *I* don't care."

"But we—we really enjoyed meeting you!" I added helplessly (I could feel Tom rolling his eyes behind me on the deck). "And seeing the firm, learning about it. Your beautiful view. The way you are— part of everything—"

Kent shrugged impatiently; placing his foot carefully on the running board, he heaved himself up into his seat and switched on the engine. I stood back as he awkwardly pulled the door closed. "Seriously, it's fine. Doesn't matter at all," he said, turning on the radio. Music blared out, twanging guitars and a man's croaky voice filling the hot, still air. "See you around." He nodded; I waved as the old truck chugged and spluttered off down the drive.

28

~

Jeanie

Dave's eyes were full of tears when I came into the bedroom. It was almost dark, and he had not switched on the lamp; he was sitting by the window, waiting for me.

I stared at him; he tried to smile, brushing the tears away with a shaking hand. "Just got a call from me dad," he explained in a rough voice. "Mam's taken a turn for the worse. Happened first thing this morning, just as I took off from Heathrow. Bloody ironic. As if she knew."

"Oh Dave, I'm so sorry," I said immediately, awkwardly kneeling beside him on the floor. "What's happened?"

"Small stroke, they think. Left side of her face is frozen, and she's not talking. Shit," he went on, putting his head in his hands, "it's back into hospital for her again, and you know what *that's* like."

Of course I did; I'd gone with Dave to visit his mam in hospital three months earler, when a fall and a hip fracture sent her into another sudden decline. The hospital building was about five miles from Dave's house, a huge, squat, hideous block of concrete with endless extension blocks and an overflowing car park. We found Mam in one of those wards you have nightmares about, eight beds of old ladies moaning and sighing and screaming against a backdrop of searing whiteness. "Nil by mouth" read the large sign above Mam's head, with "Mrs. Tickner" in blue marker pen. You could just see the name "Mrs. Browning," not quite rubbed out, underneath.

"Will it be the same place?" I whispered, and Dave nodded. " 'Course; it's the only hospital in thirty-five miles," he said wanly. "Get them in, get them out, that's the philosophy of that place. Whether they're ready for it or not. Dead or alive. Well, *you* know; you remember from last time . . ."

I cast my mind back to that awful afternoon. Mam was lying by herself when we arrived, baffled, confused, and dirty; no one had cleaned her properly since she was admitted two days before (the niceties of hygiene and cosmetics were utterly beyond Dave's dad). We set about her face with some aqueous cream from a big pot by her bedside, cleaned her teeth, and brushed out her matted hair as best we could. Then we changed her nightdress and tried to sit her up a bit higher on the pillows while Dave looked through the charts at the end of her bed. "Fuck the bastards, they *will* keep upping her dose of sedatives, anything to keep her quiet—they don't give a shit if it's actually *good* for her, wait until I find that fucking consultant," he said angrily, and off he went. Soon afterward I heard him having a furious conversation with a doctor just outside the ward ("Mr. Tickner, I understand you have your mother's interests at heart." "Yes, I bloody do, unlike you, you stuck-up southern bastard."), that ended reasonably well, from Dave's perspective; they agreed to lower the sedation and try a night of continuous nursing care. "Don't want to pay for the nurse, do they, they just want to give her some medicine that hushes her up, bloody hospital, bloody National Health, bloody government," he muttered furiously, all the way home.

I reached now for Dave's shoulder, thinking about poor Mam facing it all on her own without Dave by her side. "Is there anything I can do?"

Dave bit his lip. "It's terrible timing," he said, choking over a strange laugh. "Me here, and everything.

"Still," he went on, brushing his eyes again, working very hard to grin, "Dad and m'sister say I should try to enjoy myself out here.

First holiday in a decade, y'know. If anything changes—anything serious—they'll give me a ring. And I've only just got here, come halfway round the bloody world, I can't go back just yet. Not yet. Jeanie . . . please . . ."

He reached out to me, his hands stretching across the space between us, trying to close the gap, to bring me into his warmth. I knew what he wanted; quite reasonable, when you think about it. But it had been such a long time; and now there was this pressure, I thought, that it should somehow be equal to the occasion. And no matter how hard I tried, it was as if two people were bumping uncomfortably up against each other just when it needed to be—well, special, I suppose; a moment of togetherness. I closed my eyes, and felt his weight move above me, his body that seemed both familiar and very, very strange. Try harder, I thought to myself. This is *Dave*. He's suffering. Try harder.

29

Q

Haven't the women of your family *any* advice?" Tom asked miserably, in the cold hours of early morning, when my small family was stretched out in a damp mangled heap on the bed. "What's the point of having all these sisters? Jeanie knows nothing. And anyway, now that Dave's here, she won't be getting out of bed. You won't speak to Alison. Honestly, I'm almost tempted to call my mother . . ."

"Don't you dare," I muttered furiously, and reluctantly, faced with this threat, I called my own mother, just after lunch. She'd been very busy with her yoga studio recently; she hadn't had much space to think about me since she left to go back to England when Samuel was a week old. I dialed her number, feeling painfully hesitant.

My mother claimed, predictably enough, that all Samuel's problems were caused by my breast-feeding. "Goodness me, dear, your generation does seem to like making things difficult for itself," she announced (I could tell she'd been simply longing for the opportunity to advance her theory). "Give the child a bottle of *proper* milk, and I'm sure he'll calm down. And you won't feel so much like a milch-cow." She seemed to find it impossible to believe that a human being was actually capable of producing enough to feed a child—particularly a son ("Boys are such *feasters*!" she said indulgently, never having borne one herself. If she had, I'm sure I'd have hated him, though, since he would clearly have enjoyed the biggest portion of pie and the extra bowl of chocolate mousse throughout our childhood. He'd have been able to sleep in on the weekends, he would never have had to tidy his room, and I could just see her face when he brought home a C from school: "Justin [or whatever] just has *different* skills, dear, he can't be a whiz on the football field *and* a genius in the classroom!").

"Now then, as for the nighttime crying," she went on briskly, "try leaving the lights off when you feed him. You need to keep the room as dark as possible," she explained. "That's *bound* to help."

"Mother, of course I turn the bloody lights off," I replied, exasperated, "what, you think I'm an idiot? I could feed the child by the radiance of a glowworm, it wouldn't make a damn bit of difference."

"My dear girl, don't take it out on *me*, dear, I'm just trying to help," she returned magnificently. "And really, I think you just have to accept that babies cry. It's what they do. What were you expecting, dear? That Samuel would articulate his needs in fully formed sentences?"

I slammed down the phone.

Then, at the end of the evening, just as Tom and I discovered we had fallen asleep in front of C-SPAN (I think Tom dropped asleep literally while changing the channels), the phone rang again. When I picked it up, there was a growl on the other end, a low, inarticulate, indefinable mumble of irritation that made my hair stand on end.

Startled into hallucinatory wakefulness, I listened for a second, horror-struck. Just as I was about to grab Tom, the growl metamorphosed into a voice. "Grrrrrrwhat the *hell—what the hell*—d'you think you're doing? Huh? What? For Chrissakes?"

I stared at the phone, then cautiously put it back to my ear. "Hell—hello?"

"*You sent Emmie Cormier to me.* What do you think I am, made of money?"

"Oh—" I collapsed back into my chair, hand on my chest, trying to regularize my heartbeat "it's you, Mr Tyler. How are you? Now listen, I'm sorry about that, about Emmie I mean. I don't really know her. I bumped into her in the general store, and—"

"Well *I* know her. Emmie Cormier is a deadbeat, and always has been," came the uncompromising response. "Let's not mince words. She's a slut. Look at the way she dresses. Skirts slit to her waist, you can see her—"

"Mr. Tyler," I cut in hastily. "Listen. As I said, I don't know Emmie personally, I have no investment in this. But it does seem as if her ex is about to try to take custody of her son—"

"That's right," Kent acknowledged unexpectedly. "He is. Quite right. And a worse lowlife you'll never hope to meet."

"Really? You know him?"

"Yup. Known him since he was in kindergarten. Beat his first wife silly, then when she finally ran off to lose herself in Wyoming, he set about Emmie. Man's an absolute monster. 'Course, he's got money; works for Joseph Pinkerton, the furniture showroom, over on Route 1, they say he's the best man in the place, only one they'll never let go. If you was to meet him socially, now, you'd think he was—charming. You'd fall for him straight up. 'Good morning, how are you, and how are the little ones?' He's a born salesman, and it shows. That's how he gets the girls in the first place, of course—and there's plenty around here that've never seen through him."

"So I heard."

"Which—" gaining belligerence again—"is *exactly* why I can't take on her case! It's going to take serious man-power to defeat Ryan Cormier, if he's really set his mind on taking that kid away. You think I've got that kind of time? That kind of money? This isn't the big city, my dear! Think about what it will take! I'd have to face a man on the witness stand who's going to have half the community swearing he's an angel fresh from the Lord. That his wives have an unfortunate habit of walking slap into walls and twisting their ankles in flower beds. I'd have to find that first wife of his in the mountains of Wyoming, for a start (and they say around here she don't want to be found). Then, on top of it all, I'd have to make Emmie Cormier stick to the straight and narrow for as long as it takes, because if she gets herself drunk—or worse—even once, she'll be spotted, and someone'll take a picture on their damn cell phone, and send it straight to his lawyer. That's the thing with the country, my dear: you can't make mistakes. And I can't do that kind of case on my own! Not anymore, y'hear?"

I had been faintly protesting for the last five minutes; now, at last, I managed to lever myself into the conversation. "I'm sorry, Mr. Tyler, really I am," I began placatingly. "I see that I've put you in a difficult position. But perhaps you could—you could—I mean, if you don't help her, what else can she *do*?" I realized I didn't know much at all about how Connecticut family law worked.

"Lose her kid," Kent replied crossly. "She can apply for legal aid, of course. But they're full up to bursting, the system is strained, these days they're turning most cases down. If Ryan Cormier's set on taking that kid, it's going to be tough; there's plenty of precedent for overturning a custody order if he can just prove he has new information. I'm seeing her Monday night, at Flannigan's Bar, as it happens. Little place in the center of Sussex. Ten o'clock. I'm going to explain I can't help her. My days of taking deadbeat chicks pro bono is past. And *you*, my dear, you stop butting your nose into business that don't concern you. You hear?" The phone clicked.

I looked at it, tapping my fingers slowly on the pile of books on the side table next to the sofa, feeling slightly sick. Samuel was actually sleeping. A rare moment of silence unfolded in the evening; Tom's even, slumberous breaths punctuated the discreet purr of the air-conditioning. I switched the radio on low, and listened to a lady with a voice like sweet cream caramel talking about how to make sweet cream caramel, while wondering—I couldn't stop myself what I could possibly do to help Emmie.

30

~

Jeanie

Being with Dave again was a bit like cuddling up with a very familiar blanket. A bit worn around the edges, not particularly handsome, but warm and—well, comforting. I knew every part of Dave, every thought in his brain; had done, now, for over a year. When I looked into his eyes, there was nothing dangerous or unexpected lurking inside, just Dave-ness. A simple, straightforward, companionable, jovial Englishman. What you see is what you get.

I'd heard all the latest episodes in the saga of Badger's on-again, off-again relationship with his bank manager, a neat, tidy, professional woman who was bizarrely attracted to the loafish Badger with his weird shock of hair and multiple piercings in spite of the existence of a neat, tidy, well-dressed husband. Dave's account of the time he found the bank manager—his bank manager too, as it happens—hiding sheepish and half-naked behind the bathroom door made Q choke on her artichoke ("You've got to admit, there's never a better time to ask for an extension on your overdraft.").

I shared my stories too with someone who knew all the characters; I described the unfortunate mess-up at college, and Dave—who used to take courses with Sibelius Mordaunt, before he got kicked out of Kingsbury for nonpayment of fees—was pleasingly furious on my behalf. "Silly old codger, wouldn't last three minutes in the real world," he declared. "Sounds like he's lost his marbles, I mean, who could forget *you*?" he added, pulling me toward him. I smiled, my hand hanging limply in his.

Q was staggeringly polite to him and Tom staggeringly accommodating. Every time Dave expressed a hint of a wish, they rushed to try to find him whatever it was, from Jaffa cakes to "rough" bath towels ("These fluffy things—! I mean, I'm not complaining, Jeanie, but where's the *friction*?"). And Dave, in his turn, did his very best to make nice to the baby, peering hopefully into his little bed whenever he was sleeping ("Nothing for me to do, I'm afraid!") and swearing blind, whenever he was asked, that no, Samuel's screams did not disturb him at night. He kept pottering off to the package store and coming back with new six-packs of beer (he was fascinated by local microbreweries), which he then plied us all with ("Have another? No? Sure? Don't mind if I do . . .").

Then Dave came with me to Quiet Lanes, and entranced everyone with his tales from the frontline of the mighty eco-battle. In fact, I won a bit of reflected glory from my association with him. The old people had never met anyone like him and were touchingly convinced that he must be a genuine pioneer. They were American enough to find this thrilling, no matter what their own politics on the environment were. "We need more young men like you in this world," said Ken, an ex–fighter pilot, taking Dave's elbow in his hand. "Sometimes I think young men these days have forgotten *how* to be men," he went on, and although his palsied hand was shaking, his gray eyes were steady and serious. "That's why we get into the messes we do! You stand up for what you believe in, son; you keep thinking you can change the world. Only way to live, I think." The others nodded their heads in vigorous agreement; I felt curiously proud.

Sue-Ellen elected to read his palm ("If I can see through all this dirt, young man. You never heard of soap, perhaps?") and promised him—not riches, but a life of independence. "You're a traveler," she told him, and Dave grinned.

"Um—yes, but you already knew that," he said, chuckling. "Don't need to read my palm for that!"

She was not at all put out. "I don't mean that you came here on an airplane from England," she said scathingly. "That's *obvious*. I mean that you'll never settle in one place for long. A restless spirit. You've inherited it from your mother," she went on, and Dave gave a shout of laughter.

"My mother's lived in a tiny Yorkshire village her whole life," he said, shaking his head, "she's no restless spirit, let me tell you. A very normal housewife, in fact."

Sue-Ellen smiled peacefully at him. "If she'd lived in another generation, your mother's story would have been very different," she replied, and Dave wrinkled his forehead.

"Eh?"

Sue-Ellen patted his hand gently. "You're the son of a woman who didn't live the life she wanted," she said. "A woman who was never happy. I'm sure you picked that up as a child, children always do."

Dave furrowed his brow. "I don't think that's right," he said, confused, but then he shrugged, and laughed a little defensively.

Mrs. Forrest was looking on. "She's quite a woman, our Sue-Ellen, isn't she?" she said, happy and ineffably patronizing. Sue-Ellen looked up at her, folded her fingers neatly in her lap, and said nothing.

Dave, pulling himself together, helped us with lunch; he dashed around with plates, filled cups with cranberry juice, dove under chairs for lost napkins, and was generally very agreeable. "It's just like Mam's Day Center in here," he whispered to me as we flew past each other bearing plates laden with apple pie. "Old people are basically the same the world over, just want someone to talk to them."

"He's a breath of fresh air," a quiet old man named Joel told me, as he tucked into his dessert. "Thank you for bringing him to us, my dear." I smiled proudly.

In fact, as long as we were in public, we were having a lovely time together. Dave and Jeanie: "You seem like such a team!" But when the light faded, when Q and Tom yawned themselves up to bed, it was a different matter. Then I felt something horrible stirring in my stomach, something cold, gelatinous, and a bit twitchy. Something that made my skin shrink onto my bones. And when Dave slipped into bed, slid his hand in my pink check pajamas, and felt for my breast, my heart sank. Everything changed.

"Blimey, Jeanie, must be the water around here or something. Never seen you so ill," Dave said after our Quiet Lanes excursion, bewildered. "Can't I make you—better, love?" I pushed his reaching hands aside, and gabbled something incoherent. Everything is fine, I said; I just need to sleep it off. My head is throbbing. I'm very tired. And so I put off explanations for another day . . .

I didn't *want* to be different, especially not now, with his poor mother lying ill on the other side of the planet. I wanted to be the same girlfriend, the Jeanie I'd always been; there was so much pain in his eyes, and I wanted to take it away, not add to it. But something in my body seemed to be pulling me away from him, and no matter how hard I tried, I couldn't stop myself.

31

~

Q

I was swinging myself out the door at ten p.m. to go down to Flannigan's Bar and surprise Kent and Emmie when Jeanie appeared
in the front hall. "Where are you off to?" she asked, astounded,
I suppose, to catch sight of me dressed to go out. When I explained,
a wistful look appeared in her eye. "A—bar? *Really?* Do you think I
could come too?"

I was perplexed—but something in her eye inspired me to silence. "Of course," I said therefore. "God, we haven't been for a
drink together in years. Do you remember that time we went out
with—now what was his name?—the funny bloke you swore was
'the one.' Codger. No, Lodger. Oh, yes! How could I forget? Arty,
the Dodger . . ."

We set off arm-in-arm through the darkness, down the dirt
driveway, then along the narrow footpath bordering the coastal road
and into Sussex. There is not much going on in the town at nights,
just a few dog-walkers out for a last-minute stroll round the block,
some kids waiting listlessly around the gas station, and the drone
of the occasional passing car. The white clapboard houses looked
untouched by the centuries. After a moment's silence, Jeanie's grip
tightened. "So how did you know that Tom—you know—that he was
really—really the one?" she asked unexpectedly.

I tried to read her face, pale orange in the glare of the streetlamps. "Are you wondering if Dave—?" I began, interested, but she bit her lip and looked down.

"No. I mean, that's not why I'm asking," she returned hastily. "I mean, Dave obviously . . . But it's not because of Dave. I was just wondering."

I cast my mind back to the early days with Tom. I knew that I loved him, I suppose, almost immediately. Marrying him never seemed like a decision, it was obviously going to happen.

"In my case it all happened rather quickly," I explained. "But I think it's different for everyone. Some people take years settling into a relationship."

She nodded shortly, her face preoccupied.

"Do you—are you enjoying being with Dave?" I tried.

"Of course. I mean, he's funny, and kind, and—stuff," she answered. I had the strong sense that there was a "but" hovering on the edge of her words.

We had come within sight of the small bar, set in a purpose-built block atop a large parking lot; I felt almost regretful as we entered the circle of bright floodlight. Things were just getting interesting.

"So what are we trying to do here?" she asked quickly. "With this old man, I mean?"

"Well, we're going to be very strategic," I explained, navigating a parking truck. "Kent doesn't even know I'm coming, you see. I'm going to try to persuade Emmie Cormier, the young mother, to talk more about her life with her ex. The beatings, the violence, and so on. I want to see if she can inspire Kent's sympathy so he'll take her on as a client and help her keep custody of her kid. I want to see if I can help change his views about her."

"But why? I mean, why are you getting involved?"

"Because she can't pay him," I told my sister, pushing open the door to the busy saloon. "And—" ruefully—"you know, Jeanie, I just can't bear to stand by and watch a young mom lose her kid."

I saw Kent immediately, slumped on a stool at the far end of the bar, staring ruminatively into the depths of a double whisky. Above him a game of baseball blared on a huge TV screen suspended on the wall, a wiry pitcher preparing to throw at a batter whose mountainous neck began an inch above his ears. Kent was clearly utterly unconscious of the action—of the batter uncoiling into one swift pump, the sharp crack, the ball flying high, high, high into a forest of outstretched arms. In repose, the old lawyer's face looked older than normal, the lines around his face more sharply etched. The corners of his mouth were pulled down, and his cheeks looked gray and papery. I noticed (as I slid onto a stool beside him) that a nerve was twitching repeatedly in his eyelid.

He looked at me. "Huh. You here?"

"Well, yes. I thought I would. I—uh—came for a drink with my sister. Can we join you?"

He acknowledged my question and Jeanie's hovering presence with a neutral nod. "I guess we'll need a booth, then," he said, stretching out his limbs awkwardly.

He led the way to one of the bright red faux-leather booths lining the wall, beneath posters of sports stars and framed match tickets. As we were arranging ourselves along the benches, Emmie herself appeared in the doorway. She looked nervous and high-strung. She was wearing a cropped white top that showed too much bone, and a skinny faded jeans skirt from which too-lean, too-straight legs protruded. Her pale blond hair, in need of cutting, was loose about her face.

Emmie's expression, when she caught sight of me, was bewildered. She folded herself into the remaining seat with arms and legs that seemed all angles. She said nothing until after she had ordered herself a beer from the diminutive, curly-haired waitress, then stared me full in the face. "Who are you?" she asked, her eyes narrowing slightly. "You look sort of familiar—"

I opened my mouth to explain, but Kent got there first. "Pretty much the best friend you'll ever have, so quit the tone, all right?" he interjected belligerently. I blinked; Emmie flushed.

"Mr. Tyler, now don't be hasty, I just thought—" she began uncomfortably, but Kent waved his hand impatiently in the air.

"Shut up. This here is Quinn, a young friend of mine, and over here is her sister. From England. That's all you need to know. Now I want you to get on with it. Your story, I mean. Start with the background."

Jeanie and I exchanged baffled glances. Emmie shrugged, and took a quick slug of her beer.

"I . . ." She paused, and briefly shaded her eyes with her right hand. "I don't know what you want to know, exactly. Ryan—that's my ex—he says he's going to—he's going to take Paulie away from me," she said at last, her voice so low we had to strain to hear her above the noise and another explosion of jubilation on the enormous television monitor above us. "My little boy."

"And?"

"He says Paulie will be better off with him. He says everybody knows it. He says there's no point in fighting it, not since I lost my job. He says he'll tell everyone I'm an alcoholic, a drug addict, and a—"

There was a long pause. Kent, head cocked on one side, watching her, prompted her again. "A—?"

"A—you know, a whore," she finished at last, with visible reluctance. "He has—" (she looked down at the table) "he has some photos," she continued stiffly. "From a few years back. It was a stupid thing, down in a basement, this girl hooked me up with a photographer to earn money. Before I was married, I was kind of desperate. I'd lost—my little girl, my first baby, she died of—" (she gulped) "crib death. Woke up one morning, realized I'd slept through for the first time in months and—there she was. I went crazy for a while after that, missing Angela so bad, my Angel; people saying it was my fault, I shouldn't have got knocked up in the first place. You know how folks can be. Well, I went and got myself into real bad credit card debt."

I reached out and took her hand almost without thinking; she seemed so young. "Well, I guess I must have told Ryan about the photos." Emmie smiled a tiny, wan smile. "Now he's tracked them down. He said—he said he'll show the court. He says I'll lose Paulie for good. I don't even know—Christ—I don't even know why he *wants* Paulie, except—he wants everything, I guess. And his mother said he should take Paulie away from me, 'cause she's always hated me. She used to say bad stuff about my Angel. But I won't let it happen, Mr. Tyler," she continued, with sudden and unexpected force, banging her bottle down on the table until the beer fizzed and bubbled in a golden froth all over her hands. "I won't let him take my son away from me. I'll—I'll tear his heart out first! I'll rip him to *pieces* if he even *touches* my little boy!" Her lip trembled; a large tear slipped down her face.

Kent shushed her disapprovingly, peering theatrically over his shoulder. "Give it a break, Emmie, okay? Think about how you'll sound in front of a court!" But I found myself imagining how I would feel if someone tried to take Samuel from *my* arms. I'd kill them.

Kent was still looking around, muttering peevishly about "death threats," and how "judges don't take kindly to them, young lady," when I leaned over the table. "Emmie, I've got a baby myself," I told her. "I think I know—a little bit—how you feel. He's called Samuel. He's a couple of months old."

"Really? Who's got him now?"

"My husband. You?"

"Grandfather. You nursing, then?" (A quick, evaluative look at my figure.)

"Yes. Did you?"

"Uh-huh. Although I—"

"Okay, okay ladies." Kent was irritable. "Jeez! Let's get back to the point, okay? Keep to the subject. Now let me get this straight, Emmie. Are you saying Ryan beat you?"

Emmie became instantly interested in a piece of skin at the base of her thumbnail. "Uh-huh. Sometimes. When I—when I forgot stuff, y'know. Or—when I was late." She shoved her thumb oddly up-side down in her mouth and started to chew; we could hear the little click of her nail flicking backward and forward over her teeth.

"You reported him to the police, right?" pressed Kent.

Self-consciousness flickered in her eyes. "The nurses begged me to, of course, the one time I ended up in the hospital—overnight, I mean. That was the time he broke two ribs, blew out my knee, smashed in my nose, gave me *this*" (pointing at her face). "I was a *mess*" (she sounded almost, appallingly, proud). "But I didn't press charges. There was no point. Lieutenant Driscoll was at school with Ryan, they go drinking most Friday nights at O'Rourke's. You think I'm going to tell *him* about it? And Ryan—like he always said to me, *he's* the kind of man people believe. I'm the kind of girl they don't. That's just the way it is."

She finished off her beer with the air of one who had communi-cated a deep truth about life.

Jeanie was watching her. "Did your family ever see the bruises?" she asked suddenly.

Emmie shrugged. She was now picking the foil off her beer bot-tle. "My dad saw them all the time, he used to come by and help me with stuff around the house when Ryan was at work," she answered. "He got himself killed in a motorbike wreck on Route 1 a year ago," she added evenly, "so I guess that won't help us a whole lot. Besides, he got so damn mad at Ryan about the beating he used to get in fist-fights with him all the time. Driscoll was out at our house at least once a month, and usually wrote up the report to make Ryan come out looking good. So I don't think Dad's word would've counted for much in court. If that's what you're asking."

"And your grandfather?" prompted Jeanie.

"He don't see what he don't want to see," Emmie explained. "He likes Ryan, actually, 'cause Ryan fixes him a free breakfast every Sunday. The way to Gramps' heart is through his stomach, Ryan knows that. Basically Gramps thinks I should just quit the whole thing and settle down with Ryan again, although he's loyal to his own blood too; he won't stop me from leaving, he just won't help me either."

We asked a few more questions about the details of her married life with Ryan, and her divorce (which had been handled by a young, newly qualified lawyer from Yale, whom she'd been put in touch with by Legal Aid. He had now left the state "for something big in Chicago, I heard.").

"I've got to get back; Paulie's been waking up about this time recently, he hates it when I'm out," she finished, tugging her skirt over her skinny hips as she stood up. Then she looked down at us. "Legal Aid isn't going to help me," she said, hazel eyes huge in her face. "In case you're wondering. I spoke with them already. They said they've got to do the divorce, because of the state, I guess. But custody disputes is different. If you can't help me, I'm going to lose my son." Her eyes felt out mine. And then, to Kent, blushing a little: "You'll call me, right?" He nodded briefly, and raised his bottle to her as she flitted like a restless, awkward little ghost out of the bright, bustling bar.

Kent's eyes were fixed on mine. There was a long silence while I debated my move.

"So what do you think?" he asked suddenly.

I stared. "You mean about whether she's telling the truth? I think—"

Kent clicked his tongue impatiently. "Of course she's telling the truth," he interrupted. "Jeez! That's obvious. I'm talking about *you*, my dear."

I glanced down, astonished, as I felt Jeanie's fingers pinching my hand. "What the—?"

"Q—" Jeanie was laughing—"you are *such* an idiot!"

"I am?"

"Sweetheart, this is not about you twisting Kent's arm. Haven't you got it yet? This whole thing? *He's* twisting *yours* . . ."

32

~

Q

We packed the bags, cleaned the house, spent as much time as we could handle with Dave, and gave Jeanie a kiss. Then we got Samuel's car seat ready, complete with beguiling toys to help him pass the time on our trip to the city. We entered the car in quite good spirits.

∞

Four hours later, we felt rather differently. *I'm never driving anywhere ever again with him*, I told Tom, slamming the car door outside our apartment, Samuel hysterical and retching in my arms. It looked as if full-scale world war had broken out in the backseat.

In between Samuel's screaming fits, Tom and I had a circular conversation on the journey about whether to try a nanny after all rather than daycare. "You could do with the extra help around the house, you don't cope so well with the crying, I think you need more domestic support," Tom said fretfully, and I lost it, and shouted at him, because he didn't seem to understand he'd just weighed up my motherhood and found it wanting. And anyway, nannies are expensive in Manhattan. If Tom lost his job . . .

But it wasn't just about the money. What I couldn't quite bring myself to say to Tom in the car was that, in my mind, a nanny was either a horrible know-it-all Mary Poppins who'd do everything better than I and make our child love *her* best while making *me* feel hideously inadequate, or an organ-thieving axe-wielding murderer who would appear sweet and trustworthy and then kidnap/slaughter/ sell Samuel the second our backs were turned. Often, she was both. Tom tried suggesting we hire an au pair—"quite a bit cheaper"—but I couldn't figure out how an eighteen-year-old was going to cope with a screaming Samuel given that he sent me, a career woman in her late twenties, to the brink of insanity. At least I knew I wasn't going to throw him down the stairs in a fit of pique. (I was nearly sure I knew this.)

The next morning, Tom went out for brunch with someone from work, so I was left on my own with Samuel. We went to the Met first, and after examining Ingres's solid beauties we moved upstairs to the flourish and gay chaos of the late Renaissance. It was full of paintings of delighted mothers and fat, giggling children. Samuel goggled owlishly at them for ten minutes, then began to complain. Old ladies and gentlemen, out for their morning constitutional, pulled away and stared reproachfully at us; "It really isn't a place for children," I heard one of them murmur discreetly into her guide. Her companion, a dapper little man in a waistcoat with huge, rheumy eyes, nodded sadly. I ran downstairs to the medieval galleries, where I felt much more at home. The babies were all long and lean and tortured-looking, and the mothers were wailing.

In the sway of the baby-carrier, Samuel eventually dozed off, and I walked down the steps through the sunshine to a small Upper East Side trattoria to meet Brianna, a friend and colleague from work. Not one of the people in Caroline's orbit, obviously: Brianna was a paralegal. To someone like Caroline, she was indistinguishable from the copier machine.

It was hot, a grilling sort of day. Tourists swirled around me, damp, unfolded maps spewing from their unzipped bags, shirts knotted loose around their waists, calloused feet tripping out of worn flip-flops. Red-faced, red-eyed, hair glistening with sweat, they stumbled blindly toward the Met, looking as if they really hoped it might be closed.

Brianna was waiting for me; flicking her gleaming hair over her shoulder, she tried to enfold me in a huge hug. Samuel rather got in the way. "So great to see you, Q, I've missed you like *crazy*!" she screamed, jumping up and down. Adjusting Samuel's sun hat, I said everything that was needful, then settled with her under an umbrella on the sidewalk and sipped a spritzer while Chihuahuas sniffed hopefully at our chair legs.

With some difficulty, I'd managed to maneuver myself behind the table and into the chair without waking the baby (a complicated dance that at least three other women nearby watched with private smiles of recognition). Apart from the presence of a slumbering child on my chest, the lunch was, therefore, quite like old times— two friends having lunch together.

"I was running out of ideas for takeout," Brianna began brightly, referring to the last time we really saw each other—just before Samuel was born. "It's so great you're out of the house at last, after all those months in bed. You can take a real vacation. He's very good, isn't he?" (Peering at his crumpled face.) "But then, babies this age don't really *do* anything, do they? Just eat and sleep. My mother always said you needed maternity leave when they get to be, like, two. This first bit's *easy*! Well, that's what she always said . . ."

She trailed off a bit, which may have been because I was baring my teeth at her. Now, as it happens, I was actually trying to smile. But I'm not sure that's how it came across.

She changed the subject. "We're so glad you're back. I wish you were staying for longer. Mark was saying just the other day—" she gulped a bit—"that he was really missing Tom . . ."

Something indefinable had changed in her posture; her shoulders had rounded slightly down. They hadn't slumped—nothing as dramatic as that, but still, I knew immediately that something was wrong. She'd been dating Mark, one of Tom's oldest friends, for a year or so now, this in spite of the fact that Mark's soon-to-be-ex-wife, Lara, was pregnant with their third child.

I sipped at my water. "And *how* is Mark?" I asked politely. Fond as I was of Brianna, I couldn't forgive him for the way he'd behaved.

"Fine," Brianna replied. She looked miserable.

"How do you find living together?"

"Really wonderful," she went on, blinking hard. "Like, we just get on so well. We both love to—to shop. He's such a foodie. And we go out a lot. Mark says he's making up for lost time. All those years with Lara—and the kids—"

We fell silent as the waiter appeared; he fussed with our plates for a moment, officiously rearranging the glasses and the cutlery, then produced our hors d'oeuvres with a flourish: scallops for me, a big plate of garlic bread for her. (As if *that* wasn't enough of a clue.)

Brianna picked up her bread and ripped it in two. "Work has been all-consuming—for him, I mean. You probably heard. He just had a big case managing a takeover. There's a firm out in LA—Badden and Scutzer—that wants to hire him. He's seriously tempted to accept; Badden and Scutzer is doing really well by its partners at the moment. So, you know, financially, given the realities of life these days, it would make a lot of sense for him to jump. Particularly because I—well, let's just say, I don't think I'll have a job past the end of the month. The paralegals are all being pink-slipped."

"Oh, Brianna—I'm so sorry. That's just terrible."

Her long hair had fallen around her face; her nose was just about visible, a little bronzed point peeping delicately through the heavy dark curtain. Rip, rip, rip; she was tearing the bread into smaller and smaller pieces. I squirted my scallops with lemon and began to wolf down my plate—partly because I was starving, partly because I calculated I had six minutes before Samuel woke up. "At least Mark has options, I suppose. How do you feel about living in LA?" I went on, through a full mouth.

"It's not—I mean—I have family here, and—it will be a big transition for me," she replied desperately. I watched as the seasoned chunks rained down; her hands were now literally dripping pale green olive oil. "I've always lived on the East Coast, and—and I really love the city, y'know? This is my home, I can't quite imagine living anywhere else. But LA—people say it's a fantastic place," she went on feverishly. "If you have a car, obviously. And I suppose we'll have a villa with oranges in the garden. And peaches. And a swimming pool. So it'll obviously be great. A dream life. Most people would jump at it. We're so lucky."

"What about the children?" I couldn't restrain myself. "Mark's kids, I mean. How does he plan to see them if he's living on the West Coast?"

She had picked up her napkin and now began methodically wiping oil from each finger. "Mark thinks it's good for them," she returned, attentively contemplating her right hand. "I mean, the kids have friends who are being pulled out of private school because their parents lost half their savings. He thinks, these days, it's enough to have a dad with a good income. Plus he says they might find it easier if he's on the other side of the States. It'll be a clean break after the divorce. Less messy." She had now started on her palms. *Scrub, scrub, scrub.*

"And what do *you* think?" I asked, laying my fork and knife down. The waiter walked over and, stiff with disapproval, began to clear our plates. Hers looked like a product of the apocalypse. Mine was picked so clean you could have sutured a wound on it.

"I think—I think they're really suffering, if you want my honest opinion," she said, sitting back, watching the waiter with brimming eyes. "I think Lara's all over the place. I think the kids are bewildered and hurt and terrified. I mean, they're losing friends from school at the rate of, like, one kid a week. Mark needs to stay here and help them work it out—*I* think. But he says I don't know what I'm talking about. He says I don't know the first thing about how to raise a kid. He says I don't really understand what being a parent is like. Of course, he's probably right . . ."

I miss Jeanie, I thought to myself an hour later, as I walked back to the apartment along the burning sidewalk, with a little start of surprise. I miss having my sister around. My conversation with Brianna had reminded me somehow of her. In a sense I was pleased with the thought; it made me feel terribly sisterly, and it had the added pleasure that in just a few days we'd be back in Connecticut, in the spacious coolness of the house, all together. For years (I thought, as Samuel and I picked our way carefully through the steaming traffic) my relationship with Jeanie had been on hold; there's only so much of a friendship you can build with someone over the phone, after all. We'd been stuck at the time and date I got on the plane to come to live in America, stuck in a sort of holding pattern. But since she touched down in the US, we'd been getting to know each other as people, as adults, not just as the kids we used to be.

In a burst of enthusiasm, when I got back to the cool of the apartment, I picked up the phone to tell her this. I'm so glad we're having this time together, I said, and I can't wait to come back to the house and be with you. How's Dave? How are you guys doing?

Fine, she told me. Really wonderful. We get on so well together. And—I can't wait to see you.

It was only later, when Tom was cuddled up to me sleepily on the sofa, Samuel in the bassinet at my feet, that I thought again of Brianna, partying the night away with a man who was using her to try to forget his own mistakes. And, for that matter, of Emmie Cormier, struggling against all odds to keep her child by her side.

I looked at my son, breathing slowly in and out, and at my husband, and remembered to be glad.

33

⁓

Jeanie

On Dave's fifth night in Sussex, I slipped into the slithery cotton sheets with a stomach that seemed to have a slab of lead in it. I'd cleaned my teeth so hard the gums were bleeding. I'd brushed my hair so much the brush resembled a small marsupial. My face was red with scrubbing and—for good measure—I'd polished every nail on my feet and my hands with three full coats of "SunGlo Orange." Eventually, I let myself out of the bathroom and tiptoed across the bedroom floor, listening to Dave's breathing, wondering if he was already asleep.

As soon as my head was on the pillow, Dave's arm came snaking through the covers toward me. "Give us a hug, love," he said softly in the darkness.

We hugged uncomfortably. His hand started wandering downward. I jumped out of bed.

"What the bloody hell's the matter?" he asked angrily, sitting up and staring at me, rumpling his hair in the gray light.

I danced about nervously. "Um, nothing. Stomachache. And a backache. And you—you tickled me," I enumerated unconvincingly.

"Since when've you been ticklish?" he growled. He watched me in silence for a second or two. "Ah *shit*," he said at last, subsiding back against the pillows. "Stop playing around, Jeanie. You're finishing with me, aren't you?"

His gaze was unwavering. "Is that right, Jeanie?" he pressed.

He started out strong, but then his voice cracked on my name; he got stuck somewhere on the N, stumbled heavily, lost his balance, then failed to lift up the last syllable. Somewhere, because I knew I had to, I found the answer. "Yes."

We stared at each other as the word left my lips.

I sat down on the very edge of the bed, hands pressed hard between my knees. It was too late—not to mention absolutely cruel—to back down now. "Dave, I'm so sorry—" I began helplessly. "I don't know what's happened. It isn't working for me anymore. I don't know why."

He closed his eyes. "That's that then." Then, suddenly, he turned to me, his face set. "There's someone else." It wasn't a question.

"Wha—? No, no, of course there isn't—"

"There is."

"No, Dave, honestly, there isn't—"

"Are you sure?"

"Yes, of course. Dave, I haven't even met anyone here in Connecticut except Q and Tom and—"

"And?"

"Now, don't get the wrong idea, Dave. There's a friend of Tom's, the man who owns this house, and he came for a weekend, but *he* isn't—I mean, we haven't—"

Dave's face was as cold and set as stone. "What's his name?"

"It doesn't matter—"

"It does to me. What's his name?"

"He's called Paul, but I'm telling you, nothing has happened between us. Nothing *will* happen. He has a girlfriend—"

"I see. You've bothered to work this out, of course."

"It just came up in conversation. Dave, there's nothing going on between me and Paul, I don't even like him, he doesn't like me, I'm telling you, he's got nothing to do with it—nothing to do, I mean, with *us*." I was very earnest.

"Are you sure?"

"Yes, I promise you!"

Dave's suspicious look gradually faded; at last, he sighed. "All right, I'm sorry. I know you tell the truth. I just thought—it's funny really. There was me, trying to make you jealous about Ellen—I mean, even Badger said he thought you were trying to break up when you came here. Find a way out. But when you chucked half a dinner service at me I thought he was wrong. I told Badger . . . Christ. And we've had such laughs. I thought we were *strong*, Jeanie! I thought" (long pause) "you *loved me*."

I stared down at the floor, and began counting the knots in one board. (*Four, five, six . . ,*)

"I don't know why you even bothered to arrange my ticket to America, unless—was it—was it—pity?" His voice was rough as bark. "Did you just feel sorry for me, Dave the loser, can't afford to pay his own way?"

"Oh Dave, God, no, it wasn't that," I said desperately, looking up again at last, wanting to save him something. "I wanted to see you, of course I did. We've been together for so long, and besides, I really do like you—"

Like—not love. He saw it immediately and groaned, reaching over to the bedside table for some tea-tree gum, which he pressed out of its wrapper and slipped into his mouth. Then he rubbed his arm across his nose. " 'Nuff said," he replied at last, through the thick wedge of gum. "I get it. I'll go back to New York tomorrow, by myself, you don't have to come with me." He was bitter. "I'll go back to London, you don't need to see me ever again."

"Dave, that's not what I want—"

"Well, it's what you'll get."

I nodded slowly. I wasn't in a position to negotiate. "I'm so sorry, Dave" (wailing a bit)—"and you're being really good about this. Much better than I deserve."

"Don't give me self-pity, Jeanie, I don't want to deal with it."

"I'm sorry."

"Yeah. Well."

His face was like a window that was abruptly closed, a screen that reflected but gave nothing away. "I'll sleep on the sofa downstairs," he said suddenly, standing up and sliding out of the enormous bed in a soft *sooosh* of the sheets. "Get out of your space."

"That's okay, I quite understand, thank you, not a problem," I gabbled, with strange formality. I clutched my pajama shirt to my breasts as he walked past. But he disappeared out of the room without a backward glance, shutting the door with a sharp, final bang.

I sat on the bed, my knees tucked awkwardly into my shirt, and listened to the sound of the cupboard opening and closing in the corridor—Dave's hasty footsteps on the stairs—the sitting room door clicking open and slamming closed. The sounds of pulling and shoving and dropping, followed by the blare of the TV. The sounds of Dave walking out of my life. I started to cry.

He must have been watching a movie downstairs, because when I finally fell asleep at four a.m., I dreamed I was making love to Warren Beatty in the kitchen when poor Dave came in, saw us, and started begging me with loud tears and lamentations to marry him.

34

Q

It's funny what a difference a couple of months can make.

Our first few visits to see Dr. Templeton, our lean, homely-faced pediatrician, were exciting adventures, offering exquisite moments that seemed to validate our entry into the mysterious world of parenting. In the waiting room we enjoyed a rather pleasant feeling of entitlement: Tom and I were parents at last, the kind of people who could legitimately pore over leaflets about car seats and vaccines and shake their heads dolefully over the cost of nursery schools. At our nine-week visit we rushed in, sat down, and inspected our watches impatiently until the nurse called Samuel's name.

"So what's going on? Samuel sleeping through the night yet?" Dr. Templeton asked cheerfully, when Samuel was naked on her table. She kneaded his skinny hips with long, probing fingers; he looked surprised for a moment or two, then began to whimper. No, he's not, Tom replied, testily; that's why we arranged to see you today. He's not even close to sleeping through the night. And he cries *all the time*.

She shrugged her shoulders, all sympathetic understanding, and checked through her sheaf of notes. He's a breast-fed child I see, she said—hmm. Bottle-fed children often sleep through the night a little bit sooner than those that are breast-fed, formula takes longer to digest, but he's sure to catch up soon. And it's a wonderful thing you're doing for him, she added, turning to me, a wide smile stretching her face. Breast-feeding is the best start you can give your child. So many wonderful health benefits!

"But I'm a little surprised to hear he's not settling down," she went on, a slight frown creasing the skin between her eyebrows. "Getting into more of a routine, that sort of thing. How much of the day does he cry, exactly?"

Samuel, as if on cue, switched from whimpering to wailing, arching his body away from the doctor's cool hands. She watched him in a detached fashion for a few moments, writhing on the table; within about a minute, he was crying full-force.

I couldn't stand it anymore. I pushed past her, scooped him up, and rocked him gently in my arms. I could feel her watching us.

Samuel continued to scream, a horrible sound—desperate, lost, pained, hopeless. His eyes rolled up in his head, his body became suddenly stiff, his skin flushed purple. "I'll have to nurse him, it's the only way," I muttered, frantically trying to get my son's resisting lips to my breast. He opened his mouth, bared his gums, and kicked away from me so hard I almost dropped him. Great, I thought to myself, this is looking good. Introducing Quinn Boothroyd, World's Best Mother.

"Yes, I do see what you mean," Dr. Templeton said, or rather yelled at us, finally, after a few strategic retreats into another office to "look something up." "At this stage I'm inclined to diagnose it as colic—he wasn't crying when he first came in, there's nothing obviously wrong with him, no tender spots, and some babies do keep this sort of thing up for three months, six months, even beyond. But it can't hurt to get another opinion; there are some obvious possibilities, and we might as well investigate them properly. Reflux, for instance, is a likely candidate. How often does he vomit?"

We discussed Samuel's eating and digesting habits as best we could over the din, establishing finally that (a) it might be reflux and (b) it might not. She decided to send us to someone called Dr. Ezekial Sykes who apparently specialized in infant gastric disorders and who might be able to tell us more. Or might not.

"Have you tried swings?" Dr. Templeton asked us brightly, just before we left, "or swaddling? Maybe both at once? With music?" I managed to avoid pressing my fingers into her eye sockets (barely), although on our way out of the office I did see a leaflet for a "patented colic-soother," which I stowed in my pocket. Parents across the nation swore by it, apparently, and it had long been a staple in homes in Sweden. "My child used to cry for hours a day. Then we tried the patented colic-soother and everything changed. Now people tell us our daughter is the happiest baby they've ever seen," said Birgitta from Stockholm. It was a special bouncy chair that played soothing sounds of the sea while moving from side to side in a way designed to recall the gentle rocking of the womb. Tom told me I was being suckered in by advertising, and loudly prohibited me from buying it.

"Apart from anything, Q, we've got to start thinking more carefully about how we're spending money," he said later, when we were home. He opened his wallet up to me with a comical expression. "Empty, see? And now you've decided you want us to give up our lucrative careers and become small-town lawyers, we just can't afford to waste cash on snake oil."

"It's not snake oil," I protested faintly. "And your friend sent us to Kent in the first place! Besides, I haven't—I mean, I haven't said that we should *commit*, we're just going to see how—"

"Q, I simply said we should meet the guy. *You're* the one who's got swept up in some case. But if I'm wrong, great; let's just dismiss the whole idea. We'll call Kent and say, 'Sorry, you got the wrong guys. Find someone else to take over your practice.'"

"Tom, it's not as easy as that. Think about Emmie."

"I have been thinking about her," he replied coolly. "And frankly, she's not our problem. You barely know her. Plus Kent is obviously sympathetic to her. He'll take her on whether we come on board with the firm or not." He sat back on the window seat.

"I don't think so, Tom." I came and sat beside him. "You're right that he's sympathetic. But he told me he simply hasn't got the space or energy at this point in his professional life to deal with a woman like her. And I believe him. He needs associates to help out if he's going to take on her case. After all, it's going to involve real digging to find something on her ex-husband to shake his testimony in court. Ryan is polished, good-looking, and affluent; he's cool under pressure, he makes great eye contact, and Kent has heard stories about him buying up half the toy store for Paulie. He's going to look great in court. While Emmie is rough, down-at-heel, out of a job, and let's not forget that bunch of explicit photographs that'll support his claim she worked as a prostitute."

"Q" (my husband looked exasperated), "you do choose strange people to get exercised about! I have to ask you this: what *is* bugging you about this woman? About this case? Because honestly, at the moment I don't get it."

Outside, the blue sky was paling in the late afternoon; the moon, almost transparent, was emerging over the skyscrapers.

"I *know* she's a good mother to that kid," I said slowly, rubbing a space in the grit on the inside of the window around the outline of the moon. "Don't ask me how I know, but I know. And that little boy loves her."

"Well—" (with a heavy sigh) "I hope you're right, darling. And I hope—God, I hope—*I've* done the right thing."

Tom met with Luis at Crimpson this morning; the meeting, as Tom explained it to me, was difficult and intense. Luis outlined a deal he'd brokered for Tom to stay on at Crimpson "of counsel"— which meant, effectively, that they would keep him at the firm for his skills as a bankruptcy lawyer, but with no chance of making partner. The pay cut would be substantial too. Luis clearly thought Tom would jump at the offer ("At least it'll keep you at the firm, eh? Thank God for that. You know, your being out these last few weeks was actually a pretty sharp move, my friend," he went on, laughing, "made them realize how much they need you. The recession's kinda helped you, too—who knew bankruptcy could get so hot?").

Tom thought the offer through for approximately twenty-five seconds. Then he politely declined. Luis metaphorically fell off his chair.

"Maybe I should have taken up Luis's offer," Tom fretted now, and I pulled him close. "We've got a child to support, after all. And we still don't know what's going to happen with your job. Oh God, maybe I've been completely insane . . ."

Maybe, but at least we had a plan to keep money coming in for the time being. Tom would get a modest severance package from Crimpson, and Paul had offered to help get him set up with consulting work ("Your skills are hot property right now") to bridge the gap until we decided what to do next. "Of course you've done the right thing," I assured him therefore, nuzzling his neck, trying to feel as confident as I sounded. "Crimpson would have worked you to death, Tom. Taken your heart's blood all over again. Sucked you dry. We don't need riches, you know."

35

Jeanie

You might not want to come to New York now—I mean, Paul will be here tomorrow night, he's coming to talk to Tom about work things, and I know you don't think much of him."

Q sounded as if she was plumb in the intersection between baffled, appalled, and ecstatic when I explained to her that Dave had already left—that rather than coming down with me to New York for the weekend, as we'd originally planned, he'd gone to the airport to talk himself onto an earlier flight. I was still in a mild state of shock about the whole thing. "But why did you—but why did he—but I thought that you—oh, listen, you'll have to tell me all about it later," Q went on urgently, "and I want *all* the details. But in the circumstances it seems a bit pointless to come all this way when, as I said, Paul is coming for dinner."

"Well," I began uncertainly, but Q cut in again. "On the other hand," she added thoughtfully, "we could do with you on the car journey back. The trip here was just dreadful. You could help me keep Samuel entertained, so if you don't *mind* . . ."

That settled it. "Of course I'll come, Q," I said immediately, realizing suddenly that there was nothing in the whole world I wanted as much as a few days in New York. The sights—the cocktail bars—the shopping; Alison asked me to look for a particular belt in Bloomingdale's, and she'd even offered to buy one for me if it was in stock.

"I'll get a train down from New Haven and I'll phone you to let you know what time I arrive," I explained.

I spent the afternoon working my way through a packet of "English muffins" (i.e., not cakes) dripping butter over the computer keyboard as I searched databases for jobs in social work (having been passed over for the job in Cumbria; not a surprise). There *were* still positions out there, of course; if you fancied spending a hundred-odd hours a week sorting out methamphetamine addicts for £16,000 a year, your options were legion. Of course, with that salary, the only place in London you'd be able to live was a cardboard box under Tower Bridge, and you'd be finding your evening meal in the bins outside Starbucks, but who could be so churlish as to care about that?

But appealing positions that paid a living wage were few and far between. If I wasn't careful, I knew I'd have to take up my old job at The Firefly Theatre to keep me going when I got back (I'd been working shifts in the front of house there for three years). They would be thrilled, of course; Marge was at her most seductive the day before I left. "None of the new staff know a thing about the theater, darling, we'll miss you dreadfully," she said fretfully through her pink Sobranie. "Sergio will have to take over your job, but seriously sweetie, he's not a patch on you, no organizational skills at all, and he will keep trying to hire his little friends. Half of them don't even speak English, and I just *can't* have them jabbering in the boxes, Val would kill me. Sweetheart, say you'll come back to your old job when you return from America, mnnn? We've got a mad schedule starting in September; I'd love to know you were taking up the reins again. Val was talking about you just the other day, you know, in the most *adulatory* terms!"

It's nice to be wanted, even by Marge, The Firefly's diminutive, fey, narrow-minded front-of-house director and Val, the stomping, sallow-faced general manager. But I stubbornly resisted their blandishments. I hadn't spent the last year getting a social work degree to go back to shift work, particularly not at The Firefly (lots of responsibility, no job security, and no chance of advancing as long as Marge was in bed with Val. I only got the job in the first place because Alison knew Marge at university). So I told her no, consented to be kissed and cried over, and swore blind to myself (when I'd firmly removed Marge's hand from my left breast) that hell would freeze over before I went back.

So I sent off three applications through cyberspace to who-knows-what bored recipients, crossing my fingers as I did so, although I wasn't entirely sure if that was to help me *get* the jobs or *not* get them. Then, just as I finished, I received a phone call from Una. I wanted to tell her all about Dave but she kept sighing pointedly and asking if I could *possibly* talk more quietly. Aggrieved, I was in the middle of asking her why she'd rung in the first place if she didn't want me to talk when she cut me off mid-sentence to ask if I *really* need my room next month, because her sister was coming to stay and she'd promised her my bed. I asked her sarcastically if she'd like me to live in the States permanently, just so her sister could have my room. She actually brightened for a moment and asked if I was serious.

36

~

Q

M y conversation with Fay on the Friday of our New York visit
went something like this.

Me: Hi lovely to see you again nice to see the offices everything
   going well Schuster's clearly still on the up you'll hardly miss
   me think I need a few more months Samuel not very well how
   are you?

Fay: Huh?

Me: Um. . .

Fay: What did you say?

Me: When?

Fay: Just now?

Me: About what?

Fay (taking a deep breath): Q, what did you say two minutes ago
   when you sat down, please? You spoke so fast I couldn't catch
   a word of it.

Me: Ah. Yes. Well.

Ten minutes later we more or less understood each other, although there was a glint in her eye that suggested she understood
rather more than I necessarily wanted her to understand. We agreed
I'd put together a letter for the partners, explaining my request for

two more months of leave ("It won't be on full pay, you know, Q, but I'll see what I can manage."). "And that's *all* you're asking for, is it? You've been an extremely productive associate. This isn't a preliminary to a resignation, I assume?" My heart was pounding; I gulped and dragged a smile onto my face. Of course not, I said brightly, knowing that if I said it was, the whole game would be over.

Walking out through the building felt strange. After my meeting with Fay I took the flight of steps down to my office, expecting to find everything changed: Fay told me they had to let a couple of summer associates share it last month, but neither of them seemed to have left much imprint of their personalities on the room. In fact, I found things almost as I'd left them the day I went on bed rest, five months earlier. On a pad of fluorescent-green Post-it notes I discovered a doodle I suddenly remembered working on, a series of interlocking curls with what looked like a hamster at the bottom (I think it was actually a self-portrait: me at twenty-six weeks pregnant). My screen-saver—an old photograph of our garden back home in Kent— faded in and out, in and out, eerily reminding an empty room of my childhood. The plants on the windowsill were unexpectedly thriving: Jayne, a new secretary, stopped by and shyly told me she'd been feeding and watering them. I felt oddly touched, as if someone had been looking after me all this time, and I hadn't even known about it. Of course the desk was tidied, the chaos ruthlessly rearranged by some unknown hand, and all the file notes for ongoing cases were sifted, sorted, and refiled. It struck me, as I gently pulled the door closed, that the office looked as if it belonged to me, but a *better* me. An organized, hardworking me with a workable filing system, a neat array of highlighter pens, and an excellent supply of Miracle-Gro.

I exchanged greetings with my colleagues as I walked along the floor and then down in the elevator ("Hey, Q, how ya doing? You look—uh, great!" they enthused, not entirely convincingly. "Did you hear about Ed and Delilah?"). Then, just as I reached the heavy revolving doors—almost safe!—I bumped into Caroline in the hall. Just my luck. She was with a client. He was clad in a formal gray suit, Caroline in spotless, pitilessly tailored black. "What are *you* doing here, Quinn?" she asked sharply.

"I came in to meet with Fay," I explained, smiling politely.

She looked expectant.

"You'll be getting a letter from me asking for extended leave," I added reluctantly. "I need to take a couple more months."

"I see." Her lip curled.

No, you don't, I thought to myself, you don't see anything unless it's directly related to your professional reputation, but I didn't say anything. Instead, I shook hands with the client—he was someone I'd met before and, remembering that one of his children had cerebral palsy, I asked after his health. The man looked slightly surprised, I thought, but he was friendly, and even asked after Samuel. Caroline, who was obviously not listening, was tapping a glassy foot on the great marble floor. I caught sight of her checking her slim silver watch.

"Give me a call the week before you come back, Quinn," she said abruptly, turning toward the elevator, when the client and I had finished speaking. "We must talk."

"Of course, Caroline, I'll be happy to." The elevator doors smartly shut them from sight.

I left the building feeling unsettled. I had a job I should love. I had a job I'd spent half my life trying to get. But I hated it. I hated the office politics, the sly backstabbing, the atmosphere of distrust. I hated the awful superiority of people like Caroline. I hated the exhaustion, the intensity, the unstated expectation that the firm owned your existence. What I want (I thought, as I scooped my son lovingly into my arms, when I finally got home) is to be in charge of my own life.

37

Jeanie

Just my luck, my train was delayed; I arrived at Tom and Q's flat dripping with sweat, hair starting from my head like Medusa serpents, a bare two minutes before Paul swung into the sitting room in a pressed Armani suit, cool and poised as always, with a very expensive bottle of chilled white wine under his arm. He then produced, from a pristine paper bag, an expansive collection of takeout boxes from a place called Jo's Shanghai in Chinatown: "Best soup dumplings in the city!"

At first I tried to use Samuel as an excuse to avoid him, but my nephew seemed to have forgotten me and struggled skittishly in my arms. Q worked extremely hard to persuade me that he'd actually been missing me these past four days. "I think he only really began to get over you yesterday, and then he probably thought he wouldn't see you again, so it was a sort of *coping mechanism* to forget you . . ." she told me anxiously.

Paul, it must be said, was a model of politeness throughout the evening. The food was scrumptious, he kept our glasses topped up with wine, and he even cleared away most of the mess, pushing a laughing, faintly resisting Q back into her seat. I went into the kitchen to help him. "Hold open the trash bag for a second, Jeanie, let me get this in—okay, great. And—" he cast his eyes quickly around the room—"I think that's it. So why did you stay in Connecticut by yourself, then?" he asked curiously, as we strolled back together into the sitting room. "Why didn't you come down to New York with Q and Tom?"

This was the moment I'd been waiting for. "I couldn't leave my work at the Home," I said airily. "You know how it is. The old people expect me now, I wouldn't want to disappoint them . . ." Paul looked—surprised, but then Tom, who was pouring the scotch, jumped in.

"*And* she was spending time with her boyfriend," he explained chirpily. "Nice guy. Name of Dave. Only she dumped him, just when we finally got to thinking he was okay . . ." Q kicked him, and he turned to look at her, eyes wide open with surprise. "Wha—? But didn't you . . ." Q kicked him again. Hard.

I felt myself flush. "Yes, well. Things didn't go—er, very well," I said uncomfortably, feeling exposed before Paul's suddenly penetrating gaze. "We—er—decided it would be better to—um—part," I said foolishly, sounding like something out of a 1940s radio play. I flushed even deeper. Where did that come from?

Paul looked away, brown eyes faintly embarrassed. "I'm sorry None of my business, of course."

But now an awkward silence fell, and for some reason I felt absolutely compelled to fill it. "Mmm. It was time to move on," I suggested, dragging a few more clichés into the mix. "Er, call it a day, you know. Quit while we were ahead. Give it a rest, finish the deal." I realized some woman was gabbling pointlessly on, and since I appeared to have control over her mouth, I shut it.

There was another, even more awkward silence. Then, to my complete astonishment, Paul, who was now sitting on the window bench, started talking instead—and, in a quiet, measured voice, he told us all about his breakup with Tina last week, and he wasn't using the language of clichés, he was actually *telling* us, in detail, what really happened. Tina, he explained, was lovely and talented, and clearly a catch, but somehow, to him, brain-deadeningly dull. He'd kept it going for months, he continued, hoping they'd click; he'd taken her off for romantic breaks in Paris and Prague until she was half off her head with love for him but he'd only proved to himself that he couldn't, in fact, care for her. But by this point her mother was making discreet inquiries into the availability of certain high-class hotels on Saturdays in June and she (he had it on good authority) had actually tried on a Vera Wang.

As he talked and talked about the awful mess he'd found himself in, where a perfectly nice woman was thinking thoughts he himself thought she had a perfect right to think, I couldn't help saying, *I know exactly what you mean*, and *yes, I felt that way too*. Then we moved on to the failings of our former partners, the justification for our need to ditch them; and, gingerly stepping over the barrier, and coming to sit beside him on the bench, I told him about the time Dave broke off, while we were kissing, to scrawl "Portsmouth 2, Spurs 1" on the cover of a paperback on the bedside table. And instead of looking shocked or disgusted at the disclosure, Paul laughed, then told me about the time he saw Tina checking her hair in the mirror at a similarly inti-mate juncture. An hour later we'd talked ourselves to a standstill—at which point we looked up to discover that Tom and Q were passed out cold on the sofa, snoring slightly. And I swear to God, I don't know how it happened, but suddenly Paul's lips were on mine, and he was kissing me.

Dave's kisses are brief and cold, a short match-opener before the real thing begins—hand moves down, underwear off, and the whole thing's done in a few short minutes. With Paul, something else happened entirely, a sort of suspension of consciousness. I know we moved out of the sitting room into the hallway, just out of sight of my sister and Tom, and I have a strong mental picture of my banana-yellow top lying, cast off, on the floor. But when or how those things happened, I can't really say. Time passed in a haze. I remember he told me (fingers wound in my hair) that I was beauti-ful, that he hadn't thought about anyone else, about anything else, since the first moment we met. I remember I told him that he was quite impossible, and I didn't like him at all. But I didn't stop kissing him.

Then suddenly Samuel squawked. We heard Q start off the sofa like a race horse at the sound of a gun.

The woman only sees her child, thank God. Paul and I, laughing foolishly in the darkness of the hallway, righted ourselves hastily, I locating and dragging on the battle-torn top, he fastening his shirt with (I flatter myself) still-shaking fingers while Q flurried about anxiously in Samuel's basket. The two of us then assumed casual, we-were-just-fetching-this-new-bottle-of-scotch poses and sauntered into the room. When Samuel was calm, Q sighed thankfully, glanced at Tom (who was still sleeping), then over at Paul and—just perceptibly—above his head at the clock on the wall behind. He immediately took the point. "I'm so sorry, Q, I must be going now," he said hastily, spotting his polished wallet on the floor, and sliding it into his pocket. "Say good-night to Tom for me, okay?" he added, looking down at my brother-in-law's recumbent form. "And I'll—um—call you," he added to the air in the middle of the room as he walked out of the door.

Q turned to smile at me, wearily. "Sorry we fell asleep on you, love, and you must be tired yourself. I hope you didn't mind keeping Paul entertained for us," she said. I looked at her face closely, trying to see if she was being discreet, but there was nothing knowing in her expression at all.

"No problem, anything I can do to help you both out," I said with an air of great virtuousness, as I padded off to the bathroom through the hall. "Really, anything at all."

38

~

Q

We heard from a secretary in the office of Dr. Sykes (the gastric specialist) on Monday, offering us a cancellation spot for the next afternoon. "Thank God," I said to Jeanie fervently as I put down the phone. "Maybe he can give us some answers, you know?"

My sister, who was radiant on Saturday morning, had turned inconceivably grumpy on Sunday. She groused about everything from the bread in the local bakery—too many cranberries, apparently—to the thinness of our toilet paper. "What is this stuff, tracing paper?" she said scathingly, appearing in the sitting room with one sheet suspended disdainfully between thumb and forefinger. "We got rid of this in Britain in the 1970s!" Tom, who had been getting increasingly irritated with her, said some things at this point that he later regretted. Or at least, I hope he did.

"I don't know how much longer we can keep going. I wish I knew what was wrong with Samuel—if there *is* something wrong, that is," I continued fervently. "I can't tell you how much I hope this Dr. Sykes can help us. Maybe there's some medicine that will help him, even a painkiller, who knows . . ."

Jeanie, dressed in my robe, was preoccupied and bleary-eyed. "Mmm," she offered vaguely, clasping her coffee to her chest. She looked shattered, wrapped up in herself.

"I mean, I love Samuel," I went on, sliding onto a seat beside her, "but sometimes I think my head is going to explode. All that crying is destroying my brain cells. And sometimes—" I dropped my voice anxiously—"sometimes I can't help worrying that he isn't developing *normally*. I have a book about child development, and it tells you what a child of his age should be doing. It talks about tracking, you see, which means—"

"Following an object with his eyes; I know." Jeanie's tone was irritable; she put her fingers tenderly to her forehead. "I didn't sleep too well last night, Q. Things on my mind . . ."

I ignored this, since *I* was up half the night with a screaming child. "Actually, he's not tracking well *at all*, Jeanie, to be honest. I'm quite worried. I've been trying with a red pencil the last few mornings, the way it tells you in a book, skimming it in front of his gaze, and his eyes only follow the object for *twelve*, not *eighteen* inches in an arc. I worry—"

"You got the ruler out, did you?" Jeanie's voice was now frankly acerbic. "Twelve, not eighteen inches? Christ. You'd better sign the child up for special schooling straight away, Q."

I stared at her. "There's no need to be so catty," I said, wondering what on earth had gotten into her. "Is there something wrong?"

She reached over, picked up the carafe, and poured herself another cup of coffee. "No, there isn't. I'm sorry Q, I'm just ve-ry tired," she replied, sighing. "A lot going on. And you know, Alison says children with colic often experience minor developmental delays, so I think you should just forget about those six measly inches. No point worrying yourself over small things like that."

For a second, the world seemed to have stopped turning on its axis. "Alison says—*what*?"

Jeanie choked on her coffee. "Alison says—I mean, that is to say, she once told me—I remember her talking about somebody *else's* child who has colic—"

"Jeanie, have you been talking to Alison about Samuel?"

The expression of guilt on her face was ludicrously obvious. "No. I mean. Not really. A bit, I suppose. Now and again. She guessed—"

"Oh my God, you have! You've been talking to Alison. I don't believe it," I gasped, rigid with fury. "What else have you told her?"

She shrank away from me, her eyes wide and round. "I didn't mean—I just—I wanted her advice about Samuel, you see, and—and—" She swallowed; her face turned red."Christ, Q, you are *such* a prima donna!" She stood up to face me, robe hanging open, hair loose and tousled. "You don't want Alison to know anything! But she just wants to help, you know. She's worried about you, she's on the other side of the world, but you cut her out, you behave as though she's some sort of monster. What, because she has a nice house and she dresses her children in white?"

"Jeanie, I can't even believe you're saying this," I retorted. "You know Alison as well as I do—or at least, I thought you did. She's not just any old sister, she's—Alison. She's been itching to prove I'm failing at motherhood for months. I thought we were on the same side; now it seems you've been going behind my back for—how long?"

"For bloody years!" (We were both panting now.) "If I want advice, I go to Alison actually, did you know that? I don't go to you Q, because you just tell me to 'grow up.' Alison actually listens and tries to help. She gives me practical advice. *You* condescend to me. And you think Alison's superior? Take a fucking look in the mirror, sister dear!

"And you tell everyone—like those rich people we met, Adjile and Lily—that you and I feel the same way about her. 'We think her art is terrible. We don't really like her.' Did you ever think to ask *me* before you announced my opinion to the world? Of course not! As it happens, Q, I think some of her recent stuff has been bloody good, and I'm not the only one who thinks so. She's had some really good write-ups in the press, not that you'd know anything about it. I think if one of the three of us is going to be remembered fifty years from now, it's going to be *her*."

"Well, I'm sorry, I didn't realize she had her very own fan club. With you as the president." The floor seemed to be dropping away under my feet; I was so tired, so utterly bone-shattered, and now *this*!

"Don't belittle me, Q." Jeanie was mutinous. "Don't put me down. I'm not an idiot."

She swooped out of the kitchen in a violent *swoosh* of pink velvet, robe tie trailing behind her. I stared, baffled, at the space where she had been sitting.

39

⁓

Jeanie

Hello." His voice was warm and husky. "Can you meet me at the juice bar across the street?"

I was sitting on the floor in the bathroom, knees hugged to my chest, sobbing in the aftermath of a vast, terrible fight with my sister Q, when the phone began to ring. I waited, expecting her to pick it up, but she didn't; eventually I went and answered it. The apartment was empty.

His voice came pouring like thick honey into my ears. *Can you meet me*? Of course, I murmured, forgetting Q, forgetting the two nerve-straining days of no phone call, in a second, forgetting everything. I threw myself into the shower and into some clothes. (Not too many, of course. Just an olive-green top trimmed with lace and a black skirt made from chiffon that might just blow away in a breeze. Hair up, neckline down; the old adage. He wanted to see me!)

This is too soon, it's too soon after Dave, I shouldn't be doing this— the thought thrummed in my brain as I dodged the cabs that dart through the traffic like so many tropical fish, and flew across the road. I saw him waiting for me on a barstool by the window of the juice bar, and all conscious thoughts evaporated from my mind. He looked up through long lashes, his expression amused, quizzical. One hand was loosely in his trouser pocket, the other casually, delicately, twirling a straw. He stood up as I came in, a funny little show of old manners, then stooped down to kiss me, swiftly, on the lips.

I sat down on the stool next to him, wishing away the space between us, although he arranged himself so that his knees were touching my hip. Hot as sunburn. "So?" His voice was low. I had to bend closer to listen.

"So?" I returned, pulling slightly away again, playfully stupid. He put his head on one side, looking quizzical. "I'll have something— with raspberries, I think," I went on, demurely, ponytail nodding.

He went to order my drink, appearing a few moments later with a tall pink beaker armed with a swizzle stick topped with a plastic raspberry. "There, is that what you wanted?" Standing behind me, he murmured the words in my ear; I could feel his hot breath on my skin. Everything prickled. *I don't know you, I don't know you* . . . For a second the thoughts throbbed inside me, then I looked up into his face.

"What did you tell your sister?" he asked.

"I didn't say—er—anything," I replied, a little consciously. "She's—out." I investigated his broad, handsome face. "What are you doing here? Shouldn't you be at work?"

He grinned at me. "I'm skiving—isn't that what you Brits say? I'm on my way to visit a client uptown, the car found itself on Second

Avenue, and I couldn't bring myself to sail straight past your apartment building. Driver's waiting over there for me, actually."

He nodded out the window. A long black car was parked on the street corner; a man in a black suit with dark glasses was standing beside it, smoking a cigarette while drumming his fingers against the roof. He seemed hot and uncomfortable in the morning sun.

"He looks warm," I said, feeling sorry for him.

"That's New York for you. It's been a terrible summer. Listen, I'm sorry I was out of town this weekend. When can we have dinner?"

"Well" (I sighed heavily), "we're going back up to your house in Connecticut the day after tomorrow, so . . ."

"Tonight or tomorrow, then," he replied, musing. "But tonight is difficult for me, it would have to be late, I've got a midnight deadline for filing papers at the courthouse. I'll have more time tomorrow night . . ." He pulled his organizer out of his pocket, and flicked through some screens with the stylus. I can honestly say it was the first time I'd ever been out with someone who had to use a Black-Berry to schedule me in.

"It's a shame you're a lawyer," I said, watching him. "The hours, I mean. Q complains about them all the time. And Tom too. I don't know how you live like this. So little free time. Were you working all weekend? I mean it's like that film, *The Firm*, isn't it?"

He laughed. "Not really. And yes, I had a series of meetings with some people from IBM."

I blushed and twiddled my fingers. "But you do have to defend all kinds of awful people."

"What do you mean?" He looked surprised.

I blushed even more deeply. "Well—murderers and fraudsters, I mean. You have to take on their cases just because they're rich. Isn't it terribly unfair?"

Paul had drawn back from me slightly, but after a moment his face relaxed in a smile, and he took my hand. "Jeanie, you'll have to come with me into the office sometime," he said. "You might be surprised. It's not just defending 'murderers and fraudsters,' as you put it. Firms don't just do criminal law. And besides, there are plenty of innocent people . . ."

"Well, but that's just it, they aren't all innocent, are they? I mean, how do you feel, defending someone you know is guilty of raping a woman, and he has the money to hire you, and she doesn't? Or some company has dumped tons of toxic waste into a river, and half the residents glow bright green in the dark, but they can't afford you while the company can? Isn't that terrible?" It wasn't clear to me that this was the best line to take with him. But for some reason I was cross, I didn't want him to think I was impressed by his big Lincoln town car, and my mouth kept on going.

Paul stared at me, brows deeply pronounced. "Is this a settled antipathy to lawyers, Jeanie? Or just the opinion of the moment?" he asked coolly.

It was the BlackBerry that finally did it, I think. It made him seem so unaccountably alien.

"No, I mean—well, I'm just asking . . ."

"And that's what I like about you." Leaning even closer, he took my hand. "Listen, Jeanie, some time we can talk properly about this, I can explain more about what I do. It'll have to be over dinner, though; I can't keep my client waiting any longer. So you'll have to keep imagining me as Satan incarnate for the next twenty-four hours, I suppose. What do you think: are you willing to eat with the devil tomorrow night?"

He was utterly beautiful, and he was looking back at me with an expression that was frankly desiring. Vague ideas of lawyers and their wrongs evaporated entirely from my mind. I lifted my face, and for answer—feeling nervous, a tiny bit shocked at my own daring—I touched my lips to his.

A businessman on the stool on the other side of Paul hastily lifted up his newspaper; at a nearby table, two thin girls with lashings of hair giggled and muttered something spiteful. I vaguely noticed their expressions, and for about a second I felt a tiny part of me that was uneasy in the bottom of my stomach quite acutely, like a pea beneath the mattress. And then it dissolved, or maybe I simply didn't notice it anymore. Even in a brightly lit juice bar at ten o'clock on a Monday morning Paul made me think of mojitos and salsa. You just wish *you* had a man like this, I telegraphed to the spiteful girls with a small, smug smile. He had his hand on the small of my back, where the olive-green top met the waistband of my chiffon nonsense, and he was pulling me half off my stool into him. I had the same hazy feeling of the other night, as if I was losing myself in his body.

He pulled away at last, and rested his forehead against the top of my head. "This isn't the place," he whispered into my eyes (I could see his chest thumping through his perfect white shirt, the cotton vibrating gently to its rhythm). "And I really have to go . . ." He reached down and lifted up my chin with delicate, gentle fingers. "We can't forget about Brett outside in the heat now, can we?" he said, laughing. "I'll call you later today." I nodded, or maybe I shook my head, I don't quite know, and he kissed me again, hard, then reached down and picked up a briefcase from under the counter. I saw Brett chuck away his cigarette butt as Paul approached, then smartly open the door. Paul got in, and his tall form was immediately lost behind the car's smoky windows. The long black limousine pulled off into the traffic.

I started drinking my weird raspberry drink without really knowing what I was doing. I think I swirled the swizzle stick around a lot, and I clearly spent a great deal of time pleating a napkin. When I eventually glanced up, it was to discover that the newspaper-reading businessman was looking at me as if he was wondering if I offered the same services to all men in suits. The girls at the nearby table looked as if they wanted to strike up a conversation. The little people with white-and-blue hats behind the counter were glowering at me as if I'd besmirched their work environment. I hastily put down the beaker (secreting the raspberry swizzle stick in my handbag as I did so, as a small memento), then slid off my stool and left.

I walked slowly to Q's flat. She was back now, and was sitting with a newspaper spread out in front of her. "Just popped out to get—um— some hankies," I announced, not very convincingly, to her poker-straight back.

"We have plenty of Kleenex," she replied suspiciously; "right *there*," and she pointed to a large, rainbow-colored box smack in the middle of the table.

"Well, I needed some pocket ones," I explained, feeling as guilty as if—well, as if I was having an affair.

My sister looked dour. "Another secret, Jeanie?" she asked sarcastically, and then she turned round, and went back to her newspaper.

40

Q

It took me three attempts to reach Alison. She was out, she explained, preparing for a meeting at the Arts Council to discuss potential funding for a new exhibition of young women sculptors "seeking to capture the life force." I was so irritated, so pent up, so desperate to vent my frustration on her, I could hardly sit still for the four hours I was forced, by circumstance, to wait. I remembered a time when I was eight, when she told our mother—something or other, I don't even remember now—but it wasn't true, and I was desperate to accuse her. It felt just like that.

"What the hell have you and Jeanie been talking about?" I began furiously, when she eventually picked up my call; there was an astonished pause.

"I'm sorry—?"

"I know you've been talking about me. I know she's been telling you all about Samuel. About his colic."

"Is that so terrible?" Alison's tone was mild as milk toast. "She's very worried about you, darling. And so am I. We talk about you, and I talk with Mother. We wonder how best to help you. Would you rather we didn't?"

"You know, Alison—" I was almost breathless, choking with rage, but struggling to force my thoughts into coherence—"you know I find your intervention *very* difficult to take."

"Yes, I do know that, darling." There was a long pause; through the faint sound of her quickened breathing I could hear that damn clock of hers in the background. It was an heirloom, a wedding present from Sir Evelyn Farquhar, granddaddy and patriarch of the Farquhar family, and its resonant tick, marching on inexorably through the centuries, reminded me of everything I found so frustrating about my sister and her new life.

"You don't understand the first thing about me, Alison, but you use everything you *do* know to get one over on me," I continued wrathfully. "You would just love to know that I'm a disastrous mother, wouldn't you? Q may have a career, you can say to all your friends, but she's simply terrible at bringing up a baby. It doesn't come naturally to her, somehow—"

"Oh, *don't* be ridiculous—"

"And the idea that you've conscripted Jeanie in this endeavor makes me just furious."

"You've made your feelings about *that* perfectly clear. Q is angry with Alison. Here we are again. I thought we were starting to understand each other a bit better during your pregnancy, when I came out to visit you. But obviously not." *Tick, tick, tick*; Granddaddy Farquhar marched on.

"No. And we won't be making any progress as long as you try to undermine me." I matched her tone, feeling triumphant.

There was a long silence; Alison was clearly debating her next move. When it came, though, it wasn't what I expected at all.

"Geoffrey had colic," she blurted out, and at that moment the clock struck loudly in the background, a deep, sonorous bass that for a second dominated everything. *Bong, bong, bong* . . . the tones were rich and golden, the clock's voice filling her room, my ear, with confident noise. It was eight o'clock in London. Even as I took in the meaning of her words I found myself wondering where her husband was.

"He had colic? Really?" It is a sign of how poor our relationship had become that I didn't quite believe her.

"Really."

"I—*when*?"

"From about five weeks to four months, or thereabouts," she went on. "I'm not making this up, Q, so you needn't sound so suspicious! It was the worst experience of my life. By far. I thought I was going to go mad. I'm not sure why I didn't. Maybe—maybe in a sense I did, looking back. One night I was so desperate to sleep I—I almost threw him out the window. It was about five o'clock in the morning, he'd been screaming for the best part of forty-eight hours, I hadn't slept for two months, and I was right on the edge. *Right* on the edge. It was only the feel of the night air on my skin, when I actually opened the window, that stopped me."

I took this in. "You never said anything," I said at last.

"No." *Tick, tick, tick*. She laughed mirthlessly. "Like you, I suppose."

I tried to think what to say. "Alison, I—"

"I mean, how could I even *think* about hurting my son?" she cut in; to my utter astonishment, tears flooded her voice. "Every time I look at him, even now Q, I think about what I almost did. I remember how detached I'd become, how I—almost hated him. I suppose at least" (she half-laughed, half-gasped) "I know the worst part of myself now. The bottom; the blackest part. I couldn't explain it all to Gregory, you see, he's not—" she stopped herself—"I mean, he's a wonderful father in lots of ways, but he couldn't bear it when the baby cried. He said he had too much to do at work, he just couldn't bear it. He wanted me to make it all go away, make the crying stop. But I couldn't, I couldn't!

"Sometimes he'd send his mother over, but *she's* one of those people who thinks you should just give babies to a nursemaid until it's time to pack them off to boarding school. She's from a very different generation, or maybe it's the class thing, I don't know. Anyway, every time she came to the house she positively *reeked* disapproval. She told me I was smothering him, that boys need to learn to stand alone; one day, she even said *that* was why he was crying. I didn't believe her, but I—I couldn't fail, do you see, Q? I couldn't fail. I had to prove my way, the loving way, would work. And then when Geoffrey kept crying, on and on and on, no matter what I did, I got so angry . . .

"So you see, Q—" with a strange, hollow bitterness—"you don't need to worry that I'm judging you. I wouldn't have a leg to stand on, would I? I—I meant it when I said I wanted to—help."

"Alison—" the words came slowly, dragged out unwillingly—"I don't think you're the first mother to be tempted in—in that way."

She laughed mirthlessly. "No, maybe not. But I almost did it, Q. I actually got as far as the window."

I thought back suddenly to a night, a few weeks ago, when Samuel was screaming and screaming in my ear, when the noise was like a blade stabbing and slashing through my brain, when every nerve inside me was flayed and raw and red—when the only thing I wanted was to be asleep, unconscious, beyond sensation. And in that moment I had a flash of a thought, clear as a church bell in fog: if I killed him, I could sleep. Horrified immediately, I buried the appalling thought as deep as I could. I put it in a box, and I shut the lid, and I locked it tight, and then I put it inside another, bigger, stronger box, and I dug and dug through the deepest layers of my consciousness, and when I got to the very bottom of everything, I put it there, and I covered it up again, and I hoped it would never emerge. I didn't actually take my son to the window, but—

"Alison, I've had Tom by my side, particularly these last few difficult weeks," I said, almost apologetically. "Whereas you, and Gregory—"

"He's never been able to do 'the baby thing,' as he calls it," she remarked. "He would actually leave the room when the crying began, or go upstairs to the spare bedroom if it started during the night. And the only thing that calmed the baby was nursing, so there was nothing he could *do* anyway. There wasn't any point in him suffering, you see, since he couldn't really help anyway. I was—everything to Geoffrey. Well, *you* know."

"The law doesn't police thought," I said. "You didn't *do* anything, Alison."

"Oh, darling!" Her voice was bright and hard, through tears. "Would that make *you* feel any better?"

Tom came home ten minutes later to find me lying on the floor, the phone still gripped in my hand, talking earnestly. Samuel was, for a blessed moment, clasped quietly to my breast. "Who?" he mouthed at me, curiously, and the expression on his face when I whispered back, "Alison," was a sight to behold.

41

Jeanie

I want to take you to my favorite place tomorrow," he explained on the phone on Monday night. "It's in the Village. I'll pick you up outside the apartment building at seven. We'll have cocktails first, then we'll go for dinner."

And then, I thought to myself. And then . . .

No sleep for me that night, I was too busy staring at the ceiling thinking about what Paul looked like and felt like and smelled like, trying to remember if he had a mole under his neck or if it was just behind his ear, if his eyes were brown-gold or brown-black, if he used aftershave, and for the life of me I couldn't quite conjure up the sound of his voice in my mind's ear. I was looking forward to getting the answers to those questions properly cleared up on our date. And I had a few more lines of inquiry to pursue.

I spent Tuesday morning choosing/washing/ironing a delectable outfit. I told Q I was seeing an old friend from school—I happened to have a friend who'd moved out to Brooklyn—although quite why this necessitated borrowing her Versace heels was somewhat unclear. She was not particularly sharp at the time, though. "Oh God, if someone can get some use out of these things, I'm pleased," she said, inspecting the lovely black spiky things as if they were purchased in another lifetime.

"Alison and I have—reached an understanding," she told me

then quietly. "There are some things we find we've shared, I can't quite explain, but—I don't want you to worry that you've made things *worse*." I wasn't quite sure what to make of this (what on earth had Alison told her?), but at least I seemed to be out of trouble. I apologized for being so horrible, feeling very contrite, then Q asked me seriously how my comparative study of Cumbria and Connecticut was coming along. This was tricky, because I hadn't given it a second thought since Cumbria rejected my job application. So I suggested I was "narrowing my focus" and planning a study of Connecticut's geriatric care instead. She insisted on asking me for details, which was quite wearing, although I think I got away with it by diverting her with stories about the people at Quiet Lanes.

I was not ready to open up to Q about Paul just yet. I wanted him to be my secret. As soon as I told her "I'm seeing Paul," I knew what would happen: "You're not at all like his last girlfriend," or "you *are* a bit like his last girlfriend," or "Tom, do you remember that time with Paul when we . . . ?" or "Tom, when we had Paul over for dinner three years ago, didn't he . . . ." I knew she'd want to tell me about him. But for the time being, I wanted to find out about him all by myself.

Dress: gold. Hemline: fluttery. Nails: metallic. Lips: red. Undies: tiny (almost invisible, in fact. I debated the "Access All Areas" pair for comedy value, then decided uproarious laughter has not actually what I wanted to produce if we reached the underwear stage).

Q's in-laws were coming for lunch, and in the afternoon they were taking Samuel to the doctor's. Which would keep them delightfully out of the way. I decided to go shopping. A new pair of stockings, perhaps—?

42

~

Q

Lucille was the first in through the door at a little after noon. "Hello and where's my darling grandson?" she called, charging in like a predator in search of its prey, all feline grace, thrusting elbows, and pointed archness. She plucked Samuel out of my arms and cuddled him to her bony bosom with what I imagine she thought was grandmotherly fondness; he, of course, immediately began to yell.

"There, there, oh, oh, little one, what's da matter den, cutie-pie?" she crooned to him through pursed pearly-pink lips. Samuel, no doubt appalled by the overpowering scent of Chanel, screamed, did a double back-flip, and nearly fell out of her arms.

"Now then, for God's sake, Lucille, be careful," Peter chided her, and I saw her thin painted cheeks flush faintly. "You were never any good with them when they were that size." He had settled himself down on the sofa, legs crossed, hands locked behind his head. Peter was an international authority on minimally invasive coronary artery bypasses. His knowledge of the emotional workings of the heart was quite a bit less developed than Samuel's.

Oh no. It came upon me suddenly, almost without warning. I felt sorry for her.

"It's not your fault, Lucille," I said kindly, "he's a bit—um—fractious these days. Even Jeanie's finding him tricky at the moment," I assured her, and I saw, a second too late, anger flash across her face. *Even* Jeanie. She drew herself up tall. "Yes, well, if *I*, his *grandmother*, had had the opportunity to spend as much time with him as your *sister* has, I'm sure he'd be perfectly used to me by now," she returned frostily, and subsided, like the Boston debutante she once was, into our brown leather armchair.

"Anyone for some food?" Tom said helpfully into the silence that followed, and he vanished off into the kitchen and reappeared with a dish of vegetables, a plate of cheese, and some pâté on toast. Lucille attempted a carrot while Peter wolfed the minced pork with carnal delight.

"So you're going to do some consulting?" he began, eyes watchful as Tom launched into a description of the contacts he was making and the clients he was hoping to take on. Tom was halfway through when Peter cut in impatiently. "Seriously, you need to think about the long term, Tom. I mean it's one thing to fuck around for a few months, but what about your retirement funds? And what, are you on your *wife's* health insurance now? I mean, c'mon . . ."

Tom was determinedly keeping his face expressionless. "Thanks for the advice. We've got our insurance needs all straightened out, actually. But that's enough about me. Let's talk about you," he went on generously, although I heard a dangerous tightness in his voice.

Peter allowed himself the faintest, smuggest smile, and looked over at Lucille, who was smiling slightly too as she smoothed her navy skirt of its lone hair's-breadth wrinkle. "Yeah, well, funny you should ask. Things are going very well, as it happens. My article on stented angioplasties was, as you may have heard, nominated for . . ." I switched off; I'd heard some version of this speech about seventy-five times, and it always ended with the words "Nobel Prize" and "possibly next year" hovering in the background. I pretended Samuel's diaper needed changing in the other room, and excused myself.

I assumed that Peter's litany of marvelous success would still be ongoing when I returned. Somehow, though, in my absence, the conversation had moved from Peter's account of his own brilliance back to Tom's failings. I stood outside the sitting room door, electrified by the sound of raised voices, Samuel tight in my arms. We looked nervously at each other.

"I didn't *get my wife pregnant*, Dad, what the hell kind of language is that? It was a joint decision, we're a team, for God's sake!" Tom was shouting. "And shut the fuck up about the firm, what, you think I'd still be working at Crimpson if it wasn't for Samuel? Even if that's true—which it isn't—it's a trade I'd make again in a heartbeat. I don't care about the money—not as long as we're covering the bills. And as for our decision to start a family, that was ours, nothing to do with you. So butt the hell out of our lives . . ."

He paused for air. I wanted to run into the room and hug him, but something stopped me.

"How can I 'butt out of your life,' as you so charmingly put it, when you're *fucking it up*?" yelled Peter, and then came the loud bang of his hand meeting a table. "*When* are you going to move back to New York properly? A holiday's one thing. But this—!"

"Not yet," Tom replied, his tones now pointed and icy. "We're not coming back yet. In fact, I'm not sure if we'll ever move back here. Q has got us involved in this case—"

"What are you talking about? 'Involved?' What do you mean? What case?"

"It's—just something local to the area."

"The Long Island Pipeline case?" Peter sounded hopeful for a moment. "There's a lot of money at stake in that. Look, I'm not saying it's *impossible* to find good work in Connecticut—"

"That's not what I'm talking about, Dad. It's much more small-scale: a young woman's custody battle, actually."

"Do you mean that young Hollywood actress—what's her name—

the one living in Fairfield County?" It was Lucille's turn to sound hopeful. "Isn't she fighting with some young drug addict over her twins—"

"No, Mom," Tom sounded torn between frustration and laughter, "really, it's nothing like that. We've agreed to help a small-town lawyer with a very simple domestic case, out of good will. Although—" I could visualize his expression—"we are using the opportunity to sort of *feel out* what small-town law might be like. As a lifestyle for us, I mean."

"Feel it out? Why would you need to *feel it out*?" Peter howled. "You don't need to feel it with a ten-foot pole, young man! You've got a whole damn city here of opportunities to feel out first, and if that isn't enough for you, there's Washington, D.C., just a few hours away. And I can help you there, Tom," he went on (the cajoling was starting now), "a couple of boys from the club have offered to introduce you to some real important people. There's a whole new career out there for you, Tom; you just have to grasp it."

"And you would make such a wonderful politician, Tom; you're so polished, so articulate. And just think: you could serve the interests of the people. At times like these—well! It's truly a noble calling. Surely a little self-sacrifice is called for . . ." Lucille's voice, as she picked up the argument, was like chocolate: smooth, sweet, and nearly irresistible.

There was a pause. Samuel, tucked under my chin, muttered something. "What's your daddy going to say now?" I whispered to him, holding him a little bit away as I spoke. His head wobbled backward as he tried to look into my eyes.

"That's kind of you, Mom," Tom replied, at last, quietly. "I appreciate it. Really, I do. And you're quite right, times have changed; these days we need to think about helping people, not just servicing our own needs. But I can't see myself doing that by becoming a politician. Maybe one day in the future—when my kids have grown up—who knows? But I want to *watch* them grow up first, and it's hard to do that in politics. As a small-town lawyer, on the other hand, I can help people who are struggling in the face of the recession *and* spend time with my family. For a while I wasn't sure about it—this firm we've discovered in Cheasford—but now I'm really starting to see the advantages. In fact, the more I think about it, the more I think this is a real opportunity for us. The firm has a large client base, you see, and an excellent reputation."

I couldn't see him, so I don't know if he crossed his fingers. Just in case, I did it for him.

"It would be a very different life for us, obviously. In a good way. We would be able to buy a reasonably sized house, send Samuel to public school—"

"Public school!"

"—and, most appealing of all," Tom continued remorselessly, "Q and I could arrange our working life around each other. We could develop a more—a more *organic* professional life, instead of the old grind of nine-to-five—or, more realistically, seven-to-one-the-next-morning."

"In other words, you're going to ruin yourself."

Tom laughed; Samuel, hearing him, turned his head curiously toward the sound of his voice. "Well, if I am, you'll have to go ahead and let me do it, Dad," Tom said simply, and suddenly the door opened, and my husband ushered me inside. "Don't wait out there any longer, Q," he said, grinning, taking Samuel tenderly from my arms. "No need for you to lurk in the dark."

I walked cautiously back in to see Peter and Lucille grabbing jackets—or, rather, Lucille nervously grabbing the jackets while Peter stood, cold and furious, in the middle of the room. "We are leaving," he announced.

Tom nodded cheerfully. "Won't stay for lunch, then? Oh dear."

Peter walked past without even glancing at me or at Samuel. "Call me when you have come to your senses," he intoned as he swept from the room.

43

~

Jeanie

I took the subway down to 42nd Street while Q, Tom, and Samuel entertained the in-laws then went to visit their baby-specialist person ("Will you be all right by yourself? Will you find something to do all that time?" "Oh, I think I can manage.").

Once I got out of the station, I walked, feeling the sun on my face and a deep happiness inside. This is me, Jeanie Boothroyd, in New York; this is me, Jeanie Boothroyd, about to be wined and dined by a ridiculously eligible American who for some reason is obsessed with me. This is me, Jeanie Boothroyd, in a rather nice pair of shoes, with a brand-new bag from a shop on Fifth Avenue. This is me, Jeanie Boothroyd, living a dream. I smiled as I walked, and swung my arms, and felt the breeze lifting my hair. I wondered what Una would think of me now. How could I ever have lived with her?

Crowds of people swirled around me. Ragged, tired-looking homeless people loped side by side with uptight businessmen in linen suits. Women in tailored jackets and pencil skirts darted in and out of the throng in sensible trainers. Ladies with tiny shaved dogs inched along in heels, tourists struggled with subway maps and hot pretzels. This is New York; I'm a part of this, I thought proudly. I'm so glad I came.

So many appealing-looking restaurants, so many interesting boutiques; I stared in fascination at the sheer, extraordinary variety of New York. I passed flower shops, paper shops, pipe shops, shoe shops, wine shops, electronics shops, and toy shops; shops selling postcards, shops selling suitcases, shops selling organic coffee in hundreds of tight gold packets lined up against the wall. Chocolatiers nestled beside corner shops, artisanal bakers beside doughnut vendors. I love this, I love this, I love this, I whispered to myself, feeling the blood sort of *zing* in my veins.

I must (I thought to myself suddenly, with a start of contrition) pick up something nice for Q, a treat of some sort, she's been so weary of late. So I stopped off at a little hushed patisserie and bought three cakes, one lime, one lemon, one with milk chocolate layers. They cost a shocking amount, but as the woman wrapped them up in a gold box, topped with stiff ribbon, I felt pleased at the thought of Q's face. She loved sweet things. I pushed the door open and maneuvered myself back into the street, armed with my elegant box of bullion.

Only then, suddenly, I stopped. On the other side of the road, ahead, just visible through the press of people walking toward me, was Paul. I blinked, half-convinced for a second I must be hallucinating; perhaps I was thinking so intensely of his face I'd conjured it up in midair . . . But no; it was him. And with him was Lily.

Lily of the gold eyes—I thought, for a second, I could actually see the light reflecting off their extraordinary depths—but I can't have done, because she was looking up at him; looking in his face with an expression of passionate love. She was smiling, touching his face so tenderly that I caught my breath; he was smiling down at her too, as if she was all the world to him, and even through the noise of the traffic, the footsteps of a thousand people, I heard him laugh at something she said. I ducked into the entryway of a pharmacy, feeling suddenly sick, headachy in the bright white light of the sunshine, and watched. It *couldn't* be. . .

As they drew level with me, on the other side of the road, I saw Paul reach out his hand, and snake it around her waist, then gently—

oh so gently—it slid down, down, until it was cupped firmly around her bottom. He tugged her toward him. For a second, they both stopped, still against the stream of people, suspended, body touching body. The traffic screeched to a halt for a red light; I could see the two of them quite clearly in the space between a bus and a car. Lily drew playfully away from his grasp and then (I saw it all) came back toward him, and leaned into his chest; she slipped her hand inside his jacket, and pulled him into her body. He didn't resist; instead he leaned down and said something to her, serious for a second, and she nodded.

After what seemed like an eternity, she removed her hand from inside his jacket—in spite of myself, I could imagine her fingers, hot on his skin—and they moved on, still intimately close. At that moment the light must have turned, because the traffic started up again. Seconds later, they were lost to my sight.

I stayed still for about five minutes in the pharmacy entryway, my hand pressed to my throat, barely able to see through the sunshine that seemed suddenly oppressive. I literally thought I was going to be sick, and it was only when a disapproving-looking security guard came toward me that I fled, stumbling and knocking over a basket of beach balls. Fraught, I stared down at the green and pink and orange balls rolling in every direction, tumbling toward startled pedestrians, even rolling out into the street—cars honked, there were shouts of anger—and I ran off, in the opposite direction from Paul and Lily, away from the pharmacy, away from the guard, feeling the tears on my cheeks.

Paul and Lily, Paul and Lily. But she was married to *Adjile*, to kindly Adjile, and Paul was planning to meet me that evening—we were seeing each other now, how could he? How *could* he?

Suddenly, I felt like the stupidest person alive. I'd been so proud of myself all that time: I'd imagined I was in a relationship with Paul Dupont. Paul Dupont! How idiotic: we'd shared a few kisses, no more. He knew I was in the city for just another day, then a month or two more in the States, and after that I'd be gone. Of course, I was just a bit of fun for him. What was I thinking?

I cast my mind back to all those things he'd said—about how I was the most beautiful woman he'd ever met, about how he couldn't think of anyone else—and I realized (reality came sharply into focus) that I'd made one of the oldest mistakes: I'd thought my holiday romance was *real*. I was no better than some middle-aged woman kicking her heels up in Spain, a backpacked teenager falling in love with a long-haired stranger in Budapest, I realized disgustedly. What was I thinking?

Lily was his lover—it was suddenly startlingly clear. Had he been with her all along? I felt dazed. Perhaps the time we saw each other in Connecticut—I rifled feverishly through my memory, trying to recall a moment of particular intimacy—they'd begun an affair. Perhaps *she* was the real reason he split up with Tina. Or perhaps Tina was only ever a cover for his feelings for Lily; perhaps they'd been together for years. Perhaps he had flirtations on the side—perhaps they were all just a cover! I wondered numbly if he told Lily about them, his dates and dinners and kisses with women like me?

In fact, maybe *that* was what he and Lily were talking about just now, I thought suddenly, starting to walk again, and it was as if the volume had been switched on in the little tableau I'd just watched. "I'm having dinner with Jeanie tonight," Paul said to Lily, putting his arm around her; and she pulled away from him, briefly upset. "With Jeanie? Q's sister? What, are you *serious*?" And then she thought for a moment, and came back toward him. "I don't mind you having dinner with her, but you won't take it any further, will you?" she asked. "Of course not. It's all about us, Lily," Paul replied. It seemed terribly plausible.

I'd been walking for half an hour at least when I looked up and realized I was utterly lost; I'd been stumbling and crying without paying the slightest attention to where I was going. The nearest sign said "27th Street." There was a coffee shop on the other side of the street, so after a moment's hesitation I crossed over, and ordered myself a bucket of latte.

It was only as I got up to leave that I remembered the patisserie box, dropped and lost somewhere in the hot busy streets of New York.

44

~

Q

Sussex, Connecticut

Such joy to be in Paul's lovely house again, Tom, Jeanie, Samuel, and I. We spent our first few days back on the beach, the evenings on the deck, enjoying the view of the sun fading into pastels over the tops of the trees with freshly caught fish for dinner, accompanied by fiery wild arugula from the garden and glasses of chilled white wine.

Only Jeanie seemed sad and low, even though I told her she was forgiven for talking to Alison. "I know," she replied gruffly. "I mean, it's not that I—well, all right." I watched her carelessly splash out another large glass of wine.

Dr. Ezekial Sykes's assessment of Samuel, the day before we left New York, was unenlightening. "Not an obvious case of reflux," he remarked thoughtfully, "it doesn't sound as if his crying is linked closely to feeds." He then went through a long checklist of possible gastrointestinal causes of severe infant crying, none of which, he remarked judiciously, appeared to apply to Samuel. In the end, he simply lifted his shoulders. "I don't know why he is crying so hard. I'm sorry. I don't think it's serious. I'm sure he will grow out of it." The door closed softly behind him.

I called Alison as soon as we got home to tell her all about it; she was sympathetic and unsurprised. "Of course there was nothing, and of course he'll grow out of it," she said stoutly. "I'm glad you've had him properly checked out, but I think you'll just have to wait. And learn that you can be a good mother and still leave him sometimes, darling, so you can get rest and a change of scenery. The mistake I made was to think no one else could look after my baby.

"Is Jeanie being helpful?" she went on, and I explained that she seemed strangely low-spirited. "Do you think it's about Dave?" she inquired, and I gasped, because I hadn't even thought of this.

"You don't think she's regretting breaking up with him, do you?" I asked, and she clicked her tongue.

"I wouldn't have thought so, but this is Jeanie we're talking about. She's always had a penchant for—" she stopped herself awkwardly— "losers," I finished ruefully.

The first morning after our arrival in Connecticut, we called Kent. "If you'll take me on as an associate—on a temporary basis—I'm in," Tom explained. "Q's still technically a Schuster employee, so she'll have to be involved on an informal basis. And I'm not committing long-term yet, okay? This is just a tryout, so to speak, for us and for you."

If we were expecting a joyous response, we were to be disappointed. There was a brief silence. Then: "Come to court with me tomorrow," Kent growled. "I'll introduce you to Judge Ackerman and the other lawyers. You've got to get it over some time," he added gloomily, with the air of one guiding a couple of sheep through a huge ravine. "Might as well be now."

And so, on Friday morning, I left Samuel with Jeanie after

breakfast, then Tom and I set off for Middleford, a town a little over fifteen miles north of Sussex, on the banks of the Connecticut River. It had the faintly seedy air characteristic of all half-abandoned New England ports. A large highway separated the downtown area from the river, and only a few businesses fronted directly onto the broad water, which therefore seemed strangely incidental to the business of the place. There was one small park with a few wooden benches tucked around a bridge, but it was partly flooded and liberally strewn with trash, occupied only by occasional flurries of muddy pigeons. The main street cut a long, wide swath through undistinguished Victorian buildings, which were now occupied by a motley collection of cheap restaurants and regional clothing stores. Pansies burned paper-thin by the summer sun fluttered along the sidewalk in cracked stone urns.

The court building, which sat on a quiet side street, was red-brick, with six white Doric columns and a grandly sweeping stair-case leading out of the spacious round front hall. We met Kent on the other side of security at a few minutes before nine o'clock. Pausing to whisper something to Brenda, one of the security guards, that brought a blush to her cheeks, he led us to the elevator and into the third-floor courtroom.

There was a cheery hum of conversation in the paneled room when we entered, a hum that was perceptibly checked by our entrance. Four lawyers, clustered together in the central aisle, looked over at us and frankly stared.

Kent raised his hand in mock salute. "Mick—Sue—Freda—oh, and Charlie, didn't see you hiding there—how're y'all doing?"

"Morning, Kent," said one of the women, her eyes keen and appraising. She looked about forty-five, and her expression was redoubtable, Margaret-Thatcher-like in its formal intensity. Her blond hair was short and curled close to her head; her suit was a serviceable navy, without much style to it. She wore a simple gold necklace and tired-looking, low-heeled shoes over ugly brown pantyhose. "Heard you're trying out a couple of city lawyers for your practice, is that these two over here?" She looked us over, her right eyebrow twitching upward.

Kent grinned back at her, and shooed us toward the front of the court. "Sure are, Sue," he said, with a chuckle. "Fancy Wall Street lawyers, no less. Want to try out life in the backwoods, I guess. Mick, heard your son made the honor roll at school the other month, he's a kid to be proud of, eh? Mick's kid is a smart one, you ought to meet him," he explained. I had the bright idea of asking which college Mick's son was hoping to attend.

The ice was broken—or, at least, the surface of the ice was chipped, and soon we were chatting as best we could with the band of lawyers about family matters and then—in lower tones—local politics (" 'Course he's corrupt, but at least you know where you are with him," Freda told us, of one rising politician, with a broad wink) until the clerk announced, in deep bass tones: "All rise for the Honorable Alan Ackerman!"

The lawyers flew back to their seats and stood respectfully while a sprightly man in his sixties strode along the bench. Judge Ackerman had bright eyes and a paternal-looking fuzzy gray beard, although, Kent whispered to us, beneath the rustling cover of fifteen people settling back into their seats, "He's a pretty tough one, much harder than Judge Field. *He* looks like an Old Testament prophet, but he'll give *any* defendant a break if you can only get 'em to cry."

The business of the court proceeded briskly, Judge Ackerman listening to the array of driving offenses, tenant-landlord disputes, and divorce cases with an appearance of undivided attention. Which was impressive, because there was something almost inescapably soporific about the proceedings. Both Tom and I struggled to swallow yawns that threatened to split wide our faces. The expanse of carpet covering the floor muffled the sounds of human activity (chairs moving, people walking) like a thick, deep blanket of snow. The loud hum of the air-conditioning focused our thoughts to a single monotone that became, as the minutes passed into an hour, and then into a second hour, and then a third, a trancelike state.

Finally, though, it was Kent's turn at the lectern—case #1124—to ask the judge to consider community service instead of incarceration for his client.

Jay Axelrod, a hopeless-looking young white man in his early twenties, had been found with a glassine envelope of heroin in his jeans pocket when he was pulled over for a driving offense six months previously. Once the prosecutor, a fresh-faced, bespectacled young man, had finished outlining the case, Kent detailed Axelrod's life with considerable emotion and pathos, lingering over physical abuse from a biological uncle and stints in three separate foster homes. Judge Ackerman listened to Kent's plausible story of neglect and mistreatment with narrowed eyes. In the midst of a particularly harrowing account of how, as a child, the client had been torn from the care of the foster mother he loved in the middle of the night, when the woman was found to be a drug user herself, the judge cut in abruptly. "Yes, yes, Counselor; very tragic I'm sure. And he never saw her again, and his life was blighted. But let's be practical here, please. Perhaps you'll be so good as to tell me, Mr. Tyler, what evidence you have that this young man will *benefit* from the Community Service Labor Program? What reason do I have to think that your client is a candidate for a rehabilitative approach? You have known me many years, Counselor; I have long been concerned about the need for a punitive response on the part of the state judiciary in such matters. So tread carefully, Mr. Tyler, tread carefully . . ."

Kent bowed his white head deferentially, locking his hands together in an almost prayer-like gesture. "We have indeed known each other many years, Judge," he said somberly, "and you know that I only take on clients I have *confidence* in." He paused, allowing his words to settle into the faint buzz of the courtroom, which, in response, fell into almost complete silence. Kent held the stillness, then flashed a cheerful grin around the courtroom. "Of course, we can *all* make mistakes, Your Honor; I am guilty of plenty, you know!" His colleagues—even the prosecutor—laughed appreciatively; the judge concealed a small smile. "But it is a man's ability to stand at a crossroads and say, *now* is the time to change, *now* is the time to forge a new path, that marks him apart from the entrenched villain," Kent went on, bringing in all the theatrical flourish at his disposal, including a few bangs with his hand on the lectern for additional emphasis. It was a sterling performance.

"Mr. Axelrod here has been dealt a terrible hand by fate, but he *does* want to make something of his life. He has a lovely young girl-friend, a child on the way, and a new job as a painter's apprentice, which he found in spite of the economic downturn," Kent contin-ued, adroitly turning Mr. Axelrod's fractured life into a narrative of partial redemption. "Today, Judge, he stands in this courtroom at the crossroads of his life. Today he looks at the different roads open-ing up before him. He has said to me, Judge, that both are rocky; yet one has the promise of fine scenery unfolding in the distance! Your Honor, I believe that we, that the state, must allow him to get off on the right path today, that we must help him stay clear of the wrong one. And that, Your Honor, is why I ask for a rehabilitative approach in place of incarceration." His words rang in the air. Even Mr. Axel-rod was sitting up a bit higher at the end of Kent's stirring speech, his mouth half-open.

Judge Ackerman, who seemed entirely used to Kent's style, looked as if he was resisting its theatrical sway—"Mr. Tyler, I shall nominate you for a Golden Globe one of these days"—but he ruled in his client's favor. Mr. Axelrod punched the air delightedly and kissed his heavily pregnant girlfriend loudly on the lips; Kent sat down with a self-satisfied smile. The prosecutor yawned, and turned to his next case.

"If *you'd* come in and defended Axelrod, you'd have been home-towned," Kent told us afterward, tightening his ponytail over a cup of greasy coffee in the court's small, ill-stocked dining room, "meaning you'd have lost. No question about it. Ackerman's no friend to the 'drug court' program, not his politics at all. But he'll work with us, you see," he explained, " 'us' being the local lawyers, that is. He knows us and he trusts us. If you think your client is truly beyond help, you make a bland case and the judge picks up the cues. He knows you think there's no point in trying to rehabilitate, the client's a hopeless case. But if you crank out something really over-blown, he knows you mean it, and nine times out of ten he'll rule your way. But if a lawyer comes from out of town, the judge doesn't know if he or she understands the score, see? He doesn't trust the lawyer to flag the truth for him, make the whole case clear. So he'll almost certainly rule against them. It's just the way things work," he added, seeing the expression on our faces. "In a rural criminal court, anyway. You'll have to get in good with Ackerman if you're go-ing to make a success of the practice."

The door opened and Judge Ackerman himself appeared in the dining room; Kent, grinning, hailed him over, then introduced us.

The judge had his hands thrust in his pockets. "My, my, my, if I'd had a dollar for every city lawyer who fancied a new life overlooking the water," he remarked, rocking back on his heels with a rolling laugh. "Beautiful place, slow pace of life, that's what you think, eh? Ha ha! Still, maybe you two'll be different . . . Ha ha ha . . . Kent tells me you have potential, although Kent—well, you haven't been firing on all cylinders recently, have you, ha ha ha! Still, if you two are here next month, I'm hosting a small dinner for the local lawyers, I'll tell Betty my secretary to send you an invitation. *If* you're still here, that is . . ."

He went off, crowing to himself, to bury his head in a large piece of apple pie on the other side of the room. Kent was visibly irritated. "Acts damn high and mighty sometimes, but we were the ones who got him elected," he muttered in a furious undertone. "We decided who it should be, we told him to run; that's the way it's always worked around here. Us lawyers got together, we sorted the whole thing out for him. What, he thinks he can tell me how to run *my* practice now?" He glowered blackly at the unconscious judge across the room. "I may have to remind him about that before too long . . ."

The door opened a second time, and the lawyer named Mick strolled in to make himself a cup of coffee from the machine. He slopped in the milk, hesitated for a fraction of a second, then came over and slid out the fourth chair at our table. He took a sip of his coffee, watching us reflectively over the rim. "Bumped into Mc-Colley the other day," he said at last, casually. "Al McColley, from Sussex. Representing Ryan Cormier. You're representing the wife, right? Emmie—used to be Vaughan, before she was married?"

The three of us immediately organized our features into the appropriate expression of pleasant disinterest. "Yeah, nice girl," Kent said, uncommunicatively. He paused a moment. "*Very* nice girl. And a damn good mother," he added.

Mick raised his eyebrows over his cup of coffee, then charitably took the bait. "You think so, huh? That's not what McColley says, but you'd expect that, I guess. He's an honest man, though; not the kind to make stuff up. He says he's got big-time, tight-as-can-be evidence Emmie Cormier is a real neglectful mother. I kinda took it seriously, coming from him. Then I saw Ryan a few days later at The Fisherman, that new bar across from The Lobster Pot, crowing all about it to his buddies, saying if his—ah—glamour photos of her don't win the case, he's got other evidence that will."

Kent's face was smooth as the sand on the ocean floor. " 'Course he is, he's claiming all sorts of dumb stuff, that Ryan," he said neutrally. "McColley's just spouting what Ryan says. I wonder which one of his half-assed claims he was talking about this time, though . . ." He kept the question mark out of his voice, but left the sentence hanging.

Mick clearly knew he was being played; for a moment or two he watched a heavyset cleaner mopping the table beside us with slow, deliberate swipes. Then he turned back. "Kent, I've never known you take a case you didn't believe in," he said seriously. "And I'd always thought well of young Emmie Vaughan. McColley wasn't specific of course, but I think it had something to do with the first child's death. Something that came up in the autopsy. I suggest you put in an application to the local registrar to get a copy of the death certificate," he added, draining his cup at last, and standing up. "Ryan was talking about the whole thing pretty publicly at The Fisherman, so I'm not breaking any confidences here."

Kent slowly put out his hand, and grasped Mick's. Then he leaned back and inspected the table top. "Word is," he remarked, "that old man who died of pancreatic cancer three months back, Chuck Monro, never got around to signing the divorce papers from his first wife down in Florida. Anyone trying to sort out the Monro estate might want to check out all the S. Monros living in Tallahassee."

Mick stared at Kent, who continued his careful investigation of the melamine surface beneath his teacup. After a moment, Mick placed his free hand briefly on Kent's shoulder, squeezed it, and left.

"That's one of the reasons I never miss court," Kent said to us in a low voice as the door banged closed, looking up with suddenly sharp eyes. "The gossip. Amazing what turns up. Right then, I'll stop off at the registrar's office on the way home, get a copy of the death certificate. God knows what Ryan's talking about, but we got to be prepared . . ."

"He sounds dodgy to me," my mother said, suspiciously, of Kent when I described our morning's experiences, "very *American*, don't you think?" as if the two were synonymous. "All this stuff about playing the court, about corrupt local politicians—it sounds highly dubious to me. Things aren't like that in England, I can promise you that," she added, proudly, in ringing tones (although just the other day she was telling me about how her local MP had been forced to resign for taking "cash for questions" in the Houses of Parliament. This entire event seemed to have slipped her mind, although I didn't fail to point it out). "Well, anyway, this Kent chap—I bet he's trying to reel you in," she went on. "He says he's got to get out of his firm sharpish—have you ever wondered why? What the real reason is? I bet he's got some disasters hidden in the woodwork, I bet the business is going to hell in a handbasket, he's going to leave you with no end of problems, Q. Still, it's your business I suppose; you never listen to me . . ."

I relayed this conversation to Tom, expecting a burst of hilarity ("ridiculous as ever, your mother"), but instead he shrugged. "Frankly, she may have something," he said. "I've been wondering exactly the same thing. Why does he want to get out so fast? Wouldn't be at all surprised if Kent has the odd skeleton in his cupboard. Not much we can do about it, I suppose, just wait for it to rattle."

45

~

Jeanie

I would have liked to go home, if I could, away from the entire continent that housed Paul, but my sister was relying on me and, given that she'd paid for my flight out to the States, I couldn't really leave. Particularly not once she'd started working again (well, sort of). But living in Paul's house was a torment. I had to take his graduation photo off the desk in my bedroom, wrap it in a tea towel, and hide it in the bedroom cupboard. Even so, I was acutely conscious of it. I was constantly fighting the temptation to go and unwrap it. I could have hidden it somewhere else in the house, of course, out of my own reach, but I was worried Q and Tom might find it, and I couldn't think how I would explain a photograph in a dish towel. I knew I would look completely mad.

But he was in my thoughts constantly. And I also missed Dave. He wasn't perfect, but he was my friend. I kept wanting to pick the phone up to tell him something, and was so sad to remember I couldn't. I tried to tell Q about this; she was irritable and impatient. "For goodness sake, Jeanie, make up your mind!" she said, shaking her head. "First you want him, then you don't, then you do. Honestly . . ." Alison, to my intense frustration, said almost the exact same thing on the phone.

I dialed Paul's number two hours before he was due to collect me on that longed-for Tuesday evening. "Paul, I'm not coming," I said abruptly, before the sound of his voice could put me off my stride. There was a pause.

"I'm sorry," he said at last, politely. "Are you ill?"

"No, no, it's not that. I'm not coming tonight, Paul, because I know *everything*. I saw you this afternoon. And I'm not saying what you're doing is evil, maybe some people could put up with it, if I was more sophisticated about these things perhaps I could too, but I'm not, and I can't," I gabbled, wishing even at this late stage that I could manage coherence in front of him. If only I could sound like the kind of women I was sure he normally went out with, women who were brought up to speak in full sentences in the midst of the apocalypse! "I can't, and that's final, I can't, and I'm sorry but I don't want to see you again," I finished miserably, tripping over the words, feeling like a six-year-old, hating myself and hating him all at the same time.

"I see," he said slowly. "Or rather, I don't. Perhaps you'd like to take me through it again—? I seem to be extraordinarily dense."

Righteous indignation and sick disgust were mixed in with a physical longing for him that, like a wave, threatened to engulf everything else. Somehow, though, I stuck to my guns. "Let's just say I saw you around lunchtime," I said meaningfully. "On the street. I went to this patisserie and—and I saw you, Paul. I saw what you were *doing*, and who you were *with*."

"I see." I could hear the guilt in his voice. "I see. Look, Jeanie, I'm not saying it's the best thing I've ever done, but there are—extenuating circumstances," he went on carefully. "If you'll have dinner with me this evening, I think I can explain them to you."

"Do you deny that you're—screwing her?"

"Screwing her? Well, I wouldn't put it quite like that, although . . ."

"How would you put it?"

"I'm—I'm—okay, I am sort of screwing her. It's true. That's the starkest possible account of what I'm doing, I suppose. But—"

"You people!" I exploded furiously, hearing the ridiculousness of this claim. "My God! You're 'sort of' screwing her? Either you are, or you aren't! There's no room for 'sort of' here. What, are you going to start questioning the meaning of 'is' now?"

"You mean Clinton? A lot of people misunderstood that argument, actually . . ."

"Well, I'm one of them!" I said furiously, panting for breath. "Don't patronize me, Paul. Words mean something. They just *do*. Let me tell you something, and we'll see if you misunderstand it: *you disgust me*. I think your behavior is repulsive. You should be ashamed of yourself. I want nothing more to do with you."

"Indeed, Jeanie, there's no room for misunderstanding there," he replied. The phone, pressed against my ear, seemed to turn cold.

"I'm sorry I ever met you," I went on, because I couldn't help myself. "I wish I'd never seen you. I wish you'd never even touched me."

"Really? Then let me assure you, the feeling is entirely mutual," he returned angrily. "You *are* an opinionated little minx, aren't you? I see now that I should never have interrupted your happy little relationship with the delightful Dave," he added, his voice dripping scorn. "Tom told me all about him. Clearly, he was perfect for you, rank sneakers and all. Now that you've come to appreciate his sterling qualities, you can achieve a full reconciliation. I assume that is what this is really about. I wish you both joy, Jeanie," he continued abruptly. "I'm sure you'll be very happy together." There was a click, and suddenly I realized I was holding a silent phone in my hand.

Every night after that brought wakefulness and tears. In the morning I'd sit for half an hour on the edge of the bed with a mirror in my hand, waiting for my face to look normal, but try as I might, the tears *would* come, my cheeks *would* turn mottled and spotted and red. I mopped my eyes again and again, I thought about raindrops and kittens and copper kettles and all the rest of it, but I still looked like someone from a Shakespearian tragedy in the final act. "Jeanie? Jeanie, where are you?" my sister would call fretfully, and eventually I'd have to go downstairs and plead allergies. I'd siphon down a cup of coffee and discover myself dreaming of brandy or vodka, or at the very least a bottomless box of red wine.

46

Q

Q, are you ready? Come on! We're late," Tom yelled upstairs to me at nine o'clock one morning, about a week after our trip to the courthouse. When I arrived in the kitchen a little breathless, Samuel tucked under my arm, Tom was busy stuffing Kent's old files into his briefcase. "I'm up to F," he announced proudly. He brandished a memory stick. "Everything from *there* is on *here*—well, the basics that is, and the major facts, I figure we can get a secretary to input the smaller details later."

"Very impressive," I said, laughing, and he grinned in response.

"What do you think the Crimpson partners would think of me now?" he said. "Uh—No, actually, don't answer that."

Tom seemed rejuvenated. He'd moved into high gear over the course of the week, working to familiarize himself with Kent's business, its history, and its full range of clients. He obviously loved the challenge, although I wasn't sure Kent did; he had a faintly haunted look in his eye ("Do you have to keep making such a mess? That file—no, leave it where it is, young man, it doesn't need to—oh my God, what're you *doing*?"). When we arrived at his office to join him and drive on to Emmie's, he eyed the memory stick with grave suspicion. "That itty bitty thing? Looks like a stick o'gum. You'll lose it, and the entire practice will fall apart. Still, it won't be my problem, I guess."

On the way to Emmie's house, the three of us crammed in the front seat of his battered two-tone truck, Kent explained what he'd just found out. Producing a crumpled document from his breast pocket, he passed it sideways to me. "That first child, Angela, didn't die of crib death at all. Mick was quite right."

A horrible fear that had been collecting on the edge of my consciousness since our conversation with Mick now clutched at my throat. "You're not saying that—that—she—"

Kent threw me a curious look. "*If* you'll let me finish—! She died of something called 'Reye's syndrome.' You ever heard of that?"

I shook my head, deeply, intensely relieved. But Tom cut in: "*I* have." I turned my head to look at him.

"Really?"

"Dad's a surgeon; I've been around medical research all my life. And I thought about becoming a pre-med for a while. I did a placement with one of Dad's friends, Ian Whittaker, at Johns Hopkins; he was finishing up a report on the causes of infant mortality. Sudden Infant Death Syndrome means the baby's death can't be explained after all causes have been ruled out through autopsy, death scene investigation, and review of the medical history. Reye's, on the other hand, is a neurological illness."

"You wouldn't happen to know what the symptoms of this syndrome *are*, would you?" Kent asked hopefully.

Tom shook his head. "No. But I can find out." He unclipped his cell phone, and dialed. "Ian? It's Tom here, Peter's kid," we heard him say, and then, "Can you give me a quick summary on the presentation of Reye's? I have a professional reason for asking . . ."

The conversation was as brief as men's conversations usually are, a simple fact-finding affair sandwiched between slivers of politeness. After a moment or two, Tom snapped his phone shut. "According to Ian the classic symptoms of Reye's are vomiting, fever, severe drowsiness, and, in its most dangerous form, seizures. Pretty serious, in other words."

"*Christ!* The kind of thing no mother should have ignored," Kent groaned; and then, as Tom agreed: "She *did* say she was awful tired around then, remember, Q? Maybe she just wasn't thinking straight."

"Ian says any child suffering from Reye's would—or at least *should*—have been in a hospital for treatment and monitoring in the days, maybe even weeks, before she died," Tom continued. "He says he's never even heard of a kid with Reye's dying at home. Bottom line is: Angela should have been in medical care, and Emmie should have seen she was dangerously ill."

"Which is presumably what Ryan's lawyer found out," said Kent. "He's going to say she's a careless mom who let her first kid die. As the icing on the cake of all the *other* claims, it's likely to fly with a judge—particularly if McColley hints (which I would, if I was bringing the case) that she was on drugs or drink when the kid was sick."

The truck banged along a pitted dirt path in the middle of some open fields, past a disused stone quarry, and into the driveway of a modern prefab Cape set at the bottom of a low hill. Ducks and geese and a few rangy cats scuttered about the yard; a car sat rusting under a tarp. The windows were dark, the blinds closed; the house had a strange, shut-up feel that was faintly threatening.

"The state medical examiner must have required a full statement of the scene of death," Tom remarked quietly, as Kent switched off the car. "Emmie's baby died at home; a detective must have been called, and he would have taken evidence from Emmie and her family about what happened in the week before the child died. If we can get our hands on the medical examiner's form, Kent, it might help us establish what state Emmie was in at the time of Angela's death."

"True." Kent nodded. "We'll get onto that. For now, though, let's get the story straight from the—er—horse's mouth."

We fell out of the truck, legs bent nearly double. Kent watched us ("Are y'all right? Know you city types are used to limousines"), then leaned past us into the truck's passenger side and removed something from the glove compartment. The something was long, hard, bigger than a man's hand, and wrapped in brown paper. "Lawyer can never be too careful hereabouts," he murmured, gesturing to the packet as he slipped it into his jeans' back pocket. "Never know when you might need this." Tom and I exchanged glances.

Kent led the way to the green front door, and pushed the buzzer.

A dog immediately barked fiercely inside, a dog that sounded as if lawyers were his favorite treat and he hadn't had any for a few long, hungry days. We heard the sound of someone approaching, then a dog's scampering feet coming closer, closer. Kent reached behind him, extracted the brown-paper parcel, and began to unwrap it, his face watchful. Tom moved me sharply behind him as the door opened—the dog's face and slavering jaws were suddenly visible behind the screen, sharp teeth pulling away from huge black gums. The dog charged out—

"Here you go, buddy," Kent said, producing from the long paper package . . . a dog biscuit. A long, bone-shaped, entirely inoffensive, pink dog biscuit. The dog, a curious mix of many breeds, nosed Kent's hand, accepted the biscuit thankfully, and slumped down on the door-step with it, head resting comfortably on Kent's left shoe. Kent grinned back at us. "What the hell are you doing over *there*?" he called, gesturing to us to follow him, "don't tell me you're scared of this old boy!" He stepped over the animal's recumbent body and into the house.

An old man was hovering in the shadowy depths of the hallway, dressed in blue jeans, grubby white sneakers, and a stained blue check shirt. As we stepped inside, he grunted, then let the door slam behind us and preceded us down the hall into a sitting room that—on brief inspection—bore more resemblance to a garage than a place of family gathering. Pieces of car and generator were strewn around the chairs and tables; oil cans reposed on blackened pieces of news-paper, and a large toolbox was spilling wrenches onto the carpet in front of the television.

"Emmie! EMMIE! Mr. Tyler's arrived—get your ass in here!" the old man yelled, picking up a piece of what looked like an exhaust pipe from the coffee table. With a brief nod, he vanished through the hall and into the yard.

Emmie greeted us with limited enthusiasm. "What can I do for you?" she asked wearily, appearing in the dark hallway with a tea towel looped round her neck. "You'll have to make it quick, I've got to get a stew done for the church supper tonight and then I've got to get Paulie ready for a visit to his friend's house."

We followed her into the kitchen. A neatly swept butcher's block stood in the middle of the room; the wood counters were scrubbed clean. There was a vase of wildflowers, not particularly fresh, but still pretty, by the sink, and a few framed photographs of Paulie on the wall. Emmie produced a slab of beef from the fridge and a meat tenderizer, then a bag of carrots, a sack of potatoes, and six onions from a cupboard. "You can help me with the vegetables," she said flatly, dumping the lot on the counter.

I set about the potatoes while Kent and Tom harassed some onions and carrots and Emmie pounded the beef into submission. "So what is it" (*bang, bang*) "you want to" (*bang, bang*) "talk about?" she asked.

Kent watched the meat tenderizer cautiously. "Well, see here, Emmie, something's sort of come up," he began carefully.

"What do you mean?" *Bang. Bang.*

"Well, you see, my dear" (*bang, bang*) "it's—it's a bit of a tricky subject actually—it's about—well" (*bang, bang, bang, bang*) "maybe you should put down the—" (*bang, bang, bang*)—Kent threw me a piteous look.

"Emmie, it's about Baby Angela, actually," I cut in. "About her death," I went on, into the crashing silence that followed.

"Angela didn't die of crib death." I said slowly, very slowly, watching to see the effect of my words. "According to the certificate, she died of Reye's syndrome."

Emmie's face was white. "What do *you* know about it?" she said, her voice low. "What are you talking about?"

"Mr. Tyler has a copy of the death certificate. He—er—thought he should take a look. And see—" I gave her the document—"cause of death: 'Reye's syndrome.' Now, did you ever hear of that?"

Emmie collapsed into a chair at the table, baby daughter's death certificate clutched tight in her hand.

"Have you ever heard of it before?" Kent pressed. Emmie shook her head; her lips formed the shape of a "no."

"From what we've been able to find out," Kent went on, more gently, "it's a—real bad illness that makes you sick, and gives you a fever, and—ah—do you want to explain?" he asked hopefully, turning to Tom.

Tom came and sat beside Emmie. "Reye's syndrome is a very serious disease. No one knows exactly what causes it," he explained, "but it's got something to do with disturbances in the chemical levels in a child's blood. It leads to swelling of the organs—liver, kidneys, even the brain. Symptoms include fever, vomiting, drowsiness, and even seizures."

"Emmie, was Angela ill in the weeks before she died? Did she have any of those symptoms?"

Emmie stared at us all, one after the other. She looked a little bit wild. "I—I—" She gulped. "Angela had a cold, a real bad cold, starting a few weeks before she died; then it sort of got better, the cold part I mean, although she seemed—not herself, you know? I had the doctor up here almost every day, I kept telling him she wasn't right, he kept telling me I was being silly . . . was it my fault, then? *Was it my fault?*"

Kent caught our eye; he had seen the thing we saw, I knew it immediately. His body had stiffened, just as mine had, just as Tom's had, at something in Emmie's words. "You had the *doctor* out here? Which doctor was that?"

Emmie brushed his words aside. "Dr. Reid. He's our family doctor. Was it *my fault*?"

"Emmie, listen to me," Kent said urgently. "How often did you have your doctor out here? What did you tell him when he came? What did he say to you about Angela? *Think*."

But Emmie had her head down on the table now, her forehead cradled in her fingers. "It was my fault, they were right, I should have explained better. I should have made him understand," she groaned. "It's just like they said, just like they said . . ."

I went and put my arms around her. "That's not what we're saying at all," I told her. "Emmie, we need to know exactly what happened." Kent got out a notepad and a leaky blue pen.

Angela, as Emmie explained slowly, painfully, had caught a cold from a neighbor's kid, and was for a week a very miserable two-and-a-half-month-old baby. The family doctor, who lived nearby, came out to see her on several occasions and, when she seemed to be in real discomfort, "he told me to give her some aspirin, just a bit of aspirin to take the edge off the pain, and then a few other things—some kind of lotion in a bowl of water, and this plastic thing to squeeze out her nose."

However, as the symptoms of the cold got better, Angela seemed, oddly, to get *worse*. She became, in Emmie's memory, lethargic, lying still in her bed, staring blankly ahead, slipping in and out of sleep. Emmie eventually suggested taking her daughter to the hospital, but the doctor insisted she was overreacting.

"Dr. Reid said I should just learn to 'enjoy' my baby, he said I was being silly, an overanxious mom," she told us, fingers white, knuckles blenched. "He said young moms 'can't read their kids.' He said most women are happy if their babies lie quiet, he said I didn't appreciate what I had. Then the day before Angela died she was real sick, she threw up everything I fed her in the afternoon. I was frightened. So I called him out again; that time he said my milk must have been bad. I believed him," she went on, turning to face us, "I believed him. That's why I bottle-fed Paulie, you know; I was so frightened my milk poisoned Angela. Was he wrong, do you think?"

I could see Kent carefully writing this down in his book, heavily underscoring some words, his pen spluttering with the force—*"Angela vomits day before death; Reid blames milk; Reid dismisses Emmie's concerns."*

"Emmie, who told you that Angela died of crib death?" Tom asked.

"Dr. Reid," she replied, eyes half-closed. "Of course it was Dr. Reid. He called me a few days after the death, said he had the results of the autopsy, wanted to tell me as soon as possible so we could get on with the funeral. I was crazy the whole time, thinking of my baby in that cold place. Dr. Reid said he wanted to put an end to it all, get her decently buried. That was when he said it was crib death."

"Are you sure about that? He definitely used the phrase 'crib death'?"

"I wrote it down. He said there was nothing anybody could have done. Said I shouldn't blame myself. And I asked him—I said, what about the cold and the sickness, and he said, 'Babies don't die of colds or an upset stomach, it was just a coincidence.' So I learned the words 'crib death,' so I could say it to the folks in town. And Dr. Reid was so kind: he helped me with the funeral. Dad was crazy, Gramps locked himself in the shed, it was the doctor who helped me arrange everything. He even gave me money for a dinner in the church hall afterward."

"Reid gives Emmie money for funeral expenses," Kent wrote in his looping script; and then, discreetly, *"??"* by the side. "Emmie," he said, looking up briefly, "did you see the death certificate? Did you get a copy?"

Emmie shook her head. "Dr. Reid picked up the certificate and gave it to the funeral director," she explained. "He said he wanted to save me the trip." We sat in silence, listening to the slow sound of Kent's pen moving across the paper.

"Did you never hear from the medical examiner's office? Did nobody call you to explain what had happened, to offer to help you?" I asked. "That would be typical state practice."

Emmie thought. "I—you know, maybe someone *did* call," she said finally. "It was all such a mess, I didn't really know what was going on, I was half out of my mind, you know? But I—I think Gramps took a phone call from someone, said she wanted to get me some counseling—counseling!" She laughed shortly. "Why would I talk to some stranger about my Angel? What could they possibly tell me? So I never called her back," she finished fiercely. "I don't need people poking their noses into my life, I had my family to take care of me, my neighbors, Dr. Reid . . ." her voice trailed off.

"You're saying it was *his* fault." She half-stood, her hands strangling the table.

"Yes, dear, that's exactly what we're saying, but for God's sake don't go after him with that meat tenderizer," said Kent firmly, closing his notebook and stuffing it into his pocket. "Do you understand me, young lady? We'll follow this up, we'll go talk to Reid, find out what the hell he has to say for himself. But if you start threatening him, you'll get yourself into trouble and you'll lose Paulie for good. It's one thing to menace an abusive ex, it's another to go waving a gun at the local doctor. You do that and McColley will have your head for sure. You stay out of this like a good girl, and we may be able to get you compensation from Reid *and* keep Paulie safe at home. No promises, but I'm feeling better about this than I have in a while."

He nodded at her curtly, then gestured to us to stand up. "What're you doing these next few days?" he asked, a grin creasing his face. "Something tells me we've got a house call of our own to make. Boy, I'm glad we won't have to go to Wyoming to sort this one out after all . . ."

47

~

Jeanie

I was walking past Mrs. Forrest's office at Quiet Lanes, cheerily swinging a bag of new knitting wool for Sue-Ellen and a magazine about airplanes for Ken, when the unmistakable sound of a sob brought me up short. I stopped for a second in the hallway, irresolute, hoping I'd imagined it—but there it came again: a deep, snuffly, miserable sob. Bright, chirpy Mrs. Forrest was crying.

I knocked gently on the office door, and walked in; Mrs. Forrest was sitting by the window, holding a letter. "Oh, Jeanie, it's you. I mean, hiya!" she said, in a ghastly imitation of her usual cheer. Her fuchsia scarf was trailing forlornly over the back of her chair; without it she looked unexpectedly drab. A large cup of tea sat beside her on the windowsill, a filmy skin of cooled milk floating horribly on the top. "How lovely, gee, everyone's going to be thrilled you're here," she went on, struggling to manage a toothy smile, but her hands remained dropped in her lap, motionless. Something was seriously wrong.

"Mrs. Forrest, is there anything I can—er—do?" I asked hesitantly, hovering awkwardly on the edge of the room, and then, in response to something in her face, I walked in, closing the door carefully behind me. "Have you had bad news?"

"Oh, my heavens, Jeanie, how did you guess?" Mrs. Forrest looked genuinely astounded.

"I—um—you've had a letter," I pointed out tactfully.

She looked down at the document, then up at me again, tragically. "You are quite right, Jeanie. It seems I may not be able to keep Quiet Lanes," she added, now dropping the pretense, the sentence ending in an open wail. "Oh, Jeanie, I don't think I can bear it. This is my life, Jeanie. My life!"

Mrs. Forrest was not the cleverest woman I'd ever met, but the place ran with the peaceful hum of organized inevitability. And the more time I'd spent there, the more I'd come to recognize the little home manager's affection for her patients. "Why on earth will you have to leave?" I asked her, surprised.

Mrs. Forrest adjusted her wire glasses with trembling fingers, glanced at the letter again with an expression of utter hopelessness, then permitted herself another small sob. "I've known for a while, Jeanie, that I'm not up to the job of care manager, not—well, not in these days. Once upon a time it was just a question of—of caring, you see. Caring for old people. But now there's all this technology. And—*management*." Her voice, as she uttered the dread word, dropped to a spectral whisper. "*Efficiency*—it's all about efficiency, especially in these difficult economic times. I can't do it, and they know I can't—the managers of the SeniorOne group of care homes, that is, who own this place. The letter—it says I have six weeks to—to implement—something or other, but really it's just a way for them to get rid of me. I know it!" She ended with a howl; tears began to stream down her face and plop onto her shirt. Wordlessly, I handed her a pink tissue from a pink floral box on the desk. She blew her nose, loudly.

"But Jeanie, this isn't your problem!" The wobbly smile appeared again, a flash of brilliant white. "You go join the residents. I know Sue-Ellen and Joel and Ken are just *longing* to see you," she added. "If I have to go—*when* I have to go away from Quiet Lanes, the one thing I'll always be pleased about is hiring *you*," she remarked tragically. "You have just shaken us all up in the most wunnerful way, and I—"

"Mrs. Forrest, may I read the letter?" I interrupted briskly, cutting through her tremulous praise, and when she nervously held out the paper, I plucked it from her hands, sat down on the edge of the desk, and read the epistle through carefully from beginning to end.

It was from someone called Andrew, a vice-president of the SeniorOne Elder Care Group. (A great deal of money had clearly been spent producing a spangly logo that adorned the top third of the cream-colored page.) Andrew's first paragraph was fairly straightforward (hello, how are you, the once-yearly inspection of the cooking facilities will be at such-and-such a time). The part that clearly had the little home manager in a tizzy was a section entitled "New Mandates" in the middle of paragraph two:

We have become persuaded, after several focus groups, that collaborative enterprise is the most effective tool to promote elder care excellence in recession-era America. We are therefore enclosing a leaflet which encourages health-care providers to learn to work together through active problem solving and decision making. Our goals in response to this new initiative are three-fold:

1. socializing health-care providers in collaborative work, in mutual experiences of shared problem solving and focused decision making, thereby enabling greater patient benefits;
2. creating and enabling mutual understanding of, and respect for, multi-disciplinary contributions; and
3. producing, enhancing, and developing the necessary abilities for successful and institution-changing collaborative practice.

We expect that all care home managers will implement this new strategy, and plan an inspection in three weeks to evaluate its progress. All managers must construct a detailed twenty-page report (FAO Lina Shwartz) on their implementation strategy by next Wednesday, and a further 20 pages in advance of the inspection to indicate goal achievement success rates (numbered one, two, three).

Mrs. Forrest watched me read this nonsense with eyes like deep pools. "You see," she said at last, miserably, when I put down the letter, one more tear spilling over, "I can't do that. They *know* I can't do that. Jeanie, I don't even know—" again, that low, horrified whisper— *"what it means!"*

I started to laugh—I just couldn't help it. But it was a mistake, of course; looking deeply offended, the little care home manager drew herself up to her fullest height. "I cannot see why you think this is funny, Jeanie," she said, sounding deeply hurt. "I may not be the best manager in the world, but I try my best, and—"

"No, no," I interrupted, putting out my hand apologetically, "it's not funny, I mean, it *is*, but *you* are not. Look, Mrs. Forrest, I've just finished a master's degree in social work. I've plowed through whole textbooks full of government initiatives and strategies for geriatric excellence, and all the rest of it. *I understand this*." I waggled the letter at her.

Mrs. Forrest looked at me as if I had just plopped down in her garden in a spaceship, fully equipped with antennae and three arms. *"You do?"*

I grinned at her. "How much responsibility are you willing to give me, Mrs. Forrest?" I asked, and she gasped.

"Responsibility? Do you mean—?"

"If you want, I will" (tapping the letter) " 'construct a detailed twenty-page report on our implementation strategy.' It'll take me about fifteen minutes, I reckon. I've got some essays on my computer, I'll just cut and paste stuff into a new document, add a few more syllables and bullet points, and you can sign the thing."

"But—how can you do that? I don't even understand what they want me to do!" She was wringing her hands now, twisting them up to her face; I was delighted to see them engaged in more normal activities.

"This? All it means is, they want us to learn to work together," I said, grinning, "which we don't need to learn, because we do it already. Look, we'll have a few tea parties and a couple of games of pass-the-parcel, I'll describe them as 'entertainment events designed to facilitate greater collaborative understanding of mutual shared goals,' Andrew will be delighted, and you'll keep your job."

Mrs. Forrest flung her arms right around me. "Jeanie, I think the Lord sent you to me," she said seriously, snuffling like a bunny into my T-shirt.

When I walked into the day room, quarter of an hour later, I was almost immediately barraged by questions about "how that in'eresting young man of yours is doing." He's very well, I said; he's gone back to London. I don't know when I'll see him again. Ken kept trying to push me, but Sue-Ellen weighed majestically in: "We will leave you in peace," she commanded, and Ken raised his eyebrows, took his magazine, and submitted with a very good grace. But several of the other old people seemed keen to take up the challenge, so, without looking at me, Sue-Ellen began to tell a very long story about her first husband, who apparently made his money diving for lost ships and recovering their treasure. She showed us a locket she was wearing that went down in 1587 off the coast of Sicily, and described the tea set she had given her daughter that still had salt deposits deep in its glaze. By the time she'd finished, everyone had stopped thinking about Dave, and even I was so enthralled by her narrative of danger and gold and lost ruby necklaces I lost track of time, then suddenly realized I'd stayed more than the requisite two hours. "See, Jeanie? I'm telling you; time just *flies* at Quiet Lanes," said Mrs. Forrest, who now seemed almost restored to her twinkly self; her fingers fluttered as she spread her hands gleefully wide.

I was just about to walk out the door when I felt a soft touch on my shoulder; I wasn't surprised to see Sue-Ellen. "Honey, we need to talk," she murmured in my ear, and a little reluctantly I followed her through the French doors onto the patio. Carefully tended pots of ivy and bright red, richly fragrant flowers lined the weed-free concrete; Sue-Ellen settled herself on a bench, and crossed her ankles.

Her English counterpart would probably sport tweed two-pieces from Jaeger and burgundy leather court shoes. Sue-Ellen, being American, wore pressed trousers and T-shirts with bright white trainers instead.

"I'm worried about you, Jeanie," she began abruptly. "You're going around with a face like a camel from Cairo; you're obviously in some kind of trouble. Is it about that young man you brought here?" I nodded slowly.

"I'm not surprised. He's here, there, everywhere, zig-zaggin' all over, reminded me of a rabbit. There's someone else, I think?"

Again I nodded, more bewildered this time. How did she—? "And on top of that, you don't know what to do with yourself, you're nervous of putting yourself out on the market in difficult times like these. Life passes you by so fast, Jeanie! Figure out what you want, and get on with it. Make the times work for you, my dear; there are opportunities out there if you can just grab them. Now, one other important piece of advice," she continued—I leaned forward, head spinning, wondering what on earth would come next—"good sex is worth fighting for! You make sure you get plenty of it. That's my strategy. Worst thing about Quiet Lanes, I'll tell you, is having Mrs. Forrest walking the corridors when you're trying to get it on . . ." I tried neither to laugh nor to think about exactly who Sue-Ellen was trying to get it on with (although since the options were limited, it was hard).

"Where did you learn to tell fortunes?" I asked her suddenly; and she laughed.

"Ah, my dear, that was from husband number two," she explained, rocking gently backward and forward in her seat. "*His* aunt was a Romany, you see, a genuine Romany. We visited her in Bucharest in the second year of our marriage. Philip, my husband, obviously inherited the gift, but I—well, Aunt Sofia said I had potential," she remarked modestly. "She lived in a small house with another old lady, the two of them were known for miles around. I remember sitting with them in their front room, a tiny dark box, the air filled with heady perfume and walls hung with bright woven scarves. We learned the craft by lamplight. There's no skeptic alive could've come out of such a place untouched," she added. "You could *feel* the force of the future in their presence."

"You've never told my future," I said, and I reached out my hand with a smile. "You told Dave's, but you didn't tell mine." I held it steady before her. "Why don't *you* tell me what's going to happen in my life, Sue-Ellen? Really, it'll make everything so much simpler!"

Sue-Ellen's faded blue eyes were sympathetic beneath her towering sweep of golden hair. "Oh no, my dear," she said gently. "No, no, no. That's just what I'm talking about. *You* have to work your future out for yourself."

I felt oddly embarrassed, but still I kept my hand outstretched. "Oh come on, Sue-Ellen," I said, managing a confident chuckle. "If I cross your palm with silver, I'm sure you'll spin me a good story. That's all it is anyway, this fortune-telling business. It's not as if I was going to—you know, *believe* you, or anything."

Sue-Ellen stirred a little beside me, and brushed some soft yellow pollen off her trousers. "Really? Well, if you say so. Listen, my dear: some people need a little push in life. And you are one of them. There are no shortcuts," she added seriously. "Whatever it is you believe in, you've got to work out your future, Jeanie, before it's your past."

I sat still on the bench for a moment, thinking of an e-mail I'd received from Una the other day, telling me I had to leave the flat: "Lolly says that now you're not a student anymore, I'll have to start paying council tax, so sorry about that. Just can't afford to keep you, haha! And anyway, Lolly wants to move in with me next month, so we'd probably have asked you to sod off anyway. Lolly's amazing, you'd really like him. He's using your room right now to stash his record collection. And Dukey's sleeping there sometimes too, I said I was sure you wouldn't mind." I hadn't had a clue who Dukey was. (Frankly I was a bit hazy on Lolly's identity as well.)

"I know I have to—decide what I'm doing, but it's hard!" I said into the warm breeze. "I'm fond of Dave, and I miss him, but we aren't right for each other. Paul Dupont is—not the man I thought he was. I was totally wrong about him. I want to be a social worker—I think, but it's hard; when I started my course there were still some jobs out there, now they're all drying up—what am I supposed to do with my degree? I need a new flat, but I can't afford the rent until I get a job, and if I don't have a place I can't get a job. And you wonder why I'm hanging out over here! I'm *trying* to decide what to do with myself, you know, but it's not easy. It's not easy being twenty-four in the middle of a recession."

"Quite honestly, it's not easy being seventy-four either," replied Sue Ellen.

48

~

Q

Four days later, Tom was up to S.

And he was looking like a different man, although so was Kent; the old man developed a pained, long-suffering expression whenever he saw my husband. His shoulders sagged, his mouth rounded down, and I caught him sneaking surreptitious drags from a silver hip flask he thought we hadn't noticed under his desk. Tom, meanwhile, had a new spring in his step, and whenever you asked him what he was thinking about, he mentioned the travails of some local mechanic or postmaster or veterinarian he'd never actually met. "I think we can get the shed removed," he told me suddenly, over dinner one night, "I think I've figured it out!" I hadn't a clue what he was talking about, but Tom was so pleased with himself he got up early and went into the office to talk through his discoveries with Kent.

Dr. Philip Reid's practice had been serving the residents of a small town near Sussex called Branton for some thirty-five years. "Most people around here won't hear a word against either of the partners, Reid or Craig Warwick," Kent told us, as we drove there through a dull haze on Friday morning. "They're well known for getting up in the middle of the night, traveling to the remotest corners of the state, doing whatever it takes to help their patients. This is going to be an unpopular case, I'll tell you. Shouldn't be surprised if I lose clients over it. If *you* lose clients over it, that is . . ."

As we entered, a woman in her fifties looked up at us from behind a wooden desk. Her graying hair was twisted into a bun on top of her head, her ample form was clothed in a simple cotton dress, and a pair of steel spectacles were propped on her nose—spectacles which she immediately lifted from her face and dropped onto the desk as she caught sight of Kent. "Mr. Tyler!" she exclaimed, a hint of red in her cheeks. "What brings you here?"

Tom and I hung back discreetly near the circle of listless patients while Kent went over to the doctors' secretary. He leaned over the table and cupped his face in his hands about six inches from her nose. "Elizabeth Summers, it sure is lovely to see you again," he said; we could just hear his voice, low and caressing, as he smiled at her. "Tell me, how are those puppies you picked up a week or two back from the Mansons?"

She smiled happily "Oh, they're *wonderful*, Mr. Tyler, I got two of them, you probably heard; they're beautiful dogs, wonderful proportions . . ."

"And you'll be winning gold rosettes with them all over the state before the year is up, I'll bet," Kent murmured. "Never knew anyone like it, you could take a cur from the street and have him looking like a champion in a few months, Elizabeth."

"Oh goodness, I don't know about that," she said, her face flushing with pleasure, looking down at the desk, and idly playing with a small net purse that lay on top of the appointments' ledger. "You can't say a thing like that, it's all to do with breeding you know . . ."

"Well now, listen here, Elizabeth, I need to ask a quick question of the doctor, Reid that is, about one of his patients. I wonder if you could get me five minutes?" he asked.

Her brow furrowed a bit, and she dropped her voice even lower. "I don't know about that, we're running behind today, Fridays are always terrible, Dr. Reid had to go up to the hospital in the morning, we've been forty minutes slow ever since, people are waiting . . ." She nodded over to the group of patients, her eyes widening curiously as she caught sight of us.

Kent leaned over and said something quietly in her ear. Her face flushed bright scarlet. "Well, well—okay then," I heard her say at last, reluctantly, "if you promise you'll keep it to five minutes, I suppose it's all right, just this once. And I'll . . ." He twisted his ear toward her mouth to catch her words, and she whispered something inside we couldn't quite hear, although I could swear it involved leaving a door unlocked at half past ten on Sunday night.

At that moment, a little red buzzer on the desk flashed and sounded. Elizabeth glanced over at the patients anxiously, then jerked her head in the direction of a door. "Go on then," she said, in a hushed whisper, "but hurry up, or there's going to be a riot in here."

Kent stood up immediately. "Come on," he called shortly to us, over his shoulder, and Elizabeth watched, bewildered, as we filed past her in Kent's wake. "Who—why—who are they—" we heard her quacking, faintly, as we threaded our way along a corridor.

Kent rapped smartly on the doctor's door, and we filed into his examining rooms.

A well-preserved man of about fifty, in shirtsleeves, was sitting at his desk, hunting and pecking on an elderly-looking computer. He turned to look at us over half-moon glasses, and his smooth, pink brow furrowed.

"Unless my medical skills have completely deserted me, you are not an eighty-year-old lady with a broken thumb," he said calmly.

Kent grinned and sat down, while we crowded in through the door behind him. "True enough. How're you doing, Phil? These are two—ah—new associates of mine. We want to talk to you about Emmie Cormier. Won't take a minute."

Dr. Reid sighed gently. "Elizabeth is losing her grip, I fear," he said. "And I've long known she has a—partiality—for you, you old reprobate. Well, well, since you're here, what is it you want to know? Bearing in mind—" he went on, as Kent began to speak, his hand raised in warning, "I cannot break doctor-patient confidentiality. And I will not."

Kent nodded. "I won't ask you to. Got a letter here, authorizing you to talk to us. I just want to know, on behalf of my client, why you told Emmie her first baby died of crib death, not Reye's syndrome."

Dr. Reid, after examining the handwritten note for a moment, put his head on one side, and considered Kent's face. "Excuse me?" he said coolly.

"Simple enough question," Kent went on briskly. "She says you told her Angela's death was diagnosed as SIDS, but the death certificate says Reye's syndrome. Can you explain that?"

Dr. Reid stared first at Kent, then at us. "I wish I had more seating for you," he said to us, ever so gently, "but I'm afraid I'm not used to entertaining *parties* in my office." The edge in his voice was just palpable. He looked back at Kent. "My dear Mr. Tyler, I'm not entirely sure what you're getting at. Of course I told Ms. Cormier—Vaughan in those days—that the child's death was attributed to Reye's syndrome in the autopsy. I explained the cause of death fully to her, what on earth are you suggesting? But it didn't mean anything to her, she barely remembered her own name at the time, let alone complicated medical terminology. I suppose she has simply internalized 'crib death,' it's quicker and easier, something most people have heard of. I am not in the business of deceiving my patients," he finished, drawing himself up, his expression gently aggrieved.

Kent had got out his dog-eared notebook again and was scribbling away. He looked up now at his adversary, unabashed. "I see. It was her mistake, then. And what about all those trips out to the house in the days before the baby died?" he went on. "Did you suspect Reye's syndrome then? Why didn't you get the kid admitted to the hospital?"

Dr. Reid put his head on one side and contemplated Kent rather as a blackbird examines a worm that's not worth the trouble of pulling from the earth. "My dear man, I only saw the child once, when she first got sick with a cold," he said, with a hint of exasperation. "There was no reason whatsoever to suspect Reye's syndrome at the time; she had a touch of nasal congestion, it was a minor respiratory illness. The next time I saw the baby, she was dead. Reye's syndrome sets in in the *aftermath* of a respiratory infection; when I saw her that one time, the disease had not taken hold. The young mother was all over the place, she obviously didn't notice that an entirely new condition developed after our meeting. She was too young and inexperienced to spot the signs. To be fair, it can be hard sometimes. But what on earth makes you think I went there more often?"

"The fact that that's what Emmie Cormier told us herself," I interjected. I held Dr. Reid's gaze.

The doctor had an expression of mild surprise on his face. "Did she really, Mrs.—er—? Well, I can only say her memory is failing her, then. And if she wants to release to you copies of her daughter's medical notes, you will see that I'm right. Or you can ask the medical examiner for his report—it will contain full details of the circumstances surrounding the death. I went to the Vaughan house to see the child once, and once only. Of course people in grief remember strange things, I'm not saying she's deliberately making up claims, of course . . ." He lifted his shoulders gently, as if to say, *I'm* not the person making wild accusations.

"Yes, well," said Kent, clicking his pen closed, "Ms. Cormier will certainly want us to see copies of those notes. And the medical examiner's report as well. You'll be hearing from us again soon," he went on, "*very* soon, Dr. Reid. Good-bye."

"One last thing, doctor," Tom said suddenly, his hand resting casually on the doorknob. "Just for our records: do you happen to remember the name of the detective who attended the scene of the baby's death?"

Dr. Reid was writing something on a large piece of card, and he did not look up. "Driscoll I believe," he said coolly. "Good-bye." We filed back down the corridor and out of the offices. Kent paused to blow a kiss discreetly to Elizabeth on the way out.

"Good thought, that one," he said judiciously to Tom when we were back in the car. "Driscoll, eh? Driscoll. Hmmm."

"Isn't that the detective Emmie said was friends with Ryan?" I asked, and Kent nodded.

"It's a small police force, there's only a handful of them, it had to be Driscoll or– what's his name?—Johnson, but Driscoll is the younger man, and he's known all around as a bit of a pushover. If only we could get our hands on the report he filed . . . could be tricky, he's unlikely to just hand it over . . ."

"We should start with the medical examiner's report," Tom pointed out, "we're entitled to a copy of that." Kent agreed.

"Sure, but ultimately the responsibility for filing it lies with Reid; it'll be just Reid's official version of events. Still, I'll talk with Emmie and see if I can get a copy faxed to my offices today, before the weekend. It's a good place to start."

When we arrived home, Jeanie delivered Samuel into our arms with a small smile, a rare sight these days. "He's been very good, actually," she told us, stroking his cheek. "No trouble at all. He barely cried once. Now what would you two like for dinner?" she went on in a bracing tone. "I was thinking of making a stew. Or perhaps a pie, I could take whatever's left over to Quiet Lanes, show them what English baking tastes like—?"

49

～

Jeanie

I produced the first fifteen pages of polysyllabic nonsense in a mere two hours. I took my computer to Quiet Lanes the next morning, where Mrs. Forrest read through the document with an expression of admiring astonishment. "You know what this all means?" she asked eventually, wildly gesticulating.

"Of course not," I explained briskly, "but neither will Andrew. Now, in the meantime, I have an idea: let's think seriously about what you'd *actually* like to do at Quiet Lanes in the next year. We'll put it in the kind of language he wants, and see what we can wrangle for you and the Home."

So we sat down together, and she sketched out her wish list. More tea parties ("economically low-impact opportunities for dynamic collaborative interaction"). More visits from outside speakers ("focused interdisciplinary events developing skills in patients and health professionals alike"). And "I'd—I'd love to be able to take them all for a day by the sea," Mrs. Forrest remarked wistfully, clutching her hands dramatically to her chin. "Sue-Ellen just loves lobster, and Ken was saying the other day he's been dreaming of fresh oysters. And Joel loves reading on the beach." After referring back to my course notes, and a few of the essays that Sibelius Mordaunt actually liked, I typed:

An essential component of collaborative enterprise involves challenging health-care professionals to perform in nonconventional settings. This encourages those in care positions to communicate both verbally and nonverbally, thus developing crucial skills across disciplines. Our goal, therefore, is to create, through a series of focused single-day excursion events, opportunities for employed and volunteer health-care professionals to enhance and develop these vital skills in order to heighten patient benefits and enhance institutional excellence. An ocean-oriented event exploiting Connecticut's vibrant natural resources would allow us to target goals one, two, and three from the current collaborative mandate.

"And that means—?" Mrs. Forrest pondered, after reading this aloud carefully.

"We'd like to go to the seaside, please," I finished, grinning, and she stared at me with gratifying admiration.

"Does it really?" she asked, turning her head this way and that, as if reading upside down would make the whole thing clearer. And then, with a reluctant sigh, "Words *are* funny things, Jeanie!"

She bustled off into the day room to start lunch; I sat in her potpourried office with my computer and a plate of Twinkies editing, moving things around, and then—as a final touch—adding serious-sounding subheadings in different typefaces. By the time I was finished, the document was, I must admit, quite impressive. I printed it out on her little workhorse printer, adding a title page and a list of chapter headings (1: Introduction: Implementing Mandate in Quiet Lanes Setting. 2: Socializing Care Workers: An Overview. 3: Collaborative Enterprise Revisited. 4: Business Plan: Projecting Future Goals in Uncertain Times). I walked into the day room and presented Mrs. Forrest with the fat little bundle. She waved her arms around so much I thought she was going to take off.

I was walking out through the front hallway when I became conscious, suddenly, of a presence behind me. I turned to see Sue-Ellen, hovering strangely in her own shadow. There was something more insubstantial about her than normal; her hair was wispier, flatter, not its usual magnificent golden edifice. "There's something I've been meaning to tell you," she said softly. "Don't want you to hear it from one of the others, I guess." She reached out, and adjusted a seashell collage on the wall, which had slid fractionally to the side; with great attention, she touched it this way and that with her finger, until she had it exactly, perfectly straight. I waited, wondering.

"My cancer is not—well, it's not curable, Jeanie," she said at last, standing back to examine her handiwork. "Doctor confirmed it a day or two ago."

For a moment I couldn't think quite what to say. The news should not have surprised me—Mrs. Forrest had told me about her mastectomy on my very first day—but somehow Sue-Ellen seemed like one of those people that death can't touch. She had a timeless quality to her, a simple, peaceful elegance that had nothing to do with being sixty or seventy or ninety.

She did not look up at me now but stayed where she was, rearranging a few poems and a Childe Hassam reprint. "So I'll be moving out of Quiet Lanes in a few weeks' time," she went on, her voice quiet and level, profile impassive. "I'm going to go into a hospice in Old Saybrook, unless I get worse before that, of course. Cancer's spreading, so I guess it's just a matter of time." Unconscious hands stole upward to her breast. "But I think I have a few weeks here left to enjoy. I like it here, Jeanie. I like the folks." She smiled briefly, turned around, and started to walk away.

"Sue-Ellen!" I called, and she turned hesitantly to face me.

"Yes, honey?"

"Sue-Ellen, I'm so—so very sorry."

She reached up and patted her golden hair. "Yes, my dear, so am I," she replied, and walked back into the day room.

50

~

Q

The next morning Samuel was surprisingly peaceful, so I decided to risk giving him a proper bath. (We'd mostly given up on these, since the water appeared to drive him to distraction; we'd been making do with an occasional quick rub-down instead.) He was obviously not thrilled at the idea of the tub. Every time I touched his feet to the water he squealed worriedly, so after giving the matter some thought I stripped off my clothes and got in with him, propping him up on my stomach. Much better, he gave me to understand, waving an experimental leg in the warm soapy water. "This little piggy . . ." He observed me solemnly, head on one side, as I counted each tiny toe and finger, then crinkled up his chubby little neck to stop the piggy finding its way home under there, and giggled.

After lunch, I left him sleeping—a peaceful sleep, one he drifted into contentedly at my breast—and accompanied Tom on his way through the slow-moving Saturday traffic to Kent's office at Cheasford. My shoulder muscles felt unusual, and it took me a while to understand why; ah yes, I realized, with a sensation of shock, I haven't actually had to carry the baby *all morning*.

"Jeanie's being very helpful at the moment, isn't she?" I said brightly to Tom; he'd been irascible at times about what he persisted in calling her "adolescent" schedule ("I mean, who the hell sleeps until noon? Seriously?"). He agreed vaguely, although I could tell her visit was losing its appeal for him. "She's okay with Samuel—not great, though—and her cooking is good—when she bothers to do it. But it never seems to cross her mind we're footing the bills. I mean, does she never think about money? Has she never thought to contribute something? To give us a gift, at least? Would it *hurt* to get a box of cookies?"

"You looking for *him*?" There was a sharp tap on the car window; it was Luna Lilly jerking her Alice-banded head in the direction of Kent's office. We nodded.

"He won't be down today, not if I'm any judge," Luna remarked, leaning into the car, a trace of triumph in her voice. The smell of sandalwood flooded in around her, hot and heady, laced with an acrid tang of sweat. "I heard him yesterday afternoon. Singing, banging about. After you left. I called up to him, I said, you'll party on your *own* tonight. Don't you come looking for me, I know what you've been up to with that cleaning assistant." She nodded sharply in the direction of the dry cleaner's shop. "I mean, who needs their goddamn socks dry-cleaned? The drunk, cheating, two-timing bastard—! I could still hear him when I left for home, yelling, shouting, carrying on. He'll be dead to the world today. Dead, dead, *dead*."

She was clearly pleased to be the bearer of bad tidings; her small mouth was twisted into an angry smile, her eyes needle-bright. "Just thought you should know," she finished righteously, then, pausing only to peer curiously into the backseat of our car, her eyes taking in the baby seat and the mess of stuffed toys, she waddled back to her office. Tom got out and went after her, loudly jangling his keys; I followed behind.

"You ignoring me?" Luna turned around, hands on her cello hips. "Fine. But you'll see. There's not much you can do to help him, he's past it now. And you won't need *those*; he won't have locked his office door, never does. Anybody can take anything they want from his place, any confidential documents. You can get anything you want out of those big filing cabinets." ("We'll see about that," Tom muttered.) "Not that I ever go snooping, you understand, through people's private affairs. Well, you do what you want," she finished, watching us wend our way up the blue-carpeted interior stairs, "he won't get up for you today unless you're a glass of whisky sour."

We pushed open the door to Kent's office, which was, as Luna had forecast, unlocked. The place reeked of booze, vomit, and cigarettes; the curtains were drawn, and it took us a while to make out Kent's form collapsed in a chair. The phone lay next to him on the table, cable pulled out of the wall, an empty glass upturned beside it.

"Kent—Kent, wake up," Tom said, crouching down and taking the lawyer's thin white hand in his. Kent's hair was loose and half-covering his face; I kneeled over him and pushed it away from his nose, eyes, and mouth. "Kent, are you okay?"

He groaned, opened his eyes, and said something like "rrrm-mmf." His unbuttoned red shirt exposed his too-thin chest, the lines of his ribs, his dry, mottled skin. "I've got a bottle of water in my bag," I said. I rustled through half a dozen tissue pouches to find it. "Here, Kent, take this. It's just a little water . . ."

His arm shot out, suddenly and unexpectedly, and he pushed the bottle out of my hands. Half of it slopped out onto the carpet; I grabbed it a second before the entire contents were lost, then looked hopelessly at Tom. "What are we going to do?" I hissed, sitting back on my haunches.

Luna Lilly, we suddenly realized, was standing just behind us, arms akimbo. "I told you, there's nothing you can do," she said glee-fully. "He's a low-down dirty drunk, has been for years, there's noth-ing anyone can do. It was bound to happen, always does, he can't stay off the stuff, specially not when a bill comes in. He'll sleep it off, then as soon as he can lift a glass to his mouth he'll start on the next bottle. Leave him to it, that's my advice."

"We'll take things from here." Tom was cool; under his unwavering gaze hers eventually dropped, and a few moments later we heard her heavy footsteps on the stairs.

"Kent. Kent—are you all right?" I tried again hesitantly, peering into Kent's face, then pulling back in spite of myself. The stench of alcohol on his breath was almost overpowering.

"Uh—yeah, fine—fine. Just had a little—uh—party last night." Kent's voice was creaky, as if he hadn't used it in years; he licked his dry, peeling lips with a hint of a grayish tongue. "Nothing—to worry about. Now then—uh. Medical examiner's report—on the table. Faxed yesterday. Time for you two to make yourselves useful. Take it. Then—leave me alone."

He lifted a shaking hand to the side of his head and covered his eyes. "Don't want to—" He licked his lips again, and coughed hard. "Go on, I said! Make yourselves useful. I've got my own things to do—uh, business letters and such. You get out of here."

Tom, I realized, was holding a copy of the medical examiner's report, which he had pried from the lips of the ancient fax machine. He scanned it, then folded it up and put it in his pocket. "All right Kent, if that's what you want. Let's go, Q," he said, placing the remnants of the bottle of water within Kent's reach.

I looked at my husband, then at the figure on the chair. "We *can't* just leave him here, Tom, he's in a terrible state, he might—choke on his own vomit or something . . ." I hissed, aghast.

Tom shook his head. "Ms. Lilly will keep an eye out, even if it's just because she wants to come up and crow over him."

"But—"

"Unless you want to pick him up, take him home, and hose him off."

"Well—no."

"Right. I don't think that's what he wants either."

"Ya *still here*?" Kent asked blearily, blinking up at us with rheumy eyes. "Why do I have to do everything 'round here? Can't a man get

some time to himself, attend to his own affairs? You two—seriously—
it's time! Time for you to act like a couple grown-ups for a change.
Jesus . . ."

He was still grumbling as I followed my husband doubtfully out
of the building and into the sunlight. "Behold the skeleton," Tom
said, as we got into the car.

51

⁓

Jeanie

When I arrived home from Quiet Lanes, Q met me with a
letter. It had taken over three weeks to find me; Ann Dougins received it at college and forwarded it onto the flat,
where Una would normally have used it to snort lines, but I suppose she was feeling guilty about kicking me out on the street (and
possibly about allowing Dukey, whoever—or whatever—he may be,
to sleep in my bed). So she actually bothered to send it on, complete
with a big "Love Una" and a lipstick smackeroo on the back.

Dear Ms. Boothroyd,

it began politely and with due political properness:

We recently contacted Professor Humphrey Sibelius Mordaunt at Kingsbury College to ask if he could recommend recent graduates of the Masters in Social Work and Social Policy as applicants for a new programme to be established in the London Borough of Southwark. This new government-funded programme, part of a nationwide Supporting the Third Age Initiative, has two major goals: firstly, to provide support for older people (65+) who are struggling financially in weekly day centres; and secondly, to provide counseling for those caring for pension-age citizens through a monthly magazine and twice-monthly morning drop-in. We are seeking well-qualified applicants to manage this exciting new programme for older people in Southwark and Professor Mordaunt enthusiastically suggested your name and suitability for the position. If you are interested and would like to find out more, please visit us on the Web, where you will also find an application form (see "So you want to apply?", bottom right, third column, red bubble). We hope to hear from you soon.

I hastily logged onto the Web site and read the information about the Supporting the Third Age Initiative, hardly able to believe my eyes—"*in our modern times of economic hardship, extra support for those struggling on diminished pensions is crucial.*" But more surprising even than the thought of increased government funding for old people was the thought that Professor Mordaunt "enthusiastically suggested" me for the position. He *did*? *Why*? It couldn't have been my stellar B- performance, after all, so clearly something else possessed the man to put forward my name—unless, of course, he still had me mixed up with Cindy or Amy, or someone else entirely from the course.

And then I thought about it as I worked my way ruminatively through a bran muffin, and I realized with a sensation of shock that even if Professor Mordaunt suggested me in a drunken haze after cavorting with his secretary one night, I actually wanted this job—

really, truly. And not just because it would pay the bills (although let's face it, that was recommendation enough). I loved working with older people; I loved Quiet Lanes. It was something I could actually build a life around. Everyone else on my course in London enjoyed helping children—because there was hope for their future, I suppose, and because children (even the ones who've set their parents' beds on fire with a blowtorch) look sweet and vulnerable, little round faces covered in goo. Me, I liked the stories older people told; I loved hearing about Sue-Ellen's husbands and Teddy's lost wife and Ken's raids over northern France in 1944. I liked the peaceful order, the familiar routine, the cheery hum of conversation. No one was going to put their fingers in the electric socket or grow up to murder their sister at Quiet Lanes, it was all rather more predictable. Serve tea, lift people, clean hands, water plants, talk. I was no Florence Nightingale. But I loved it.

So I punched in my application details with a fervent sense of purpose. I can help the older people of Southwark, I thought; I can help them get something out of life in the community, and—well, there was nothing about improving the standard of nursing care in the job description, but I could spend the next five years of my life banging my head against the system trying to improve things, couldn't I?

Only then I got to the bit where you press "send," and I couldn't; it wouldn't accept the application because I was three days past the deadline. "Please e-mail us by clicking *here* to learn about future job opportunities in the London Borough of Southwark," invited a cheery pop-up. "Thank you for your interest in the London Borough of Southwark." I stared at the screen, feeling my newfound sense of purpose and inspiration ebbing away. A near miss. Good try, but not this time. No, not yet; no, not here.

I clicked *here*, and up popped a small box for my e-mail address and a second, larger rectangular message box. "Please tell us your field of work, so that we may send you details of suitable positions as they become available." And then, because my school motto (patience and humility) was obviously a nonsense, I punched in a message explaining that I wanted *one* job in particular, the one whose deadline had passed, and suggesting they should consider my application in spite of its lateness. Professor Mordaunt of Kingsbury College recommended me for this position, I went on, confidently. And I *am* amply qualified for the job. Of course it wouldn't let me attach a CV, so instead I typed in everything I could possibly think of that might persuade them of my suitability—every placement, every bit of work experience, every piece of course work on "issues facing our ageing community," and my volunteer work at Quiet Lanes ("a first step toward a comparative study of geriatric care in the States and in south London in a time of deepening recession"). I really want this job, I said at the end. I want to make caring for older people the focus of my career.

I pressed "send," and held my breath. Everything went blank. There was a pause, in which I stared at the large screen of white and wondered why I forgot to *save* my epistle of self-confidence before sending it off into the vortex. And then: "Thank you for contacting us, your message has been received"—a rush of relief!

I literally ran downstairs to tell Q all about it—the job, Professor Mordaunt's recommendation, my application. When I'd finished, she nodded approvingly. "I'll admit I thought it was weird when you said you were going to work at Quiet Lanes," she said. "Frankly I got the impression Paul maybe maneuvered you into it. I couldn't think why. But I was obviously wrong," she continued. "I hadn't realized you were so committed."

"Didn't you?" I said. "Really? How strange!"

"Phone Alison and tell her all about it," she prompted, "she'll be really pleased. We were talking about you just this morning, actually. She was saying she wondered if you'd really considered all the options in social work. She even said perhaps you needed an interview with a career counselor. I mean, I know she can be a bit officious, and to the best of my knowledge she's never sat down with a career counselor in her life, I didn't know she even knew they existed, but I still thought it was a really good point. I told her I could arrange something down in New Haven for you, and she—"

Honestly, I liked it better when they didn't talk to each other.

52

Q

Tom was onto his second memory stick, and he had the look of a man possessed. Every time we wanted to eat a meal, we had to wade through tumbling piles of files on the dining-room table. And books began arriving in the mail all week from Amazon, with titles like *Running Your Own Private Practice*, *Practical Law*, and *So You Think You Can Cut It in the Real World?*

It was early fall; we were moving into our second season in Connecticut, thanks to Paul's generosity ("No, no, you're doing me a favor; old houses don't like to stay empty."). And now at last there seemed to be a rhythm to our lives, a regular beat of gentle expectation as the leaves began to flicker with color and the nights turned cool. The sea in the mornings was like cold glass against my skin.

The woman who sold fish from her white van to locals on Mondays knew my name, and I knew hers. I knew when fresh lobsters arrived at The Lobster Pot. The general store had begun to stock my preferred brand of diapers in Samuel's size and extra portions of dried sweetened pineapple—Tom's favorite afternoon snack—in the "serve yourself" bins (new deliveries arrived on Wednesdays). I'd finally persuaded the *New York Times* to deliver to our mailbox. I'd weeded out the leggy yellow flowers from the arugula in the garden, so we had fresh salad each night for dinner. Tomatoes were ripening in pots along the deck.

Every morning I collected cicadas in cupped hands from the floor of the bathroom and dropped them gently out the window. I knew to avoid bustling wild turkeys on the road by day and soft-footed deer at nights. We watched flaming cardinals in the trees at lunchtime, while at night a raccoon snuffed at the back door and possums hesitantly vacuumed up the crumbs of our meal upon the deck. I knew to stay clear when the skunk made his leisurely evening shuffle past the front door as the moon came up. I heard the creak of wood board floors contracting with the fresh cold air in the dead of night, and I was not afraid.

Every afternoon, when Samuel took his nap, Tom and I made ourselves cups of coffee, which we brought onto the deck, and then we talked. It was a precious time of peace and quiet. The day after Kent's collapse, we called Luna Lilly to check up on the old man again ("Oh, *he's* all right, can you hear him?" she asked scornfully, holding the telephone up so we could listen to his high-pitched rendition of "The Star-spangled Banner"), then we discussed Emmie's case. Tom smoothed out the medical examiner's report that we'd collected from Kent's office, and we pored over it together on the round wicker table.

According to the document, filed at the State Medical Examiner's Office, Angela Vaughan was pronounced dead by Dr. Philip Reid at 9:07 a.m. on May 1, 2001. There were no signs of violence in the home, and the child's body was not covered by blankets or any other obvious suffocation hazards. She was lying on her side in her crib, and appeared to have been dead for three to four hours when the doctor arrived on the scene.

Dr. Philip Reid, the document claimed, had seen the child once in the two weeks prior to death, on April 19, at which time the child had been suffering from a slight cold but had seemed, in all other respects, healthy. The mother reported that nothing unusual had taken place since the doctor's visit, although she now recalled that the child's cold had appeared to worsen, rather than improve. "Mother was intending to take the child to see Dr. Reid on Wednesday morning (May 2) if child not better," the notes remarked.

The report was filed by Lieutenant Anthony E. Driscoll, his signature a careful flourish along the bottom. Unless we could find a chink in his story, a gap in the narrative, it was going to be hard to prove Emmie's account of the facts.

"We need to talk to him," Tom said, standing up, "to Driscoll, as soon as possible. I'll call to make the appointment for Monday."

"What if Kent's not sober by then?"

"We'll go by ourselves."

"By *ourselves*?" I returned disbelievingly. "Are you serious? Why on earth would Driscoll talk to us? He's never met us before."

"He's bound to have heard we're working for Kent. Everyone around here has."

"Well—okay. But like Kent said, he's the only one who understands how the local system works. I think he'd want to be involved at an important meeting with the local cop."

"I've been thinking about that, Q." Tom propped his arms on the deck railing. A pair of blue jays was screeching in the branches of a reddening maple on the far edge of the garden; we watched the bright flashes of blue darting in and out of the fire-tipped leaves. "I think he's stage-managed this whole thing to get us to take over— oh, not consciously. But he set us up all the same. He couldn't bring himself to hand the firm over to us sober, so he's done it drunk, forcing our hand into the bargain. He knew perfectly well we were coming, you know—didn't it strike you as strange he tumbled off the wagon hours before we arrived? He can't handle the firm anymore, not in these times. He wants to retire on whatever savings he has left and catch sea bass. I think he got us the medical examiner's report yesterday afternoon, and decided he was done."

The blue jays shrieked and jeered; I could hardly hear myself think. "I can't imagine you're right. Now he's seen us he's bound to sober up," I said firmly. "He'll be a bit embarrassed, he'll drink a pint of water, and by tomorrow, Monday at the latest, he'll be fine. I think Kent will be able to come with us," I continued, standing up as Samuel's sleepy snuffles turned to wails on the monitor. "It's probably just a weekend thing. He fell off the wagon on a Friday—he's not the first alcoholic to do that, I'm sure."

Tom cocked an eyebrow. "I think I'll make that phone call," he returned coolly.

53

~

Jeanie

With Samuel propped on my knee, I typed "geriatrics" into every social work database I could find, while Tom and Q were out. I found about seventy-five jobs that required the applicant to manage several hundred octogenarians and a fleet of undertrained volunteers. I found one job that involved running a day center for geriatrics with mental health problems, but it would require moving to Poole. I applied for it anyway; I'd never been to Poole.

Then I took Samuel to Quiet Lanes, which I'd been meaning to do ever since Paul suggested it. The fascination of a small child drove everyone "crazy," as Mrs. Forrest inevitably predicted, clutching her hands to her pointy nose, and Samuel was so entranced by the attention he didn't cry once. Passed from hand to hand, from knee to knee, he felt soft faces with a gentle hand, and even laughed when Ken made loud farting noises against his stomach. Sue-Ellen thrilled everyone by doing her palmistry (Samuel will apparently enjoy an extraordinarily long life, vast quantities of cash, and a beautiful wife from India) and Tim gave Samuel a cranial massage that sent him into a peaceful doze. He really seemed to be getting better, just as Alison predicted.

"I'm thinking of working with old people—seniors, I mean," I explained to Sue-Ellen, in a quiet corner, "for my career. I've applied for a job back home in London. If they accept my application I think there's a good chance I'll get it."

"Marvelous idea, honey!" she exclaimed. "It's been wonderful, having you around these last few weeks, someone who comes because they *want* to, not because their school tells them they have to." She patted my hand. "You volunteered to work with us out of the good of your heart, Jeanie; we appreciate that. You've restored my faith in young people. The others feel the same way. We've had some kids here, you can tell they're just thinking of a grade at the end of a page, we're just a means to an end. Not like you."

My heart lurched. "Sue-Ellen," I began, and she looked innocently up at me.

"Yes, dear?"

I opened my mouth, and then I closed it again. I couldn't—well, put it this way, I didn't tell her the truth. What would be the point in puncturing her illusion? Instead, I returned the pressure on her hand. "If I've found my way, it's got a lot to do with you," I explained, and I was absolutely sincere about that. "If things are making some sense to me now, I think it's because I met you. I really mean it. Thank you."

I arrived in our kitchen at home an hour or so later to find Q murmuring in hushed tones on the telephone. She looked up and reached immediately for Samuel; then an expression of conscious guilt passed over her face: "Oh, *Jeanie*, hello, I didn't realize you were—uh—home," she said, in the loud tones you use to tell someone on the other end of the phone that the person they're talking about has just walked into the room. Alison, I presumed, or possibly Mum. I scowled.

"Yes. Would you rather I wasn't?" I replied irritably.

"Of course not, Jeanie, don't be silly," my sister returned patiently. "But you did say you'd help me clean up the sitting room this morning, I was waiting for you, and then you *completely* disappeared."

I stomped upstairs. Alison didn't seem to phone me so much these days, she'd opened up a permanent line to my sister instead, so when I saw a message icon on my mobile, which I'd left on the table, I wondered for a dizzying second who it might be. I dialed my messages and pressed the phone a little closer to my ear.

It was Dave. "We haven't been in touch for a while. Thought you might want to know I got back all right. I've just got back from Ranger and Magsie's; fancied a break. So I went down to their place in Brighton. They're planning a trip to the Netherlands to meet a bloke who's going to teach them about harnessing the power of the wind, and I might go with them for a bit. It's something to do. Just wanted you to know in case—well, in case you tried to reach me."

I put down the phone, feeling faintly sick. Poor rudderless Dave, meandering around the countries of northern Europe, blown hither and thither by the wind.

But there were no other messages.

54

~

Q

All day Sunday we called Kent's offices; no reply. Finally, at four o'clock, we put Samuel in his car seat and drove to Cheasford. The two-tone pickup was still in the parking lot, but there was no answer at his door—which was now unexpectedly locked, the chain slid into place. "Maybe he's—you know," I said nervously, not quite meeting Tom's eye above Samuel's head, and then, just as I was debating whether to dial 911, we heard a thin, bleary, but unmistakable voice. "How many times do I have to tell you to—leave me in peace? I have a lot of things, invoices and papers and stuff, to do here. Are you two working, or what?"

Tom shrugged. "I'm not wasting any more time on this," he said impatiently. "He obviously wants us to take charge. And frankly, he's in no condition to take control of Emmie Cormier's case anyway. This has gone on long enough." After peering through the keyhole and assuring myself that Kent was on a chair, not ready to jump off a rafter, I reluctantly followed my husband back down the stairs.

"We're here to see Lieutenant Driscoll," Tom announced, when we arrived on the premises of the small purpose-built block just after lunchtime on Monday. The bald desk clerk was blandly bored.

"Kenton Tyler's associates—yes, yes—I remember. I'll let him know you're here."

We sat down in the small, empty waiting room. After a few minutes we heard a buzz; the door opened, and the clerk appeared on the other side. "He'll see you, but he's only got ten minutes to spare, he's *very* busy at the moment," he told us, managing to achieve an expression of official officiousness as he ushered us into an interior office. Lieutenant Driscoll—who was about forty, with a simple face, sandy hair and eyelashes—was fiddling aimlessly with a pen when we entered; he began hastily typing at his computer, then gestured to two plastic chairs. As I sat down, I noticed a picture of a little girl in a pink tutu facing him on his desk.

"Old man Tyler said he had a coupla city lawyers working with him," he began. "You think you can cut it up here, eh?" he added, with a short laugh. "If lawyering's anything like police work, you don't stand a chance. You need to be *from* a town if you're going to understand it, the *heart* of a town, that is." He sat back on his chair and looked over at us with a vastly superior expression.

"I'm sure you're right, Lieutenant Driscoll," Tom answered respectfully. "We've only been here a few months, but already we can tell that working in a town like this takes real care, real commitment. But we'll try to help Mr. Tyler as best we can."

Driscoll nodded. "Sure, sure, I get it. Not much you can do for that girl Cormier, though; she's a—harrumph," he finished lamely, looking at me.

"We know the score," Tom said. "Look, we just need to get a few answers, get the story straight, so we don't look like idiots in court. Some of this stuff—" he got out his BlackBerry—"some of this stuff Tyler wants us to get, it's real obvious, you know? Just details. Like, what was the name of the doctor on the scene when her kid died?"

The policeman visibly relaxed. "Jeez, half the folks in town could tell you that. Between you and me, Kenton Tyler needs to walk out of that practice before he *falls* out of it, or *off* of it, know what I mean?" he added, guffawing. "It was Reid, Phil Reid." He leaned back in his chair. "Phil Reid has been the family's doctor for years."

Tom tapped *Philip Reid* into his BlackBerry. "That's great. You're being a tremendous help to us! Now then, the other people in the house were—I'm guessing the mother, her father, and her grandfather, right?"

Driscoll nodded again, fingertips held lightly together. "Sure. Terrible upset they were," he added soberly, a quick glance at the tutu girl on his desk.

"We have a baby boy ourselves, actually," I put in suddenly. "My husband here, and I. His name is Samuel. He's just a few months old. Now I'm a mother, this kind of story—I feel it very differently, don't you? Before I had kids I didn't quite grasp what the death of a child would mean. But now—just think—think what it would be like if you could—y'know. Never kiss her good-night . . ."

Lieutenant Driscoll gulped. "I can't imagine it," he said gruffly. He reached out unconsciously for the photograph.

"The thing we don't understand is how a child can just die, without warning, in the middle of the night," Tom picked up the thread. "I don't mind telling you, Lieutenant Driscoll, since we heard the story about the Vaughan baby my wife has hardly been able to leave our son's bedside. She's too frightened to part from him in case he vanishes like that, without warning or symptoms. One minute healthy—the next minute gone." He snapped his fingers for emphasis.

Driscoll had put down the photograph and was leaning forward to face me now. "I know what you mean. Yeah. But it wasn't quite like that," he explained earnestly. "The kid had been ill for a week at least, maybe longer. Emmie told me at the time, I remember. She kept saying she wished she'd taken the baby into the hospital."

"Is that right? Well, that does make me feel better!" I said. "Do you happen to know what those symptoms were, Lieutenant?" I went on. "It would really put my mind at rest, I think."

"She had this cold that got worse and worse, then she was out of sorts, acting kind of funny; Emmie said she'd had the doctor . . ."

He stopped himself suddenly. There was a silence. Tom and

I kept our eyes off each other. "Said she'd had the doctor—?" Tom prompted.

But Driscoll's face had clouded over. "Had the doctor out a week or two before she died. Just like I said before." His body was stiff with suspicion.

"But Dr. Reid wasn't able to help her?" I asked politely.

Driscoll drummed his fingers against the long metal desk. "You'll have to ask Reid what it was they discussed," he said, his tone now distinctly surly. "The way I remember it, when he came out to see the kid, there wasn't a whole lot wrong with it. Emmie should have called him out again, when the kid got worse, but she didn't. I submitted a report about all of this to the medical examiner. You'll find the details there." He stood up abruptly.

Tom made one last attempt. "I don't suppose we could see your own notes on the death scene, by any chance, Lieutenant?" he asked, standing up to face the young police officer. "The internal police report? Just in case there's something there—some small detail—that might help us—?"

"Help you with what?" Driscoll said immediately, fronting up to Tom, and when my husband mentioned something vague about Emmie's court case with Ryan, Driscoll's answer was short. "Emmie Cormier is a deadbeat, always has been, always will be. Whatever you need you'll find in the medical examiner's report." He opened the door. "If Emmie Cormier loses that kid, she'll have no one but herself to blame. You tell old man Tyler that, from me. If he's sober enough to understand you, of course."

55

⁓

Jeanie

Just as I was beginning to give up hope, I was asked to schedule an interview in Southwark. A formal "please contact us at your earliest convenience" e-mail accompanied by a second "dear Jeanie" message from someone named Sandra arrived on Monday morning. "Sorry our initial letter got delayed, we received your message though, loud and clear. Can you send us a hard copy for the files?"

Someone in the world really seemed to want me—for a job! A real job! Ludicrously excited, I spent half the morning sketching out plans for "Third Age" day centers. I would bring in financial counselors to help people who'd lost their savings and masseurs to improve morale, I decided. I'd ask Mum for advice on yoga for the over-sixties, and perhaps Alison could help with contacts for a program in sculpture and art. And perhaps I could collect stories from the seniors on how people survived financial crises in the twentieth century—in the 1930s; after the war—to make them feel like useful and valued members of society. We could even turn the stories into a book—!

My happy sense of purpose was only briefly checked when Dave phoned me a few hours later to tell me (sheepishly, with deep embarrassment) that over the weekend he got together with—*Ellen*.

I won't deny that at first I gulped. The thought of them together brought a strange lump to my throat—Dave finding consolation in those plump round arms, Dave burying his head in that generous white bosom—but, as he nervously explained how they'd got together, I found myself making peace with it all. Mam died late Friday night, poor lady, breathing out her last with Dave and the rest of the family arranged by her side. Ellen was there, weeping salt tears for the confused old woman, and their hands met in grief, and the rest followed quite naturally.

"You're not cross with me, are you?" Dave went on anxiously. "I mean, it was a bit quick and all . . ." his voice tapered off into embarrassed silence. I laughed with the sudden happy consciousness of complete delivery from guilt, then told him I was actually *looking forward* to seeing them together, as a couple. When I got home.

"To be completely honest with you, Dave," I said—although frankly I wasn't, there was some stuff I missed out—"I need to come back, see my friends, get on with my life. It's all right over here, but after a while you miss your mates, people you can really trust. And I've got an interview for a social work job, so things are really coming together in my career," I went on semi-self-importantly, because *I* needed to have a story to tell him too, I couldn't quite bear to be upstaged by Dave.

"I'm glad for you, Jeanie," Dave said. His voice was sincere. "And I'm glad you don't mind about me and Ellen. You and me—well, we weren't really right for each other, were we? Whereas Ellen . . . she's suggested I pick up carpentry again, Jeanie, she found this little stool I built as a kid, and—she thinks maybe I can sell them, earn a bit of cash. I know it's just been a few days but—it's *so nice* to be with Ellen. I'm really happy, Jeanie! And I did want you to know . . ."

Then we talked about Una and Lolly—who was, apparently, the enormous basketball player my flatemate got her paws on just before I flew to America. Apparently, he more or less moved into her bedroom that night, and never moved out. Dukey was his enormous German shepherd, and since I'm allergic to dogs, the whole thing worked out quite well. "Would you like me to help you move your stuff, Jeanie?" Dave asked earnestly. "I think I can get Badger to help, as long as you rent a hybrid van to move across town." I laughed, and promised him I'd think about it.

56

~

Q

Driscoll was about to tell us that Emmie called Reid out to see Angela more than once, but he stopped himself in time," Tom remarked after dinner Monday night. He'd just spoken to Paul, who apparently wanted advice on a property conflict he'd run into, involving a Brooklyn-based judge. Jeanie was snoozing on the sofa, half-listening to music on her iPod. My husband poured two glasses of cognac, a small one for me, a large one for him. "For some reason, Driscoll's gone along with Reid—he filled in the report just as Reid asked him to do, and he's protecting Reid now."

Of course we'd checked in on Kent once more after seeing the lieutenant, but he claimed he couldn't see us "because I—uh—got some important file—uh—arranging to do."

"How are we going to prove anything?" I asked gloomily, resting my head on Tom's shoulder. "We could try to subpoena Driscoll's notes, I suppose—"

"Good luck," Tom retorted. "I'm sure he's doctored them by now."

High up in the sky a plane cruised by in the darkness, a steady receding drone.

"Q, we need to think of a different way into this," Tom said at last. "Let's go over it again—what we know, what we don't know." He walked over to the table and opened his laptop.

We talked through the case, through our conversations with Driscoll, Reid, Kent, and Emmie, while Tom tapped out notes. Noticing the clicking keys, Jeanie looked up. "What are you doing?" she asked curiously, and when we explained, she pulled out her earplugs, swung down her legs, and came over. "Ooh, this is just like an Agatha Christie," she said comfortably, pulling out a chair. She watched the timeline unfold on Tom's screen, her head tilted to one side. I caught the expression of disapproval in Tom's green eyes as he glanced sideways at her; we could just hear the faint tinny thump of her music still going full-blast.

"So what are the gaps?" he asked finally, when we'd filled in every detail we could think of. "I don't just mean about Driscoll and Reid's relationship, I mean about the circumstances surrounding Angela's death. We've got to find something to help us shake Reid's credibility, Q." He rubbed his dark head. "This is serious. Unless we can call the medical examiner's report into question, Emmie will go into court against Ryan looking criminally negligent. Ryan'll clean up."

"This Reye's syndrome, where does it come from?" my sister asked, gazing attentively at the screen, hands resting on her jean-clad hips. "I mean, is it a virus? Can anyone get it? Or just kids? I've never even heard of it. It can't be that common, can it?"

Tom and I looked at each other. "We don't know much about that, actually," I replied, considering. "I thought about that when you were talking to Emmie, Tom. You described the symptoms, then you said no one knows exactly what causes it. Is there a suggestion in the research that some children have a genetic predisposition to it, maybe? Is *that* something Reid missed?"

Tom shrugged. "No harm in asking Ian, I guess."

He picked up his phone; after a brief conversation with his father's colleague, he closed the cell again with a frustrated snap. "Nothing to do with genetics. Nothing at all, or at least that's the current state of research. It's a strange disease: Ian says it's only been identified in the last few decades, and it's not much understood. As happened with Angela, it often follows a fairly minor respiratory illness, and leads to serious chemical imbalances in the body's major organs. But it can be misidentified because the symptoms are sort of nonspecific." Tom topped up his glass, and then—after a second's hesitation—splashed a drink out for Jeanie. "It's also unusual; Angela was unlucky. It's become rare since aspirin was contraindicated for children and teenagers a decade or so ago. Apparently there seems to be some causal connection, although no one quite understands . . ."

My last sip of cognac rose into my nose; I felt it burning up the tubes from the back of my throat into my head as the meaning of Tom's words hit my brain. I inhaled and choked, and choked again. *"Aspirin?"* There seemed to be fire in my eyeballs.

Tom and Jeanie began frantically thumping my back. "What's wrong, Q?"

I stood up coughing, gasping for air, and knocked over the chair. It fell with a tremendous bang that seemed to shake the house. *"Reid prescribed Angela aspirin!"* I panted, wiping my streaming face and nose on my shirt sleeve. "He did, he did!"

"What? He *did*?"

"How do you know?"

"Emmie told us," I explained, gaining breath. "I only remember because I was surprised to hear of a child's taking something other than acetaminophen—Tylenol, you know. That's what we were told to use when Samuel had his vaccines, don't you remember, Tom? I remember thinking, maybe different states suggest different painkillers for infants, I meant to ask Alison what parents use in

England, and then I forgot all about it. But I know—I just know—that Emmie said Reid told her to give Angela aspirin."

"My God. I wonder, I wonder," Tom began slowly, "I wonder if she still has the box! I wonder if it was on prescription . . ."

"Phone her, phone her!" yelped Jeanie, virtually throwing the phone at me. She was jumping up and down, eyes brightly delighted, ponytail jiggling. "Phone her *right now*!"

"Emmie," I began nervously, when the young mother picked up the phone a few moments later, "I need to ask you a question, and it's going to sound pretty weird . . ."

"Oh, it's you." Emmie's voice was flat. "I can't talk now, I've got my Bible study group here. Call again when we're done. In about half an hour." The phone went dead.

I called back immediately. "Emmie, I'm sorry to bother you, but I need to ask you a really important question," I began carefully, before she could speak. "It's about old medicines you may have in your cupboard. Well, one in particular . . ." I heard her talking to someone else at the other end; it was a few moments before she came on the line again. "Medicines? Are you collecting for developing countries too?" she asked interestedly; and then she added, "you're too late. Elizabeth Summers took all that old stuff. At the beginning of the meeting, as a matter of fact. First come, first served, you know? And it's all in a good cause. Listen, like I said, I'll call you when I'm done. Thanks."

She hung up again, and this time, when I redialed, she didn't pick up.

A knot seemed to be tying itself in my intestines. "Someone called Elizabeth Summers just collected the medicines. Something about needing them for developing countries, apparently," I explained, and Tom's face paled.

"Elizabeth Summers—Elizabeth Summers . . . wait, Q, wasn't that *Dr. Reid's assistant*? The woman Kent was sweet-talking the other day?"

"Tom, do you think—"

"What's going on? What are you talking about? Who on earth is Elizabeth Summers?" Jeanie screeched, but we ignored her. "I don't know," Tom mused, "it could be a coincidence, but maybe . . . maybe Reid realized we were onto something the other day, in his office. Maybe he remembers the aspirin, maybe he'd hoped no one would ever realize—it's certainly possible. Let's drive over to Emmie's house now. We'll see if we can catch this Summers woman before she leaves the house with the medicines. There just *might* be time. Jeanie," (touching her awkwardly on the shoulder) "um—Jeanie, will you babysit, please?"

Jeanie's face was a comical mask of frustration. "I *knew* you were going to say that!" she said exasperatedly as we flew out of the house.

57

~

Jeanie

So when are you going to see your young gentleman next, honey?" Sue-Ellen asked me in the afternoon at Quiet Lanes, grinning. "The one you want, I mean. The one who keeps you up at night, thinking about him."

I patted her hand gently. "You don't understand," I explained. "He's not right for me. *Really.*"

Sue-Ellen shrugged, then heaved herself carefully out of her chair. "You know best, honey," she said, with a sigh. "Of course in my day it was all about men, about getting a husband. Now you can make your own way. But I still think you're pining for this man, yes I do!" I watched her walk back slowly to her bedroom for a nap. Already she was much less steady on her feet.

When I got back to the house, I phoned Alison to tell her to stop gossiping with Q about me; it'd been getting very irritating. Not surprisingly, she denied she'd been doing anything of the sort. "Really," she said crossly, "the two of you seem to take it in turns to get annoyed with me. It's very dysfunctional. Here I am, sitting all by myself in England, wondering how my two sisters are doing on the other side of the world, wishing I could be there helping them, and they—they badger me, one after the other. Really, I don't think it's fair. Now tell me," she went on, without pausing, "*when* is that handsome American coming back to the house?"

"What—what handsome American?"

"Paul Dupont—isn't that his name? The fabulously rich man who—yes, I Googled him—rowed for Oxford in the Boat Race, dated a film star for two years, and owns two quite important Gauguin sketches, not to mention an Audubon. And surfaces repeatedly in the *Tribune* and the *Times* as 'one of the most brilliant legal minds of his generation.' *That* handsome American. Don't worry, I haven't said anything to Q about him," she whispered. I could hear a purr of self-satisfaction in her voice. "You underestimate me," she continued silkily. "Would I betray you to Q?"

"By which you mean," I returned furiously, finding my voice, "that *you* like being the one in the know. Or am I underestimating you again, Alison?"

"Almost certainly, dear!" she replied, sounding utterly delighted.

"My love life isn't just a source of amusement for you and Q," I scolded. "What, are you living vicariously through me?"

"Jeanie, do you even know what that means?"

When I'm running half of Southwark, she won't be able to speak to me like that anymore.

Later, much later, while I was waiting for my sister and Tom to return from their frantic trip to see Emmie, I reread the article that appeared about me today in the local newspaper. I carefully cut it out, put it in an envelope, and addressed it to my sister. Then I wrote AIR MAIL in big, confident pink marker all over it. Alison didn't know that I was a "prominent British researcher." She would soon!

BRITISH RESEARCHER COMPARES
SENIOR CARE IN UK AND US

by Julie Van Der Veeze,
Cheasford Times. *A CT exclusive!*

Jean Bothroyd, a twenty-four-year-old researcher from London, has demonstrated what different countries can learn even in a recession by comparing strategies for senior care.

After an intensive study (and hands-on experience in our own Quiet Lanes Senior Care), Boothroyed has identified a series of strategies implemented in certain US centers that, she says, UK-based geriatric care can easily and cheaply develop. "I have compared a number of institutions in Connecticut with centers serving a comparable demographic in London. British Senior Care centers are chronically short of cash. Many are underfunded by the NHS, not to mention caught between responsibilities to local social services departments and to fee-paying individuals. But the focus on collaborative decision-making that many US centers now espouse, can easily be implemented in UK centers, by adopting and adapting existing support networks and entertainment strategies. In fact, I think the British government may be starting to catch on," said Bouthroid with a smile.

Joan, who is twenty-six, was full of praise for Quiet Lanes. "The patients have their own rooms," she said. "And the flowers are really pretty."

I was rather proud of that bit about demographics. I was almost tempted to send a copy to Paul.

58

~

Q

We sprinted to the car—or, rather, Tom sprinted; I puffed ten paces behind, cursing the extra twenty pounds of baby weight I'd gained and somehow clung on to grimly these past months. "Do you actually remember the way?" I gasped, levering myself into the passenger seat as Tom revved the engine. "Sure. Of course. Er—maybe," he finished, less confidently, peering into the darkness.

"Maybe" was right. "Tom, I think we're heading toward the sea," I offered at one point, and after much swearing and yelling he finally admitted that I was right, as we rounded a sharp bend at the bottom of a road and the ocean reared up in front of us. We turned around and began to crisscross lower Connecticut, shouting at each other, rip-

ping at maps in our hasty efforts to read them, craning to read faded
street signs in the moonlight, and generally making a complete hash
of the twenty-minute drive to Emmie's house. I threw us completely
off course at one point by swearing that a disused mine we passed was
the one near Emmie's house (it wasn't); we finally arrived at Emmie's
home a full forty minutes after the last Bible study guest had left.

When Emmie answered the door, and explained that Elizabeth
Summers had gone, we both collapsed wearily onto the steps of the
deck at the front of her house, shivering and roundly defeated. Emmie stared at us. "Do you mind telling me what in the world is going
on?" she asked, arms crossed over her loose black T-shirt.

I explained that we had hoped to find a bottle of aspirin drops in
her medicine cupboard—a bottle that Dr. Reid prescribed for Baby
Angela. "I remember you saying that that's what Reid told you to give
her for her cold," I added. "Maybe you just bought a generic, but we
were wondering if he actually wrote out a prescription . . ."

"For Angela's aspirin? Yes he did," she said. "He did, because
then I wouldn't have to pay for it. Prescriptions were covered by my
insurance. In those days I had a pretty good policy, through Dad's
work. Not like now, these days I got a high deductible, you wouldn't
believe . . ."

"Emmie, did Elizabeth Summers take the aspirin drops away
this evening?" Tom cut in abruptly. "When she came to clear out
your cabinet, I mean?"

Emmie regarded him. " 'Course not," she said.

"But you said she was taking old medicines, she claimed she
needed them for some program to aid developing countries . . ."

"Yeah, she did." A strange, half-angry expression passed over
Emmie's face. "*Jeez*, you may be a mother, but anyone can tell you
haven't lost a child. Wait in there."

She pushed us into the sitting room, then reappeared a few moments later with a large cardboard box, which she gently laid on the
sofa. We craned over her shoulder to look at it.

The box was painted pink, and small magazine pictures of animals—teddy bears, rabbits, kittens—were lovingly glued to the sides. The word ANGELA was carefully picked out in red and glitter on the top, and a long, broad strip of pink ribbon was wrapped around the whole box. Emmie clipped back her hair, then sat down on the creaky bed, unfastened the ribbon, and opened the box.

Inside nestled five tiny, slightly stained white onesies ("Sometimes I think they still smell of her."). Beside them was a small brown teddy bear, a few pairs of pink newborn socks, and a strange assortment of baby equipment—a blue rubbery aspirator and a swaddling cloth, a half-used tube of diaper cream and three diapers ("That was what was left of the packet when she passed away."). And then there was a plastic crib mobile and a pink hat, a hand-knit wool blanket edged in white, a birth certificate, a sheaf of Xeroxed notes from the hospital on "Newborn Care," and a Polaroid in a silver frame of a tiny, red, scrunched-up baby with her eyes tight-closed. And finally, in the midst of it all, a brown bottle. "Angela Vaughan, April 23, 2001. Reid, M.D. Aspirin. One dropper (.8 ml) to be taken twice a day."

"Is that what you're looking for?"

We looked down at it, and at each other, and then back at her, momentarily lost for words.

"What, you think I just kept Angela's stuff in some old cabinet, jumbled anyhow?" she chided. *"My baby's things?"* she went on, stroking the photographed face gently with her finger. "I don't have my little girl anymore, I don't have her to hold in my arms, but everything she had, everything she used, everything with her name on it is—precious. I packed it all up, and sometimes, when I feel she's gone so far away from me, I take it all out, and look at it, and I see her name on this bottle, 'Angela Vaughan,' and it makes her seem real to me again, you know? I like to imagine, for just an hour, that she's still alive. I think about what she'd look like now, how she'd come into this room, calling *'Mommy!'*—hair all over the place, dirty knees and a torn dress, teddy in her hands, those big eyes smiling up at me. She'd be a pretty girl, don't you think?" She smiled down at the tiny, scrunched-up face. The face that would never become the girl her mother longed so desperately to know.

"Well, anyway," Emmie went on, after a moment's pause, "I guess what you're telling me is you need to take this bottle. Tell me *why*, please."

I took the bottle and slipped it into my pocket. "Reid should never have given this to Angela," I explained. "It's not safe. This bottle is crucial evidence. Apart from anything, it proves he came more than once to see you, because the date on the bottle is April 23; the medical examiner's report Driscoll filed claimed Reid came just once, on April 19. We're going to need to file a medical malpractice claim against your doctor. And if we can prove that he sent Elizabeth Summers today to fetch this bottle, well . . ."

Emmie looked bewildered. "Reid always prescribes aspirin, he says modern medicine has a—a prejudice against it, he says it's good for the blood . . . you're telling me that—*that* made her sick?"

Tom explained what Ian had told him—that aspirin doesn't *cause* Reye's, but that medical research has found a correlation between children treated with aspirin for respiratory illnesses and the development of Reye's. That aspirin use has been limited in children and teenagers for the past decade now, for precisely this reason. "I had no idea," she said, when he was done, wiping her cheeks. "I just did what he told me."

The small brown bottle would go a long way toward validating Emmie's claim that Reid visited her multiple times in the weeks before Angela's death *and* that he either lied to Driscoll or persuaded him to omit this fact from the form he submitted to the medical examiner's office.

Emmie listened to us describe the seriousness of falsifying a death report. "You say Driscoll was supposed to fill that form in after talking to me?" she asked suddenly. "Ha! He didn't ask me a damn thing. Reid gave me something when he came that day, something to make me sleep, he said it would dull the pain. When I woke up, Driscoll was gone. I didn't think anything of it—wasn't thinking about anything except Angela—but I guess he and Reid cooked that thing up together while I was out cold. Gramps'll tell you the same thing, for what it's worth.

"But one last thing," she went on anxiously. "How is this going to help us with Ryan? How's it going to stop him from taking Paulie away?"

"This goes a long way toward reestablishing your credibility as a good mother," I explained.

"It'll help us prove you didn't miss the signs that Angela was seriously ill," Tom added. "Practically speaking, we'll probably ask the judge to hold up the decision about custody while we pursue the medical malpractice claim—a successful verdict in *that* suit will help exonerate you in the custody fight."

"Ryan'll have a job taking Paulie away from you once we've proved medical malpractice against the doctor and, with any luck, secured damages," I added.

I watched her in the side mirror as we pulled out of the driveway, waving slowly to us in the moonlight.

When we got home, Jeanie was so agitated to learn what happened she hardly let us get in through the door. "What happened? Did she have it? Can I see it? Will you get him? How *incredibly* thrilling this is . . ." So great was the general excitement that she and Tom actually exchanged energetic claps on the back—and even, after a moment or two, an awkward, hasty kiss.

59

⁓

Jeanie

My last day at Quiet Lanes was Sue Ellen's as well. She went downhill fast those last two weeks, the cancer taking vicious hold. She should probably have moved to the hospice before, but there was no space, so Mrs. Forrest struggled to provide for her at Quiet Lanes, in spite of the lack of appropriate facilities. The other residents did what they could to help.

I came to clear out her room. I put her few valuables into a small leather monogrammed case—the locket and her wedding ring, which had started to slip too easily off her bony finger—and gave it into the hands of the nurse who had come to take her along the coast to the Old Saybrook hospice. As she was wheeled toward the waiting van, she looked up at me and grinned slyly. "Someone's coming tonight," she said suddenly, raking my face with her sharp blue eyes, and I laughed in sheer disbelief. (Not for the first time I wondered if there was something to her "Romany" training after all . . .)

"Now how can you possibly know that?" I asked, shaking my head at her. "You've been prying somehow, you naughty old woman!" She laughed back, delightedly.

"Honey, I see it in your face," she drawled softly. "He's coming to Connecticut, and no matter what you say, you're just *crazy* to get your hands on him."

"He's coming, you're quite right, but it's nothing to me," I corrected her gravely, as her wheelchair was hauled carefully up into the van. I walked around so that I could still see her through the sliding door. "He's not the right man. There's someone else in his life, and that's the end of it."

"Honey, it's never the end," she said, smiling tremulously at me. "It's never the end. Until it's *really* the end, that is." I nodded, and didn't speak; I wouldn't for worlds. Instead I waved at her as the door slammed closed, and I kept waving at that neat, erect head, with its perfect wave of golden hair, long after the van had pulled out of the drive.

Paul was, indeed, coming in the evening, although how Sue-Ellen guessed I can't imagine. We'd had a phone call from him late one night, about a week previously, saying he needed to come up again to "winterize" his boats—in other words, put on their little socks and coats to keep them warm.

He arrived just in time for dinner. I was in the middle of finishing the salad dressing when there was an almighty knocking on the front door. (Presumably, just in case I happened to be swanning around buck-naked again. You should be so bloody lucky, I thought to myself sourly.) When the four of us sat down, the atmosphere was chilly. Would you pass me the salt, he asked, and I crashed it in front of him with an expression designed to convey the words "you are an evil bastard and in an ideal world I'd pour this straight down your throat." This continued for half an hour. Then Tom, in what was clearly a desperate effort to get the conversation moving in a more positive direction, asked about life at Paul's company, and he began to talk.

Of course I switched off and examined my manicure—but then some stray word, or perhaps it was the tone of his voice, unexpectedly caught my attention.

"You know, this is really why I joined Prince in the first place," he was explaining, leaning forward, the light of the low silver chandelier reflected in his eyes. "My work with New York nonprofits has been incredibly rewarding these past few years. I'm certain that

PHMP Pro, in particular, would have collapsed if we hadn't been able to help them. But we managed to restructure the company, purchase supporting industries to help them finance themselves, and this year they've been able to get AIDS medications to people in some of the poorest countries in Africa. Then last month, I thought I'd made a total mess of the Marathon case, but it worked out okay, the tax exemption will stick, they'll be able to stay in business after all. Which is good, because their outreach program to inner-city kids is making a real difference."

Tom began to ask about how he was negotiating the bureaucracy of the New York State Charities Bureau, but I cut in. "I don't understand," I said abruptly. "*What* have you been doing?"

Paul looked at me. "I was just talking about my work at Prince," he replied. "Defending the indefensible, as you would put it. Or, as I like to say, specializing in supporting nonprofit organizations and charities of all sizes."

I stared at him. "Really?"

Paul put his fingertips together. "The reason I went to Prince and Cohen in the first place, Jeanie, was that they offered me the opportunity to head their nonprofit services. It's become particularly important now given the state of the economy. We can't let these vital enterprises fail." His body was rigid, but I saw his foot twitching under the table like the tip of a black cat's tail. "I once offered to describe my work to you, as I recall, but you didn't wait to let me."

Just as I was beginning to feel a creeping embarrassment, the other, more serious charge I'd directed against him rose into my mind. "Fine, so I got that wrong, I suppose," I said bitterly. "It doesn't really matter, does it? What you do in your professional life, I mean. You're not exactly a paragon of virtue in your *personal* life."

Paul looked over at me. "Jeanie," he said, abruptly standing up, dropping his napkin on the table, then leaning forward on his hands to face me, "I want to tell you, here and now, in front of Tom and Q, that I am *not* having an affair with Lily Olawe."

I gasped; Q gasped; Tom snorted with laughter. "With Lily? Good God, I should think not! Why would anyone think you were?" he said, gazing disbelievingly from me to Paul, and back again.

"I saw him with her," I said firmly. "I saw him touching her, holding her. I saw her stroking his chest," I went on explanatorily. Q furrowed her brow.

"Would you be kind enough, Tom, to tell your sister-in-law what all good lawyers know about the veracity of eyewitness statements?" Paul said suddenly.

Tom raised his eyebrows. "About—? Uh, okay. There's no proven correlation between the *confidence* of a witness in what he or she saw, and the *accuracy* of the statement."

"Precisely." Paul nodded. "In other words, people don't always see what they think they've seen. And they're notoriously bad at judging whether they're interpreting events correctly. This makes eyewitnesses tough to handle in court. People will swear blind they saw a black man coming out of a window, but what they actually saw was a man in the shade. They're not lying, they truly believe they know what they saw. As a lawyer, you have to trust the jury to see that just because the witness is confident, it doesn't mean they're correct. Or you have to find a way to prove outright that they're wrong."

I stared. "Okay, well, thank you for this little lecture, mister law professor, but what has it got to do with you and Lily, please?"

"Jeanie, let me take you back to that day—the day you saw me with Lily," Paul said, moving around the table and folding his arms lightly across his chest. "How far apart were we? What stood between you and me?"

"Oh, I see what you're doing, and it won't work—but, fine, all right. You were on the other side of the road. And there was traffic between us. But it stopped."

"What kind of a day was it?"

"Sunny."

"And was I on the bright or the shadowy side of the street?"

"The shadowy—but—"

"So the sun was in your eyes. Thank you. Now what did you see as we walked down the street?"

"I saw you stroking Lily's bottom," I said mutinously.

"As we walked down the street?"

"No—I mean, at first you were just walking. And then you reached out your hand, and put it round her waist, and then it sort of moved down. And you stopped walking."

"Okay, so I put my hand around her waist, then moved it to her hip. Did you see stroking or touching? Did I move my hand and caress her?"

I thought this through for a moment, remembering the position of their bodies, the bright sunlight, the traffic and confusion, my distress—"I'm not actually sure," I said doubtfully, at last. "I thought you did—but I could have been wrong about that. But I'm *not* wrong about—"

"Thank you. What did Lily do at this point?"

"At first she pulled away, and then she came back and slipped her hand inside your jacket."

"Could you see what her hand was doing?"

"No, not exactly, but—"

"Why not?"

"Well, because it was inside the jacket, obviously—"

"Did I kiss her?"

"No, but—"

"Did I pull her toward me?"

"No, but—"

"So there was no actual sexual contact between us? You didn't see anything happening except a hand placed on a hip, and another hand placed in a jacket?"

"No, but—"

"So what made you think the interaction was sexual? If there was no sexual contact?"

"It depends how you define 'sexual,' I suppose—"

"Yes, it does, doesn't it? I quite agree," Paul returned coolly. "Isn't it possible, Jeanie, that you simply saw two people laughing and enjoying each other's company? Two friends, who've known each other for a long time, who were sharing a joke?"

I tried to argue that there was very little possibility of an "innocent" explanation when hands were actually inside clothes, but Paul ignored me.

"I'm going to tell you what actually happened, Jeanie," he went on, coming to stand in front of me. "Lily and I went out for lunch that day—*with Adjile*. I paid. Adjile and Lily tried to split the bill with me; I told them I wouldn't take a cent, they'd given the four of us that wonderful day on the sea. Straight after our meal, Adjile went off downtown to see a friend, and I walked Lily back to their New York apartment. But the whole way there, Lily kept trying to slip a bill in my pocket. Just before you saw us, I realized she'd managed to stuff it into the back pocket of my trousers, so I tried to slip it back into her skirt pocket when she wasn't looking. It had become a game. She noticed what I was doing, laughed, told me it wasn't going to work, and put the bill into my inside jacket pocket, begging me to accept it this time. I asked her if it really mattered, and she told me it did, that she and Adjile felt—for reasons I won't go into—that the debt was all on their side. So at that moment I said, fine, Lily, if you feel that way, I'll accept the money. And we walked on. That was it."

My throat felt very dry.

"Were we flirting a little bit?" he went on thoughtfully, "yes, I suppose we were. Would I have acted the same way if you were there, if Adjile had been there? Absolutely. Did I do anything I'm ashamed of, or that I think you have any right to be angry over? No, not at all. I think you saw something innocent and friendly, but turned it into evidence of a treacherous affair. Why? Because you'd already decided I was so lost to morality I would betray one of my best friends, a guy I've known for a decade. You thought I—that all lawyers, as far as I can tell—are villains without souls, Jeanie, so you weren't a bit surprised to 'discover' that I was also a liar and a cheat. The kind of person who exploits the system, and other people, for his own personal gain."

Tom and Q were looking reprovingly at me. "You really think that about us?" Q clucked faintly, and Tom said something angry about the social value of lawyers and the imperative need for a legal system with "socially acclimated moral underpinnings." I stared at their three accusing faces.

"Well," I began desperately, and then looked to Paul hopefully, somehow expecting him to save me. I caught sight of his expression—ah. No help there, clearly.

"But you said you were screwing her!" I blurted suddenly. "You actually admitted it."

To my astonishment, Paul began to laugh. "Oh Jeanie! I couldn't think what you were talking about, so I assumed you'd seen me with Martha Lundquist (a judge who happens to live in Brooklyn Heights) that day. We met for coffee. I was feeling guilty about it, so my mind jumped immediately to our meeting. I am 'screwing' her, I'm afraid. I'm trying to get planning permission for a drug rehab facility in her neighborhood, but I've told her it's going to be an educational institution. She knows the purchaser is a client of mine, she asked to meet with me because she's worried about property prices, and I—well, I obfuscated the facts, shall we say."

Suddenly, I realized we were alone, although I had no idea where Q and Tom had gone, or when they went. Somewhere upstairs I heard a short yell from Samuel, followed by hush, as if a breast or a pacifier had been shoved hastily into his mouth. Outside the wind stirred in the drying autumn leaves; the cold sea cast glass and shells at the shore.

"Words are—" I stopped, and flushed. "When did you realize I'd got it all—er—wrong?"

"About twelve hours after I put the phone down."

"Really?" I was aghast. "Why didn't you try to explain?"

"It had something to do with being told I was repulsive, I think."

"Oh. Did I say that?"

"Yes."

"Ah."

"Jeanie, maybe it was silly, but I'm not used—I'll be honest—to being spoken to like that. And when you launched into your attack, I thought to myself, who needs this? I certainly don't need some woman who comes snooping after me—"

"I *wasn't* snooping—"

"Well, whatever you want to call it, then, 'observing in secret,' if you prefer—I don't need that, and I don't need someone who jumps to the worst possible conclusions about me at the drop of a hat. Particularly not when she comes from England, and when visiting her is going to involve ratcheting up serious frequent flyer miles—"

"You were thinking like that? About coming to see me? At that point?" I was astounded.

"I *was*, until you told me—let me see if I have this right—that I 'disgusted you,' that you wished my hands had never touched your body."

I stared at his hands. I really, really wished, at that moment, that they were on my body.

"Dave's got a new girlfriend, she's called Ellen," I babbled suddenly. "She's three times as buxom as me, and four times as pretty, and she is understanding and very loving, and I bet she never, *ever* jumps to conclusions."

He cocked an eye at me. "And does this bother you? That Dave is with Ellen, I mean?"

"*No.*" I was emphatic. But I couldn't say anything else. My lips were somehow sealed closed. I looked up at him, appealingly.

Paul reached out a hand and pulled me up to him. "Jeanie, you've got to say something. Frankly, I've gone out on a limb here," he added. "I've driven three hours to see this English girl who's done nothing but yell at me, who's accused me of every kind of evil. I've come to see her because it turned out I *couldn't* forget her, because it turned out that I—God only knows why—want her in my life. I don't know what that means yet. But I do know I don't want to let her—let you—slip through my fingers. Now tell me what *you* think."

"It is—possible," I said haltingly, "that I—"

"That you—" he prompted, leaning fractionally closer toward me.

"You're going to make me say it, aren't you—"

"Uh-huh—"

"Do I *really* have to say it?"

"Absolutely—"

In a big, hurried gasp now—"that I care about you, and that I'm sorry . . ."

Somewhere in Old Saybrook, Sue-Ellen cheered.

60

Q

Kent was off the wagon for a full three weeks, during which time Tom more or less took over the firm. On one of Kent's better afternoons, we shifted him back to his tiny house on the edge of Cheasford; over the course of the next few days, we watched him seesaw in and out of sobriety. For much of the time he was in a pathetic state, and we were frantic with worry about him, not least because the stairs in his house were hellishly narrow. We tried hiding every bottle we could find in the house, but he seemed to have an almost endless stock of concealed spirits in rafters, under beds, in the basement. Tom threatened him with hospitalization repeatedly.

Then, one day, we arrived to find a short, quiet Asian woman in a pale green pinafore with the words OCEAN VIEW CLEANERS on her breast pocket standing beside him, helping him dress. There was a pot of green tea on the desk, and periodically—in response to gentle chiding from her—he sipped at it, and from a glass of iced water. His eyes were still bloodshot, but his hair was combed and his face was fresh-scrubbed. The windows of the house were open, and the fuggy yellow air was pouring out. Warm autumn sunlight rippled across the floor.

"He stupid old man," the woman offered disapprovingly, nodding at Kent as he tried to do up his shoelaces. Kent rolled his eyes.

"Whatever, whatever," he said, but there was a hint of shame in his voice. And then, "How've you two been getting on, then?" He looked over at us from under his bushy, white-black eyebrows, then nodded impatiently at the door to the woman. Giving him a look that clearly said, I'll come and go in my own good time, mister, she moved with measured pace to the stairs.

We'd told him nothing about Emmie's case; there seemed little point, and, in fact, for most of the three-week stretch, any reference to the business of the firm made him terribly, desperately anxious—which prompted more drinking. Now, therefore, we observed him cautiously. "Do you really want to know?" I asked at last.

Kent coughed. "'Course I do. Assuming—" he paused, and the faintest hint of anxiety flittered through his eyes again—"assuming you're taking over the firm now. For good. Right?"

Tom laughed, and eased him into a chair. "Yes, I think we're taking over the firm, Kent; don't worry. We're going to give this a real shot. Q officially resigned from Schuster on Friday. And I, as a matter of fact, have already taken the Connecticut bar exam; a date came up, I saw the opportunity, and took it. Q will do the same this winter. So we just need to come to final terms about the transfer."

The old man closed his eyes briefly. "Right. Good. And—the—er—rent on the offices, I'm just wondering . . ."

"—Is all paid up."

"Ah. Glad to hear you're not—ah—falling behind."

"We're obviously insane, Kent, but—somehow, this life seems to suit us," I contributed, touching my fingers to the rope cable veins on the back of his hand. "Samuel's happier, I'm happier, Tom's happier. We like it here. We've even started looking at houses. And if we're not happy a year from now—well, I guess we'll sell the firm ourselves, and move on."

Kent pulled himself up, looking for a second his old cantankerous self, then thought better of it, and shrugged. "All right. That works. I can live with that. So—come on then, I can see you've got something else to tell me: how have you managed to wrap up young Emmie Cormier and that piece-o'shit husband of hers?"

So we told him the story, from our meeting with Driscoll to the revelations at Emmie's, and the medical malpractice suit that was now substantially prepared and simply awaiting his signature.

"Pretty good work," he said, when the story was told. He chewed his lip thoughtfully. "Pretty good work."

And then, face cracking into a smile as he poured himself a thumping big glass of tea, "I *knew* you could do it! I just *knew* it! That Judge Ackerman, what does he know? I showed him! " he crowed. "He was laughing at me, saying I didn't know what was best for my firm. Did you hear him? Said I was losing my touch! Other people said the same thing—what, you think I didn't know that? I heard them, in the market, the liquor store, the diner. Over their pancakes. Kenton Tyler's all washed up, they said; he wouldn't know a piece of evidence if it was covered in blood and fingerprints. *I* heard them! Well, people won't be able to talk about my judgment after this, no way! We've tied up Phil Reid nice and tight, there's going to be a lot of press about this. *Everyone's* going to be talking about me. About us. About—the name's already over the door, you know—*Kenton Tyler's Associates . . .*"

Epilogue

Q

Samuel has just turned eight months old.

Yesterday, flakes of snow whirled in the bare branches of the maples, and settled for an instant on the black-green needles of the pines. We lit a fire in the stone fireplace, and the scent of wood smoke lingered in the garden all day.

My little son will never be a Renaissance cherub, all chub and easygoing smiles, that's clear enough. He is determined, and cautious at the same time; fascinated by details, yet quickly overwhelmed. He can sit and stare at a piece of lint on the floor for hours. Five minutes of TV sends him into a howling meltdown.

But I've stopped asking him to rake small objects with his fist to check his hand-eye coordination, I'm too busy fretting he'll shove them all down his throat and choke. I've stopped worrying whether he can see a moving pencil, I'm too busy worrying I can't see *him*, as he nimbly evades my grasp and hares at breakneck speed—legs and hands moving like tiny pistons—across the carpet into the other room.

So things have changed at home, but perhaps they haven't really; there are just new worries, new things to check for. ("Well, that's mothering, dear," says Alison.) Still, I think we're understanding him better now, and he seems to be making better sense of the world. The improvement we'd begun to notice around the time Kent fell off the wagon continued, and now it's a rare day that begins, and ends, with crying. He loves his daycare, loves tumbling about on the floor with the other children, loves battling for the best toys, and when we pick him up after work (Tom, and I, on alternate days), his face lights up at the sight of us, then he yells at the sudden realization he can't take every single yellow truck home.

I went down to New York to clear out my desk at Schuster on a chill November morning. I knew, as soon as I walked into the office, that something was seriously wrong. People were clustered in little groups, talking nervously in the corridors; several people actually jumped when they saw me, as if I was a ghost from another world. "Oh Q, hi, what are you—doing here?" asked Julie, who was standing irresolute in the corridor, a stack of files in her arms; she looked as though she hadn't slept in months. When I explained, she shrugged her shoulders, her face twisted into a painful smile. "Looks like we'll all be doing the same thing soon," she said. "You got out just in time, you know."

"You mean—?"

"You haven't been reading the blogs? Watching the news? Good God. Well, seventy-five—yes, seventy-five—associates were fired three days ago, and the rest of us—put it this way, Q, the news from the top isn't good. We've had about six town hall meetings, they keep telling us the firings will be 'proportional to the firm's needs.'" She laughed mirthlessly. "Marta's out, of course. Michael jumped to

Badden and Scutzer two weeks ago, as did Fay—nice to be a partner, I suppose. Although—I suppose you haven't heard—Caroline—"

She fell abruptly silent as a shadow appeared in the doorway; Caroline herself, dark rings around her eyes, stumbled out. Her white silk shirt was crumpled, and there was a stain on the hem of her skirt. "Oh, Q," she said vaguely. "How—are you doing? Good, good. I'm er—very busy. I have—lots of papers to—deal with, and—stuff. Need to get back to—work." She pulled her phone out of her breast pocket, glanced at it for a second without seeming to take anything in, then walked off down the corridor. "So—y'know, bye. See you around."

Julie waited until she was out of sight. "As I was saying. Caroline hasn't been able to find another firm to take her on. I mean, she's got the wrong skill-set for this economy, and besides, no one likes her. Turns out that actually sort of matters." She laughed grimly. "Who'd have guessed it? So she's all tied up in Schuster, for good or for ill. If the firm goes down, which it looks like it will, she goes down too. She's been drinking hard for a good week now. People say she did really badly in the stock market crash too. She's probably going to lose that house."

I felt sorry for Caroline, I decided, listening to Julie, watching Caroline's retreating back and bowed shoulders. But not that sorry.

I cleaned out my desk and walked out of the building into the fresh, cold air, feeling as if the whole world had changed.

The world has changed for Jeanie, too. She went home in early October to interview for her job, which she got, then started the following week. She'll worry her local borough councilors into miserable submission over the course of the next five years, I'm sure, and the older people of south London will be better off because of it.

Paul flew out to London two weeks after she left, to stay for almost three months. He's taking up a temporary placement to help set up a new British branch of Prince, which has just opened in London (Prince is one of the few firms, like Badden and Scutzer, that is actually managing to thrive). And there's an opportunity for him to stay in England in the longer term if he wants. I don't know whether Paul would have gone to Britain anyway, or whether something about Jeanie's "go away" a while back convinced Paul that it could become a "come hither" with a touch of persuasion and the undoubted convenience of a London home (contract signed, rent and six weeks' deposit already paid). But if it was the latter, it was brave of him, I think, to go ahead with the plan, and she thinks so, too, "but also terribly nice of Prince to move into the London market, don't you think, Q? It'll be very easy for me to commute into Southwark, or maybe we'll just live halfway in between . . ." And then she stopped herself, and blushed, and looked as conscious as she did that first night, when she came inside from a walk in the garden, holding Paul's hand as if she'd never let it go.

Alison, of course, was fascinated to know every detail. "I take a bit of credit for the whole thing," she said airily. "Their relationship, I mean. I played my cards very close to my chest. I knew if I told you everything you'd put your oar in, Q, then Jeanie would get all defensive and find some loser just to make us cross, and the whole thing would be *ruined*. It was hard for me, obviously, but I just watched, and waited . . ."

"You just didn't want *me* to be the one to get them together!"

"Nonsense!"

"It isn't nonsense, Alison. That's typical of you. If you'd told me what was going on I might have been able to sort out the mess long ago, but oh no—"

"It's just like Mummy always says, you think you're the only person in this family who makes sensible arrangements. Q the career woman, always in charge. I may be a full-time mother but that doesn't mean I'm utterly impractical, Q."

"I would never say that! I would never think that!"

"Oh really? You don't secretly think that your advice to Jeanie is weightier than mine because you have an office job, and I don't?"

"I don't. Alison, honestly!" I said, and we only managed to make peace when I remembered to ask after Serena's croup.

This morning, I woke up in our brand-new Connecticut home, and was immediately invaded by a sense of strangeness. I sat bolt upright in bed, and looked around me. My husband was lying still, face collapsed into the pillow, arms scissored beside him; warm, heavy, unconscious. My son was lying in his bassinet on the other side of the room, a hint of sprouting hair just visible above the rim of the basket and—I lengthened my spine and craned to see—chest gently heaving his sleep sack.

I looked at the clock, glowing blue on the wall in the gloom created by the heavy blanket we've put up to help Samuel sleep. Around the edges of the blanket I could see the creeping light of an early morning winter sun, orange pricking through the thick navy woolen threads. It was seven a.m. Eight hours had passed since we last switched off our light. *Eight whole hours!*

I almost woke Tom up to share this incredible news with him. But then, just as my hand was about to touch his shoulder, I stopped myself, and looked down. Tom smacked his lips gently in his sleep, then settled a little deeper into his warmed cocoon of mattress, sheet, and pillow. I smiled at his childlike pose, then lay down again, curving my own body carefully toward his, knees and foreheads gently touching. And as I closed my eyes, and felt his steady, hot breath on my face, I enjoyed the tiny miracle of a morning lie-in with the man I love.